GRANDFATHER'S TALE

GRANDFATHER'S TALE

▼

The Tale of a German Sniper

Timothy Erenberger

Writers Club Press
New York   Lincoln   Shanghai

Grandfather's Tale
The Tale of a German Sniper

Writers Club Press
an imprint of iUniverse, Inc.

For information address:
iUniverse, Inc.
2021 Pine Lake Road, Suite 100
Lincoln, NE 68512
www.iuniverse.com

Any persons names mentioned are purely coincidental.

ISBN: 0-595-16462-5

Printed in the United States of America

DEDICATION

▼

I would like to dedicate this book to my grandfather, James Goodding. It is a tribute to him, as well as all other veterans of the Second World War. He served in the US Marine Corps in WWII, and was placed on a ship headed for Japan as part of the US invasion force. Before the invasion force reached the Japanese mainland, two atomic bombs were dropped on Hiroshima and Nagasaki. Japan surrendered, and the invasion never took place. If it had, I would probably not be here to write this wonderful book. He also served in China after the war ended, and saw some combat there.

I would also like to thank the four people I interviewed for historical information: my grandfather, James Goodding (Private First Class, USMC) described previously; Dennis Miller (A-1, USAF), who was a heliocopter navigator during Vietnam and was shot at several times while flying low over the Vietnamese jungle, and has a scar to prove it; Duane Brown (who is a fellow history buff); and Robert H. Cropp (Lt Col, USAF), who was a strategic bomber pilot in the European theatre during WWII. Robert gives a first hand description of what it was like to have flak cannon shells exploding all around him, while flying over Germany.

I would also like to thank my mother, Judi Erenberger. She is an attorney and a graduate of the University of Oregon.

A special thanks goes to my father, Doug Erenberger. He gave me a Kar 98K for Christmas a couple of years ago, which became one of the main "characters" of this book.

Finally, I would like to thank the many friends and relatives who read the book before publication. They gave me a lot of good advice. I would also like to mention my friends Chris Moorhead and Sean Pachow. They really liked the idea of the book and encouraged me to write it.

CONTENTS

▼

PREFACE

▼

As Americans, we are constantly shown movies and television shows which depict German soldiers during WWII as sadistic monsters who deserve to be put to death. In this story I have portrayed them much differently. I learned that they were conscripted, for the most part. This means that they were unwillingly forced to serve in the German Army. Some of them were cruel and monstrous, but the vast majority of them were just frightened soldiers, fighting to stay alive against all odds.

I do this not as a disrespect to American servicemen. I hold them in the highest respect. I hope the reader can appreciate the skill of some of the German soldiers whom they had to fight. As you read through the story, you will learn how the Germans became expert soldiers by winning battle after battle for the first several years of the war. The Americans, although victorious, must have surely respected the German's ability as soldiers. They were quite ferocious.

For reasons of simplicity, I have converted the ranks of the German soldiers to their US equivalent. If it pleases the reader to note what they would have been called in German, I have included this chart to convert them back (it's also pretty fun just to know what they are).

US—German
Private—Soldat
Lance Corporal—Gefreiter
Corporal—Unteroffizier

Sergeant—Stabsunteroffizier
Staff Sergeant—Feldwebel
Warrant Officer—Oberfeldwebel
Senior Warrant Officer—Hauptfeldwebel
Second Lieutenant—Fanrich
Chief Warrant Officer—Stabsfeldwebel
Lieutenant—Leutnant
Senior Lieutenant—Oberleutnant
Captain—Hauptmann
Major—Major
Lieutenant Colonel—Oberstleutnant
Colonel—Oberst
Brigadier General—Brigadegenerel
Major General—Generalmajor
Lieutenant General—Generalleutnant
General—General

CHAPTER 1

▼

MIDWESTERN USA, JUNE 2000

George was walking home from school with his friend Andy. They each had a very large, completely filled backpack. They had both just cleaned out their lockers.

They were both in a very good mood, because this was the last day of the school year.

"Maybe you could spend the night tonight?" asked Andy.

"No, I can't."

"Why not?"

"My dad is driving me up to my Great-grandpa and Grandma Frick's house. I am going to visit them for a couple of weeks."

"Man, you are going to be bored out of your mind," laughed Andy.

"Yeah, I know, but my grandfather's really old. He could die any day now, so my dad thinks I should spend some time with him."

"How old is he?"

"I think he's at least eighty."

"Eighty years old? Wow! Have you got anything fun to do up there?"

"Yeah, it's kind of fun, actually. It's out in the country, and they have a lake, and Grandpa has a bunch of guns. He lets me shoot them."

"Well, that does sound pretty fun." Andy thought for a moment. "Maybe I should go, too!" He had lived in the city all his life. He had never spent any time out in the country. He had never fired a gun.

George thought about this for a moment. "Yeah, that could be really fun. I'll ask my dad."

They continued walking to George's house. It was a beautiful summer day.

When they arrived at George's house, he walked in and found his father Ron in the kitchen. He was washing the dishes, and had his back turned to them.

"Hi, Dad!" he said to his father, who continued washing the dishes.

"Hello, George. How was your last day of school?" his father asked, without turning around.

"It was great. We didn't have to do anything except clean out our lockers."

"Sounds like fun. Have you packed your suitcase yet? Mom has dinner in the oven."

George noticed the smell of food filling the air. "No, I haven't packed yet, Dad." He peeked in the oven and saw a casserole cooking inside. "This smells great!"

Ron turned around and saw the two boys behind him. "Oh, hi, Andy. I didn't know you were here."

"Hello, Mr. Frick," said Andy. He was trying to be extra polite. He usually called George's father by his first name.

"All right, boys, what do you want?" Ron had instantly picked up on Andy's attempt at being extra polite.

"Would it be all right if Andy came with me to visit Grandma and Grandpa?" George asked, smiling.

"For two weeks? I don't think so. You're going up there to spend time with your great-grandparents, not Andy."

"But Dad, it's boring up there. Andy will keep me entertained."

"I'm sorry, George, but I think that is imposing on Grandma and Grandpa. I want you to spend some quality time with them."

With the attempt an obvious failure, George had no alternative but to turn to Andy and say, "Sorry, Andy." Then he thought, *Oh, well, he invited himself anyway.*

"It's all right. I will find something else to do," said Andy.

"You can stay for dinner if you would like, Andy," said Ron. He didn't want Andy to feel bad.

"Okay," replied Andy with a smile. "Is it all right if I call my mother?"

After dinner, George went upstairs to pack his things. Andy went home.

"Make sure you take plenty of clothes, George," advised his mother.

"All right, Mom."

George filled his two suitcases as much as he possibly could. He not only packed plenty of clothes, but also his toothbrush, deodorant, and face cleansing soap. He threw in four paperback books he had not yet read. When he was finished, he zipped the suitcases up and carried them downstairs.

"Dad has the car running, dear," shouted George's mother. She gave him a hug and a kiss, and George walked out with his two large suitcases.

They were soon halfway to George's great grandparents' house. George had been napping, but now awoke. He asked his father how much farther they had to drive.

"Three more hours. You can go back to sleep if you'd like."

"No, that's all right." He stretched his arms and yawned. He was tired of sleeping. It was difficult with the sun shining in all the car windows. Even with his sunglasses on, it seemed very bright.

"Dad, did Great-grandpa ever do anything cool?"

Ron laughed. "Like what?"

"I don't know. Was he ever in any wars or anything?"

Ron got a serious look on his face, but continued to watch the road. "My dad always told me that his father was in World War Two, but said never to ask him about it."

"Really? Why not?"

"Because he probably was in the war, and he probably saw some bad things happen that he just doesn't want to remember. Either that, or just being a German makes him resent the whole thing."

"Is he really from Germany?"

"Yes, he is. He moved here after the war ended."

"That's kind of cool."

"What?"

"Being from another country. I don't know anyone else from another country."

"Well, that's good. I'm glad you're interested. Grandfather loves to tell stories about the past. You can ask him all you want to about Germany. Just don't mention the war unless he brings it up first."

"Okay, Dad. I won't."

"Thanks, George." Then his father began to think. "Oh, George?"

"Yeah, Dad?"

"If he ever does bring it up, try to remember all of the details."

"Sure thing, Dad. Why?"

"Well, Grandpa is getting pretty old. Anything he tells you is kind of like family history. It's knowledge about our family that probably can't be obtained from any other source."

"I'll do my best."

"Thanks, George. You're a good kid." He rubbed George's head with his right hand. George loved it when his dad did that.

"Thanks, Dad."

Three hours later, they arrived at George's great-grandparents' home. It was a large house, surrounded by a huge yard filled with trees and neatly trimmed grass. A lake with very still water was nearby. It looked like a great place to swim. George had gone swimming in it before on previous visits. He had never stayed here by himself, though.

As they neared the house, the screen door opened and George's great-grandparents walked out. They were smiling and waving.

George's great-grandfather's name was George also. His name was well known for its strange spelling, which was G-e-o-r-g. He had white hair, which was balding in the center and cut very short everywhere else. He had a very intense gaze, and deep blue eyes. The skin on his face was wrinkled, and had age spots on it. He still looked like a handsome man, though. He wore faded jeans and a white tee shirt.

George's great-grandmother's name was Ingred. She had snow white hair, which was pulled back into a ponytail. She had gold wire-rimmed glasses and brown eyes. She looked very happy to see George and Ron. She was wearing orange slacks and a white pullover shirt. She had large silver earrings, a necklace, rings, and a bracelet. She was well-known for being fond of large silver jewelry.

They got out of the car, and Ingred was already moving close to give Ron a hug. He opened his arms and squeezed her gently. "Hello, boys!" she said pleasantly. Her German accent was obvious.

"Hello, Grandma and Grandpa!" said Ron. George echoed this greeting.

"How the heck are you doing?" asked Grandpa Georg as he looked at Ron. He also had a thick German accent.

"I'm doing fine, Grandpa. How are you two doing?"

"We are doing very well. Better, now that you and George are here," replied Georg. He smiled broadly. "We have missed you so."

"I missed you too, Grandpa," said George. He gave his great-grandfather a hug.

After this warm greeting, George walked into the house with his two large suitcases. The first room he walked into was the kitchen. It was filled with older appliances. George could smell fresh baked bread. He carried his luggage to the upstairs bedroom. It was in the upstairs loft, and occupied the entire top of the house. It was simple, with finished walls, hardwood floors, a small bed, a nightstand, and a dresser. He placed his suitcases on top of the bed and went back downstairs.

In the kitchen, Ingred was already feeding George's father some apple strudel. It smelled as if it had just been baked. "Here, George. You sit and have some as well."

They ate, and it tasted even better than it had smelled.

Georg spoke, "We used to eat apple strudel in the old country all the time."

George looked into his father's eyes, and they both smiled. Georg instantly saw it. "What's so funny, boys?"

"Oh, nothing," said Ron. "We were just discussing how you two moved here from Germany after the war. George was curious about what it was like in Germany."

Georg smiled. "Germany. That's the English name. The real name is *Deutschland*. The English think they can change the names of everything. It's a silly thing to do."

This was a new concept to George. "You mean they don't call it Germany in Germany?"

"That's right," answered Ron. "They call it the *Deutschland*."

"Wow! I have never heard of that before," said George.

"That's because you grew up in America. They teach you the English way, and nothing more. There is much outside of this land which you should see," said Georg.

He continued, "In the *Deutschland*, we ate many of the same foods you eat here, like potatoes, apples, and sausage. We also ate lots of sauerkraut, apple strudel, and bratwurst."

"Sounds really healthy," Ron joked.

Georg laughed, "Healthy it was not. It all tasted good, though."

"I'll bet," offered Ron.

They continued to talk about the mundane aspects of the *Deutschland* for about half an hour. Georg and Ingred told them how expensive it was to live there, how everyone liked to drink beer, and how different the workplace was. It was indeed like a whole other world.

Then Ron began to get tired. He spoke to George. "I am going to get some sleep upstairs. You get the couch tonight. I'll go back in the morning, and you can have the upstairs to yourself, George."

"All right, Dad."

Ron then went to bed.

"Have you ever played poker, George?" asked Ingred. He hadn't. She got some cards out of a drawer, and they spent the next hour playing cards. George had at first thought it was going to be boring, but he was enjoying it after a short while. They bet with poker chips, instead of money.

Ingred gave George several helpings of apple strudel as he played. She also gave him a glass of cold milk to wash it down.

After an hour of playing cards, Ingred and Georg began to get tired and said goodnight to George. George went into the living room. It was decorated with antiques on the walls. The furniture looked very old, as did the console television. George laughed when he saw the antenna on top of it. He found a pillow and blanket on the couch. He laid down, and was soon asleep.

Ron woke George in the early hours of the morning. "See you in a couple of weeks, George. You be good, all right?"

"Okay, Dad. Have a safe drive home."

"I will. Don't go wandering off. Stay on Grandma and Grandpa's land."

"All right, Dad. You don't have to worry about me. I'm a big boy."

"Yes, you are." He rubbed his head. With that said, he turned and left.

George was still tired, so he quickly went back to sleep.

After about an hour, he was awakened by the sound of someone cooking. He stretched and stood up. He was still very tired, but the thought of food motivated him to get up.

George's grandmother was cooking waffles in the kitchen. She smiled at him, saying, "You look like a hungry boy. Do you like waffles?"

"I love waffles, Grandma." He yawned, and stretched like a cat. His hair was pointing in every direction.

Georg walked into the kitchen. He was wearing boxer shorts and a white tank top shirt. His hair was in disarray as well. "Good morning," he said to both George and Ingred.

"Good morning, dear," said Ingred. She removed two waffles from the waffle iron. Steam rose from them. George could see that blueberries were baked into them. His mouth began to water.

"Good morning, Grandpa Georg."

Georg rubbed George's hair. "You have Grandpa's greasy mop, George." He said, laughing.

George reached up and felt his hair. "I need to take a shower."

"Not until you've eaten!" joked Ingred.

They all sat down and began to eat waffles with butter and maple syrup on them. Ingred also poured each of them a glass of milk and a smaller glass of orange juice. It was delicious.

"Tell us about your school, George," urged Ingred.

"Well, it's over now, thank God." George joked. "I'll be in fifth grade next year."

"Did your father buy you a car yet?" asked Georg, teasing him.

"No, not yet. He said I needed to get a job, and I haven't gotten around to it yet." He didn't mention the fact thaat it would be a few years yet until he would be old enough to have a driver's license.

"Don't be in a hurry, George. Things such as jobs and cars can wait. You still have time to be a boy," offered Georg. "Once you start working, you will never stop until you're old like me."

George considered this. He wanted a car very badly as soon as he was old enough, but had never considered a lifetime of employment. His father had frowned upon his decision to put off looking for a job. He could see the deep wisdom in his great-grandfather's words, and vowed not to forget them.

After telling his great-grandparents about every aspect of school and filling his belly with as much food as he could, George went upstairs to get his bathroom necessities.

He went into the downstairs bathroom to take a shower. This room was modernized. It had oak cabinets, both over and under the sink, and a large one next to the shower. George found it full of clean multicolored towels. Some of them had holes in them and were worn thin. He could tell from the out-of -tyle designs on them that they must be very old.

After showering, George walked upstairs into the guest bedroom to get dressed. He put on denim shorts and a red tee shirt. It was a rather warm day, and he didn't want to be uncomfortable. The house was air conditioned, but he was sure he would be outside.

He noticed a small closet door at the far end of the room. He had been in this room several times as a boy, but had never noticed it. It was painted in the same light green shade as the rest of the room, and was not very noticeable. He wondered what was stored inside it. His father's parents, who were George's grandparents, lived closer to him. He had extensively explored their home, and had found many treasures inside, such as ancient books, games, and electronics. He found such things very interesting. He made a mental note that he should look in the tiny closet some time.

When George went back downstairs, Ingred was in the kitchen washing dishes. "Where's Grandpa?" he asked.

"He's taking a shower now."

"Oh, all right. I'll go up and read a book while you are cleaning up." Now would be a perfect time to explore the tiny closet. George quickly walked up the stairs. He could hear the shower running as he walked by the bathroom.

The small door was a bit difficult to open. It seemed to have been added to the room in a rather unprofessional manner. It did not have a finish around it like a regular door. It was much rougher.

When the door opened, it made a slight noise. George looked at the stairs, but did not really think anyone could hear the small sound. It was dark inside the closet, and the ceiling was only about four feet high. It was a storage area which fit under the sloped section of the roof, which was too low to use as part of the bedroom. A wall divided this area from the rest of the bedroom.

George could see a large box just inside the closet. He quietly dragged it out into the bedroom. It was quite heavy, and spilled over the top. The cardboard felt old and damaged by dampness.

Inside, George saw many boxes. Several were full of old coins. Some of the coins were American, and others were from many European nations, including many from Germany. These had a symbol of an eagle on them, and George saw many from the years 1892 to 1948 as he studied them.

Another box was made of wood, and it was closed. There was a small brass key in a keyhole on the box. This box looked much nicer. The other boxes were cardboard cigar boxes. This box looked rather expensive. It made George very curious, and he found himself turning the tiny key. It stuck for a moment, and then made a click. The lid opened.

Inside the box were many military medals. They were all German. Some had Nazi symbols on them; others had crosses, swords, or eagles. One was in the shape of a shield. One depicted a pillbox fortification with a shovel and pick ax above it, and above these was an eagle. Several depicted a flying eagle with a swastika in its talons. Many were dated. The dates ranged from 1939 to 1944. George was amazed by what he found. He had never before seen anything like it.

"I really don't like it when people snoop through my things," said a voice behind him. George was startled, and dropped the box. The medals spilled out onto the floor.

"Don't be frightened, George," said Georg in a softer tone. "I used to look through my grandfather's closets, also. I think it's something every boy does."

"Sorry, Grandpa. I was just curious." George quickly picked up the spilled medals. "Where did you get all of these?"

"From the war." Georg sat down next to George on the floor. He looked very solemn.

"You earned a whole box full of medals? That's amazing, Grandpa!" George thought there must be more than forty medals here.

Georg smiled. "Yes, I suppose it is. I was a very lucky man. Many men never got to return home."

"What did you do to earn all of these?"

Georg was silent for a moment. "I'd rather not talk about it. I still have nightmares about it. It was terrible. That's all I can say." He stood and walked toward the stairs. "Please put the box back, George."

"Yes, Grandpa," said George. He quickly slid the heavy box back into the closet and closed the door.

George came downstairs and saw that his great-grandmother was out on the porch. She was sitting on a wooden lawn chair, enjoying the fresh air. He could not see where Georg was. He guessed that he was in the master bedroom. It was down the hall past the bathroom. The door was closed.

George walked outside. "It's a nice day out today, isn't it?" he asked Ingred.

"Yes, it is, George. I can smell the flowers all the way from here." She pointed to a row of rose bushes which grew near the driveway. The flowers were red and very beautiful.

"Yeah, I can smell them too," he said as he smiled. "They're great."

"Thank you, George." She smiled back at him. "Why don't you sit down here in the shade with me?" She pointed to a nearby lawn chair. George sat down.

Georg emerged from the house. He had two rifles in gun cases and a pile of targets. "Want to do some shooting, George?" he asked. He was smiling.

"Sure, Grandpa!" George responded. He had shot guns with his great- grandfather before. It was the only chance he ever got to shoot.

Ingred stayed on the porch, as they walked behind the house to a field with a large pile of dirt at the far end. There were wooden posts for holding targets. The posts were full of bullet holes.

"Wait here, George. Leave the rifles in their cases." Georg walked toward the posts with the stack of targets.

"Okay, Grandpa," said George. He watched as his great-grandfather walked across the field and tacked the targets onto the posts. He put five targets on each of the three posts. The targets had ten rings and a white bullseye in the center. Each ring had a number on it, which was for scoring shots.

Georg returned and took one of the rifles out of the gun case. It had a scope on it. "This is a twenty-two," he said. "It's not very powerful, but it's a fun gun to shoot."

George watched as Georg produced a box of ammunition from his shirt pocket. He set it on a table, which was used as a rest while shooting at targets. He opened the box and began feeding bullets one by one into a tube under the barrel. George could hear them slide down into the tube. He counted them.

After putting eighteen rounds in the rifle, He put the cover rod into place, and screwed it down. He then pulled back the action on the side of the rifle until it clicked when he released it. "Ready to fire," he said. "Let's see you get a bullseye!"

"I'll do my best," promised George. He began to look through the scope. At first, he could only see the green grass around the posts.

"Just shoot at the targets on the left post, George. Save the others for later."

"All right, Grandpa." He could see the target through the scope. The cross hairs were like a black spider-web. He tried to hold them over the bullseye. Despite resting the gun on the shooting table, he could not hold them perfectly still on the target. He pulled the trigger and there was a sharp crack. He could see the bullet hole through the scope. It was near the outer rings. He had probably scored a three. A bullseye was a ten, and each outer ring went down by one point.

Georg held a pair of binoculars up to his eyes. "Three," he said.

George fired again. The gun was semi-automatic, so all he had to do was pull the trigger. This time he hit closer to the center.

"Five," reported Georg.

George fired several more rounds in rapid succession. It was fun to snap several bullets so close together. He saw holes appearing all over the target, but had an even harder time holding it still.

"Slow down, George. We're just target shooting."

"I know. It's just fun to shoot them fast once in a while."

"I see a six, and a couple of fives. The others are all worse than four."

George took another carefully aimed shot. "Bullseye!" exclaimed Georg. "That's the way we do it! You just needed some practice."

George pulled the trigger again, and nothing happened. "It's empty," he said.

"Remember to always count your shots," admonished Georg.

"All right," said George.

"This weapon holds eighteen rounds." Georg took the gun and quickly loaded it as he had before. "It's important to keep guns very clean. That keeps them from jamming and getting corroded."

George smiled. He wondered why his grandfather was telling him such things. He felt like he was in basic training for the Army. "Yes, Sir!"

Georg smiled. "You never know when you might need such knowledge, George. It's good to know."

"Yeah, you never know. I might join the Army some day." George had entertained thoughts in the past of joining the Army. It seemed like fun. He liked to shoot guns. They probably got to shoot machineguns in basic training.

Georg looked serious. "Never join the Army, George." He motioned for George to move. "It's my turn to shoot."

George got up. "All right, Grandpa. Let's see what you've got."

Georg looked through the scope. He put the gun very close to the top of the table. He turned his left hand, palm up, under the barrel, to rest the weapon. He seemed to be in deep concentration. "You never pull the trigger, George. You squeeze it slowly. He quickly inhaled and held his breath. The gun fired. A second later, it fired again. The shots rang out, one after another, about one per second.

George wanted to see how Georg was doing. He looked through the binoculars. "Which target are you shooting at?"

"Top center, George." He held his breath again. The bullets continued to fly.

George looked at the top center target. "I don't see any hits."

Georg smiled. "Look closer."

Now George turned up the magnification. He adjusted the various controls on the binoculars until the target appeared to be twice as large, and he could see holes in the bullseye. Each time the weapon fired, the center moved a bit. He could tell the bullets were all passing through the bullseye.

"Wow!" George was truly amazed. "That's incredible! Are you holding your breath?"

"Yes, George. I also fire in between heartbeats. The gun is empty again." George smiled. "Squeeze the trigger, George."

"Yeah, you got it Grandpa." George had to close his mouth. He had never seen anything like that before. That target was fifty feet away, and Georg had just put eighteen bullets through the bullseye. He hadn't even hit the line in between nine and ten. Every shot was a perfect ten.

Now Georg removed the other rifle from its gun case. "This is a Kar 98K. It's a sniper rifle."

George began to understand how his grandfather had earned so many medals and survived so many battles. He watched Georg expertly, and quickly put the bullets into it the gun's internal magazine. The bullets were huge—about three inches long. The smaller twenty-two shells were about an inch long. This weapon was also fitted with a scope.

"How much bigger are those bullets?"

Georg held up one of the sniper bullets. "These are seven point nine two millimeter. That's about the same as thirty-caliber. They are much more powerful, because they have a lot more gunpowder in them. This pushes them out of the gun at a much higher speed."

Georg turned toward George. "Hold your ears." He held his breath in, after sharply inhaling.

George covered his ears with his palms, and he noticed that Georg had a hearing aid in his ear. It was deep inside the ear canal, and not very noticeable. He also noticed that he was missing half of two fingers on his left hand. His pinky and ring fingers had been cut halfway off.

The skin had long since healed, but the ancient wounds were obvious. Georg had before claimed that it was a farming accident. Now George began to suspect a much different cause.

"Bang!" The sound of this gun was many times that of the smaller rifle. It made a fast shock wave, which George felt several feet away. It was as if the air had slapped him very lightly in the face. George looked with the binoculars, and could see a hole that looked about as large as a dime. It was in the bullseye of the second target from the top on the center pole. He heard Georg rapidly work the bolt-action on the Kar and fire another round. This only took about two or three seconds. "Bang!" The previous hole was now distorted by another bullet. It was more like the number eight than a perfectly round hole.

Georg quickly fired three more shots from the Kar. They were also all bullseyes. He then rapidly pushed five more shells into the bottom of the gun and loaded one into the firing chamber.

"You want to shoot the Kar, George?" He stood up.

"You bet I do!" George sat down, and tried to imitate his great-grandfather's firing pose.

"Good, George. Hold your breath while you shoot. Hold the crosshairs as still as you can on the target."

They continued to shoot for half an hour, until the targets were filled with bullet holes and all the bullets were gone. Then they walked back to the house.

When they got to the porch, Ingred was looking at them. "Did you boys have fun?"

"Yeah, Grandma. I can't believe the way Grandpa can shoot!"

She smiled. "He has had lots of practice over the years."

"George is a good shot as well. He scored six bullseyes!" exclaimed Georg.

For the rest of the day, George spent his time swimming in the lake and exploring his grandparents' land. He saw many interesting plants, and a pheasant, which flew away as he approached it.

When he returned to the house, it was time for supper. Ingred had prepared a large meal. It included roast beef, mashed potatoes with gravy, a giant bowl of corn, and green beans. The table had already been set. George was the first one to sit down, and was soon joined by his grandparents.

"George, Grandpa has a surprise for you."

George's eyes opened wide with anticipation. "Really?" he smiled.

"He would like to tell you the story of what happened to him in the war."

"Cool!"

Georg remained solemn. He looked as if he was thinking. He stared at the bowl of mashed potatoes.

"This is a great honor, George. Grandpa has never told anyone the story, including me."

"Really? Wow!" George had a look of surprise on his face. "Are you going to listen to it too, Grandma?"

"You bet I am. I have been waiting more than fifty years to hear this!" she smiled.

"Why are you telling it to me, Grandpa?" George asked.

"Because you are my great-grandson. I do not want the memory of what happened to me to be completely forgotten. The war was terrible, and you must never forget this: war is a very bad thing. It's worse than any disaster you can think of. I want you to know this."

"I will begin when we have finished eating," stated Georg. He held out his hands, and the three of them held hands as Georg prayed out loud. "Dear Heavenly Father, for this meal we are about to receive, we are truly thankful. We know that it is much more than many have to eat tonight."

"Amen," they all said in unison. The began to eat. The food was delicious. George especially liked the mashed potatoes. He poured plenty of gravy on top of them, and he had a little corn as well.

When they had finished, Ingred and George cleaned up the table. Both of them did so quickly. They were anxious to hear the tale of adventure. They all went into the living room.

Georg sat down in a reclining chair and pulled the lever. The footrest opened up, and he pushed the the chair backwards until he was almost lying down.

George and Ingred sat on the couch and watched Georg as he began to speak.

"Before the war started, your great-grandmother and I had just gotten married. We lived in an apartment with my mother. It was located above the bakery that our family used to own in Hamburg. My father had started the bakery. He was killed years before in the Great War."

"You mean World War One?" asked George. Ingred put her finger to her lips, silently asking George not to interrupt.

"Yes, George. He was a sniper, and a good one."

George's eyes opened wide. He had never heard anything about his great-great-grandfather before.

As Georg told his story, he began to relive the experience.

CHAPTER 2

▼

THE OLD COUNTRY, SEPTEMBER 1937

"I was working in the family bakery one day. Working alongside me were my mother, Anna, and my pregnant wife, Ingred. Ingred and I were both eighteen years old. We had gotten married only two months earlier.

"For years, I had helped my mother run the bakery. Now that I was grown, we ran it like a partnership. It was too much work for Mother to do on her own, and she was happy to be able to work alongside her beloved son.

"Two old women entered the bakery. They looked at all the different breads and pastries for several minutes, talking to each other in hushed tones. Then they selected some pastries and cookies and purchased them from Mother. As they left the store, the postman held the door for them. He then walked inside.

"'I have a draft notice for you, Georg,' said the postman. That was the moment I remember the world changing. I had heard of young men being drafted, but never thought that I would be one of them. I accepted the small yellow envelope and looked at it. It had my name and address typed on the front.

"'Thank you, Michael' I said to the postman. I handed him a cookie. 'Take this.'

"Michael accepted the cookie and smiled. 'Thank you, Georg.' He tipped his hat to Mother and Ingred and exited the bakery.

"Mother looked at me with a very worried look on her face.

"I smiled, trying to reassure her. 'Mother, don't be frightened. We are not even at war.'

"'Your father was drafted, Georg.'

"I opened the envelope and read the draft notice. It said that I had three days to report to the recruiting officer or face arrest. It gave the address for the recruiting office. It was a few miles away.

"The next three days went by very quickly. My mother told me anything she could think of that might help me. 'Tell them that you've just gotten married. Tell them that you have a child on the way.' She also gave me advice on surviving combat. "Don't be brave, Georg. Use your head, and be careful! There are many dangers on a battlefield. The one you don't see is the one that kills you!"

"I listened to many lectures that day. I also gave Ingred many long hugs and kisses. 'Promise me you'll be careful, Georg,' she begged.

"'I promise, Ingred.'

"'Promise me you'll come back to me.'

"'Promise me you'll wait for me,' I implored with a sad face.

"'I promise,' she said. 'Now you promise you'll come back.'

"'I promise I will come back.' I smiled. I couldn't believe Ingred was so scared for me.

"'Tell the baby, Georg.' She looked quite serious and pointed at her belly.

"I got down on one knee and gently spoke to her swollen belly, 'This is your father speaking. Your mother has asked me to promise you that I will come back. I promise that I will.'

"Then I found myself walking to the recruiting office. Ingred walked with me. When I arrived, I saw a long line of young men. Some of them were with their wives, girlfriends, or mothers. Some had children with them, kissing them goodbye.

"I got in line. Ingred stood next to me, squeezing my hand. I said 'Don't worry. They probably just want us to guard the border.'

"Many changes had taken place in Germany in those last days. Adolf Hitler had come to power in 1933. His Nazi party ruled the nation with fear. To even joke about Hitler could mean imprisonment. The few Jews that used to come into the bakery had disappeared about two years ago. I didn't know if they had fled the country, or been imprisoned.

"He hesitated, then began to speak again. "I was not a Nazi, but I feared them. Everyone did. There were many of them standing outside the recruiter's office. They were handing out leaflets about the Nazi party. They wore brown shirts, and armbands with the Nazi symbol on them.I accepted one, and I tried to smile at them. I didn't want any trouble.

Georg closed his eyes, as he remembered that as the line moved, he neared the entrance to the recruiting office. And then he began to recount the events as if they were happening right now. "I have to go, Ingred. I love you. Goodbye. I gave her a strong hug, followed by a kiss."

Ingred wept as she spoke, "I love you, too! Be careful, Georg. Goodbye." She stepped back, and watched as he stepped inside.

"The line continued into the recruiter's office, until it reached a desk. Behind the desk was a fat Sergeant. He was asking the conscripts questions, and taking their draft notices.

"When I finally reached the desk, the Sergeant asked for my name, address, age, weight, and a number of other similar questions. He did not smile or pause between questions. He was very much like a machine. He had me sign a document, which said I was enlisted for four years. I signed it.

"After this, I was told to walk into another room. There, a group of young men were being sworn in. When they were finished, the group I was assigned to moved in, and placed their hands upon their hearts. We were told to instead hold them high in the air, palm outward. We repeated a pledge of allegiance to Adolph Hitler: 'We pledge our unconditional obedience to Adolph Hitler, leader of the Reich and People.'"

As Grandpa continued talking, it was like I was there, watching it. It did not seem like words any more. It was more like a movie—and I was a part of it. I could not hear it, but I could see it. It was alive!

"Soon afterward, we were in another line. This time we were getting our pictures taken. A photographer took a snap shot of each of us as we sat in a chair.

"After the photograph, we went to another line. This was where we were each issued our own personal book. We were told to sign it on the inside. Soon afterward, my photograph was glued inside. It also had my personal army number.

"Another Sergeant stood on a chair, and held up his personal book. 'This book will be kept with you at all times. It contains your personal information. You are to now fill out the blanks for next of kin, and any special training or skills which you have which may prove useful.'

Young George imagined himself to be a soldier, standing alongside his great-grandfather, watching his every move.

"I put Ingred and my mother down as next of kin. I wondered what this was for. *Perhaps in case I get killed*, I thought, matter-of-factly.

"For special training, I wrote that I was a good marksman, and that I was a baker. I could think of nothing else.

George once again heard the words fill the room.

"From the recruiter's office, we boarded a truck. I sat with many other conscripts in the back of the truck. It took us to a train station, where we were loaded onto a train.

"Within a few hours, we arrived at a German army training camp. We exited the train in a line. Another Sergeant was awaiting our arrival. He yelled in order to be heard above the sound of the train, 'I am Sergeant Krauss. I will be turning you men into battle-ready soldiers.' He continued with a lengthy speech, and then told us to follow him into the barracks.

Again, young George was watching, not just listening. He followed Georg's every movement. He was not hearing him; he was actually watching him—in his mind.

Georg selected a bunk. This is where he would sleep for the next three months.

Georg was issued a uniform. This included a gray-green field jacket, long gray trousers, knee high black jack-boots, an oval ID disc in two halves on a necklace, a belt, and a helmet.

The field jacket showed Georg's lowly rank of Private on his upper left sleeve. It had two pockets on the outside, and one on the inside, made specifically for his personal book, which he immediately placed inside the pocket.

The belt had an eagle emblem with the motto "Gott mit uns" (God be with us). There were three bullet pouches on each side of the belt. Each bullet pouch could hold ten bullets.

He was also issued a spade, which would fit into the back of his belt on the left side. It folded up for easy carrying.

There was also a musette bag, which would later hold rations. A field flask with a cup hung beside it.

The final item seemed to make Georg nervous. It was a gas mask, with its own accessories. These included chemical warfare tablets, and a gas shield.

The recruits were also given a military haircut. Georg usually had short brown hair, but it had never been that short. He did not like the way it looked.

Over the next week, the recruits were given vigorous exercises. These included marches and jogs with full packs, push-ups, sit-ups, and running an obstacle course.

They also practiced shooting on a firing range. Georg's exceptional skill was noticed almost immediately. The Sergeant informed him that after basic training, he would be attending a school for snipers. This caused Georg to remember his father. He pictured the bullet taking him by surprise, putting a hole in his head.

Georg learned that two of the men in his squad had gone to elementary school with him. Their names were Anton Keller and Misha Gaus. The three of them quickly became friends.

Anton was also a very good shot. He was of medium build, like Georg. He had serious-looking brown eyes, and could also run very fast.

Misha was a large man. He boxed for a hobby, and had wrestled for many years in school. He had very large muscles. His hair was blond, and his eyes were very blue. Despite his size, he was friendly and he laughed a lot. He loved to show off his strength by doing more push-ups than anyone else could do.

Georg and Anton trained with Misha until they got his accuracy to be almost as good as theirs. This took a couple of weeks. When the drill Sergeant saw Misha's improvement, he listed him for sniper school as well.

Basic training covered many things, including navigation, the use of equipment, the meaning of different commands. They were also taught how to deal with many dangers, including tanks, snipers, and poison gas. They learned the uses of many weapons. These included the Kar 98K rifle, the eight-centimeter mortar, anti-tank grenades, rifle grenades, and the S24 grenade.

The S24 resembled a potato masher. It had a stick handle, and a round metal body, which contained an explosive charge. There was little or no shrapnel. It used primarily the force of the blast to kill enemies. To activate it, you unscrewed the bottom and pulled a detonation cord. It had a four-second delay before exploding.

The Kar 98K rifle was a heavy battle rifle. It weighed more than eight pounds, which felt like much more when one was marching for many hours. It had bolt-action, and an internal ten-round magazine. Most of the soldiers were not issued a scope. They used the mechanical sight to aim.

The eight-centimeter mortar had a muzzle large enough for a man to fit his hand into. It could shoot a shell that weighed over seven pounds: more than two kilometers. It was aimed by changing the direction and elevation controls.

George watched as they learned to use improvised weapons, such as a spade or rifle butt.

Some men were trained with special weapons, such as flamethrowers, artillery guns, and the MG 34. The MG 34 was a heavy machine-gun which could be used against ground or aerial targets. It fired the same 7.92-millimeter cartridge that the Kar 98K fired. Its ammunition was fed on a 50-round belt.

After their three months of basic training, the three friends spent another month and a half at a special sniper school, where they practiced shooting much more than before. They practiced at much longer ranges, and trained to use a scope. Georg learned how to adjust the scope for range and wind.

They were also taught how to prioritize targets. They would attempt to shoot enemy snipers first. These were the soldiers who would be hunting for them. Then they looked for artillery spotters, officers, artillerists, heavy weapons users, and finally infantrymen.

They practiced extensively with camouflage. They learned to make improvised camouflage. This could be done with soot, dirt, weeds, or any number of things.

"Remember," the instructor said, "you shoot once, then you move. If you stay in one place and keep shooting, you'll make yourself a target."

After the completion of sniper training, Georg was given a leave. He went home for two weeks. He received warm greetings from both Ingred and his mother.

Georg told them how his skill with a rifle had been noticed, and his rank had been increased to Lance Corporal. The men who only went to basic training were still Privates. His new rank was sewn onto his sleeve already. He gave most of his wages from the army to Ingred, keeping only a little to buy beer with. "I don't need any money. The army pays for my food and lodging. Save it, Ingred."

"I will, Georg," she said.

Again, George heard his grandfather's voice. "The two-week leave was over all too quickly. I again gave Ingred and my mother a tearful goodbye and boarded another train. This one took me to a huge army base near Berlin, where I spent the next several months. I had two more leaves to go home during that period." He paused, remembering. "I was thankful for them, even though they were short."

"Ingred gave birth to our son Kurt in June. I was given my second leave at that time." Even now, all these years later, he grinned widely. "I rushed off the train and found Ingred proudly holding our new son. I hugged both of them. Mother was nearby, smiling. I spent the next two weeks with them. I enjoyed this brief period very much. Ingred again made me promise the baby that I would return safely. I did promise."

George glanced at his great-grandmother. Her eyes sparkled with tears, even now. He could sense the fear she did as she had prepared for her husband to leave again.

"'See, Mother? They only wanted me to guard Berlin. There's no war.'

Mother wasn't convinced. They didn't draft so many men for nothing. 'I hope you're right, Georg,'"

Grandpa breathed loudly. "I think that's enough for tonight," he said, sitting up in his recliner. "We'll talk about it more tomorrow night." And he slowly climbed the stairs, leaving George and Ingred alone.

CHAPTER 3

▼

THE ANNEXATION OF THE SUDETENLAND, SEPTEMBER 1938

The Sudetenland was a large section of Czechoslovakia—almost one third of the entire country. Hitler made a deal with the French and the British which allowed him to annex the Sudetenland. The Czech people were never even consulted. Their land was signed away September 29, 1938. He had already annexed Austria in the month of March. It had gone very peacefully. The Deutschland was growing at a very rapid pace. Hitler was trying to expand the borders, and unite the "Volk," who were the mythologized German-speaking people. Many of the Volk lived in surrounding countries, including Austria, Czechoslovakia, and Poland. There was also a great need for more living space, or "Lebensraum."

As George listened, he felt like he was in a private history class, except this was much more interesting.

"I was part of the invasion force," Georg continued. "They had expected no resistance, but anything was possible. I rode with my friends Anton and Misha, along with seventeen other snipers. We made up one squad of German infantrymen. The squad was packed into the back of a canvas-covered truck, and was riding behind a column of light tanks."

Again, almost daydreaming, George watched. Many of the infantrymen in the squad were smoking cigars. They were each issued two of them per day. They had also been issued their weapons, and ammunition.

"I was issued a Kar 98K rifle, complete with a bayonet and snipers' scope. The scope magnified 2.5x. It was only a slight improvement over normal vision. I held it tightly in my hands as we rode in the truck. Visions of enemy soldiers shooting at me flashed through my mind. I could scarcely believe that such a thing was happening. My hands were shaking.

"There were some hushed conversations in the truck, but most of the men remained silent. Anton and Misha sat near me. They also had rifles with scopes. Misha was looking out the back of the truck, where another squad of infantrymen rode on horses. Anton just sat and looked at the floor in silence.

"All of the other men in the squad had also been issued Kar 98K rifles, complete with scopes and bayonets.

"The infantry squad's leader's name was Sergeant Keller. He quietly rode near the rear of the truck, holding his rifle. He had already told the men that he had been in the First World War. They could see that he was nervous, but was trying not to show it.

"Suddenly, I could see a German tank pass by as the truck rolled past it. Three German Soldiers were looking at the engine. It must have broken down.

"A minute or two later, the truck stopped. Sergeant Keller stood up, and walked toward the front of the truck. He asked the driver what the delay was. The driver pointed ahead to what I later learned was another broken down tank. Black smoke poured from its engine.

"Other tanks and trucks began driving around the disabled tank. Soon the truck we were in began to move again, and they drove around it, too.

"Over the next two hours, I counted fifty broken down tanks. This made me feel very nervous. What if the tanks were urgently needed?

How could seemingly brand new tanks break down so easily? I kept these thoughts to myself, not wanting to get into trouble.

"After several more hours, we crossed the border of Czechoslovakia.

"As we rode through the many small cities of the Sudetanland, I could see many peasants weeping as they rolled by. This surprised me, because we had been told that the people of the Sudetanland longed for independence from their oppressive government. I began to wonder about the truth of these words. Nowhere did I see a happy face.

"The column of troops finally reached a large encampment. It had been a farm, but was now covered with many German army tents.

"The men were part of a German occupation force. There was no armed opposition. The Czechs were obviously not very happy about them being here, but they did not fight them.

"I received only one leave while I was part of the Czech occupation force. When I got home, I told Ingred and Mother how sad the Czechs seemed. I warned them to tell no one of this, because I did not want them to get into trouble. The eyes and ears of Hitler were everywhere, and any hint of negative propaganda was something you only whispered.

"I also told them that I had been issued a low-powered scope. On the last day of my leave, Ingred and Mother presented me with two gifts. One was a locket with small pictures of Ingred and the baby. It was made of silver, and in the shape of a heart. I think I wept as I put it on.

"The other was a new scope, which they had purchased it at the local gun store. It was a 6-power "Zeiss" scope. It was like a telescope with crosshairs in the center, but much smaller than a telescope. It had a black finish, and dust caps for both the front and back. There were small knobs for adjusting the scope for trajectory and wind. My army-issued scope also had these knobs, so I knew how to use them.

Oh, yes, I can see it all so clearly, thought George.

"Thank you very much! With a scope like this, I cannot miss." I hugged both of them.

"Return to us safely, Georg," Ingred said to me as she gave me a kiss.

"I then gave my young son a kiss on the head, and boarded a train. I once again had to ride in a truck to return to my post in Czechoslovakia.

"A few days after we returned to the base in Prague, I went to the rifle range. I carefully mounted my new scope on his Kar 98K. I set it high enough that I could still use the mechanical sight underneath the scope. I took several practice shots at six hundred meters. Each time I shot, I adjusted the two knobs, and the next shot was closer to the bullseye. When I hit three bullseyes in a row, I was satisfied that the gun was very accurate at that range. I also memorized how large a man looked at six hundred meters so I could ascertain the distance to my targets.

"I was stationed in the Sudetanland for several more months, until March 15, 1939. At this time, the army was again on the move. Hitler had annexed much of the rest of Czechoslovakia. The great column of tanks, trucks, half-tracks, cars, and horses rolled into Prague.

"I once again rode in the back of the truck with my squad," Georg said. "Our spirits were higher than they had been when we rode into the Sudetanland. The Czechs were not fighters.

"Again I saw many people crying as they held up their hands in the 'Hail Hitler' salute. The SS had told us that if the Czechs did not salute they would be punished, perhaps even shot.

"The SS were the elite troops, and were especially loyal to Hitler. They were also better equipped, and trained. I met a few of them in the army, and thought them to be especially cruel and vicious. I did not like them, but respected their abilities as soldiers.

"Like the Sudetanland, the Czechoslovakian capital fell without bloodshed. I learned that the Czechs had a huge arms industry, which was now in the hands of the Germans. Czech weapons, including tanks, artillery, anti-tank guns, and various small arms would soon enter the German arsenal.

"I could not help but wonder why they had failed to use any of these treasures in their own defense, though I was glad they had not.

"Six days later Germany annexed Lithuania. Like the Czechs, they surrendered to Hitler without putting up a fight.

"I remained in the occupation force inside of Prague, where I stayed for the next five and a half months. I wrote home almost every day with little to report, other than that I missed my family terribly. Things were quiet in Prague. I liked it that way, and hoped that the rest of my tour of duty would be the same."

"In May 1939, Hitler signed a defense agreement with the Italians, making them official Allies of Germany.

"On August 23, 1939, Hitler made a pact with Russia to divide up Poland between the two allied powers. I was quite dismayed when I heard this. I hoped the Poles would surrender, as the Czechs and Lithuanians had done. Two days later I was told that our division would be a part of the invasion force. I was ordered not to tell anyone or write home about it.

"Writing that next letter proved difficult. I had so much to say, but I suspected that the SS might be reading my letters, so I was very careful not to. I simply told Ingred and the baby that I loved them very much, and that I looked at their pictures every day in the small locket I always wore. I could hardly wait to see them again.

"On September 1, 1939, I was waiting inside the truck I had traveled in before. We were parked outside the border of Poland, but still inside of Czechoslovakia. The sun had not even lit up the horizon yet.

Tonight, George sensed that this was about as much as Grandpa could take for one time. He suggested they play another game.

CHAPTER 4

▼

THE INVASION OF POLAND, SEPTEMBER 1939

"At 0400, September 1st, the column began to roll toward Poland. We were about twenty miles from the border.

"The atmosphere was a bit tense this time. During our rides into the Sudetenland and Prague, we expected little or no resistance. No such assurance had been given for Poland. We could all sense danger in the air.

"This feeling seemed to be confirmed when we heard a large group of planes fly high overhead in the darkness. We looked at one another, trying to read each other's faces. I gripped my Kar 98K until my knuckles turned white. I made a mental checklist of my equipment.

"In addition to my normal equipment, I had an S24 stick grenade stuck in my belt. I hoped I would not have to use either the grenade or my gun.

"I prayed silently that we would not be killed. I also prayed for my family and my fellow soldiers. I kept my eyes closed, but my lips moved slightly. Some of the others prayed to themselves as well, I'm pretty sure.

"As we neared the border, one of the riflemen in our squad suddenly stood up and ran to the back of the truck. As Sergeant Keller told him to get back into his seat, he vomited off the back of the truck.

Goerge's head leaned backwards against the sofa. Once again, he felt like he was really there—when it all happened. He could hear them talking, feel them breathing hard, sense their fear.

"Sorry Sergeant," the soldier said. He returned to his seat, looking ashamed. "I'm just a little scared, Sir."

The Sergeant addressed everyone, "Fear is good for you. It keeps you alive. Just don't let it get the best of you. Keep a clear head, and let your training take over."

"Yes, Sir!" The men said together.

"Around 4:50 we rolled across the Odra River, which was the Polish border," Georg said as he continued to recount the story. "There were other divisions in behind ours. A division of tanks was the vanguard of the Blitzkrieg, and rolled just in front of their line of trucks. I had seen tanks and artillery in addition to infantry divisions behind them, but I was certain this was an invasion force. It looked much more dangerous than the smaller occupation force that had entered Czechoslovakia.

"Everyone was quiet as we all rolled across the border. I expected to hear gunfire, but there was nothing. I tried to hear anything over the sound of the many engines, but I could hear nothing else.

"After a long period of quiet, we heard some gunfire way off in the distance. The sun had not come up yet, so some of the guys strained to see out the back of the truck. They saw that about five trucks had pulled over, and troops were moving out of them in the direction of the gunfire. I expected the truck to be hit at any second, but that did not happen. It just continued rolling on. Soon the parked trucks were too far behind us to be visible. We could still hear gunfire, and I was sure there was a fight going on back there.

George could almost hear the trucks as they lumbered ahead.

After more than an hour of driving, the column turned north. The glow of dawn appeared over the eastern horizon. The cool morning air blew into the back of the truck, and chilled the men. George shivered.

He saw his great-grandfather, as a young man, pull his field jacket closed in an attempt to warm himself.

After driving north for an hour and a half, the truck finally stopped.

"Move out!" shouted Sergeant Keller. The men all stood up and began jumping out of the back of the truck with their weapons.

Now Georg could see that the division of tanks in front of them had left the road, for the most part. Many of them fanned out into a great line. A kilometer in front of them, Georg could see a small army of thousands of Polish soldiers. They were taking what cover they could behind small hills, trees, and farmhouses. Many of them had heavy weapons, such as machine-guns and small anti-tank guns. Georg could see that some of the soldiers had horses, and there were a great number of horses tied up behind the army. He deduced that this was one of the infamous Polish cavalry divisions. Georg's Sergeant had earlier told them all that the Polish cavalry were elite units, with better training and weaponry than most Polish troops.

As he watched it play out in his head, his eyes clamped shut and his imagination working overtime, *he* had become Georg. This was no longer his great-grandfather's war; it was now his own.

The Poles opened fire, launching a hail of bullets, shells, and anti-tank gunfire at the tanks in front of us. Most of these either missed, or bounced off tank armor. There was an incredible sound from all of these weapons going off at once, and the distinct clang of bullets bouncing off steel. Thousands of muzzle flashes were visible, as the Poles fired at us. These were like the flashes of many tiny cameras.

Sergeant Keller yelled at us, "Spread out behind the tanks, and advance. Fire at will, and destroy the enemy! Take what cover you can behind the tanks!"

Georg did just that. He put his head down, and walked up close behind a tank. They were not rolling all that fast. The tanks opened fire with their 20-mm cannons and 7.62-mm machine-guns. Georg did not look up to see what their effect was, but imagined it to be quite brutal. They also had a few medium tanks with them, which were firing heavier 37-mm guns. Several mortar and MG 34 crews set up their heavy weapons and opened fire on the Poles.

The hundreds of German tanks made the ground shake as they rolled so close together. The medium tanks jumped from the recoil of their guns as they fired.

George jerked involuntarily as he came back to reality. He vowed to listen to Grandpa tell the story. He wasn't ready for war. Not World War II—not even in his mind—and not any other war. Grandpa had been right. There was *nothing* glamorous about any of this!

"Images of my little son Kurt flashed through my mind," Georg said. "I remembered my mother's warning—not to be brave. Try to stay where it is safe.

"Suddenly a thought occurred to me. *I am a sniper.* I knew I was safer at long range, not rushing up close to the enemy, where I would be exposed to horrendous fire. I moved over toward Sergeant Keller and shouted, 'We can hit them from here, Sir!'

"Keller thought for a moment, then shouted to the entire squad, 'All right, spread out and begin firing.'

"I motioned for my friends to follow me. Anton, Misha, two machine-gun crews, and a mortar crew followed me. They ran quickly to the side and got behind a mound of dirt. I heard a few bullets whistle past my head, and I dove for cover. The other snipers in our squad took what cover they could find.

George was once again with them, in spite of his desire to stay separate from them. He no longer knew what was reality and what was fantasy. He heard Grandpa shouting.

"Remember to prioritize your targets!" shouted Georg. The others nodded. They all looked frightened, but kept doing what they were supposed to.

The three snipers took low profile positions, and began to aim their rifles at targets. The two machine-gun crews set up their MG34's on tripods, and prepared to fire.

Georg could now see that several other heavy weapon crews and snipers were moving out to do the same thing. He saw a man carrying an MG 34 get hit as he ran for cover. The bullet sliced through one of his thighs instantly. He screamed, and fell down hard.

Georg wanted to go help him, but instead he saw Misha suddenly dash out and drag this man behind the dirt mound they were all hiding behind. Georg thought this was extremely brave, because bullets were everywhere.

"Oh, my God! I've been shot!" cried the wounded soldier.

Misha took off his field jacket and tied it around the soldier's thigh. The man was obviously in pain, but he knew Misha was saving his life.

"Medic!" shouted one of the MG crewmen from Georg's squad. They could see no medics running to their aid.

George saw his grandpa look through his rifle sight in order to survey the scene. The Poles were taking losses, but they held their ground. The tanks were rolling toward them while firing. He saw many Poles cut down by machine gun fire.

Georg saw an anti-tank gun crew. They had a small caliber gun, perhaps a twenty-millimeter. They were quickly firing the weapon and loading shells in the breach. He moved the crosshairs onto the gunner and squeezed the trigger. He held his breath as the heavy Kar 98K snapped a round off.

It took about one second for the bullet to hit. Georg had put the crosshairs high, to account for the bullet dropping a bit. He saw a dark red hole appear in the unfortunate gunner's chest as he fell down.

"I froze for a moment," Georg said, and George again roused to hear his oh-so-familiar voice. "I had never shot anyone before. I watched the man in my scope, writhing in pain and screaming. Blood spurted up into the air. One of the other men tried to comfort him, while the third continued to man the gun. It took him much longer. He had been the loader, and now he was getting ready to take a shot.

"I squeezed the trigger again. The second gunner fell screaming. I was appalled at how easy it was to take a life. *You just aim and shoot, like target shooting on a sunny afternoon. Bang. Someone dies.* I wondered with a shiver if *my* head was in one of the Poles' crosshairs. I ducked behind the hill.

As Georg recounted the conversation, almost as if his friends of yore were sitting there with them, his voice lowered, almost to a whisper. It was like watching a movie being played out in slow-motion, but Grandpa was playing all the roles.

"What's the matter, Georg?" asked Anton. He continued aiming and firing.

"I hit two of them," I said.

"How the hell can you tell from here?" Anton looked at my scope. "Your scope?"

I looked guilty. "Yes. My wife and mother bought it for me. I can see everything over there."

"You have to keep fighting, Georg. We don't want to lose. Everyone is counting on us to help them." Just as he said this, one of the tanks exploded. There was not just a single explosion, because the ammunition inside the tank began to explode, too. Fire shot out of the small peek holes in the tank in instantaneous bursts. I was certain the crew was dead.

"I knew Anton's words were true. If the tanks were destroyed, there would be nothing to stand in between the German infantry and the Poles. I returned to my shooting position, and again looked through the scope.

"I scanned the enemy army for snipers. I didn't want any long-range shooters putting their crosshairs on me. The Poles were about nine hundred meters away, but looked like they were only one hundred and fifty meters away. It was like looking a block down the street.

"I adjusted the scope to account for the great distance, until I believed the crosshairs would be dead on. I then put them on a Polish soldier who was firing a heavy machine-gun, and I fired too. He was hit in the center of his chest, almost exactly where the crosshairs had been.

"I fired twice more, killing two more machine-gunners. My gun was empty, so I reloaded. I looked at the wounded soldier behind me as I did so. The man was holding his leg while biting on a stick he must have found on the ground. I could see that his pain was intense." The sweat was pouring off Georg's face as he retold this tale. And then it became less personal, and once again George felt like he was back in his history class. It was like reading from a text book as Georg's voice droned on with facts. *Just the facts, man,* George thought as he listened.

The many MG 34 and 8 cm mortar crews fired their respective weapons into the ranks of the Poles with devastating effects. The machine-gun crews fired in one-second bursts. Each group of rounds kicked up a lot of dirt, so it was easy to see where the rounds were hitting. To adjust their fire, they just moved the barrel until the dirt movement got close to and then behind the enemy.

The mortar crews could adjust their weapons' latitude and longitude settings until they were confident that they were hitting the enemy. Then they could make small adjustments, to saturate the target area with mortar shells. The shells made a loud noise when they shot out of the mortar, and a louder explosion when they landed, just a few seconds later.

"I continued to fire repeatedly at the Poles. Nearly every shot was a hit. I felt that I could have hit them even if they had been farther away. The Kar 98K was indeed a very powerful gun!

"After using up half of my ammunition, I could see that the Poles were pulling out of their hopeless position. They left many dying and wounded behind, as well as many weapons. They ran as quickly as they could toward their horses. Our forces fired at them the entire time. When they reached their mounts, they quickly got into their saddles, and began to ride them away at great speed.

"Our column of tanks and infantry followed. Wounded Poles were run over by the advancing tanks. The whole thing made me sick. *What is happening?* I wondered. *What did the Poles ever do to us?*

"I assisted Misha load the wounded German soldier onto a medical truck. He asked the doctors, 'What of the wounded Poles?'

"The doctor looked at him with uncertainty. 'We have orders not to treat prisoners. Only German soldiers.' He then went about helping the soldier with the leg wound.

"I looked at Misha. I could tell that he didn't approve either, but he said nothing.

"When we marched through the lines of dead and dying Polish soldiers, some of them cried out for help, although I could not understand them. I did as the others did; I marched right past them. I heard a loud shot, and I realized that another soldier had just shot one of the wounded Polish soldiers. I opened my mouth to shout, but Misha put his large hand on my shoulder. He urged me to keep marching. I could tell he felt terrible for doing this. The image of the dying Poles have haunted me all my life.

"We chased the retreating cavalry to the outskirts of the City of Kalisz. The tanks in front of us were firing all the while, and by the time we could see the city, the entire cavalry batallion had been annihilated. There were bloody bodies of men and horses all along the road. I silently wept as we marched along. I could do nothing for them.

"We could hear explosions on the far side of the city—Polish ground forces there were either being shelled or bombed. We were ordered to halt our advance outside the city.

"After I spoke with our commanding Lieutenant, Sergeant Keller spoke to the squad. 'We are to wait here while the enemy positions inside the city are softened up, and their supporting artillery on the north side of the city is destroyed. Take a break, men; you've earned it.' He smiled at us. 'Keep a sharp lookout for the enemy, though. They could be hiding anywhere.'

"This word of caution awakened my senses. I looked all around, imagining crosshairs on my head. I tucked my scope under my arm so no enemy sniper could tell that I too was a sniper. I could see that all twenty of the men in our squad were still uninjured. I hoped this good luck would hold.

"We sat in the grass for a few hours. Finally, Keller became restless. He ordered us to dig foxholes to sit in while we waited. We all took our spades from our belts and began to dig.

"After digging a comfortable foxhole, we sat in it and talked about the battle we had just been in. We spoke of how Misha had bravely saved the wounded machine-gunner. 'It was nothing.' Misha said modestly. 'Any of you would have done the same for me.'

"Anton quietly asked me, "So how many of them did you shoot, Georg?"

"I didn't answer for a few seconds. 'I don't know. A few.'

George realized that Grandpa had once again begun relaying the events like he was watching them—over and over in his mind—like he must have done a million times during his lifetime. He listened to the parts being played. Grandpa had become a one-man-show.

"Anton said, 'Come on, Georg. I know how you can shoot. I know I hit at least twenty of them.'

"It's nothing to be proud of, Anton."

"Georg, they were enemy soldiers. They were going to slaughter all of the Germans who live inside Poland. We got them first."

"I knew that was probably a lie, but I said nothing. I knew I could get into serious trouble for saying such a thing. 'They were young men like us. We butchered them like cattle.'

"We sat in silence for a while. Anton could see that I was upset. I lay back with my helmet over my face and took a nap.

"I opened up my musette bag on the rear of my belt. It contained my cold food rations. A field flask filled with water hung on my belt next to it. I ate my army rations, which consisted of a small loaf of bread, butter, honey, cheese, sauces, and a baked potato. I also had a box of candy and some tea bags, which I saved.

"When it got dark, some of the men kept watching for the enemy, while the others tried to sleep. It was difficult with the thunder of shells in the air. I had a nightmare about shooting the Polish soldiers, and walking by them. I saw several of them with skulls that had been crushed by tanks. I had not noticed this the day before. I woke up, and was unable to sleep again that night.

Georg was again sweating as he relived his nightmare. He shivered as he continued.

"We remained dug-in until the following morning. The shelling had gone on all night long. Just before sunrise, Sergeant Keller woke us by yelling, 'Time to get up and crack some Polish skulls!'

"Our entire squad woke up and quickly readied our gear. We walked up to the supply truck, where several cooks had been preparing greasy sausages and burnt muffins over campfires. Each man was rationed two large sausages, one muffin, and had their cold rations and field flask refilled. We were each also issued seven cartridges. This dismayed many of us, because we had used many more the previous day in a single fight. I had used up thirty of my sixty cartridges, and now had only thirty-seven.

"Once we had eaten, we were told to advance into the city and engage the enemy. This gave me a feeling of foreboding. The long-range fight the day before had been scary, but it was my specialty. I knew that today I might be fighting men only a few houses away, perhaps closer. My hands shook as I ate my sausages.

"The division of tanks went around the city on the eastern side. I could see them continue to the northwest. Artillery shells continued to rain down upon the city, causing blasts which sounded like thunderbolts. A haze of smoke filled the air and made long-range sight difficult.

"Within a few minutes we were advancing on the city. We paused a few times to look through our scopes.

"The third time we paused, I could see rifle muzzles protruding from several houses. 'Get down!' I yelled. Many men did. Others kept on marching, waving their hands at me like I was mad. Then, a swarm of bullets errupted from the Polish soldiers hiding in the houses.

"I began firing. I put my crosshairs above a rifle barrel, and snapped off a shot. Each time I saw the rifle fall, either outside of or into the window. I fired off two magazines before remembering that I only had twenty-seven cartridges left.

"Soon several German mortar crews began firing 8-cm mortars at the houses. One of the houses exploded in an instantaneous flash. I thought I saw green flames shooting out the windows for just a split second before the walls of the house fell apart.

"Heavy machine-gun and mortar fire now pounded the flimsy walls of the many houses the enemy soldiers were hiding in. I saw several German soldiers hit. Some were hit in their limbs, others in their torsos. I saw one bullet pass right through a man's throat as he fed a machine-gun belt into an MG 34. He fell, clutching his throat and choking.

"I saw another German soldier push this man aside. The soldier began feeding the belt into the gun, but he laid his head down behind the ammunition box, for any cover he could find. This allowed the gunner to fire much more rapidly and accurately. The dying soldier was making pathetic noises and convulsing as the battle raged around him.

"After reducing many of these houses to rubble, most of the fire from them died out. I went over and took some cartridges out of a dead German soldier's ammunition pockets, which were located on his belt. I found enough cartridges to be fully supplied, and I gave another five to Misha.

"There were about one thousand squads in the division, which was a total of about twenty thousand men. They now poured into the southern end of the city, using the heavy smoke as cover. It had been created by the combination of the short battle they had just been in, and the many 10.5-cm artillery shells, which had been pounding the city all night.

Georg began talking faster, almost like he was trying to run away from the visions he saw.

"There were burned out buildings all over the city. Houses, businesses, and other buildings stood with their windows and walls in pieces. Many had no roofs, or were burned to the ground. Now the sound of artillery was silenced, and I wondered if the artillery battalion had been moved farther to the northeast, toward Warsaw.

"After moving slowly forward in the city, we realized that we were pursuing a fleeing Polish division which had lost many of its men. Dead Poles, including both soldiers and civilians, were all over the city. They had been killed by the shells which had rained down upon the city overnight.

"I came across the remains of a Polish machine-gun nest. It had taken a direct hit. The two men who had been waiting for the Germans were blown to bits. Pieces of their bodies and sandbags were blown everywhere, and their foxhole had been turned into a crater.

"Shots rang out in the distance, then there were a few more in other directions. Some of the Polish soldiers must have remained behind to cover the retreat of the others. Our squad cautiously advanced through the city.

"I saw several terrified women hiding in one large house with broken windows. I could not stand to look at them. I felt like a thief who had come to steal their land from them. They all wore scarves over their hair. Many of them were weeping. They did not speak to the German soldiers, and they looked as if they expected to be shot at any second.

"There were so many similar scenes: women holding dead men or children in the street, an old man bandaging his wife's severely wounded leg, two old women helping a third who had lost her foot.

"There were houses that were now craters. I imagined the unfortunate civilians who had possibly been asleep when the shell hit their home. They were probably buried inside—dead or alive.

"The Wehrmacht ignored these scenes. They followed their orders, marching through the city in pursuit of the Polish forces. The trucks, which they had used as transports the previous day, followed behind in a great column.

"As they began to get close to the downtown area of Kalisz, they began to hear heavy gunfire. I was sure the Poles must be making a stand downtown.

"We saw many other squads of German infantry taking cover in the many houses that surrounded the downtown area. I walked alongside Misha, Anton, and Sergeant Keller. As we approached the houses that the others were going into for cover, we noticed a pile of bodies in the street in between two of the houses. Eight German soldiers were in the pile. They had been shot several times and were obviously dead.

"Keller ordered one of the riflemen to peek around the corner and look down the street. He did.

And Georg was back *in character* again. This time he even became so far removed from the scene that he described himself simply as "Georg." He was now merely a bystander—an innocent observer.

"Machine-gun nest, Sir, down the street."

"How far?" asked Keller.

"Maybe two hundred meters."

Keller pointed at Anton and Georg. "Take it out."

"Follow me, Anton." Georg said to his friend. He began to crawl with his rifle held in front of him. He moved so that he was behind the pile of dead Germans, and crawled up near them. He imagined that it would be difficult to see him, since he wore the same color uniform as the corpses.

Anton crawled up alongside him. He carefully placed his rifle on top of one of the corpses, and looked at the enemy position. "Two guns. We could each shoot at once and get both gunners."

Georg did the same, looking through his more powerful Zeiss scope. He put the crosshairs on the chin of the left gunner. "Not much of them is showing. Can you make the shot?"

Anton smiled. "Yes, I think so Georg. On my mark."

"Three, two, one!"

They both fired. Georg's shot went high, striking the gunner in the face a few centimeters above where he had aimed. He had forgotten to account for the close range. He watched the Polish soldier's eyes open wide, and he lay down out of sight.

"Keep watching them," said Georg, then he saw another Polish soldier sit up and aim the machine-gun his way. He shot him in the face. The man's nose disappeared and his head snapped back. Anton fired as well. "Got the loader!" he said excitedly. Georg could tell that Anton's adrenaline was flowing. Georg's was also. He scanned the street for enemies.

Georg turned toward Keller as Anton continued to watch the street. He used hand signals to indicate that he had taken out the machine-gun crew.

Keller nodded, and moved the rest of the squad forward. They dragged the unfortunate German soldiers off the road, and Keller took half of their identification tags, which hung around their necks. He put them in his pocket. "Poor bastards," he said.

Keller asked Georg if he could look through Georg's scope. Georg handed him his rifle.

Keller looked at the downtown area. He moved the rifle around as he scanned. "They are holed up in those concrete buildings. These houses we are hiding in are made of plaster and a few bricks. They won't stop anything. It's like hiding behind a blanket."

"What should we do, Sergeant?"

Now an officer moved up to Keller. He was a Captain, and he had several other squads with him. Georg guessed there were about eight squads. He asked Keller what the situation was.

"The enemy has taken cover in the concrete buildings downtown. Several of our men are using these houses as cover, and firing at them. We just took out a machine-gun nest down the street." He pointed in the direction of the machine-gun nest.

"Well done, Sergeant. Do you think your snipers can cover us while we move in?"

"Yes, Sir!" said Keller.

"Good. Shoot any Polish soldier who shows so much as an eyeball. Keep them pinned down"

"Yes, Sir!" said Keller. Georg thought he looked a bit frightened.

Keller turned to Georg, Anton, and Misha. "Let's show them how Germans fight!"

"We'll do our best, Sir!" stated Anton. He saluted and stomped his heel.

Anton turned to Georg. "You go first, mister big scope," He smiled.

Georg again crawled in between the two houses. The dead soldiers were now gone, so he simply used the side of one of the houses as concealment. He peeked around the corner, looking through his scope.

He soon sighted a Polish rifleman. He was shooting out of a window, while hiding inside a large building. He had good cover from the brick wall, showing only his rifle barrel and a small part of his head.

Georg pulled the trigger. The soldier either fell down or moved instantly away, because he was gone.

Using the same tactic, Georg moved his crosshairs across the building, keeping the corner of the house between himself and the rest of the building. He could hear both automatic and rifle fire from the building he was aiming at and the surrounding houses.

As many bullets struck the brick exterior of the building, he was looking at, puffs of white smoke and pieces of shattered bricks flew off. The glass was already broken from all of the windows. A mortar exploded on the roof of the building.

Georg put his crosshairs on a Polish soldier who was firing a machine-gun. He was about to fire when a bullet stuck the gunner in the chest, and he fell.

Another Polish soldier siezed the machine-gun. Georg shot him in the forehead. He then shot the machine-gun right through the barrel, to ruin it. His shots were hitting about three centimeters above the crosshairs, so he was able to place his shots with pinpoint accuracy.

He again moved the crosshairs across the building, and there were no obvious targets. He motioned for the assault team to move forward.

Keller moved up with the Captain, who was accompanied by about two hundred riflemen. They moved very quickly to the front of the building and flattened themselves against it around the front door.

The Captain motioned for a squad to move into the entrance. There was some gunfire, and then Georg heard what must have been a stick grenade going off inside.

After this, all the remaining riflemen poured into the building. Georg and the other snipers watched the windows, but saw no more Poles aiming out of them. After a few minutes, more than a few shots and grenades went off, and Keller emerged from the building. He rejoined the snipers.

"There were only about twenty of them left in there," he said. "It looks as if they have troops in most of the large buildings downtown. We can now use this building as cover."

They went back into the building and moved upstairs. Here Georg found a window and got ready to shoot at another building. The other snipers in Georg's squad did the same.

He again made himself only partially visible. He swept the crosshairs across the far building, and soon found what he was looking for. An enemy sniper was aiming at the building Georg was in. He had a small scope on his rifle and snapped off a shot as Georg aimed at him. Georg imagined him taking the life of a fellow German soldier. He would not allow him to take another shot. He squeezed the trigger and fired a shot. It went through the enemy sniper's left cheek, and he fell down.

This process was repeated over and over all day. Georg and several other snipers shot any Polish soldiers in the windows of a building, and an assault team moved into the building and cleared out the defenders. Several times Georg took cartridges out of the ammunition belts of dead German soldiers. He was dreadfully afraid of running out of bullets.

Keller noticed Georg's excellent accuracy, and told him so. "You're a good soldier, Georg. I have never seen a sniper with your skill. I'm glad to be serving with you."

"Thank you, Sergeant." Georg had never heard such a compliment, but felt sickened by the idea that he had to kill so many men to draw the Sergeant's attention.

Georg had one close call during the day. A Polish sniper fired a bullet that came so close to Georg's head it moved his helmet strap. The strap hit his cheek with such force that it left a dark purple welt. Georg dropped to the floor for a long time, until he was sure the sniper would think he was dead, then he moved to another window and scanned for him.

After a few heart-pumping minutes, Georg saw the enemy sniper. He was watching Georg's building through his scope, searching for a target. Georg shot him in the forhead.

By nightfall the Poles, who had been surrounded in the downtown of the city, were surrendering in large numbers. They were disarmed and forced to march to the South, guarded by a few hundred German infantrymen.

With Kalisz taken, Georg's division encamped for the night. They could see many refugees leaving the city, loaded down with personal possessions. Almost all of the civilians fled the city. Several squads were posted around the city as watch patrols.

The army cooks again cooked food for the men. They grilled bratwurst and cooked huge pans of potatoes with butter and salt. Georg was glad to have hot food, and he ate hungrily. He had been so busy fighting all day that he had not touched his cold rations.

That night, Georg wrote a letter to Ingred. He was able to tell her now about the attack on Poland. It was no longer a secret. He did not mention the long day of fighting. He said he had heard some fighting, but was far back in the lines. He did not want to scare her. "I love and dearly miss you, Georg" was his last line.

After rehashing the terror he felt, Georg once again returned to a more normal tone of voice and could manage to tell the story like he remembered it. A smile crossed his face as his thoughts took a sharp turn to the left.

"Young Kurt was one year old now. I looked at his picture in the light of the cooking fire. I kissed him goodnight, then I kissed Ingred's picture. She was very beautiful.

"Anton, Misha and I went into a civilian residence to sleep. It was in disorder, as if they had quickly gathered what they could, and left. We found a block of cheese and a loaf of bread, as well as some wine. We ate and drank well that night.

"I slept on a straw filled mattress. It was much more comfortable than the night before in the foxhole. I remember sleeping very soundly.

"In the morning, the cooks were cooking sausages and apple strudel. I wondered how many days we would be served sausage. I liked sausage, but we ate it over and over, and it quickly became boring. Then I realized that at least I was alive. I thought of the many German and Polish soldiers who had not lived through the previous day.

"I was issued seven cartridges. I told the ration Sergeant that I didn't eat any of my cold food, and the Sergeant seemed very surprised. I told him that I did need to refill his field flask with water, though.

"Soon our whole division was back in our trucks and rolling to the northeast, toward the Polish City of Kutno. Several other divisions had already moved near the city, and it was under siege.

"We rode for the entire day on the road to Kutno. It had been dark for perhaps an hour when we finally stopped for the night.

"Thanks to Anton and some of the other men who had witnessed my many true shots, I had gained a reputation among the squad. They all spoke of how I had killed so many Polish soldiers with head shots as they peeked out of windows. I told them I was just surviving. They said my modesty only added to their admiration for me. It was embarrassing to be admired for such awful things.

"All twenty men in the squad were still alive, and they attributed much of this to all of my bullets which had found their marks.

"The morning came too soon for my taste. I was still tired from all the fighting the previous day. I had again been forced to sleep in a foxhole.

"Once again we were served a hot breakfast. I remember that it was sausages, sauerkraut, and muffins. The muffins were baked in Dutch ovens. The sausages and sauerkraut were cooked in cast iron skillets. Several Privates were helping the cooks prepare the meals. When we had finished eating, they quickly rinsed the pans and ovens and packed them in the supply trucks.

"I was also issued my cold food rations, and seven cartridges.

Again, the history lesson narration began. Funny, George thought, how it seemed like Grandpa wasn't even there sometimes, yet he knew it all intimately.

The Polish City of Kutno was one of the major objectives of the invasion. We were now only a few hours away from it, and as the trucks began getting closer, the sounds of a battle could be heard.

The sounds of explosions thundered through the landscape like thunderbolts. There were hundreds of them every hour. This was a larger battle than the other two, with more heavy weapons. The thought was frightening.

After another hour, the shelling became even louder, and an artillery division as it fired upon the city became visible. They were German 10.5-cm guns. Hundreds of them were firing salvo after salvo of shells.

In between the artillery and the city were two tank divisions, and an infantry division. The infantry division was dug-in. They must have been there for a while, because there were several craters around them. Some of the foxholes had obviously been hit.

Outside the city there were several burned out tanks. Some were German tanks, including both light and a few medium tanks. There were also perhaps a hundred Polish tanks.

"I looked through my scope at them. I could see that they included light and medium tanks. I was surprised that the Poles had any tanks at all.

Several of the officers drove into the artillery division in an armored car. While this was happening, the men took a break and ate some of their cold food rations.

"You think they'll send us in there, Sergeant?" I asked.

"Most likely," said Keller. "At least this time we might get to bring in some tanks with us."

While we were watching the artillery shells fall on the city, we saw several German bombers drop bombs into the besieged city. These caused a colossal sound when they exploded. I could feel the shock of their blasts from where I was, which I guessed to be at least five miles away.

After about half an hour, the higher-ranking officers returned to my division. They spoke with the many lower-ranking officers, who then informed the many Sergeants about what was going on. When this process was completed, Sergeant Keller rejoined the squad, and got them all together for a meeting.

"The Poles have the remnants of one infantry and one anti-tank gun division inside of the city. They are dug-in and spread all over the city. Our tanks were already repelled once, and now they want to attempt to take the city with infantry. They are going to send a few tank squads in with us."

"I began to feel very afraid. I was lucky the day before, but it only took one bullet in the right place, and I knew I would be finished. I thought of the bullet which hit my helmet strap the day before.

"I tried to imagine what Ingred and young Kurt would do without me. Then I remembered my words to her. "I promise I will come back." I had to keep my promise!

Sergeant Keller ordered all of the men to check their equipment, and clean their rifles. All the men cleaned their rifles with a small bit of oil-soaked cloth, and a cleaning rod. If their rifles got too dirty, they could jam, so they had to make sure every inch of the inside of it was clean.

Most of the men already had blackened faces. Firing their rifles and walking through clouds of smoke had covered them with a light coating of soot. Keller told them that this would make them less visible in the crater-filled city.

As the shelling continued, the division moved toward the city. They joined the other infantry division in their foxholes.

Keller, Anton, Misha, and I crawled into a foxhole, which held three young soldiers. They each looked as if they had just finished high school, and they were smoking their army-issued cigars.

One of the cigar-smoking soldiers spoke first. "Hello, there. You ready for your first fight?" He smiled, as if eager for battle.

"We have already been in two battles, boy," said Keller, without smiling.

"Really? Wow!" The three young men looked at one another. "We have been watching the backs of these damn tanks for two days."

Misha spoke to them as if they were children, "It's not a game. A lot of men on both sides were killed. The Poles got the worst end of it, but I think we were lucky."

"Lucky?" asked the second boy. "We have better weapons than they do. You should have seen it yesterday. They had a bunch of old planes from the Great War flying around us, and our Messerschmitts were flying circles around them. The Polish planes were shot to pieces."

The third young soldier now spoke up. "They sent a tank battalion out to confront our tanks, and you can see that it was almost completely destroyed." He pointed at the many wrecked tanks.

Keller spoke up. "Yes, we have advantages in technology and numbers, but you must never underestimate your enemy. Remember, they are defending their country. They might try anything to stop us."

After this conversation, we turned and watched the city get shelled for several hours. The three young soldiers later told us that the Poles had artillery the day before and were shelling their position, but their artillery guns had been destroyed by a combination of artillery fire and bombs. They had been ordered to hold their position while the shelling was taking place. A few men got out of their holes to run to safer ground and were killed by shrapnel from the shelling. It was definitely safer to stay in your hole and wait it out, they said.

"Unless you were in one of those holes," stated one of them, pointing to one of the foxholes which had taken a direct hit. His hands shook as he smoked his cigar.

An hour later, the shelling stopped and we were ordered to advance.

We all marched forward. When we had advanced to within about one thousand meters of the city, the enemy soldiers who were taking cover in the outskirts of the city began to fire at them. Heavy machine-guns, rifles, and artillery guns opened fire at them, and more than a few German soldiers were hit. A group of men were hit by a shell, and body parts flew everywhere. It happened so fast, they never knew what hit them.

Georg's voice came in short, swift breaths.

"I dropped to the ground. I saw several men do the same, while many others kept moving forward. Those who advanced did so at a greater speed. Some of them were running forward.

"Once again, I looked through my scope for a target. I saw the muzzle flash of a heavy machine-gun in a window. I fixed my crosshairs above it and fired once. The flashes stopped. I moved the bolt-action on my rifle, and the flashes started again. I had no idea if I had hit the gunner and this was a replacement, or if I had missed. I fired again. The muzzle flash stopped again.

"I moved my crosshairs around and found a muzzle flash from another heavy machine-gun. I fired once and the muzzle flashes stopped. That gun did not resume firing. I moved on to another. Within a few minutes, I had fired three magazines and was fairly sure I had hit at least fifteen machine-gun operators.

"Several tanks advanced behind the main group of infantry. Machine-gun and cannon fire poured into the houses which contained Poles. Houses crumbled from the devastating effects of the fire. German machine-gun crews fired their MG 34's, and over a hundred mortar crews were launching a hail of mortars at the Poles. There were explosions everywhere.

"When I had fired my twentieth cartridge, I reloaded. I looked for more muzzle flashes, but I could find none. I turned around and made a hand signal to the many crews who were firing to cease fire. I stood up and advanced behind the other soldiers who had been advancing the entire time. Many of them were now reaching the edge of the city, and some had already entered a few residences through broken windows and back doors. I heard rifle and machine-gunfire from several directions within the city.

"I stopped to get some cartridges from a dead German soldier, and I was surprised to see that he was still alive. He had been shot through the abdomen. 'Help me!' the man whispered.

"'I need a medic here!' I yelled. I put my hand on the wound to stop the bleeding. The soldier cried out in pain. I pressed down on the wound, despite the man's agony.

"I could see no medics, so I lifted the man onto my shoulders and began to walk back toward the foxholes where they had come from. The other soldiers and tanks just went around us, continuing their way to the battle. I could still hear gunfire behind us.

"When I finally reached the first foxhole, I was exhausted. There were some medics there, and two of them ran up and took the man from me.

"'Thank you,' the soldier whispered to me. He had a shocked look on his face. I really hoped he would be all right. I just nodded to the man and waved goodbye.

"I turned and moved back up the hill toward the city.

"When I finally reached the city, the fighting was well inside of the outskirts. Many of the Polish houses had been destroyed. This city had taken much heavier damage than Kalisz had. There were not many places to hide.

"I had to move cautiously. I wondered where the rest of the squad was. I advanced behind cover at all times. Piles of debris, carriages, dead horses, and craters were everywhere. There was either something to hide behind or a hole to hide in almose everywhere.

"I spotted a tall building to my right. It was a business of some sort, and I could see rifles being fired from the second floor toward the center of the city. I hoped these were German soldiers firing at Poles. I had to make sure before going past it.

"I walked up to the entrance, keeping my head almost level with my pelvis. This made my profile very low, and would make me a difficult target. At least that's what I hoped.

"The door was closed, and a sign hung above it with Polish writing painted onto it. I had no idea what it said. I pounded on the door and called out, 'Are you German?' I stood to the side of the door so any gunfire would not hit me through the door.

"'Yes. Show yourself,' came the reply. I opened the door, and showed myself. I saw another German soldier at the top of a staircase, pointing his rifle down at me. When he saw me, he relaxed and pointed the weapon toward the ceiling. 'You scared the shit out of me,' he said.laughing at me. 'Come on up.'

"I walked up the stairs and saw four snipers in the room. Three of them were shooting, while the fourth had answered my knock at the door.

"'I was separated from my unit,' I said. 'Can I stay with you until the battle ends?'

"'Sure you can. Welcome!' said the soldier who had let me in. 'I am Felix.'

"As we spoke, a bullet suddenly went through the head of one of the other three snipers. There was a *Thwak!* sound and the man fell, convulsing and making a gurgling sound.

"'Oh, God!' yelled Felix. He knelt by the unfortunate soldier, but there was little he could do.

"The other snipers quickly dropped down to the floor.

"I spoke to them. 'You must remember your training. We were taught to fire and move. When you fire over and over from the same spot, you become a target. We have to get out of here."

"The other three agreed. Felix took half of the dead sniper's identification disc, and I took his ammunition. The others looked at me with disapproval.

"'They issue us seven cartridges a day. I have to make up for it somehow. I'm sorry.'

"'It's all right,' said Felix 'he won't be needing them any more.'

"A large pool of blood was growing under the dead sniper's head. His eyes were wide open and I closed them, while trying not to look at the large hole in his forehead.

"One of the other snipers threw up in the corner of the room. He was crying and vomiting at the same time. He was obviously very frightened.

"We moved cautiously out of the building. Using buildings as cover, we moved in a northeast direction, toward the center of the city. After traveling about two blocks, we met up with several squads who were watching a Polish tank from a concealed position behind some bushes. The tank was rolling toward us, moving its main cannon around. It must have been searching for a target. There were several Polish soldiers running behind it, ducking down low.

"One of the German soldiers was aiming a very large anti-tank rifle at the tank. He fired, and there was a tremendous bang. It was as if five normal rifles had been fired at once. I watched through my scope as a bullet hole appeared in the front of the tank's armor.

"A machine-gun on the front of the tank opened fire. Without thinking, I fired a round right into the eye slit above the machine-gun. The firing stopped abruptly..

"The other German soldiers opened fire. The Poles behind the tank tried to get behind it, but the Germans were spead out, and many of them were hit. One of the Poles aimed his rifle above the side of the tank to fire, and was instantly hit in the head with a bullet.

"A German soldier ran up to the tank with a Panzerwurfmine and threw it up into the air. This was a German anti-tank grenade, which had cloth fins to stabalize it. These made it look a bit like a dart as it flew through the air toward the Polish tank. 'Get down!' yelled a Sergeant in German. All the German soldiers dove for cover. I did the same.

"The grenade exploded on the front of the tank with tremendous force. It was such a fierce blast that it blew the turret off of the tank, and the machine-gun and 47mm cannon ammunition inside the tank began to explode. Shock waves and green flashes shot up through the hole where the turret had once been. It was obvious that anyone who had been inside the tank was now dead.

"German riflemen advanced on the Polish infantry behind the tank, and shot all of them to death. They were careful to stay clear of the tank, which was still exploding.

"I looked at the soldier who had fired the anti-tank rifle. The Polish machine-gunner had hit him before the tank was destroyed. I ran over to him and saw that he had several bullet holes in his chest. Blood gushed out of his mouth, and he relaxed his body. He seemed to be dead.

"Some of the other infantrymen crouched around the dead soldier. One of them prayed over him and then took half of his identification disc Each soldier had his name, rank, and serial number stamped into each half of the disc. One half was removed so that the soldier's family could be notified. The other half was kept for burial detail, for identification of the corpse. Then the infantrymen began to move on to the next house.

"The other three snipers and I, who had been with me, stopped at the body. 'Maybe we should take his rifle,' I suggested.

"Felix picked up the anti-tank rifle. 'It's like a cannon,' he said.

"I took it from him. 'It fires eight millimeter, just like our guns do. Why is it so powerful?'

"Felix held up an enormous cartridge. It had the same calliber as a sniper rifle, but a much larger powder cartridge. 'The bullets are huge!' he said.

"The sniper who had gotten sick earlier was vomiting again. He seemed to be getting hysterical. 'How can they expect me to be around all of these dead people?' he asked.

"I had seen enough dead soldiers in the last few days that little surprised me any more. 'I know it's hard, but you have to get used to it,' I told him. I wasn't really sure I was used to it. I was sure I would have nightmares about watching the sniper up in the second floor sniper-nest die. The image went through my mind again.

"The anti-tank rifle was heavy, but I took it anyway, along with the soldier's ammunition box. It contained nineteen rounds. He had fired only one round before he was killed. I felt sorry for him.

"Did you see the way that grenade blew the top of that tank off, Georg?" asked Felix.

"Yes. Those things can really do the job.'

Felix laughed. "I think it could have blown up two tanks. What a blast!"

"The four of us moved from house to house, using the broken walls as cover. We followed the infantrymen who had just blown up the Polish tank. I loaded the anti-tank rifle and put the box of cartridges in my musette bag. I carried my Kar 98K in my hands and the anti-tank rifle was slung over my left shoulder.

"We came upon an immense brick building. It looked like it might have been a school, but it was now filled with enemy soldiers who were firing out of the windows. The roof had been shelled heavily, and the entire top floor was gutted and collapsed. Every window in the building was broken.

"We were about six hundred meters from the building. The air was full of smoke from burning buildings and gunfire, so it was difficult to see every detail of the building.

"German MG 34 crews were pouring fire onto the building. The machine-gun bullets smashed bricks, and many of them penetrated the brick exterior of the building and hit the soldiers inside. We got on the ground and watched the scene through our scopes for a few seconds.

"Then I saw a muzzle flash from a rifle. I saw the rifle pulled into the window for reloading, and we waited. After about one minute, the rifle reappeared. I could see the Polish sniper as I looked through the site. I fired at him, and hit him in the cheekbone. His head snapped back and he hung halfway out the window. The Polish sniper rifle fell to the ground.

"Felix snapped off a shot. I couldn't tell if he hit anything or not.

"The four of us fired at the building for several minutes. I took three shots at the muzzle flashes of a machine-gun, with no effect. The crew must not have been directly behind the flash. Perhaps they were off to the side, firing at an angle. I fired about two feet to both the right and left of the flash, again with no effect. For a moment, the smoke cleared and I was able to see that the weapon was indeed pointed at a sharp angle, and the soldier holding the weapon was behind a brick wall. It had several bullet holes in it, but none had gone through.

"I set the Kar 98K aside, and aimed the anti-tank rifle at the wall in front of where I thought the gunner must be. I aimed with the mechanical sight and fired. The recoil was tremendous. It felt as if a mule had kicked me in the shoulder. It had made the same loud bang that it had when the other soldier had fired it. My ears rang for a long time afterwards.

"After shooting, I put down the anti-tank rifle and looked through my Zeiss scope on the Kar 98K. I saw a black hole about the size of a penny, as if it went all the way through the wall. The machine-gun had stopped firing.

"Then I saw a German soldier run up and throw a stick grenade into the window from which the machine-gun had been firing. As the soldier ran back to the house he had been hiding in, the grenade exploded loudly inside the brick building. I spotted a Polish sniper aiming out of one of the windows at the soldier who had just thrown the grenade. I quickly fired a bullet into the sniper's forehead.

"The soldier who had thrown the grenade turned abruptly toward me, and he saw that he had been firing into the brick building. He looked up and saw the dead sniper with his arm and head hanging out the window. He turned back to me and waved, while mouthing the words, 'Thank you!' He then returned to the house where he had been before he threw the grenade.

"There were no longer any Polish soldiers firing from the near side of the building. I was afraid some German infantrymen might storm the building, but none did. After waiting a few minutes, I decided to try to find out why they weren't coming. I knew a good opportunity when I saw one.

Again, George found himself in the midst of the conversation, like he was actually there himself. He could almost picture how the men looked.

"Felix, you three cover me. I'm going to see what they're doing," said Georg.

"All right," agreed Felix.

Georg ran over to the house where the grenade thrower had gone. "Don't shoot!" he shouted, while waiting around the corner.

"Come on in," came a reply.

Georg went into the doorway. He saw five riflemen and a two-man machine-gun team. "We need to storm the building before they bring more men to this side," he said. "Are there any more of you here?"

"Our Sergeant and the rest of our squad is in the house next door," said one of the soldiers. He pointed to the south. "I think there are some more squads around the building."

"We need to send an assault team in to clear out this building. I think all of the defenders are cleared on this side for now."

One of the soldiers ran over to the next house and came back with the Sergeant. He was an older man, perhaps forty years old. He looked at Georg with contempt.

"We are not going in without orders," said the Sergeant. "Perhaps we could speak with the Captain."

Georg became nervous. He was a mere Lance Corporal. The Captain probably led an entire company of men.

"No, it's all right. I don't want to bother the Captain." Georg turned to leave.

The Sergeant spoke to him, "No, you may be right. Let's go tell him what you just told me."

They exited through the back door of the house and quickly ran back a block. A large group of soldiers was standing there.. The Sergeant led him to one soldier who was dressed like the others, but had the insignia of a Captain on his uniform. He saluted him and stomped his heel.

"What is it, Sergeant?" asked the Captain.

"This sniper is from another unit, Sir. He says the defenders inside the school have been cleared on this side, and he thinks we should storm the building."

The Captain looked at Georg. "What is your name, Corporal?"

Georg stood at attention, but did not salute. "Lance Corporal Frick, Sir."

"Where is your salute, soldier?" asked the Captain.

"With all due respect, Sir, I was trying not to make you a target for snipers. I will salute if you would like, Sir."

The Captain looked around nervously. "That's quite all right, Corporal. Thank you." He pointed at Georg's scope, which was attached to his gun. "Are you a sniper, Frick?"

"Yes, Sir! I was separated from my unit."

"Let's go take a look at this building," said the Captain. He motioned for Georg, the Sergeant, and all of the other men to follow. They all stooped over and ran, while staying as low as possible.

Grandpa's voice was once again clear and present. George listened again as he spoke.

"As we ran, machine-gun fire erupted from an upper floor of yet another building. It was several blocks away, but the gunner was firing at us. Four of the soldiers who were with us were hit.

"I took cover behind a tree, put the crosshairs in the center of the machine-gunner's face and squeezed the trigger. His head snapped back and the heavy machine-gun fell to the ground.

"The four men who were hit screamed in pain. One man was screaming for his mother. Three of the soldiers who were with us were medics, and they began to treat the men.

"The Captain moved over close to me. 'Excellent shot, Frick. Very well done.'

"'Thank you, Sir,' I said, my face expressionless.

"The Captain could see that this was no new experience for me. He could see that I was from a different division by the markings on my field jacket sleeve. 'Your unit saw some heavy fighting in Kalisz, didn't it?'

"'Yes, Sir.'

"'How many men did you shoot?'

I stared at him. 'I'm not sure, Sir. I lost count.' The words sounded strange to me as I spoke them. How many had I killed? I tried to make a mental count of them. 'Perhaps somewhere from fifty to one hundred.'

"The other soldiers who heard this looked very skeptical. The Captain did not. 'You stay close to me, Georg. That's an order.'

"'Yes, Sir!'

"We continued, and soon we reached the house where I had first met the Sergeant. By now another machine-gun and some riflemen were firing out of the building.

"'Damn!' I muttered. 'We'll have to clear them again.'

"'Wait, Georg.' said the Captain. 'I have another idea.' He turned to one of the other soldiers who had come with them. This man had the rank of Lieutenant on his sleeve.

"'Take three squads and search the areas under our control for any of those Polish anti-tank guns. Bring them and any ammunition you can find for them to our meeting spot over there.' He pointed in the direction from which they had just come.

"'Yes, Sir!' said the Lieutenant as they ran out the back door with two other soldiers.

"'Can you see how old that building is, Frick?' the Captain asked me.

"'Yes, Sir.'

"'What did you do before being conscripted, Frick?' The Captain changed the subject abruptly.

"'I worked in my mother's bakery, Sir.'

Some of the men snickered. Captain Bidembach did not, although he did smile a bit. 'I was an engineer.' He pointed to the brick building. 'The building uses the brick walls for its skeleton. If we can bring them down, it will collapse.'

"He walked over to the wooden table in the house's kitchen. He pulled out a bayonet, and began scratching a rectangle in it.

"'The building is here. We are here. I want you and a few more snipers here and here, Georg.' He made some scratches a few blocks behind where they now stood. 'Can you hit them easily from here?'

"'I could hit them from here,' I told him. I pointed about five feet off the edge of the table, which was more than one kilometer away.

"The room was silent for a moment. 'All right, Georg,' he continued, 'you just go to a spot where you feel comfortable and cover the building. If you see a Polish soldier, he dies. Understand?'

"'Yes, Sir. I can do that, Sir.' I said confidently.

"The Captain pointed to the Sergeant. 'Round up ten of our best snipers and tell them to go where Georg tells them to.'

"'Yes, Sir,' said the Sergeant.

"It took the Sergeant about ten minutes to find all of the snipers. They met with me in a nearby shed. 'All right, sniper. Where do you want us to go?' asked one of the snipers.

"I sighed, hoping I would not lead any of these men to their deaths. I drew a map of the school and the surrounding houses. 'All right, I will be here.' I made a mark about one block from the school on a house where both the west and south sides of the school could be seen. 'I want two of you with me, and three of you here." I made a mark on another house which had a better view of the south side of the school. 'The rest of you will go here.' I pointed to a third house which viewed mainly the western side of the school. 'Each team should have at least one spotter and two snipers. Don't let them stick their noses out an inch.'

"'All right, you heard the man. Now let's go,' said the Sergeant. Then he turned to me and added, 'I'm going to join the colonel.'

"'Yes, Sir!' I replied..

"I could see that the infantrymen were wheeling three Polish anti-tank guns to the designated area. They also had a cart full of shells. I thought they looked very much like the German 3.7cm anti-tank guns used by the Wehrmacht.

The Sergeant soon returned to the house where I was waiting with the other two snipers. 'The colonel said to start clearing the defenders now.'

'Yes, Sir!' I said.

"'I will let the other snipers know as well,' said the Sergeant as he left.

'Let's wait until he tells them,' I said.

"We watched the Sergeant run to the next house I had selected. This house contained four snipers. Shortly after the Sergeant left the house, the snipers began firing.

"'Open fire!' I ordered. I looked through my scope. I heard the machine-gun open fire as the Poles attempted to defend themselves. The two snipers I was with fired a few shots. I saw the machine-gunner hit by two bullets at once. I moved my scope and saw the two riflemen go down as well.

"'Well done. Now watch the windows for any other defenders.'

"Soon after that, the captured Polish guns were fired into the brick walls. Four more riflemen appeared in various windows, and started to aim at us.

"I was ready for them. I shot one of the Polish riflemen in the chest. By the time I moved my crosshairs to the next soldier, he had already been hit. The other two snipers with me fired several times. The anti-tank guns continued to fire. A cloud of white smoke now hid much of the school from view.

"The gunners fired their 3.7cm guns at the walls of the ground floor of the building. After it was hit perhaps thirty times, sections of the walls began to collapse. Soon afterward, the entire western side fell, followed by the southern side.

"'That's incredible!' I exclaimed to the other snipers.

"'The Captain is smart, isn't he?' remarked one of the two other snipers.

"'Yes, he is quite brilliant, and he cares about the lives of his men.'

"I saw a white flag on a stick being waved out of one of the windows on the north side. Several Polish soldiers came out of the building with their hands up and surrendered.

"The school had been one of the main strong points of the Poles in the city. After it was taken, it took only three more hours to secure the city.

"Another German Army group, which also contained several infantry and one tank division, communicated that the other main objective would be taken by tomorrow morning. This was the city of Lodz.

"Before long I was reunited with my squad. Several of the snipers had been killed in an ambush. I was shocked to hear this, and felt guilty for being separated from them.

"'What happened to you, Georg?' asked Anton. He looked very upset.

"'I had to carry a wounded man all the way back to our foxholes. Nobody would help me. I'm sorry, Anton.'

"'It's not your fault, Georg. The same thing would have happened even if you had been there. We were moving toward the center of the city, and suddenly about five squads of Poles ran out of a building and charged at us. I ducked into a house and threw my stick grenade. I think I killed quite a few of them, but I didn't wait to find out. I ran. I ran like a coward.'

"'At least you're still alive, Anton,' I said, trying to console him. 'Sometimes it's better to run than fight. You know that.'

"'I know, but I still feel terrible.'

Suddenly we were interrupted. Sergeant Keller said 'Georg?'

"'Yes, Sir?'

"'You have been ordered to move to another division.'

"'What?' I could not imagine why they would do this.

"'Here is the transfer order.' He gave me a yellow piece of paper. I was to report to my new Captain, Captain Bidembac, at once.

"'Yes, Sir!' I said and saluted. I got my equipment, including the anti-tank rifle I had acquired earlier that day, and said goodbye to my friends. I marched over to where the 3rd infantry division was camped.

"I found the Captain, and saluted him. 'Lance Corporal Georg Frick reporting for duty, Sir!'

"'At ease, Corporal,' said the Captain. 'I'm sorry if this comes as a surprise to you, but I couldn't just let a good sniper like you get away from me, Georg.'

"'Thank you, Sir.' It was unusual to be addressed by my first name by an officer. They usually knew me only as Frick, or Corporal Frick.

"'I had to tell the Colonel about your extraordinary abilities to get you transferred. He wants you to report to him in the morning.'

"'Sir?'

"Bidembach smiled. 'He likes you, Georg. He wants to meet with you.'

"'Very well, Sir.'

"'Get some rest, soldier.'

"'Yes, Sir!' I turned to leave. I reported to my new squad. I recognized a few of them. They were some of the snipers I had been with earlier. Like my old squad, this one was made up entirely of snipers.

"'Well, if it isn't the expert sniper!' said one of the snipers I had ordered around earlier. We were of the same rank, so I would not normally be able to give him orders. In combat, a man of equal rank could technically give you an order if he was older. This man was obviously older than I was.

"'I'm sorry about that. I had no idea he was going to put me in charge of you.'

"The other sniper laughed. 'It's all right. You probably saved my hide by shooting that machine-gunner earlier today. How the hell can you aim that thing so fast?' He slapped me on the back, then he noticed the anti-tank rifle.

"'What the hell is this?'

"'An eight millimeter anti-tank rifle.' I removed the weapon from where it hung on his shoulder, and handed it to him. 'I acquired it today from a dead German soldier.'

"The other sniper looked at it. He opened the chamber, where he found a cartridge which I had loaded earlier. 'These bullets are enormous!' He took it out and looked at it. The portion of the cartridge which contained the powder was more than twice as thick as that of a normal rifle cartridge. It had a folding bipod and a folding shoulder stock. It had a carrying handle on the top, which had a leather rifle strap tied to it.

"'This thing is heavy!' said the other sniper. It weighed perhaps more than thirty pounds. This was much heavier than the Kar 98K, which weighed almost nine pounds.

"'Yes, I know, but it can shoot through tank armor.'

"The other sniper laughed. 'Are you going to lug this thing around all the time?'

"I shrugged. 'I shot a Polish machine-gunner through a brick wall with it.'

"'Have you heard about the French and the British?' asked one of the other soldiers.

"'No,' I said..

"'They've both declared war on us.'

"'Mother of God,' I exclaimed.

"The other sniper introduced himself as Joseph Enzel. I introduced myself to him as well. We spoke while sitting in their foxhole until Captain Bidembach finally told us to get some sleep.

"I sat there and thought of all that had transpired that day, and finally I fell asleep.

"And I think that's what I am ready for now. Ingred, are you coming to bed with me?"

CHAPTER 5

▼

WARSAW

George wondered how much Grandpa was going to eat. He knew the stories wouldn't begin until the last bite was swallowed and the dishes were cleared off the table. Then they would go into the living room, and he could imagine being there, right beside Grandpa, as he watched the things happening—even if they were only played out in his mind.

Finally, the last plate was removed from the table and they were on their way—not only to the living room, but to the past.

"The Wehrmacht spent most of the day regrouping on September 5th. Army Group South, which contained three entire armies and nearly a million men, needed time to complete their conquest of the cities of Lodz, Ozorkov, Rodomsko, and Brzeziny."

George listened intently, and then Grandpa was again seeing it all, just like it was happening all over again.

"I spent the morning cleaning my weapons. I also was able to get extra cartridges for the anti-tank rifle. I was issued seven rounds for both my Kar 98K and the tank rifle. This allowed me to take a few practice shots with the anti-tank rifle. I tried to fit my old 2.5 power scope onto the top of it, but I had nowhere to secure it.

"At 1100 hours, I was admitted to Colonel Holzwarth's command tent. The colonel was seated at an oak desk, looking at some maps. 'Lance Corporal Frick?' he asked.

"'Yes, Sir!' The colonel smiled. 'At ease, Corporal. It's a pleasure to meet you.' His friendly manner took me by surprise. Officers usually looked upon enlisted men as if they were little more than slaves. 'The pleasure is all mine, Colonel Holzwarth.'

"'May I see your papers?' The colonel held out his hand. I handed him my personal book, which I kept in my field jacket pocket at all times.

"He looked in the book for a minute or so. 'I see that you attended the sniper school in Berlin.'

"'Yes, Sir.'

"'I have found snipers to be particualarly useful. I have a couple of squads which are made up entirely of snipers, including yours.'

"'Yes, Sir, I noticed that my entire squad was made up of snipers.'

"A soldier who had a very soot-covered face entered the tent. Every part of his face, including his ears had been blackened. He saluted the Colonel, and stood at attention.

"The colonel spoke to this man. "Hello, Sergeant Ellis."

"'Hello, Colonel.'

"'At ease. I believe that I may have found a worthy pupil for you.'

"Sergeant Ellis smiled. 'Have you, Sir?'

"'Lance Corporal Frick has somewhere between fifty and one hundred unconfirmed kills.'

"'Really? The war just started a few days ago. Has he had prior experience?' He looked at me. I was surprised he even noticed me. They had been talking like I wasn't even in the room.

"'No. He was conscripted two years ago.'

"'That is extraordinary.'

"The colonel looked at me. 'Sergeant Ellis was a sniper in the Great War. He has over one thousand confirmed kills.'

"These words sent a chill through my spine. Standing before me was a man who was a master sniper and killer. I was to be his pupil. What was to become of me? I wanted to go home. I said nothing.

"'He's quiet. I like that,' said Ellis. 'I'll see how he can shoot.'

"'Very well, Sergeant. You two may go.' The colonel sat down at his desk, and I followed Ellis out of the tent.

"'What ranges are you comfortable shooting at?' asked Ellis, as we walked to the edge of the camp.

"'My scope is set at six hundred meters, Sir. I have hit men from at least nine hundred meters.'

"'That's good.' He looked at my scope. I had left the anti-tank rifle in the foxhole where I had spent the night. It was very heavy, and I didn't want to wear myself out carrying it everywhere.

"I followed Ellis to his tent, and waited outside for him. When Ellis exited the tent, he had several paper targets, a pair of binoculars, and some wooden stakes. He tacked one onto each stake as we walked even farther away from the camp.

"When we were over one hundred paces from the closest foxhole or tent, Ellis told me to wait. He walked six hundred paces away from the camp, and thrust the stakes into the ground. He ran back to where I was waiting.

"'All right, Corporal. Let's see how well you can shoot."

"'Sir, if you don't mind, I'd like to conserve my ammunition. Could I just fire a few shots?'

"'I'll replace your ammunition. Just shoot.'

"I lay down on my belly, and rested my rifle on my left fist while looking through my scope. I put the crosshairs on one of the bullseyes and fired. I quickly slid the bolt-action on my rifle and reloaded.

"Ellis was watching through the binoculars. 'Perfect. Again.'

"I fired at another target.

"'Excellent. Again.'

"I fired at the third target.

"'Good. Now the last one.'

"I moved the crosshairs and squeezed the trigger.

"'You are an excellent shot, Frick,' said Ellis. 'You hit the bullseye every time. You also reloaded very fast, and have a good rate of fire.'

"Ellis explained several of the finer aspects of sniping to me throughout the day. These included shooting at sunset or sunrise, when the enemy was blinded by the sun. He also gave me a camouflage net, and taught me how to put leaves and weeds into it and drape it over myself. To show me how effective this was, he had me turn around while he ran a few hundred paces away and hid in the brush. After counting to one hundred, I turned around. I could not see Ellis at all.

"I looked everywhere. I tried the binoculars, and finally the scope. I saw nothing. 'I give up!' I finally yelled.

"Ellis stood up. He had looked like a clump of weeds when he was lying on the ground. I laughed. 'Very good camouflage, Sir,' I said.

"I also learned that bullets travel faster than sound, and if you waited until an enemy was not looking, they would not even have the chance to see your muzzle flash. There would be no warning at all.

"Ellis explained how I could wait for two or even three men to line up and kill all of them with one bullet.

"'You can also snipe at night very effectively. All you have to do is look for some foolish soldier smoking a cigarette.'

"We spoke all day, until it began to get dark. I learned about using wounded soldiers and heavy weapons as bait. I learned how to locate enemy snipers, and how to out-think them. Ellis demonstrated how he would sometimes put his helmet on his spade, and then fasten the strap on the head of the spade so it was tight. He would then lift it out of his foxhole to see if any snipers were watching.

"He also explained how important was to choose where you waited for a shot. Choose the wrong place, and you die.

"'Remember rule number one,' said Ellis.

"'What's rule number one, Sir?'

"'Don't get killed.'

"'What's rule number two, Sir?' I asked, smiling at him..

"'Refer to rule number one.' Ellis laughed at his own joke. I thought that Ellis genuinely liked me. I liked Ellis as well.

"We stopped by Ellis' tent on our way back into camp, and he gave me a whole box of cartridges. 'Get some rest. Tomorrow you report back here.'

"'Yes, Sir,' I said.

"The other snipers were curious about what I had been up to all day. When I told them, some of them were obviously jealous. 'The colonel's pet,' they called me.

"'Don't listen to them,' said Enzel. 'they just wish they were as talented as you.'

"'Some talent,' I said sadly. 'I'm good at killing people. I just want to go home.'

"'I know what you mean, Georg.'

"I went back to my foxhole to sleep. I looked up at the stars, and marveled at their beauty.

"In the morning I ate my hot meal with the others and received my seven cartridges. I had nearly filled my musette bag with extra cartridges, and they were smashing the loaf of bread I had been rationed that morning. This was a small matter, though. I could handle eating flat bread.

"Our entire division was mobilizing. Men were packing up everything into trucks and armored cars. The invasion of Poland was continuing toward Warsaw.

"Ellis was waiting for me when I arrived. He already had his net over his head, and his face was black from soot. He was drinking from a field cup filled with coffee. 'Good morning, Georg.'

"'Good morning, Sergeant.'

"Ellis looked at the tank rifle and raised an eyebrow. 'What is that?'

"'It's an anti-tank rifle.'

"'A good luck charm?' Ellis said as he laughed.

"'Yes, sort of. I shot a Polish machine-gunner through a brick wall with it.'

"'Really? Your carbine can shoot through a brick wall, Georg?'

"'I know, but it was a thick one. Too thick for the Kar to penetrate.'

"'You know, it probably has a better range. I never thought about using such a weapon. Maybe it will come in handy.'

"'I hope so,' I said. 'It weighs a ton.'

"We boarded a truck which was filled with a squad of infantrymen. It soon began following a long line of trucks, which contained thousands of men. The trucks were following a division of tanks and armored cars.

"Even the roads were clogged with refugees. Polish civilians had packed all of their belongings into whatever they could muster and were trying to flee the invasion. These included horses, carts, and a few motorized vehicles. Ellis and I saw people standing along the side of the road with terrified looks on their faces. The Panzer crews must have ordered them to get out of the way.

"To me, that day was uneventful. There was no fighting. I simply rode in the truck and learned about the finer points of sniping. It was sometimes difficult to hear one another, but Ellis seemed eager to pass his extensive knowledge on to me.

"'When a man is running, you put your crosshairs in front of him and shoot so your bullet will meet him. It takes practice, but you can learn to do it.'

"I listened intently to these lessons from the master sniper. I knew that this was uncommon knowledge which would surely help me stay alive in the days to come. With Britain and France declaring war upon Germany, who knew how long this war would last? The Great War lasted years, and took the lives of millions of soldiers. I very much wanted to avoid this fate.

"As we had done before, the army stopped and made a large camp. Like the other infantrymen, I dug a foxhole to sleep in. My hands were already blistered from digging, and some of the blisters broke open as I dug. I had become very proficient at digging with my spade.

"After eating a hot dinner of bratwurst and baked potatoes, I lay down in the foxhole. The other three infantrymen who had helped me dig it also prepared for the night. There was little conversation. We were all very tired, and we had our minds on what events might come the next day.

"The sound of shouting awakened me some time later. It was still very dark, and I could hear explosions. They were very close to where I was sleeping. The volume of these blasts was tremendous. They were many times louder than grenades. The sound was deafening.

"The advantage of sleeping in a foxhole was that if your position happened to be shelled, most of the shrapnel and concussion would simply pass over you. I said a silent prayer of thanks for whoever had thought of sleeping in them, as a shell exploded some one hundred feet away.

"A division of tanks were parked in between where our division had been camped and the road to Warsaw. The shelling seemed to be coming from that direction. The shells whistled in the air before they hit.

"All four of us stayed as low as we could and kept bodies tucked in as much as possible. We had our helmets tightly fastened to our heads with chinstraps. The thunder of artillery shells was all around us. Whoever was shelling us must have known exactly where we were.

"A few minutes after the shelling began, I heard the many guns of the Wehrmacht answering the guns of the Poles. I could hear many 105mm and a few 150mm guns firing back at the Polish artillery. Soon several 8cm mortars began firing from foxholes as well.

"This shelling from both sides continued for about half an hour. It seemed like a much longer time to the frightened soldiers in the foxhole. I listened to the whistle of each incoming shell, and imagined it coming straight for our tiny foxhole.

"After one particularly close explosion, I heard men screaming. I was sure that a foxhole had been hit. I then heard someone scream, 'Medic!'

"The shelling continued, breaking up the darkness with flashes of light. The air became thick with smoke.

"Soon after the other foxhole was hit, a corporal ran and jumped into the foxhole. He shouted over the sounds of the shelling, 'We are moving out to support the tanks! They are mobilizing against the enemy! Get your gear together! Five minutes!'

"After five minutes of listening to shells pound the ground around us, we jumped up out of the foxhole and ran, with hundreds of other soldiers who were now following the tanks. The tank division was rolling along slightly faster than walking speed.

"I witnessed a group of soldiers getting hit by a shell. It exploded right in the middle of their group as they ran along. Pieces of them were flying everywhere. Most of the soldiers just kept on running. A few, who were probably medics, stopped to help them.

"It was somewhat comforting to run out of the camp. The shells continued to pound the camp, and did not follow us.

"As I ran in the darkness, I tripped over something. I fell down hard on my face, trying to hold on to my weapons. I looked down and saw it was a barbed wire fence that had been smashed by the tank division. I got up, and followed the tanks.

"After we ran for perhaps half an hour, we came within about one kilometer of the edge of a forest. I could just make it out in the twilight. Soon after, when I was able to see the tree line, muzzle flashes began to appear all over it. 'Get down!' I shouted, then I dove to the ground.

"It took about a second for the hail of bullets to reach us. I heard the bullets as they whistled by. A few soldiers had either heeded my warning or seen the muzzle flashes and dropped. Most of them did not. Many of the Germans who stayed standing were hit by the deadly bullets as they whistled through the air.

"Ignoring the screams and pleas for help all around me, I pulled back the action on my carbine and started firing shots at the muzzle flashes.

"Our entire division was in chaos. Some men were hit and scream-ing—or dead. Others followed the tanks as they rolled toward the tree line. A few helped the wounded soldiers, while others were just too frightened to do anything. Some heavy weapons crews were firing MG 34's or 8cm mortars from where they were.

"I moved the crosshairs around, methodically shooting one muzzle flash after another. I aimed high, thinking them to be about eight or nine hundred meters away. Some of the muzzle flashes were from rifles, but these were more difficult to aim at, and I thought it would be much more effective to take out machine-gun crews.

"Several of the German tanks opened fire with cannons and machine-guns as they rolled forward. The sound of bullets striking them could be distinctly heard above the many noises of the battle.

"The tanks sped up and closed the distance between them and the Polish infantry. A few tanks exploded when they were hit. The infantrymen who had been running behind the tanks were now exposed to enemy fire, and several of them were hit. Some dropped where they were and began firing. They could not keep up with the tanks after they had increased their speed.

"When the tanks were about three hundred meters from the tree-line, the Poles rarely fired at the German infantry. They were much more concerned with the tanks which were firing at them. Machine-gun fire poured into the Poles' ranks. It probably had a devastating effect on them, but I could not see well enough to know what was hap-pening.

"The battle continued like this for about an hour. I continued to pick off targets. I completely used up the ammunition in my belt once, and I took the belt off of a dead German soldier for reloads. I did not get into my emergency reserve of ammunition, which I kept in my musette bag, nor did I use my anti-tank rifle.

"The sky finally began to grow lighter with the approaching dawn. I pulled my camouflage net over my head to make myself much less visible. I then crouched down and ran out of the main army group. I headed for a barn which was in between my previous position and the tree line. The tanks had still not entered the woods, although several German infantrymen had entered the woods in pursuit of the Polish soldiers.

"I entered the barn. The smell of straw filled the air and I could see several goats and a cow. It was a miracle that no ordinance had hit them during the battle. This was a good sign, indicating that the barn had not yet come under much fire.

"I climbed a ladder and went up into the loft of the barn. There I found another sniper, who was also covered with a net. He was firing in the direction of the fighting, where the Poles, tanks, and most of the German infantry division were located. The sniper suddenly turned his rifle in my direction.

"'Is that you, Frick?'

"'Ellis!' I exclaimed. 'How long have you been here?'

"'Since the battle began. Do you have any extra cartridges?'

"'Yes.' I reached into my belt and handed Ellis twenty cartridges.

"'Thank you, Frick.' He handed me his binoculars. 'You can spot for me.'

"'Spot?'

"'Look through those and find me a target.'

I stood up behind Ellis and began looking.

"'Ellis pulled me down. 'Stay low, Frick. You want to get us both killed?'

"'Oh, I'm sorry,' I said as I got down into a crouch and pulled the net over my face. I held the binoculars over the net, so I could see through them, and then I scanned the battlefield.

"I soon found a battery of Polish anti-tank guns. These were probably twenty-millimeter guns, which resembled tiny cannons. There were twelve of them, and two men fired each gun. They also had a spotter, who was looking through binoculars.

"'A battery of twenty millimeter guns at eleven o'clock.'

"Ellis moved his rifle and looked through the scope. His scope was a "Zeiss" scope, which was identical to mine. His rifle was also a Kar 98K.

"'I don't see anything.'

"'Look higher up on that hill.'

"Ellis moved the gun up. 'Yes. I see them now. Watch the spotter.'

"I watched him. Ellis fired, and one second later the spotter fell down. 'Good shot.'

"'Now the gunners.'

"He began picking off the gunners and loaders, one by one. His rate of fire was incredible. He moved the bolt-action with incredible speed and quickly reloaded when his five round internal magazine was used up. He put five rounds in the magazine, plus one more in the firing chamber. This gave him six shots per reload. After he had shot six of them, they all stopped firing the guns and lay down on the ground behind them. I could see them speaking to each other. *They must be terrified*, I thought.

"'Their Sergeant will tell them to keep firing,' said Ellis.

"A few seconds later, they did indeed stand and resume firing their guns. Ellis shot another one, leaving the Sergeant alive. When three more fell, the remaining Poles began trying to retreat with their guns. Ellis shot two more of them, leaving only the Sergeant. He ran at a very high rate of speed, and escaped. The entire gun crew had been killed.

"'Another target,' said Ellis.

"I continued to spot targets for Ellis. He shot machine-gunners, officers, snipers, and infantrymen. There was no sign of pity, mercy, or regret from Ellis. He was truly a killing machine. He pointed, and fired, and someone died, or dropped in agony.

"When we had used nearly all of the cartridges from my belt, Ellis told me to wait there while he went back for ammunition. He told me to use his remaining bullets on any good targets if they presented themselves.

"He was gone for quite a while, and I found and shot three enemy snipers in the half-hour while Ellis was gone.

"'How did you do, Georg?' he asked.

"'I hit three snipers,' I replied.

"'Excellent!' Ellis slapped me on the back, 'They are the ones we want to hit the most.'

"Ellis picked up the binoculars and spotted for me for a while. He spotted ten snipers in twelve minutes. I shot them one by one. I tried to work the bolt-action as fast as Ellis, but could not quite achieve that level of speed and precision.

"'You are a shooter, Georg,. like me," Ellis said in his usual monotone.

"'Thank you, Sir.'

"The animals below us began to make noises. Ellis slapped me on the back and pointed down, through the cracks in the floor.

"Five Polish infantrymen had silently entered the barn. They were nervously pointing their weapons up at the ceiling. 'They must know we are up here,' whispered Ellis. He took the stick grenade out of my belt and silently walked over to the ladder.

"As the Poles readied themselves to move up the ladder one by one, Ellis silently unscrewed the bottom of the grenade and pulled the detonator cord.

"I knew the grenade would explode in four seconds. Ellis waited a full two seconds before dropping the grenade down the ladder hole, right in the center of where the Polish soldiers were standing. One of them shouted something in Polish and they all attempted to run.

"The grenade exploded, and Ellis motioned for me to follow him. He then quickly climbed down the ladder with his rifle in one hand.

One of the Polish soldiers attempted to aim his rifle as he lay on the ground, bleeding through his nose. Ellis shot him in the chest. He then worked the bolt-action on his rifle.

"I saw this as I climbed down the ladder. I saw another Polish soldier attempting to crawl away. I pointed my gun at his back, and hesitated.

"'Should we take him prisoner?' I asked. My heart was pumping hard. I had never been this close to an enemy before.

"'No, just shoot him,' Ellis replied coldly, as he shot another of the Polish soldiers.

"The soldier who was crawling turned over and held his hands up. They were black, as was his face. He was bleeding from one ear.

"I was surprised to hear the man speak in German. 'I surrender! Don't shoot!'

"I heard Ellis fire his gun again, and saw that he had shot another of the Poles.

"'This one is surrendering. I'm taking him back to camp.'

"'Whatever you say, Frick,' said Ellis in a disappointed tone. 'Just try not to get shot by a sniper while you're walking him back at gunpoint.' He shot the last Polish soldier. Only the one before me still lived.

"'You speak German?' I asked the soldier.

"'Yes, a little.'

"'Stand up. Leave your gun.'

"The Polish soldier stood up. He was crying.

"'I'm taking you prisoner. Stop crying.'

"'I'm sorry. I'll try to stop.'

"Ellis spoke to the man 'How did you know we were in here?'

"'We saw the muzzle flashes from your gun. You've been here for a while.'

"'All right, Frick. Take him back. This spot is no good anymore.'

"I told him to march in front of me. When we got outside I told him to run, and I ran behind him. I heard at least one bullet pass within ten feet of us as we ran back to the supply trucks, which had followed the tanks and infantry here. They were over a kilometer away. The Polish soldier fell once, and I yelled at him to get up. I did not want to spend any time standing still in the open. The frightened Polish soldier stood up quickly, and we continued running.

"When we finally reached the trucks, I took him to an area where there were perhaps a hundred other Polish soldiers who had been taken prisoner. Most of them looked as terrified as the one I had captured.

"I later rejoined Ellis, and we saw that the battle was over, for the most part. What forces remained of the two Polish divisions which had attacked us had fled into the forest, and were being pursued by two fresh German infantry divisions. Our division spent the rest of that day regrouping and waiting for reinforcements.

"The reinforcements arrived late that afternoon. They were fresh troops with relatively clean uniforms, and shaved faces. I guessed that they had not been in any battles yet. Some of them were quite shocked to see German soldiers with their arms and legs blown off. There was a medical company in the division, and they were treating wounded soldiers as fast as they possibly could.

"As several other divisions continued on toward Warsaw, our 3rd Infantry Division licked its wounds, got more supplies, and turned to the north. This was not in the direction of Warsaw, which was to the east. We were instead going to assault the City of Modlin, which had been made into a fortress.

"We spent half the day of Sept 8th travelling north, where we waited for engineers who arrived just before nightfall. In the morning we began erecting several pontoon bridges across the Vistula River. This took most of the day, so we did not cross the river until September 10th.

"I was very glad for this rest from fighting. I received several replacement cartridges with my seven-per-day ration and heard several more lectures from Ellis. Our conversation did turn toward other things several times, including our families, and hunting.

"Ellis did not speak much of his family, so he listened to me tell about the baby and helping my mother in the bakery. He told me that he was a skilled hunter, as well as a sniper. He frequently hunted deer in the many forests of Germany. He was convinced that hunting had made him a much better sniper, and he recommended that I try it.

"I informed Ellis that I had been forced into the life of a soldier, and I would much rather be baking breads and cookies in the bakery.

"Ellis was quiet for a time. 'Do you need an extra baker?' he finally asked. We both laughed.

"On September 10th, our 3rd Infantry Division, along with another division of infantry, crossed the Vistula River. We moved north, and then sharply turned to the east, toward Modlin. We also learned that the day before there had been a very bloody battle east of Warsaw. The German army had taken heavy losses against an entrenched Polish army.

"The city had been fortified in the past week. Miles of trenches and barbed wire spanned the entire western side of the city. The division abruptly halted when we were within rifle range, and began to dig in. Shelling began almost immediately from both armies.

"I ignored the sounds of shells, and dug. Within five minutes we had dug our foxhole, and were able to get inside to dig it still deeper.

"Suddenly Ellis jumped into the foxhole. 'Come on, Frick. Let's go.'

"I followed him. We ran away from the enemy lines, getting behind most of the foxholes. We finally reached a clump of small trees and dug another foxhole.

"Ellis carefully strung camouflage net above the foxhole, and he produced several empty sandbags, as well as a couple of boards.

"As there was no sand to be found, we filled the sandbags with dirt and placed them on top of the two boards. This was made into a roof for to ur foxhole. We still had a small hole to shoot out of for each of us, which faced the enemy lines. The sound of the shelling continued the whole time we did this.

"When our sniper nest was completed, we began to shoot at the same time. We did not need a spotter, as targets were plentiful. Polish snipers, riflemen, machine-gun and mortar crews were everywhere in the trenches. They only had their heads showing, so both Ellis and I missed more than a few times.

"Ellis produced an entire box of MG 34 belts, which contained the same ammunition that was used by the Kar 98K. We had to take the bullets out of the belts, but we never ran out of bullets.

"The assault on Modlin continued for many days. Ellis and I tracked the number of Polish soldiers we shot. After two weeks, we had each hit over one hundred men.

"We had many conversations in between shots. Ellis explained that at this long range, and with a good sniper nest such as this one, you did not need to move after every shot. It was unlikely that even an expert spotter or sniper would see you in such a hole with camouflage over you. He was right. No enemy soldiers even shot at us. They were about one hundred meters from the rest of the division, and the Poles were probably more concerned with the easier-to-find foxholes where the infantry was hiding.

"On September 17th, the word quickly spread that the Soviet Union had attacked the other side of Poland as Germany's ally. Many of the German soldiers' spirits were uplifted by this news. Poland was caught in a two front war with two superpowers.

"On September 19th, Ellis and I learned that the day before there had been a huge tank engagement between German and Polish tanks. Both sides had taken heavy losses.

"The Polish soldiers who were killed in the trenches were continuously replaced, so the Germans never assaulted the fortifications. Artillery and other long-range weapons continued to fire from both sides, but no ground was taken.

"On September 28th, Warsaw capitulated. Even with the capital taken, Modlin fought on for one more day. They finally capitulated on September 29th.

"Also, on September 29th, the 3rd infantry division moved into Modlin and secured the city. They rounded up Polish soldiers and confiscated their weapons. Almost all of the Polish army's ammunition had been depleted, and they had no food. Their supplies had been cut off, forcing their surrender.

"On October the 5th, the remainder of Polish forces surrendered. 900,000 Polish soldiers were captured, and their country had been divided in half. The Soviets occupied the eastern half, and the Germans occupied the western half.

"During the next five months, I was promoted from Lance Corporal to Corporal. This was primarily due to my large number of kills, which had been confirmed by Sergeant Ellis. I wrote several letters home, but I did not mention anything about combat in any of them. I was granted only a single leave for one week during that period, and I rushed home by train once again.

"Ingred and my mother were very glad to see me. Kurt surprised me by walking up to me and saying, "Hi, Daddy!" I picked him up as he gave me a hug. I was so thankful that I lived to hear those precious words from my son's mouth.

Ingred and Mother continuously asked me about the war. I gave them vague answers, such as 'Yes, I saw combat. No, I don't want to talk about it. It is like being in Hell.'

"I could tell that this frustrated them, but they understood. Before I was drafted, I was a young man who laughed easily. I knew my smile was gone. I kept myself busy at all times, so my mind did not drift back to the many battles I had participated in.

"Every night I had nightmares about bullets hitting me, and about me shooting other people. I dreamed of the screaming wounded German soldiers, and the Polish soldiers who were run over by the tanks. I would sit up, thinking I was sleeping in a foxhole, and realize I was safe in my bed.

"'What is it, Georg?' Ingred would ask after I awakened her.

"'Nothing. I was just dreaming. Go back to sleep.'

"The night before I had to leave, I held my son in my arms until the small boy fell asleep. I buried my nose in little Kurt's hair and inhaled deeply. I closed my eyes and just smelled my son's hair. I wanted to remember this smell, and to think of it whenever I was frightened. I knew that if I ever felt like I was about to die, I would remember this one moment of togetherness.

"The week passed all too fast, and I was back with my squad. I was stationed on a base, but this time it was in the Rhineland, which was located near France.

"On November 30th the Soviets invaded Finland. This led to a three-month war, which resulted in heavy casualties for the Soviets, and the conquest of Finland.

"It was shortly after this that Ellis asked me if I would like to join the German paratroopers, or Fallschirmjager. We had both received invitations to join, as had many other exceptional soldiers.

"'Think of it Georg, other than cutting a few phone lines and railroad tracks, they didn't even have to fight in Poland! We could watch the war from the safety of Berlin!'

"I was skeptical. They would not be so vigorous in their recruiting attempts if they did not intend to use the paratroopers.

"'What if they do use us for combat?'

"'It will probably be for some special operations. We won't be put into any major battles.' Ellis seemed quite confident of his idea.

"I agreed, and we both went through the six-week paratrooper course.

"We were issued new uniforms, which included a jump smock, better boots, and a different type of helmet. We were warned never to wear standard German helmets for skydiving because the rear edge of the helmet could seriously injure us. The new helmets were more rounded, without the extra neck protection.

"My most vivid memory of this training was skydiving. I hesitated for a moment when it was my turn to jump. I looked at the land thousands of meters below. I thought to myself, *This is what I must do to survive the war. If I fail now, my chances of survival are lower.* With that in mind, I jumped out of the plane.

"My nine-meter static line pulled my chute opened almost immediately, but for a second I was falling like a stone. It was terrifying, and yet thrilling at the same time. When the chute opened, I fell slower, and actually enjoyed it very much.

"After many jumps and much training, we learned to control our speed and direction as we parachuted down to Earth. Ellis and I took this part of the training much more seriously than most of the other soldiers. We knew it could mean life or death.

"In April of 1940, the German army invaded Denmark and Norway. There was almost no fighting at all, and our division was not even called into action. We remained on alert, just in case of an emergency.

"Ellis and I continued to practice our sniping techniques. We also became good friends. Ellis said I was a fast learner, and I respected Ellis' abilities.

"In addition to sniper training, I learned how to deploy and disarm mines. I also learned a few things about how to fight tanks. I learned that they had vulnerable spots, such as their treads and their cannon. A heavy weapon, such as an anti-tank gun could more easily damage them in these areas. I learned how to throw an anti-tank grenade, like the one I saw used so effectively in Poland.

"The Wehrmacht received many new weapons. These included various arms from the Czech, Austrian, and Polish arsenals. It also included some better tanks.

"Many squads received new submachine-guns to upgrade their close range firepower. These included captured Czechoslovakian and German MP 38's.

"On April 9th, Ellis and I were informed that we had been selected to join an elite team of paratroopers. This surprised us, since we were relatively new paratroopers.

"We were trained in demolitions and house-to-house fighting. We trained with submachine-guns rather than rifles.

"I was terrified by the prospect. I knew that France and the United Kingdom had declared war upon Germany, but I had hoped that this would not lead to any heavy fighting. My father had been killed in France, and now I was going to war there myself.

"Images of the Polish campaign flashed through my mind. I had received a medal for participating in it. I wondered if I would live to receive my next medal.

Grandma leaned forward and patted Grandpa's hand. "I think that's enough for tonight, Georg."

Young George yawned. "Wanna go outside for some fresh air, Grandpa?" he asked.

"Yes, I think we could both use some," Grandpa said as he walked to the door.

Once they were gone, Grandma sat and buried her head in her hands and wept. "If only I had known, all these years, how much he suffered…"

CHAPTER 6

▼

EBEN-EMAEL, AND THE INVASION OF WESTERN EUROPE

"Ellis and I were called into a secret meeting. It took place on April 17th, in the afternoon. We were sitting in a conference room, along with eighty-three other paratroopers. The men were speaking in hushed tones, wondering what was going on.

"A Captain entered the room, and the paratroopers all stood at attention. He walked to the front of the room, and told us all to be seated.

"'Good afternoon. I congratulate all of you for being good enough soldiers to be here right now. You have all been hand picked, and you are our very best. You have been selected for a very secret and important operation. I am Captain Dorn, and I will be your commanding officer during this operation.'

"He stood and unrolled a large aerial photograph. He hung it on the wall behind him with several tacks. It depicted a huge mountain fortress, with several artillery cannons and castle-like buildings. I had never seen anything like it before.

"'This is the Fortress Eben-Emael. It is strategically located in the Belgian Mountains, and overlooks much of Belgium.' Then he added ominously, 'It is considered to be the strongest single fortress in the world, more formidable for men and tanks than even the Maginot line.'

"My heart began to beat faster. I felt myself being drawn into a very dangerous situation. It was too late to turn back now.

"'We believe the garrison here to be about twelve hundred men. You will be outnumbered, but you will have the element of surprise.'

"'As I said previously, you have all been carefully hand picked for your various specialties. You are seventy-four of the most dangerous soldiers in the armed forces: five demolitions experts, three medics, and three communications experts.'

"He pointed at the large armored roof of the fortress. 'This is where you will land with your parachutes. It should be unguarded when you land, and will make a good landing zone.'

"He pointed to several armored turrets with artillery guns fixed into them. They had no hatches or other means of entry on the top. He then pointed to the many artillery guns and anti-aircraft guns. 'These are the reason you are attacking this fortress. As long as these two hundred and twenty-millimeter guns are in the hands of the Allies, we cannot effectively attack Belgium. In short, our entire invasion depends upon this mission. You must not fail.'

"He reached into a wooden box, which was already on the table. He removed a submachine-gun. 'This is an MP35. It fires nine-millimeter rounds and has a thirty-two round magazine. The effective range of this weapon is about two hundred meters.'

"He returned the MP35 and picked up a small black pistol with a silencer attached to the barrel. 'This is a Walther-PP with silencer. It also fires nine-millimeter ammunition, and is effective to about fifty meters.'

"Next he held up a flamethrower. The fuel tank was shaped like a round life preserver. 'This is the manpack flamethrower, also known as the flamethrower-40. It has a thirty-six meter range and enough fuel to fire continuously for about two minutes. It is recommended that you use ten second bursts, giving you about twelve shots. Twenty of you will be issued these weapons.'

"The Captain then held up a cone-shaped explosive, 'This is a shaped charge. It has been fitted with the same detonator cord that the S24 grenade uses, except the fuse time has been extended to ten seconds.' He pointed to one of the armored turrets on the picture. 'The charges are magnetic. Attach one to the armored turret, pull the cord, and get a safe distance away. It will blast through the armor and kill the crew inside. Twenty of you will be issued two of these, and your five demolitions experts will also each have two of them.'

"'You will all be issued one MP35, one silenced Walther PP, as well as two S24 (stick) grenades. Those of you who are not issued flamethrowers or shaped charges will be issued extra grenades and ammunition.'

"I raised my hand. The Captain pointed to me. "Yes, Corporal?"

"'Excuse me, Sir, but I'm a sniper. I need my carbine, to be effective.'

"The Captain addressed the entire room. 'I realize that many of you specialize in the use of various weapons. It was determined that they were too heavy for this operation. We normally drop weapon containers along with you men from the air, but because of the necessity for pinpoint accuracy in your drop, this is not possible. You will instead be carrying your weapons on your body in special weapon pouches which will be attached to your uniforms.'

"After the plan was announced, we were allowed several hours to speak with one another and plan the finer details of the attack. I was told to help the other snipers pin down the enemy inside of the barracks and take out any guards who might be outside of them. Ellis was ordered to do the same. We were among those who were issued extra ammunition and stick grenades.

"Our team was taken to a replica of the fortress. It was amazingly detailed, and was almost exactly like the picture we had seen. We drilled over and over. To increase the number of practices we had each day, special gliders were used in place of parachutes. Each day we would get into our gliders with full gear, glide down to the roof, and practice placing charges and attacking the areas of the fortress where resistance was expected. We used blank cartridges and dummy grenades and charges. Several infantrymen were inside, pretending to be Belgian guards. We did this drill at least ten times per day, right up until May 9th, when the invasion began. We each learned the location of every room, door, and corridor within the entire fortress.

"We all waited, listening to news of the invasion. German forces attacked Belgium, France, Holland and Luxembourg simultaneously. We were awakened in the middle of the night on May 10th and were told that the mission was a go, and that we would be going immediately.

"Shortly after this, we were outfitted with our special uniforms. We had a long zipper compartment on our backs to hold the MP35's. We also had a holster on our belts for our Walther PP's. The silencers were in a small pouch on the side of the holster.

"We were issued special belts which held eight magazines for the MP35, and four magazines for the Walther PP. A commando style knife was in a holster on our boots.

"At 0300 hours we were airborne and headed for Belgium. We were scheduled to drop down just after it was light enough to see the roofs of the buildings inside the fortress. Ellis and I were both very anxious, and we gave each other a handshake.

"'See you on the ground,' said Ellis.

"'I'll be there. Don't get shot, Ellis.'

"'Remember rule number one.'

"'I remember.'

"Captain Dorn turned and spoke to the group of paratroopers, 'We are going to be over the target area in five minutes. Be ready, and remember to cut away your chutes as quickly as possible and get clear for the man behind you!'

"I took out my locket, which always hung around my neck. I opened it and looked at the pictures of my wife and son. I closed it and kissed the cold metal before placing it under my shirt.

"A few minutes later the jump door was opened and we quickly began to jump out in single file. I secured my jump goggles and jumped out.

"For a moment I panicked, because I saw only darkness below me. Then I could make out the fortress and the line of parachutes leading towards it. I steered myself in that direction.

"'I can't believe this is happening,' I thought. The fortress was getting closer by the second. All of us eighty-five paratroopers were silently dropping down upon it like ghosts.

"Then we began to land. Just as we had planned, we quickly landed and released their parachutes. One-by-one we landed on the concrete roof of the large fortress.

"As I neared the roof, the silence of the night was shattered by the sounds of someone yelling in French. I knew we had been spotted. The sounds of gunfire quickly followed.

"I finally landed. I ran a few steps to stop and released my parachute. It blew away with the morning breeze. Ellis landed behind me and did the same.

"I could see and hear several paratroopers firing off the edge of the roof, toward the ground. Some were dropping off the edge of the roof into the top floor. There were several armored artillery turrets located there.

"'Stay clear!' they shouted from down below. A few seconds after that, several of the shaped charges went off one after another. I could see smoke from the explosions as it rose into the night sky.

"Ellis and I followed our planned orders and moved to cover the entrances of the four barracks buildings. I could see muzzle flashes from the doorways and windows. The men inside were finally responding. I unzipped the MP35 and loaded a magazine into it. I began firing at the muzzle flashes.

"Many more paratroopers climbed down into the top floor. Ellis and I continued to fire rounds into the barracks far below. I heard a bullet as it bounced off the wall near me. We were lying prone, using the stone roof for cover from the Belgian infantry below.

"Two of the German soldiers who had rapelled down to the ground were sneaking up to two of the windows of the closest barracks. They simultaneously threw grenades into the windows. A few seconds later, there were two loud bangs inside from the grenades, followed by screams. We each fired a full magazine from our MP35's into the windows, then reloaded. Another soldier crawled up and threw a grenade into the doorway. There was another loud explosion, followed by more screams. I then sprayed automatic fire from my MP35 into the door.

"Now paratroopers were everywhere. Several more grenades were hurled into the other barracks, and the sound of gunfire and grenades exploding filled the air.

"I spotted a Belgian soldier exiting a building other than a barracks. He had a rifle in his hands, and was aiming into the darkness. I shot him twice, and he fell.

"'Good shot, Frick,' said Ellis. He was about ten feet away from me. I gave him a thumb's up and continued scanning the scene for any sign of the enemy.

"Within ten more minutes, the sounds of gunfire had ceased in all but the last barracks. The men in that building had been attacked last, and had the most time to prepare.

"I spotted a team of paratroopers on the roof. One of them had what looked like an S24 stick grenade with the heads of six more S24 grenades attached to it. He crawled over until he was above the doorway, and hurled it in. Then he stood up and ran as fast as he could.

"It was a good thing that he did. The explosion blew green flame out all of the windows of the building, and buckled the sheet metal walls. I was certain that anyone inside had been instantly killed.

"I saw several Belgians coming out of another building with their hands up. They were quickly mowed down by one of the paratroopers. We had been ordered to take no prisoners.

"With the barracks cleared, the paratroopers could now concentrate on the main part of the fortress, which contained the artillery and anti-aircraft cannons. Ellis and I could hear gunfire and grenades going off in the many tunnels of the fortress below us for many hours. We continued to scan the courtyard below until paratroopers on the ground signaled that it was clear.

"'We should go in and help with the assault,' said Ellis.

"I shook my head, and we climbed down—two friends, together. We loaded a fresh magazine into our MP35's, and pointed them ahead as we cautiously advanced into the smoke-filled corridor behind the 220mm artillery turrets, which had been blasted with shaped charges earlier. The sounds of fighting continued about two floors down, so we hurried to join the other paratroopers.

"We finally reached a large group of paratroopers. We made hand signals, indicating that the room down the hall contained enemy soldiers.

"Suddenly, one of the Belgians tossed a grenade around the corner. One of the paratroopers held his MP35 like a cricket stick and smacked the grenade back in the direction of the Belgians. It flew through the air and exploded down the hall. The same soldier now nimbly pulled the detonator cord on a S24 stick grenade and quickly threw it in the room full of Belgian soldiers. It exploded and he quickly sprayed his MP35 in the room.

"Another Belgian suddenly appeared around a corner down the hall with a rifle in his hands. He shot one of the paratroopers in the chest. I snapped off a shot, hitting the Belgian soldier in the chest. Both of the men who had been shot fell down. A medic began attempting to help the paratrooper who had been shot.

"We came to an open area which contained a pillbox. This was a small building made of reinforced concrete, which gave good protection to the crew inside from many types of attacks. Inside the pillbox was a Belgian machine-gun crew. The heavy machine-gun crew opened fire on us, but none of us were hit. I could hear the sound of bullets ricochet everywhere, bouncing off the concrete walls and floors. They made high-pitched whines as they tumbled through the air. The machine-gun was so close to us, we could hear the brass bullet casings as they hit the floor. The air was filled with loud sounds of guns firing, bullets flying through the air, explosions, and screams. The quiet fortress had suddenly turned into a warzone. Aside from the many sounds, heat could be felt from the many explosions and flamethrower bursts. It was difficult to see more than ten meters, because of all the smoke.

"I crawled up to the wall and opened fire at the same instant another soldier hurled a grenade around the corner toward the Belgian gunner. I shot the Belgian in the face, and he fell. I also shot the loader before ducking back around the corner. The grenade exploded with an extremely loud sound, which echoed off the concrete walls of the fortress.

"The soldier who had thrown the last grenade said 'Cover me.'

"I stood and aimed at the machine-gun nest as the man advanced, and then he threw another grenade into it.

"We heard rifle fire coming from a small firing hole in a steel door, which was behind the pillbox. I fired a bullet into the hole and called up a paratrooper carrying a flamethrower.

"The soldier with the flamethrower quickly ran up and shot burning fuel into the firing hole. We heard screams and the sounds of the flames inside. Black smoke poured out of the hole.

"Another soldier placed a shaped charge on the door, and we took cover as the door exploded. Without giving anyone inside time to recover, we stormed into the room. Dead and dying Belgian soldiers were all over the room.

"There was another door in the back of the room, which also had a small hole for firing out into the walkway beyond. I looked through the hole and saw several Belgian soldiers running toward the door. I immediately put my MP35 up to the hole and began firing at them. I quickly fired a burst of automatic fire, moving the gun horizontally and firing at chest height. All of the Belgian soldiers fell down, screaming in pain.

"The quick soldier who had earlier hit a grenade like a cricket ball now opened the door and hurled a stick grenade out of it. He quickly closed the door and waited for the grenade to explode. He then immediately motioned for the others to follow, and went out of the door.

"The walkway led to an area which was tunneled out of the side of the mountain. I saw another Belgian soldier round the corner, and promptly shot him in the chest. I put a fresh magazine into my MP35. I was beginning to like the weapon because of its quick rate of fire, light weight, and large magazine capacity. It was perfect for this sort of combat.

"When we reached the next floor down, we saw a team of paratroopers who were unable to get past a corner which led into a large room. Shortly after we met up with the team, a Belgian threw a grenade around the corner at us. We were all able to find cover just before the grenade exploded with a loud bang.

"The quick soldier silently ran up as he pulled the detonator cord on his S24 grenade. He hurled it around the corner, while holding his

MP35 ready. It exploded, and he snapped around the corner, spraying the MP35. He then motioned for the others to follow.

"The next room had two of the round firing holes facing us, and we came under fire immediately. None of us were hit.

"'Give me a shaped charge,' said the quick soldier. He held out his hand and one of the other paratroopers gave him one. He pulled the detonator cord and hurled it around the corner. There was a metallic sound as it hit the steel wall and stuck to it.

"The explosion of the shaped charge was massive. The Belgian soldiers screamed as they were killed by the blast. Our group of paratroopers looked around the corner and we saw that even the armored door had been blown open. We quickly walked inside and found all of the defenders dead.

"We heard several explosions and gunshots on the floor below. The floor we were now on was clear, so we cautiously walked down the stairs. We saw two slain paratroopers at the bottom of the stairs, riddled with bullets. In front of the stairway was a hallway, which had been blocked with a waist high wall of sandbags and a heavy machinegun. Three dead Belgian soldiers were behind it. There were black blast marks all over their bodies and the walls from what must have been a grenade.

"Farther down the hallway we could see several of our fellow paratroopers firing their weapons. We could not see who or what we were shooting at. We rushed up, and one of the paratroopers signaled us to wait. One of our men hurled a grenade down the hallway we had been shooting down, and we all ducked behind walls to escape the effects of the blast. It went off, and someone tossed a small round grenade into the center of us. It came from the direction in which we had just thrown our grenade. We all took cover, but some of us still got wounded by the blast.

"'Cover me, you two,' said the quick soldier who had killed several Belgian defenders earlier. He grabbed a stick grenade from his belt, and unscrewed the bottom. He held the detonator cord, but did not pull it yet. He got down into a crouch, and stayed very low as he walked. This allowed Ellis and I a clear shot over his head.

"Suddenly a Belgian soldier's head popped around the far corner, along with an arm holding a pistol. A bullet hole appeared in the soldier's forehead from Ellis' well-placed bullet. He had aimed and fired in a fraction of a second. It was amazing. The dead Belgian soldier fell to the floor. Only his right arm and head were visible. The rest of his body was around the corner.

"The quick soldier continued to sneak up to the doorway where the man's head had appeared. I aimed my sights at the same site where Ellis had shot the Belgian soldier in the head. Ellis also aimed carefully.

"Another Belgian soldier snapped around the corner with a pistol. Two bullets instantly struck him in the face. He fell and dropped his pistol. He screamed in shock and retreated into the room.

"The quick soldier pulled the detonator cord. He waited a couple of seconds and tossed it around the corner. It exploded, and there were many anguished cries inside the room.

"The soldier with the flamethrower now moved up to the doorway. Without looking into the room, he sprayed burning fuel from his flamethrower around the corner in a large arc. Several bullets hit the wall around his hand, but he was not hit. Screams of agony erupted from the room, and the paratrooper with the flamethrower quickly retreated behind Ellis and me. Smoke from the flames inside the room crawled along the ceiling into the corridor.

"'It must be another barracks,' said Ellis. 'There must be some still alive in there.'

"'What should we do?' I asked.

"Ellis went around the room and collected six stick grenades. He produced a small hacksaw and began cutting the heads off of the sticks. He told me and the others to cover the door as he did this.

"After cutting the heads off the six grenades, he produced two pieces of wire and wrapped the six heads around a seventh grenade, which was still attached to its stick.

"'So that's how you make those things,' I said.

"Ellis nodded. 'Very effective on strong points.'

"When the super-grenade was finished, he handed it to the quick soldier, and told him to throw it into the room.

"As we had done before, we watched the doorway for Belgians, as the paratrooper with the grenade quietly walked up and pulled the detonator cord. He then hurled the massive grenade into the room around the corner. He ran back to Ellis and me.

"I did not expect the massive explosion which followed shortly after that. I thought one of my eardrums burst. I could feel the instant flash of the shock wave as it passed through my body.

"'Go!' said Ellis. He ran into the room, blasting with his MP35.

"The quick soldier, the soldier with the flamethrower and I followed close behind him. The room was filled with about fifty dead or dying Belgian soldiers. We mowed the few of them who were still standing down with bullets. They had been knocked senseless by the blast, and could offer little resistance.

"With this last pocket of resistance gone, the fortress was ours. We walked out the front of the castle-like structure into the courtyard. Captain Dorn was waiting for us with two dozen more paratroopers.

"Captain Dorn was now giving orders. 'Find their radio. Radio Berlin that we control Eben-Emael!'

"Dorn seemed to be shocked at the mission's success. He looked around in disbelief and said, 'We have done it, men! Excellent job!'

"Ellis and I found the Belgian's armory and helped ourselves to two rifles. We still had no scopes, but felt that we would be much more effective with rifles than submachine-guns. All the same, we put the MP35's back into our special jumpsuit pockets, and zipped them shut.

"The fortress was over a quarter of a mile high, and the only way up was a narrow mountain road, which we could easily fire upon. The fortress had been designed to hold off thousands of men and armored vehicles.

"As the sun rose, we could hear the sounds of shelling in the distance. It always reminded me of the sound of thunder.

"I felt a bit sorry for the unfortunate Belgians. They had cunningly prepared these massive guns for their defense, and they had not done much to defend themselves.

"Captain Dorn also informed us that Germany was winning on all fronts, and that the Wehrmacht would soon push their Blitzkrieg into the countryside below the fortress. This news resulted in an enthusiastic cheer from all of us. I hated to think what would have happened had they taken the fortress, only for the Wehrmacht to never take the ground around them.

"France was known for having one of the world's strongest and most technologically advanced armies. It was amazing that the

Wehrmacht could defeat them, even with their many allies helping them.

George sighed as he thought, *Oh, boy. Here we go back to history class. Come on, Grandpa, let's get back to the action.*

What was more, the German army of two million men was defeating an Allied army of four million.

"Captain Dorn began to give orders. 'We need to blow those guns!'

George grinned. It was almost as if Grandpa had heard his thoughts.

"The demolition specialists went up into the upper portion of the fortress and began blowing up the massive 220mm guns with their shaped charges. They were done in about half an hour.

"Several of us paratroopers watched the road and the skies for signs of trouble. Someone shouted "Enemy approaching!" at the top of his lungs. He pointed at the mountain road, which led to the fortress.

"As we looked up ahead, we saw a huge column of Allied soldiers moving up the road. Some were in jeeps, while others were on foot.

"'Take defensive positions!' shouted Captain Dorn.

"Ellis and I took cover inside a pillbox, and even though we were not in an undetectable sniper foxhole, we began taking incredibly long shots at the approaching enemies. Due to the great distance, and the fact that we had no scopes, we could not tell what weapons they carried, so we could not prioritize our targets. We just fired blindly at them. Soon after this, another pair of German paratroopers loaded one of the heavy machine-guns inside of a pillbox and began firing at the approaching column.

"'Radio command! Tell them we need assistance—*right now!*' shouted Dorn.

"The radio crew had taken over the fortress' radio station. It was inside of a room near the front gate. I looked back and saw them speaking into a microphone.

"Some of the Allied soldiers were still attempting to crawl toward the fortress. Others returned fire, but had little chance of hitting the Germans, since we were all inside pillboxes and other fortifications.

"There was a massive explosion as some of the paratroopers on the upper portion of the fortress fired a 75mm anti-aircraft cannon at the approaching Belgian soldiers. A jeep exploded and flew high into the air.

"The sound of bullets being fired in the direction of the Germans intensified as more and more weapons were fired at us. At least two heavy machine-guns were firing at one time, until Ellis and I located it and shot the crews.

"This intense battle continued for about twenty minutes. Some 3000 Belgian infantry attempted to enter the fortress under heavy fire from the seventy-five paratroopers who were firing rifles, heavy machine-guns, and eventually four anti-aircraft cannons.

"At this point in the battle, about fifty German Stuka dive-bombers began dropping massive 500-pound bombs on the enemy infantry. The explosions from these weapons killed every soldier within at least thirty meters, and several of them were direct hits on the infantry column. The dive-bomber would plummet from the sky, making a loud roaring sound as it increased to incredible speed. It raced directly toward its target, released the bomb it carried, and pulled up sharply. This exposed us to enemy fire, but made our bombs extremely accurate.

"Shortly after the bombing began, another three squads of German paratroopers parachuted down onto the roof of the fortress. They quickly released their parachutes and joined in the defense of the fortress.

"The troops that were left in the column began to withdraw. Our German troops continued to fire at them until they were out of range. The bodies of Allied soldiers were all over the road. The bombs left huge craters in the pavement.

"Later that afternoon, a German Panzer division reached the land below Eben-Emael. This resulted in a cheer from everyone in the fortress, including Ellis and I.

"We also witnessed several air battles between the German and Allied air forces. One of the formations of Allied planes flew dangerously close to the fortress, and the men who were manning the 75mm cannons opened fire on them. We shot down four of them before they were out of range.

"Shortly afterwards, a small contingent of German infantry was driving up the road in several armored cars. I saw the vehicles bounce as they drove over the bodies of Allied soldiers. They had to weave around bomb craters.

"When they reached the top, the gate was opened, and they were allowed to enter.

"A German Major got out of one of the vehicles and spoke to Captain Dorn 'Well done, Captain Dorn! You have opened the road to Brussels!' He shook Dorn's hand.

"Then he turned and addressed all of the paratroopers. 'Excellent job, men! You have pleased Thor, the God of battle today!' He pointed at the swastika armband on his coat.

"We had been taught in basic training that the swastika was the symbol of Thor, the ancient God of war, thunder and lightning. The symbol of Thor resembled a hammer being thrown through the air, which had the speed of lightning, and struck with a clap of thunder.

"'As a reward for your valor, you will remain here as a temporary garrison for the next few days. Do not allow the Allies to retake this fortress.'

"The major looked out onto the battle, which raged in the countryside below. 'It is a beautiful view, isn't it?' He got back into his armored car, and they drove back down the mountain.

"The dead Belgians were unceremoniously thrown over the side of the mountain. We rested in their bunks, ate their food, and drank out of the many barrels of wine that were found in one of the storerooms.

"Ellis and I spoke to each other about having the luxury of sitting up here in a relatively safe place, while the battle raged around us. It was much safer than being in the field. As we tried to sleep that night, the thunder of artillery shook the entire fortress.

"Sentries stood guard around the base, and early the next morning Ellis and I had our turn at sentry duty. The quick soldier walked up and joined us.

"Ellis shook his hand. 'Hello there! What is your name, soldier?'

"'I am Lance Corporal Konrad Shuler.' He shook my hand as well. 'What are your names?'

"Ellis and I introduced ourselves.

"'You move like a cat!' I said.

"Konrad smiled. 'Thank you. If it wasn't for your expert aim I would not be alive.'

"'We make a good team,' said Ellis. He made a motion as if aiming and firing an MP35. Konrad motioned as if he was throwing a grenade.

"'How can you move with such agility?' asked Ellis.

"Konrad shrugged. 'Before the war, I was in school, and I played a lot of sports.'

"'What sort of sports?' I asked.

"'Cricket, football, wrestling,' he said, smiling. 'All the things girls like.'

"We all laughed. Ellis pointed at me and said, "Don't tell Georg that. He's married and a father already!" He and Konrad laughed again.

"'What's wrong with that?' I asked.

"Konrad and Ellis wiped tears from their eyes and tried to stop laughing. Then they burst out laughing all over again, 'Nothing!' they said together.

"I began to think of home. I wondered when—or if—I would see my son and wife again. I wondered what they were doing at that moment. I pictured Ingred working in the bakery, and Kurt playing on the living room floor with his toys.

"A loud artillery blast woke me from my daydream. It was miles away, but still shook the ground.

"'I hope our army is still winning,' said Konrad. All three of us looked from the edge of Eben-Emael upon the Belgian landscape.

"We received war reports every day after that. We stayed in the fortress, guarding it from an attack that never came. It was like a sanctuary from the war. We all had plenty to eat and drink, and all of us became good friends.

"On May 20th we learned that the Panzer forces of Heinz Guderian had reached the Atlantic coast, cutting off a huge army of French and British soldiers from their supplies and communications.

"After several battles and counterattacks, the German lines to the Atlantic held, and on May 28th, Belgium surrendered.

"With the fall of Belgium, the full force of the German armies was unleashed upon the Northern border of France. German troops entered Paris on June 12th, and on June 25th, France surrendered. This surely shocked the entire world. The French government was allowed to continue running the southern half of France. The northern half was occupied by Germany.

We learned that a massive Allied army had fled the beaches of Dunkirk. Over three hundred thousand In had been evacuated, and had left all of their weapons on the beaches.

"The arsenals of Belgium, France, Holland, and Luxembourg were taken over by the German army.

"The conquest of France was followed by a nine-month period of relative quiet for the Wehrmacht. The German Air Force waged war with Britain, but the infantry had little to do with it.

"Hitler himself was so pleased with our unit that he visited us personally and presented each of us with a special medal depicting the fortress Eben-Emael. He shook each of our hands and congratulated us. This was a great honor for most of the men, but I had mixed feelings about the Fuhrer. I wanted very much to ask him 'Is the war over now? Can I go home and live in peace?' but I knew that would be foolish, and could possibly even result in my imprisonment. I simply smiled and accepted my medal.

"All of us were given a one-month leave. This was the best reward I could have possibly been given. I cared little for medals. I tossed them into a wooden box in my closet and forgot about them. I tried not to think of the many men who died just so I could earn them.

"I again suffered from horrible nightmares. I woke up at least once every night, thinking I was in combat. I would suddenly jump, scream, or wake up fully alert. The room was dark and I was disoriented. It took me a few seconds to realize that Ingred was asking me what was wrong, and that I was in fact home. She complained that I often talked in my sleep about 'terrible things.' Toward the end of the month I had fewer nightmares, but the time with my family went by very quickly.

"Kurt was two years old, and was very happy to see me. Ingred and Mother told me that Kurt frequently asked things like 'Where's Daddy?' while I was gone. They would reply, 'Daddy has gone to war.'

"'Now that the war is over, can't you come home?' asked Ingred one night.

"'I'm not sure it's over, Ingred.'

"'What do you mean?'

"'We are still at war with Britain. We're supposed to be getting more training when I get back. They might be planning to take over another country. It's all very secret stuff, but you can tell when something is being planned.'

"Ingred cried, and held me in her arms. 'Don't they have enough land? You've helped them conquer three countries, not to mention the other six they've conquered! When will it all end?'

"I shrugged. 'I have no idea. Soon, I hope. All I can do is hope.'

"Ingred became very upset. 'I can tell you one thing; if this war ever ends, we are moving out of this damn country!'

"The idea of fleeing Germany had never occurred to me, but the more I thought about it, the more I liked it. 'I like that idea, Ingred. Save what money you can, and we'll move somewhere safe when this is all over.'

"'Where is safe?'

"'I don't know."

"When I returned to the base, my training did indeed intensify. It was as if we were training for another war. We parachuted at least once a week and had weapon practice every day. We learned how to cut telephone and power lines, and how to destroy bridges and rails with high explosives.

"My friends Ellis and Konrad tried to talk me into going out for a drink with them, but I stayed on the base. 'I'm sorry. I'm not here to have a good time. I just want to serve my four years and get the hell out of here." I saved every penny of my wages and sent it home for Ingred to save. I got free food and drink on the base, and had no expenses.

Grandma put her hand in her apron pocket. She pulled out a coin. She had not kept many of the Marcs, but she still had this one. She turned it over and over in her hands, then handed it to George. "This is one of the pieces I saved," she said. "I kept it—just this one."

George sat there, a look of surprise and admiration on his face. "We'll continue tomorrow night," he said and got up and walked upstairs—to the closet and to his medals.

CHAPTER 7

▼

OPERATION MERCURY, THE INVASION OF CRETE

"In early April the German Army began conquering Yugoslavia. Before it was finished taking over the entire country, it also attacked Greece, which was defended by both Greek and United Kingdom soldiers. The Yugoslavian army surrendered on April 14th, while Greece managed to hold out until April 30th. Fewer than two thousand German soldiers were killed during this entire campaign, and the battles were relatively small compared to those in Poland and Western Europe.

"While this fighting was going on, all of us paratroopers were training for Operation Mercury. This was the code name for the invasion of the Island of Crete, which was south of Greece, and was protected by British troops.

"The plan called for elements of an entire division of paratroopers to be dropped all over the island, which would be followed by reinforcements brought to the island by the German Navy.

"Ellis and I, along with the other snipers in our regiment were armed with sniper rifles, and scopes. I once again equipped my rifle with my higher-powered Zeiss scope. Ellis did the same. We also kept our silenced Walther PP pistols, and we each had two S24 grenades. We were not issued shaped charges for this mission, as there were no heavy fortifications such as those found at Eben-Emael.

"Our new friend Konrad specialized in close fighting rather than sniping, so he equipped himself with the MP35. Unlike foot soldiers, who were assigned their weapons, the paratroopers were allowed to select their weapons to some degree.

"We also had a lot of standard equipment, including a spade, paratrooper knife, helmet, rations, and a few tools. It was surprising how much equipment we could safely parachute with. Only those who were specially trained to do so could jump with their weapons. The other paratroopers had to jump with only four grenades and a pistol, with their weapons stored in containers. These were parachuted in alongside the paratroopers.

"The invasion began when German heavy bombers bombed the airfields on Crete. The entire island airforce was destroyed on the ground.

"My two friends and I were among the second wave of paratroopers. The initial wave landed in the early morning of May 20th, 1941. It was later learned that this force was nearly annihilated shortly after it reached the ground.

"Our commanders informed us that plans had been changed, and our battalion was going to be dropped over the open country west of Maleme. We were ordered to take the nearby Maleme airport and hold it at all costs.

"We boarded a JU-52 bomber. It held one squad of twenty paratroopers, and was one of a fleet of fifty such planes. There were also several paratroopers in DFS-230 assault gliders, which were towed behind JU-52's.

"We took off from one of the many airbases which had been captured in Greece, and the sky was filled with the formations of bombers. There were no windows for us to look out of, so we had no idea whether we were over water or land. We all simply sat and looked forward at the cockpit door.

"Images of combat flashed through my mind. Would this be the mission that would kill me? I dreaded the thought. I knew I had been lucky to escape death many times. It only took one bullet or piece of shrapnel in the right place, and I would be a dead man. I again opened my locket and looked at the pictures of my wife and son. I closed the locked and gave it a gentle kiss before putting it away.

"There was very little conversation among us. We simply waited until the plane neared the drop zone. The sound of the engines would have made conversation difficult anyway.

"We had no idea that we were headed into a trap. The British had cracked the secret German codes and had known of the invasion of Crete the whole time. The defending garrison had been more than doubled and a British fleet was waiting to ambush the German fleet, which contained the reinforcements and heavy weapons that would be desperately needed during the attack.

"As we neared the island, machine-gun and cannon fire erupted from some of the areas behind the beaches. It was a very tense moment, for all we could do was hope that we were not unlucky enough to be shot down over the Mediterranean Sea.

"Someone started to sing the Fallschirmjager (paratrooper) marching song;

Red shines the sun, get ready, who knows
whether it will smile for us tomorrow?
"The others joined in, singing in loud voices;
The engines start, full throttle,
takeoff, on our way, today we meet the enemy!
Into the aircraft, into the aircraft!
Comrade, there is no going back!
In the distant west there are dark clouds,
Come along, and don't lose heart, come along!

Thundering engines, alone with one's thoughts,
Each one gives a quick thought to his loved ones at home,
Then comrades, come the signal to jump,
And we drift toward the enemy,
Light the beacon fire there!
Quickly we land, Quickly we land!
Comrade, there is no going back!

In the distant west there are dark clouds,
Come along men, don't lose heart, come along!

Our numbers are small, our blood is wild,
We fear neither the enemy nor death,
We know just one thing; with Germany in distress,
To fight, to win, to die the death!
To your rifles, to your rifles!
Comrade, there is no going back.
In the distant west there are dark clouds,
Come along men, don't lose heart, come along!"

"With the completion of the song, a large shell exploded nearby. The dispatcher stood up and yelled that it was time to get ready to jump. We secured our nine meter static lines to the cable on the ceiling of the aircraft, and stood in single file.

"When it was announced that it was time to drop, Ellis and I once again shook hands.

"'See you on the ground!' said Ellis. I nodded.

"We repeated the ritual with Konrad, who stood behind us. He smiled and nodded as well.

"Having our weapons with us had worked very well at Eben-Emael, so we three friends had insisted that we do it on this mission as well. I made sure all of my straps were secure. I did not want to lose my precious Kar 98K rifle. My heart pounded, and for a moment I wondered if I had the courage to even jump out of the plane. I pictured my son Kurt in my mind's eye.

"'I promise I will come home,' I whispered. This was inaudible under the sounds of the engines.

"One by one, we began to jump out of the plane. I followed Ellis, and Konrad jumped after me.

"Our senses were instantly filled with the brightness of the daylight all around us, and the force of the wind hit our bodies and clothing as we rushed toward the ground. After a short distance of free falling, our static lines pulled our parachutes open. This slowed our descent, and we took time to look at the island beneath us.

"As we descended, we could see that two of the JU-52's had been shot down and were falling into the sea.

"The center of the island was covered with mountains, and had a ring of light brown beach all around it. The ocean surrounded it as far as we could see in all directions.

"Machine-gun tracer bullets began shooting up from the ground. Several of them came within twenty feet of me as I fell. I was helplessly hanging from my parachute as I fell. I said a prayer out loud, hoping to avoid being hit. The heavy machine-gun fire had tracer bullets, which I could see shooting up from the ground below. I knew that for each tracer bullet I could see, there were many bullets that I could not see in between. I watched helplessly as several paratroopers were shot. Others had bullet holes in their parachutes, which only sped their descent a little.

"One of the gliders took a direct hit from a flak cannon, and exploded with a tremendous bang. It then began falling into the sea, with smoke pouring out of the windows. One of the wings was blown completely off.

"The City of Maleme was visible a few miles to the east. Beneath our feet was a flat area of farmland. It quickly rushed toward us as we fell.

"I watched several of the other paratroops land, including Ellis. I followed close behind them. Several gliders and weapon containers also descended toward the landing zone. Several paratroopers landed in the sea, and would have to swim for their lives.

"Once again we released our parachutes and readied our weapons. I pulled back the bolt on my carbine, putting a cartridge in the chamber. I did this as I was lying down against a small hill. I had no idea if enemies were nearby. I had seen none on my descent, but they could be hidden anywhere. They heard the sounds of shelling and small arms fire to the northwest.

"Soon the entire group, which had originally consisted of about 1000 men, was on the ground, and we began arming ourselves with weapons from our many weapon containers. These included not only small arms, but also heavy weapons, twenty-four 8mm machine-guns, twenty-four 8cm mortars, eleven 37mm anti-tank guns, and five 20mm cannons.

Then we began marching toward Maleme. About half of the men never made it to the island alive, leaving a force of about 500.

"After marching a kilometer, they heard the volume of the gunfire dramatically increase. Only a few hundred meters away were the remaining troops of the first wave of German paratroopers who had landed in this area. They were locked in a furious battle with several hundred British troops, who were in foxholes on a nearby hill. Dead paratroopers were everywhere.

"At that moment, a squadron of German dive-bombers dove out of the sky, and several bombs fell on the British troops who were entrenched on the hill. The sound of these explosions was tremendous. It was as if a lightningbolt had hammered down only a few paces away from me each time a bomb exploded, even though they were hundreds of meters away.

"The troops were given the order to engage and destroy the enemy. Ellis and I were ordered to shoot enemy heavy weapons crews, snipers, and targets of opportunity at long range. This was music to our ears. We did not want to get close to such a dug-in force.

"We decided to stay together. We found a spot which was concealed by brush and quickly dug a foxhole. An artillery shell landed within a hundred feet of us and threw dust and sand onto both of our heads. This prompted us to dig much faster.

"Within minutes, we had a deep enough foxhole and were ready to shoot. There were so many targets on the hill that we did not need to spot for one another.

"I looked through my scope. I could see several heads of British and New Zealand soldiers sticking up out of several foxholes. All of them were either aiming rifles or heavy machine-guns, and were firing at the surrounding paratroops, who were dug-in around the hill.

"I put my crosshairs on the head of a British sniper, who had a large scope on top of his rifle. Just as I was about to shoot I heard Ellis fire and saw a bullet hole appear in the sniper's temple.

"'How about if you cover your side of the hill, and I'll cover mine?'

"Whatever you say, Georg."

"I quickly found another target. It was a New Zealand soldier firing a heavy machine-gun. He had sandbags piled all around him, but his head was clearly visible. I put a bullet through it.

"I kept my crosshairs on the machine-gun and waited. Within a few seconds, another soldier grabbed the handles on the gun and began aiming the weapon.

"Before he could fire a shot, I shot him in the forehead. I quickly worked the bolt-action on my rifle and waited with the crosshairs on the machinegun.

"A third soldier attempted to fire the gun, and I shot him in his left eye. His head snapped back from the force of the bullet.

"After waiting about twenty seconds, I decided to move my crosshairs in search of another target. I quickly found a spotter for a mortar crew who was holding binoculars.

"The 8mm bullet went through the soldier's left hand and face in the same instant. It also went through the head of one of the men firing the mortar behind him. They both fell behind the wall of sandbags, where I could no longer see them.

"The mortar fired again, and the foolish soldier who had fired it peeked over the edge of the sandbag wall to see where it landed. He never got to see it, or anything else, ever again.

"We saw German 8cm mortars landing all over the hill. Several of them hit directly on top of foxholes, killing those who were inside instantly.

"After killing five more heavy machine-gun crews, eight snipers, and another observer, I could not find any targets of higher priority than riflemen, so I began to pick them off.

"I almost felt that shooting riflemen was a waste of my ammunition. I thought of the battle in Poland, when Ellis and I had a box of five hundred machine-gun bullets to use. We now had our standard sixty cartridges, many of which had already been used.

"After shooting seven riflemen, I spotted another sniper. This man was looking almost right at our position! He must have been looking for us!

"Crouching next to this sniper was an observer holding binoculars. He was pointing right down at my scope, directing the sniper's gaze.

"I moved the crosshairs back to the sniper and fired. The bullet struck him in the chin, instantly killing him.

"I moved the bolt to reload very quickly while moving the crosshairs back to the observer. The man had not yet realized that the sniper next to him had been shot. I shot him in the forehead.

"I stopped shooting for a moment so I could duck down behind the safety of the foxhole wall.

"'What's wrong?' asked Ellis. He stopped shooting as well, and looked at me.

"'We were spotted. A spotter with binoculars was giving our position to a sniper. He almost had us!'

"'Really? He must have been a good spotter. Did you get both of them?"

"'Yes, but I think we should move. There's no telling whether or not any more of them know our position.'

"'I agree. We have been here too long. I need some more cartridges anyway."

"We crawled out of the foxhole, staying behind what cover we could. The sounds of the battle were still very loud. We crawled on our bellies until we reached a group of dead paratroopers that we had seen earlier.

"We both began taking ammunition from the dead soldiers. I found that the first man I searched had only five cartridges left in his belt. I did not bother to check his gun.

"The next man I checked had both legs blown off. His weapon was an MP35, so he had only 9mm cartridges. I took the MP35 and four magazines, just in case I needed them later. It was a very handy weapon up close.

"The third dead paratrooper's head was almost completely destroyed. I tried not to look at it as I went through the unfortunate soldier's belt. I found this man's ammunition belt to be completely full. He must not have fired a shot.

"After searching several bodies, both of us had all the cartridges we could carry. We put them into two equipment bags, which we also acquired from the dead paratroopers. I estimated that we had about nine hundred rounds. Ellis slung the equipment bag over his shoulder and we began looking for a new place to shoot from.

"Our previous shooting position had an excellent view of the hill from a long range. We selected a closer spot which was concealed within an olive tree orchard, which was relatively close to the crater covered hill. We dug another foxhole and placed a few leafy olive branches on top of it. Each of us still had a small firing hole in between the branches and the earth.

"By now most of the British and New Zealand soldiers were keeping their heads down. They were definitely feeling the effects of the additional paratroopers who had reinforced the ones they had been fighting all day.

"Another artillery shell blasted in the midst of the German forces. Ellis and I scanned every enemy position visible to us, but we were unable to find its origin.

"We spotted a group of four British tanks, rolling down a road from the East toward the entrenched German paratroopers. About one hundred British infantrymen were following these tanks.

"As soon as they were within one hundred meters, the British tanks opened fire with machine-guns and cannons. This was followed by fire of all sorts from the Germans.

"Machine-gun bullets and 37mm shells began pounding the tanks. I guessed that an attack like this had already been anticipated, and the 37mm guns had been aimed down the road from a concealed position. I watched the two lead tanks explode.

"The British infantry began to retreat. I shot three of them with one cartridge as they fled. I worked the bolt-action on my Kar 98K and quickly fired five more bullets into the group. I opened the bolt and reloaded five cartridges into the internal magazine, and one into the barrel. This gave me six shots with each reload. It was one of the many tricks Ellis had taught me.

"As the two tanks attempted to retreat, they exploded when they were hit with 37mm shells. Another British artillery shell landed on the Germans. Most of the British infantrymen were shot by German gunfire as they attempted to flee down the road. They had no cover from the murderous fire.

"We stayed in our second foxhole for several hours, shooting at riflemen and the few who dared to work the heavy machine-guns on the hill. It then began to get dark.

"The night was terrifying. Artillery and mortar shells continued to rain down. Shots in the dark were common, and there was no way to know who was shooting or where.

"Every noise was suspicious. Several times I thought someone was sneaking up to the foxhole. Sleep was impossible, so we scanned for targets.

Several times Ellis and I fired at cigarettes which glowed on the hill. Each time we fired we would duck back down into the foxhole and a few bullets would fly our way from the British soldiers who had seen the muzzle flash. After the third time this happened, we decided it would be wiser to simply wait until morning. Our muzzle flash was very clearly visible in the darkness.

"I held the MP35 in my hands as I rested. The sounds of artillery shells and occasional shots broke the silence every few minutes during the entire night. Two of the shells were close enough to throw sand onto us as we lay in our foxhole.

"'So what do you think of this war, Ellis?' I asked.

"'I think it was a good idea for Austria, Czechoslovakia, Norway, Yugoslavia, Greece, Poland, maybe even for France. Now, it's overkill. This is getting old.' Ellis puffed on one of his two cigars he had been rationed that morning. He kept the glow of the cigar well below the edge of the foxhole. He was not about to fall for his own trick.

"'What do you think of all this, Georg?'

"I took a deep breath. 'I just wish I could live in peace and go home to my family.'

"'That would be nice, but what about the British? We are at war with them.'

"'Do they actually think they can defeat Germany? They must be insane.'

"'They probably are trying to pull the Americans into the war.'

"'Did you fight the Americans in the Great War?'

"Ellis turned onto his side, looking at me. 'Yes. We were locked into a stalemate on the western front. We were tired of fighting, and so were the French. The Americans sent in millions of fresh troops and we simply could not hold them back.'

"'Did you shoot any of them?'

"'I could see Ellis smile, even in the moonlight. 'Do you have to ask?'

I smiled back. 'No, I suppose I don't.'

"'They had a lot of snipers. Some of them were very good. A lot of my fellow snipers got killed.'

"I pictured my father being shot between the eyes. Perhaps it had been an American sniper who killed him in France.

"Ellis continued. 'I wouldn't worry about the Americans. I've heard that they are very much against entering the war. As far as I am concerned, they can stay home.'

"For a moment, I wanted to ask Ellis if he liked Hitler. I knew that if I did ask that simple question, I was asking for trouble. Those who disliked Hitler often disappeared. Ellis was a good friend, but there was no reason to risk getting into trouble.

"I had a sudden urge to move my bowels. 'I need to go to the crapper.'

"'Go in your helmet,' answered Ellis.

"This reminded me of basic training. We were told to urinate and defecate into our helmets when we were dug-in and under fire. I had considered this idea ridiculous and quickly forgot about it. 'There's no shooting right now, I can just crawl over there.' I pointed behind the hole.

"'I shoot people who get out of their holes all the time, Georg. It's always a risk, no matter how safe you think it is.'

"I attempted to hold it for some time. There was enough moonlight that a good sniper might spot me getting out of the hole. I finally relented, but decided to try an alternative. I defecated on the ground and scooped up my feces with my spade. I flung it out of the foxhole, along with a shovel full of soil which had been underneath.

"I still needed to urinate. This time I did go in my helmet. I threw the urine as far as I could from the hole without exposing my hand to enemy snipers. A few drops got on my hand, and I quickly wiped it clean on my trousers. I poured some water from my field flask into my helmet, and moved it around to clean it somewhat. I threw the soiled water out of the hole as well.

"We listened to the sounds of the night until morning, without speaking.

"Shortly after dawn, a German runner crawled into our foxhole. He was breathing hard, as if he had been running very fast.

"'Good morning, gentlemen,' he said in between short breaths. 'Our commanding officer was killed yesterday. The second in command was critically injured. The highest ranking officer still fit for duty is a Lieutenant,' he said.

"'Where the hell is that artillery gun they keep shooting at us?" I asked.

"'We don't know. We know it's behind the hill somewhere, and that it stops firing whenever our dive-bombers come close.'

"'We have been looking for it, but it's nowhere in our line of sight," replied Ellis.

"'How many of the British soldiers did you two hit so far?'

"'At least a hundred," I replied.

"The runner's eyes opened wide. 'You're joking!'

"'We killed everyone on the hill using a heavy machine-gun, almost all the snipers, and several riflemen. We also hit a few of their mortar crews and officers,' said Ellis.

"'That's very good! Keep them pinned down. We are going to be assaulting them today. We must take the hill today or we are going to die.'

"'Why?' I asked.

"'Because the hill overlooks the nearby airfield. We must clear the airfield of enemy fire so we can get supplies and reinforcements. We badly need anti-tank and heavier artillery.'

"'How many of us are still alive here on the island?' asked Ellis.

"'About fifteen hundred of us are here. We are not in contact with the other groups on the island, so there is no telling how many of them are left.'

"'My God!' exclaimed Ellis. About three thousand men had parachuted or glided into the Meleme area. That meant that about half of them were dead. "'What about the two fleets of ships that were supposed to arrive yesterday with the 5th Mountain Division?'

"'One fleet was ambushed by a British fleet and sank. The other fleet turned back. The air force bombed the British fleet all night.'

"'So the only way any troops or supplies can get to the island is this piece of shit airfield?' asked Ellis in an irritated voice.

"'I'm afraid so,' replied the runner.

"'God be with us,' I said.

"Before leaving the runner added 'We'll be stepping up our attacks in an hour. Try to clear the way for us, cover us as well as you can. We are depending on you.' He then ran back to the other group of paratroopers, who were dug-in closer to the hill. Several shots were fired at him as he ran.

"'We'll have to move again, Georg. Half of those British soldiers saw our runner leaving here.'

"We quickly moved to a third position. This one was behind a row of bushes. We quickly dug another foxhole behind us and began scanning for targets.

There were not very many British soldiers sticking their heads up the next morning. I spotted a periscope looking around. The soldier holding it was safe from being hit as he scanned the German lines. I put a bullet through it and destroyed it. I tried to imagine the look of surprise on the British soldier's face as I examined his periscope with a bullet hole through the center of the scope.

"A few minutes later, a heavy barrage of 8cm mortar fire began pounding the hill. The Germans were preparing to storm the hill.

"After firing about thirty mortar shells at the enemy, several German infantrymen began crawling toward the closest foxholes.

"I saw one British soldier stick his head up to look, and I shot him in the nose. He screamed so loud that I could hear him from three hundred meters away. He had not been killed, and continued to scream for half an hour.

"A grenade was thrown into one of the foxholes by the troops crawling up the hill. An instant after it exploded, the stormtroopers crawled into the hole. Another grenade was hurled down from the British foxholes and landed in one of the holes that contained German soldiers. It exploded, killing an unknown number of them.

"Another British soldier attempted to shoot our comrades as they were crawling into the foxhole. He was positioned farther up the hill, and had somehow sensed them coming. I shot him in the temple before he could fire a shot. I heard Ellis' gun at almost the same instant, but did not see a second bullet hit the soldier which he had been firing at. Ellis must have been shooting elsewhere.

"'Watch those upper holes, Georg," said Ellis.

"I moved my crosshairs up the hill and saw three British soldiers emerge from a foxhole at once. Two fired rifles, while a third threw a grenade. I shot one of the riflemen in the head, while Ellis shot the grenade thrower. The third rifleman ducked under the edge of the foxhole before I could work the bolt on my rifle. I held my crosshairs on the spot where he had been for a few seconds, but the man stayed hidden.

"Our troops were moving up the hill. They were blasting hole after hole with grenades. A few British soldiers attempted to fight back, only to be shot by either Ellis and I or the closer troops.

"While this was going on, three German gliders crash-landed on the beach behind Ellis and I. What we did not know was that these were loaded with badly needed supplies.

"Minutes later, about one hundred gliders landed several hundred meters to the east of the hill. I guessed that they were attempting to land in the vicinity of the British artillery gun, which had shot at us all night. Each glider contained ten paratroopers, which meant there were now about another one thousand men helping us. The sounds of heavy fighting erupted from that area almost instantaneously.

"By 1400, the remaining British soldiers on the part of the hill which were visible to Ellis and I were attempting to retreat. This was very difficult for them, because if they were out in the open for more than a few seconds several bullets were fired at them. I shot three of them as they attempted to run over the top of the hill, and I was sure Ellis had hit several more.

"Several of the paratroopers who had just arrived on the eastern side of the hill were now fighting their way up the hill, and soon the British were all attempting to retreat from the south side of the hill. Seeing this, several hundred German infantrymen got out of their foxholes and ran up to take control of their side of the hill.

"Within a few hours, the runner returned to our old foxhole. We watched him the entire time.

"'Go tell that idiot where we are,' said Ellis.

"While keeping myself as close to the ground as possible, I ran over to the man who was sitting in the foxhole looking around. 'We've changed our position.' I pointed to where our new foxhole was.

"I returned with the runner. I explained to him that every time he ran to our position we had to move. He apologized and acknowledged that he understood.

"'What news do you have?' asked Ellis.

"'The Lieutenant wants you two to position yourselves on the hill so you can cover the airfield and the surrounding area. We control the entire hill.'

"While we were having this discussion, we watched as one of the British tanks started up and drove over to the airfield.

"'Oh, we got one of those knocked out tanks to start. We're going to use it to clear debris on the airstrip.'

"The tank had just cleared one lane of the airstrip when several JU-52's began to land. Enemy machine-gun and artillery fire went by the planes as they landed, but none of them were seriously hit. Several German infantrymen jumped out of each plane.

"Ellis and I decided to find a new position on the hill. We selected one of the many foxholes already dug by the British and rearranged the sandbags to maximize our protection from fire from the eastern side of the island.

"Over the next two hours the entire 5th Mountain Division arrived in JU-52's. This included some twenty thousand men. They brought with them several 105mm artillery guns, and 75mm Czechoslovakian anti-tank guns. This greatly improved the morale of the exhausted paratroopers.

"We quickly located several British machine-gun nests which were located on the uneven ground to the east of the airfield. We looked through binoculars, which had a less magnified but broader field of vision than our scopes. We also located fourteen snipers and marked their positions before we began firing. We made a map in the dirt in the bottom of the foxhole. We used landmarks such as rocks and houses to locate the sniper positions. Each of us would attempt to take out seven enemy snipers as quickly as possible. Two of them were actually inside houses. Their rifle barrels were plainly visible, protruding from the open windows.

"When we felt that we had spotted everything, we prepared to begin shooting, 'Three, two, one, go!' said Ellis.

"During this countdown, I had my crosshairs on the face of a sniper who was sitting under a clump of olive trees. When Ellis said 'Go!' I put a bullet through the man's face.

"I quickly worked the bolt-action, my hands shaking. I wondered how many snipers were attampting to locate us. I looked for the next sniper, who was in one of the houses. I shot him in the head.

"Then I shot the rest of my seven designated targets, one after another. None of them seemed to suspect anything was happening. They were just doing their job, looking for a target among the Germans.

"'I missed one!' shouted Ellis. 'Damn! I can't see him now!'

"I looked to where Ellis was pointing. It was a group of large rocks. I put my crosshairs on it and saw nothing. 'The rocks?'

"'Yes. I must be getting old. He was right in the center of my crosshairs.'

"Then the British sniper began to run out of his spot in the rocks toward one of the houses. He must have known that the other sniper was in there. He did not know that the other sniper was now dead.

"Both Ellis and I fired shots at the man as he ran. It was much more difficult to hit a moving target. On his third shot, Ellis hit him in the leg and he went down. I finished him off with a shot to the chest.

"With that task completed, we had eliminated all known enemy snipers within range.

"'Let's find another hole,' I said. Ellis agreed. We moved to another hole farther up the hill. We were careful not to select a location which would make us visible against the sky behind us. This would make finding and shooting us easier. Instead, we chose one which was on the eastern side of the hill, where our camouflage would help us a great deal. We both had blackened faces, and had placed olive branches in the webbing of our helmets. This made us very difficult to see, at best.

"After moving for the fourth time, we began firing at the numerous machine-gun nests which were to the east of the hill.

"The 5th Mountain Division spent the remainder of the day getting all of their men safely off of planes and getting them organized. Major General Julius Ringel took control of all attacking forces. He was the commander of the 5th Mountain Division. Ellis and I learned these facts from Konrad, who rejoined us later that day.

Konrad also told us about how he had been in the foxholes closer to the hill all night, and how the shelling had come as close as five meters to his foxhole. He then told us that several men were shot by British snipers, and the sniper fire quickly tapered off after we had begun firing at the British positions.

"'The men greatly admired your ability to take out enemy snipers. It gave them courage to attack the hill today. I told them that you are both very skilled snipers.'

"Ellis and I told Konrad how we had cleared the many enemy snipers and heavy machine-gun operators from the hill. He replied, 'Now that I think about it, the heavy machine-gun fire stopped as well. I never thought that they had stopped because they had all been shot. I thought perhaps some of our mortars had hit them.'

"After this conversation about the battle over the hill, we asked Konrad if he would spot for us. He eagerly agreed.

"Within the next hour, he had spotted three more snipers and a dozen more machine-gun nests. Several of these were at extreme range, but we were still able to shoot the New Zealanders running them.

"'This is amazing!' exclaimed Konrad, 'I show you where they are, and *bang!* They're dead.'

"The artillery gun sounded again. 'Damn!' said Konrad. 'Where is that damn thing?'

"The entire hill was fortified with mountain soldiers and paratroops before nightfall. We set up heavy machine-gun and mortar nests and confiscated many of the heavy weapons of the dead British soldiers, who had been on the hill.

"Once again we spent the night listening to artillery shells and sniper fire. We only spotted two cigarettes glowing in the night, and fired at both of them.

"I ate my cold food rations and drank water from my field flask. I wondered how long it would be until I would receive a hot meal. I looked at the stars as I ate, and thought of my wife and son.

"After eating, I fell asleep. Konrad and Ellis were also able to sleep, despite the loud sound of artillery shells hitting every ten minutes.

"The next morning, another runner jumped into their foxhole.

"'Are you Sergeant Ellis?' he asked.

"'Yes.'

"'I have orders to escort you and your sniper team down the hill.'

"'For what purpose?'

"'You've been ordered to assist a battalion of mountain troops in flanking the enemy artillery. You'll receive more information when we get down to the bottom of the hill, Sir.'

"Konrad, Ellis and I followed the runner down the hill, where a large group of about one thousand mountain troops was assembled.

"We learned that the snipers in the 5th Mountain Division were inexperienced. Major General Ringel had heard how Ellis and I had shot and killed almost all the enemy snipers and heavy machine-gunners on Hill 107. He wanted us to accompany a battalion of men who were going to climb the mountains in a flanking maneuver on the entrenched British forces.

"'See what happens when you do your job too well?' joked Ellis. I nodded, and sighed.

"We were shown a map of the mountains to the southeast and told a few more details about the mission. The British infantry was dug-into the land between Meleme and Canae. This was causing the largest portion of the German invasion force to become involved in a stale-mate. The artillery batteries behind the British infantry had to be destroyed.

"We had our first hot meal since we had reached the island. It included sausages and biscuits. We also received our daily ration of cold food, a box of candy, two cigars, and seven cartridges. Our field flasks were refilled with cold stream water.

"The two bags full of cartridges we had collected from dead German soldiers still held about seven hundred rounds. We divided these up evenly, and we each carried one of the heavy bags. We did not allow any of the other soldiers to see how much ammunition we had.

"Within an hour, we were climbing up the closest mountain. The climb began with a two-hour hike up the side of the mountain, where it was not all that rocky or steep. The battalion encountered a few British snipers who were hiding on the side of the mountain, and we promptly shot them.

"As we began to climb up a rocky trail higher up the mountain, we came under fire from high above. A German mountain-soldier was hit in the chest, and fell off the narrow trail.

"Konrad looked up with the binoculars and quickly spotted the sniper. "He wears no uniform. He looks like a civilian," he said as he pointed at him.

"Ellis and I looked up through our scopes and saw the sniper. He was indeed a civilian with a rifle. He had climbed high up on the mountain, and had good cover. He fired at us again.

"Ellis and I fired at the same instant, and both bullets struck the man in the head. His rifle fell to the rocks below. It took several seconds for it to hit the ground, since it had to fall a great distance.

"'He was a partisan,' said Ellis. 'That's what civillians are called when they take up arms. Treat them as you would any other enemy.'

"It took us most of the day to climb high enough on the mountain to be safe from the view of British soldiers on the land below. We were about one mile above sea level, and we could see for many miles out to sea in every direction except east, where the main part of the island was. We could see that the mountain range was enormous and stretched across the entire center of the island.

"The temperature soared to a blistering one hundred and thirty degrees. Many of the men, including the three of us, took off our field jackets and tied them onto the tops of our heads. This at least kept the bright sun from baking our brains.

"When night finally came, we stopped on the top of the mountain and chose a campsite. We dug foxholes in the few areas of soft soil we were able to find on the rocky mountaintop. Most of the men were very fatigued.

"The temperature at night dropped to nearly freezing. We did not make any campfires, for fear of air or sniper attacks. Instead, we wrapped ourselves in our field jackets and curled into a fetal position as we slept. Needless to say, it was not a very comfortable night under the stars.

"The sounds of artillery shells and gunfire echoed up from the land to the north of the mountain, where the British and German armies continued to shell one another.

"We also heard German bombers pounding the British position throughout the night. They dropped heavy five hundred-pound bombs, which sounded like thunder when they exploded.

"The next day we began marching across the mountain again. Once again the temperature soared to over one hundred degrees, and many of the men with us had already drunk all of the water in their field flasks. We were desperately trying to find a stream.

"Shortly before noon we spotted a waterfall. We were near the top of it, and took turns getting water from the fast moving stream. We watched as the water fell into a large pool below and marveled at it. I had never seen one so close, and I rather enjoyed the experience. It made me forget about the war at least for a few minutes.

"The water was cool and tasted very good. I drank one full flask, and then I filled it again. I also dipped my field jacket into it, after removing my papers. I put the wet field jacket on top of my head, and this cooled me off very nicely.

"We each had to make a jump of about five feet to get over the fast flowing stream. Failing this jump would probably mean being sucked down the waterfall and most likely death or serious injury. We threw our heavy equipment across before jumping.

"When I threw the bag of ammunition, I held my breath, hoping that none of the rounds would go off. It landed with a loud jingle, and I was grateful when it did not attract too much attention. I then threw my spade, rifle, musette bag, and field flask, and then I jumped across.

"A few soldiers almost fell in, but were quickly pulled to safety by their comrades.

"It took about an hour to get the entire battalion across the stream. We quickly resumed our march to the east.

"The rate of our march was slow on the narrow pebble covered trails. We tied ropes around our waists in case one of us fell. The mountain division had been equipped with a lot of mountain climbing gear, including ropes, picks, and steel spikes.

"Later that day, we found the mutilated bodies of two German paratroopers. Their bodies had been shot several times, and their heads were cut off. We examined the bodies for several minutes, before continuing on.

"When Ellis, Konrad and I walked by them, we wondered who would do such a thing. The two paratroopers had probably landed on the central portion of the island and were attempting to reach the Germans who were near Meleme.

"A few minutes later, we came under fire from several riflemen. The ambush came from a group of partisans who were using several large rock formations for cover. There were about twenty of them.

"Several of the mountain infantrymen in the front of the formation had already been hit. Others were scrambling for what little cover was available, while a few returned fire at the partisans.

"Ellis and I immediately began firing our rifles at the partisans. Despite their cover, it was an easy shot for two deadly snipers like us. We shot them one after another in the head.

"After killing twelve partisans, we had to reload. While we reloaded, several of the partisans hid completely behind the rock and stopped firing. Three of them continued to shoot.

"Dozens of German infantrymen then began firing with deadly aim at them, and these three were quickly killed. Another German soldier crawled up to the rock and hurled a grenade over it in the area where there were still some living partisans hiding behind it. It exploded, and we heard several screams.

"Many German soldiers were badly wounded or dead, and a few of them were screaming as well. Ellis and I watched the top of the rock through our crosshairs, as a squad of Germans climbed up the face of the rock and shot the rest of the partisans.

"Ellis shouldered his rifle, looked nauseous, and then he vomited.

"'What is it?' I asked. This was most unusual behavior for the veteran sniper.

"Ellis got sick again, then whispered, 'I shot a woman and a child.'

"'What do you mean?'

"'The partisans, Frick. One was a woman and one was a teenage boy.'

"I wondered if I had shot any women or children. I had been aiming very quickly, and I watched more for the shapes of heads than actually looking at their appearances.

"Our column took a break to treat the wounded. There were several medics with us who were able to save seven men. Three soldiers were not so lucky, and died.

"Ellis and I did not look over the rock to see the bodies of the partisans. Ellis said nothing more about it.

"The heat was almost unbearable, but we conserved our water in fear of running out. Ellis swished out his mouth, and spat.

"Within an hour we were on the march once again. Two of the wounded soldiers were unable to march with any speed, so they decided to head back to the Meleme area. I wondered if they would meet the same fate as the two paratroopers we had found. I guessed that the partisans had killed and mutilated them. There were probably more of them somewhere.

"We spent the remainder of the day marching, and finally made camp at nightfall. It was far too dangerous to walk on the small trails at night. The area we selected for a campsight was rocky, so we were unable to dig foxholes. We did have good cover from several large rocks and rock formations.

"The night was very cold again, and our sleep on the rocky ground was extremely uncomfortable. The sounds of artillery shells, machine-guns, rifles, and bombs could still be heard.

"We spent the entire next day moving into position behind the location of the British artillery. We could hear the guns when they fired, so we had a good idea of where they were located. It was decided that we would rest, then attack in the morning.

"The following day was May 25th. We moved into position, over-looking the dug-in British troops, and we quickly spotted a line of trenches, covered with camouflage nets and very difficult to spot. The sound and smoke of the guns confirmed that they were located in this well-concealed spot.

"Ellis was asked to instruct two squads of snipers, totaling forty men. He told them to get behind good cover and locate as many snipers as they possibly could before opening fire. These would be their first targets.

"We had also had several 8cm-mortar crews, who aimed their weapons at the British artillery.

"Several MG-34 machine-guns had been carefully positioned. All of the crews got ready for action.

"When the commanding officer gave the signal, the entire battalion of Germans opened fire. Machine-gun, rifle, and mortar fire hit all over the British soldiers below. They were completely taken by surprise.

Several of the British were in line for breakfast when they were mowed down by machine-gun fire.

"The many German snipers immediately began shooting the British snipers. I had selected five of them as targets. I methodically shot four of them in the head. By the time I put my sights on the fifth, he was already dead. Another sniper must have shot him.

"The closest British foxholes were only about five hundred meters away from us. We were about one hundred feet above them on the side of the mountain. The foxholes did not give them much cover from this angle. Most of their sandbags had been stacked to protect them from an attack from the west.

"Mortar shells were pounding the battery of British artillery guns. Heavy machine-gun fire was raking up and down the trench, which contained the guns. Many of the wooden poles that had been stuck in the ground to hold up camouflage nets over the guns were splintering and falling apart as they were hit by bullets and shrapnel. This caused the large nets to collapse, and the outline of the guns could be seen within the fallen nets. The guns never fired a shot in their own defense.

"The British were taking heavy losses all over, but they continued to fight. The German troops near Meleme were not visible. Tracer bullets from heavy machine-guns flew out of scores of British foxholes.

"Ellis and I were both shooting heavy machine-gun operators as quickly as we possibly could. Konrad had the binoculars and was help-ing us find targets. We did not need much assistance, as targets were plentiful.

"The other snipers were following Ellis' instructions and were also shooting heavy machine-gun crews. One of these snipers, ten feet away from me, was shot through the head and fell down. His body con-vulsed, but he was obviously dead.

"Some of the other snipers looked down at him, and Ellis shouted "Keep firing! You'll end up the same if you don't keep firing!"

"Hearing this, they all kept firing—with increased speed. A mortar shell exploded on the hill above them. Dirt and blood was thrown everywhere, as were several German riflemen.

"I heard screams from all around me, but they were definitely louder within the British foxholes. I quickly reloaded my weapon and resumed firing at heavy machine-gun crews. I saw dead and dying British soldiers everywhere I looked with my scope.

"Another mortar struck the area above us. A piece of shrapnel nicked my helmet and bounced off. It made a loud metalic clang that made my ears ring. I felt my neck and looked at my hand for blood. I saw none, so I kept firing.

"'Find me a mortar crew, Konrad!' I shouted.

"'Acknowledged!' replied Konrad. Both of us were worked up from the excitement and danger of the battle.

"I shot two more machine-gun crews, then reloaded my weapon.

"'Right there, next to the jeep!' exclaimed Konrad, as he pointed a grimy finger.

"I looked, without my scope, and spotted the jeep. I pointed my rifle at it and looked through the scope again. I saw two mortar crews firing repeatedly.

"One of the loaders was hit instantly. The bullet went through his pelvis and into another soldier's head, which had been holding the base of the mortar.

"The next bullet passed through the pipe of the second mortar and into the holder's belly. He screamed and went down. The mortar was ruined.

"The loader of the second mortar attempted to duck behind the jeep. I could still see his boot sticking out from behind it. I moved the crosshairs and fired a bullet through the center of the jeep, right where the seats were located. I looked back at the boot and it was moving, as if the soldier was writhing in pain.

"'There's another one, and there's a tank!' Konrad yelled, pointing.

"I looked and saw the tank, which was parked in its own foxhole with sandbags piled all around it. I saw its cannon and heavy machine-gun firing in our direction. Next to the tank were two more mortar crews in a foxhole.

"I tapped on Ellis' helmet and pointed as I yelled "Tank!"

"At that moment, there was an utterly massive explosion near the artillery guns. One of the German mortar or machine-gun crews must have hit the artillery ammunition and it went off with the sound of a hundred artillery shells.

"Such was the force of this explosion that all of the Germans stopped firing, and dove for cover. This was done a second too late, for some of them had already been hit by shrapnel.

"The British soldiers, who were affected much more by this explosion, also stopped firing. I saw several of them decapitated by shrapnel just a second before a huge cloud of smoke covered all of us.

"Despite all of this, the German mountain-troops were still badly outnumbered. Before the smoke cleared, we were all ordered to withdraw back up the mountain. This we did with as much haste as possible. Wounded soldiers were dragged along. Sergeants and officers took the identification discs of dead soldiers from around their necks.

"Ellis, Konrad and I were quickly marching back up the side of the mountain along with the others. Some of the British soldiers had resumed firing, even though they could not see us. This was largely ineffective.

"When we reached safer ground, I saw the commanding officer standing next to a radio operator. I could hear him saying, 'Say again, enemy artillery has been completely destroyed. Objective completed. Awaiting further orders.'

"I could not hear the reply on the radio. We three friends continued walking past the commanding officer, and eventually found a spot to rest.

"We quickly removed our shirts. With the battle behind us, our primary concern now was surviving the heat. I sprinkled a few drops of my precious water onto my head, and rubbed it into my hair. I then took a large drink.

"We ate lunch quietly. Several of the mountain-soldiers did the same in small groups around us. The only available food was our cold rations. These were kept in our musette bags.

"One hour later, the sounds of German artillery and bombing intensified. The sounds of the battle were several miles to the west.

"A Sergeant approached us and addressed not only us three snipers, but also many of the mountain-soldiers near us.

"'Listen everyone, you need to clean your weapons and get a little rest. As soon as the rest of the division gets to the beach below us, we have orders to descend and assist in mopping up the British forces around Canae.'

"Several groups were assigned to set up foxholes around the perimeter of the camp to watch for possible attacks from enemy soldiers or partisans. Ellis, Konrad, me and three mountain soldiers dug a hole on the outer edges of the camp.

"I found digging difficult, as my palms were covered with blisters. My feet also had blisters from days of marching on rocky mountain trails. My entire body hurt. I wanted to go home.

"I still found the strength to dig. I knew he had a much better chance of surviving in a foxhole in the event we were attacked.

"The sounds of fighting grew nearer throughout the entire day and on into the night. We could tell that our comrades were making progress, but it was slower than expected. The British were putting up a nasty fight, despite the loss of their artillery guns.

"Once again the temperature plummeted that night to near freezing. I reminded myself to bring some extra socks the next time I went into battle. I also hoped there would never be a next time.

"Konrad produced some playing cards. He asked Ellis and I if we were up for a game of cards. At first we said no, but then we relented. Konrad was insistent. Soon the three mountain soldiers joined in as well.

"As we played cards, the commanding officer of the entire group approached us. He stepped down into our hole. We stood up and saluted, and he told us to be at ease.

"'You men did a hell of a job today. I am glad that we brought you along.'

"'Thank you, Sir!' said Ellis.

"The Lieutenant shook hands with each of us. 'You'll have to give me a shooting lesson after the war is over.' He smiled.

"'As long as you bring the beer, Sir,' I said. This brought laughter from all four of us.

"'That sounds good. You men get some rest. Goodnight.' He walked out of the foxhole, and back over to a larger foxhole which contained his personal tent.

"We all three shivered through the night and lay next to one another to keep each other warm. Our paratrooper smocks and field jackets were not very warm at all.

"In the morning, we could hear that the shelling was perhaps twice as close as it had originally been. Our comrades still had a long way to go to reach the beach below us.

"We ate the last of our cold food rations for breakfast. I saved my box of candy, in case I got hungry later. I also traded my two cigars to a mountain-soldier for half his bread ration. I saved this as well. I did not smoke, and I found the cigars to be useful for bartering items.

"'They should have given us double rations before sending us up here,' I complained to Konrad.

"'I heartily agree with you,' replied Konrad.

Ellis cleaned his gun while the others ate.

"'Not hungry, Ellis?' I asked.

"He remained silent for a moment. 'I keep thinking of shooting those partisans.'

"'It was them or us,' said Konrad sympathetically. 'You had no choice.'

"'Do you know why we invaded this island?' asked Ellis.

"Konrad and I looked at each other for a moment, then shook our heads.

"'Oil,' Ellis said with a sober face. 'It's within bombing range of the Hungarian oil fields.'

"'What's so important about the damn Hungarian oil fields?' asked Konrad.

"'Hitler needs oil to wage war,' answered Ellis.

"'On the English?' I asked.

"Ellis shrugged. 'Perhaps.'

"I knew that Ellis had been befriended by several officers. He divulged no more information about the oil fields, or Hitler's possible motives. He did have a bit of a mysterious tone in his voice, though.

"We waited there until that afternoon. The day became cloudy and a little rain fell. This was very much welcomed by all of us. We were tired of baking in the sun.

"Shortly after 1300 hours, we saw a group of German Dornier bombers approaching. Many of the men waved at us as they approached.

"'Maybe they'll drop us some food!' shouted Konrad. He waved at them.

"As the planes passed over, several of them dropped what might have been food containers.

"'You see?' He smiled at me. 'I told you!'

"As the container hit, there was a massive explosion. I watched as at least ten men were instantly killed. The other bomb exploded on the other end of the camp. The explosions were so forceful that the very ground beneath our feet shook from the impact. The sound was deafening.

"'Take cover!' yelled several soldiers from all directions.

"Konrad, Ellis and I got down in our foxhole. Konrad had a large cut on the side of his head from one of the bomb fragments. Ellis and I bandaged it the best we could by cutting strips out of our rags we used for gun cleaning strips. It was the cleanest cloth we had.

"The bombers turned and came back for another pass.

"'For God's sake, shoot some flares!' shouted Ellis.

"Someone must have had the same idea, for several flare guns were fired within seconds after this. The planes ignored the signal and continued their bombing run.

"'What the hell are they doing?' I asked as I braced myself for another blast.

"'They must think we're British,' yelled Ellis. The three of us were now getting as low as possible in our foxhole, crouched down low with our helmets on.

"Another bomb hit. A bloody severed arm landed in the center of the foxhole. The fingers twitched. I kicked it to the far end of the foxhole and one of the mountain soldiers threw it out.

"I then raised up, and aimed my rifle at one of the planes as it sped away.

"Ellis pushed his rifle down. 'No, Georg! You must not shoot at them!'

"'Why not?'

"'That will only confirm to them that we are the enemy! Our only chance is that they realize we are German!'

"I got back down in a defensive position and crossed my arms crossed over my face, helmet down and my legs pulled in. Another bomb hit the closest section of the camp, which was only fifty feet away from us. The blast wave shot over the foxhole. The ground shook even more violently than it had before. I felt my teeth slam together and wondered if I had chipped some of them. A second later another bomb exploded with such force that some of the dirt fell from the edges of the foxhole. I looked up and saw that the head of one of the mountain soldiers was gone. He had been peeking out of the foxhole when the bomb hit. His headless body fell and convulsed, as blood filled the bottom of the foxhole. I began to scream, and I was joined by the other four men in the hole. The blood formed in a pool on the floor of the foxhole, which slowly oozed into the dirt, forming black mud. Despite this, we dared not get or look out of the foxhole. The bombing continued.

"Again and again and again, I felt my entire body hammered by shock waves from the bombs. For a minute I thought I could no longer take it, and I wanted to jump out of the hole and run. Then I looked at the body in the center of the foxhole. The flow of blood had ended, as had the convulsing. I did not want to end up the same way.

"This attack went on for fifty minutes. After dropping most of their bombs, the planes flew back to the north where they had come from.

"Ellis and I got out of our foxhole and helped with the wounded and dead soldiers. We learned that the foxhole with the radio had taken a direct hit. Several German flags had been laid out for the pilots to see, but they did not see them. The morale of many of the men was very low. They were complaining about incompetence, and the Lieutenant did not discourage this. He was furious.

"Ellis showed me that one of the fillings had been shaken out of one of his teeth.

"I held the hand of an eighteen-year-old soldier who lost an eye during the ordeal. The boy was sobbing and calling for his mother. A medic placed a bandage over the eye as I spoke to him.

"'You're lucky, boy. They'll send you home for sure now. You'll be back taking care of all those single women in Germany for us.'

"The boy attempted to laugh, and then began crying all over again. 'It hurts. What woman wants a man with one eye?'

"This made me wonder what Ingred would think if I returned missing an eye, or an arm, or a leg. I shuddered at the thought.

"By then the shelling was right below us. The Lieutenant gave the order to begin moving down to assist in the attack on the remaining British.

"We climbed back down to where we had been when we ambushed the British earlier. About twenty percent of the original force which was traveling with us had either been killed or wounded. These casualties included six of the mountain-soldier snipers.

"The German lines were now visible. They were about two hundred meters to the west. German infantrymen could be seen throwing grenades into foxholes and then advancing into them. German artillery was constantly pounding the remaining British forces, and many of them were attempting to retreat from the onslaught.

"I took a moment to take in what I was seeing. There were many things happening at once. Several British soldiers were attempting to save some of their dying comrades in a large foxhole. Mortars shells were landing everywhere among the British positions, like explosive hail. A mortar shell landed right in the middle of this group, killing almost all of them.

"German machine-gun fire raked across the many British foxholes, hitting several of them as they attempted to either fight back, or run away.

"Some of the British were dug-in even more than they had been during their earlier assault on the area. There was barbed wire strung everywhere and it was snapping and moving around, as hundreds of bullets sliced through the wire.

"The order was given to fire at will. Once again, the mountain-soldiers unleashed a massive amount of fire. This included their heavy weapons and rifles. The snipers began shooting any available target. There were far fewer targets than there had been the day before.

"The German infantry on the beach saw their comrades above and sped up their advance. Several British troops stood up and raised their hands in surrender.

"Within an hour the entire defensive force around the capital City of Canae had been destroyed, captured, or routed.

"There were bodies everywhere in the British foxholes. Burned out tanks, which had been hit with bombs, were everywhere.

"Our entire force climbed down from the mountains and rejoined the rest of the 5th Mountain Division on the beach. We were already entering the City of Canae.

"The army halted and allowed the soldiers who had traveled through the mountains to rest, eat a hot meal, and reorganize. There was a medical platoon of doctors, nurses, and medics. They were set up a temporary hospital inside of a large warehouse on the outskirts of Canae. The wounded soldiers from the mountain force then began to receive medical treatment.

"We three paratroopers rejoined the rest of the paratrooper force. They were choosing which houses to sleep in. The city had been abandoned for the most part, so several houses were sitting empty.

"The other paratroopers were anxious to hear the story of what had transpired in the mountains. They were appalled when they heard about the brutality of the partisans, and the ferocious bomb attack from the German airforce. They cheered when they heard how the British artillery had been destroyed when its ammunition exploded.

"The other paratroopers told us how glad they were when the British artillery guns were silenced. They heard the massive explosion. They thought an enormous bomb had been dropped on the British. The British could not hold the German forces back after the loss of their defensive artillery. The flanking maneuver had been a great success.

"We were given double rations the following morning to make up for our hunger while traveling over the mountains.

"The 5th Mountain Division was then divided in half. Half of the force was to travel east, toward Retimo. The other half would go south, to Sphakia. Their mission was to drive the British off of the Island of Crete. We paratroopers were ordered to go with the eastern group.

"We traveled along the foot of the mountains, with the sea a few miles to the north. We followed the trail of the British infantry, which was in full retreat.

"It was not long before we met resistance. There were several enemy soldiers dug-into well-concealed foxholes. This was only the rear guard of the British army, and we German snipers quickly took them out.

"I watched one German infantryman walk up to one of these foxholes. He was going to toss a grenade into it. When he was within twenty feet, a mine suddenly exploded beneath him, blowing his foot off. He began screaming, and three medics rushed to help him.

"'Stay away from their holes! They're probably all mined!" yelled a Lieutenant. He also ordered us to use metal detectors in front the army.

"Ellis and I, accompanied by several other snipers, were ordered to accompany the men with metal detectors. We were told to watch for dug-in British troops, and snipers. I knew that this would probably be very hazardous. I held my heavy rifle in my blistered hands.

"Konrad walked along with Ellis and I to help us watch for danger. We did not speak. We instead concentrated on our senses of sight and hearing.

"It was not long before one of the men holding a metal detector signaled for them to stop. I thought he would dig up the mine, but he instead marked it with a small flag on a stiff wire. He then simply walked around it.

"The rest of the infantrymen walked behind us, staying in the trail, which had been checked by metal detectors. We did not walk near the bright colored flags.

"Ellis told me to walk in the footprints of the British soldiers. This was the easiest way to avoid mines, he said. I liked the idea and began doing just that. The thought of having my foot blown off by a mine was horrifying.

"A mile later, one of the infantrymen with a metal detector was shot. We heard the sound of the sniper's rifle about three seconds later. We all got as low to the ground as we could and hid behind weeds and small bushes. The only sound we heard the moment was shot was a very quiet *thwak* sound made by the bullet passing through his flesh. It hit him in the leg, which caused him to scream for help.

"Ellis spoke to Konrad and I. 'Long range shot. Probably a British sniper.' He then looked through his scope to find the sniper.

"Konrad looked through the binoculars and I looked through my scope. We looked for several minutes, but we saw nothing. The man who had been hit was dragged back by another soldier. He was careful to keep his head down so he would not be shot, too.

"Ellis placed his helmet on his spade and held it up above the rock he was hiding behind. 'Watch for a muzzle flash!' he told me.

"An instant later I saw one. The bullet was in the air for two seconds, then hit the helmet with a metallic sound. It was in a clump of trees almost two kilometers away. I put my crosshairs on the exact spot where I had seen it, and fired. I fired three more shots into it. I told Ellis where I had seen the flash. Ellis showed me his helmet, which had a round bullet hole going through both sides. The hole was in the very center of the helmet. 'Not bad for two kilometers,' whispered Ellis.

"We resumed pursuing the British army.

"After walking thirty meters I saw another distant muzzle flash. 'Get down!' Ellis shouted as loud as he could, while diving down on the ground.

"All of us within shouting distance did the same, and none of us were hit. We could hear the bullet as it ripped through the air above our heads.

"I had a good idea where the sniper was hiding. I looked at a clump of trees on the side of one of the mountains with my scope. The trees were over one kilometer away. I saw another muzzle flash.

"Knowing that the bullet would take a second or two to hit, I rolled to one side. I had no idea where it was going, but it could very well be coming after me. I heard it pass through the air, in the exact spot where I had just been.

"I looked through the scope again, and saw another muzzle flash. It was right in the center of my crosshairs. I fired and rolled again, this time in the other direction. I was breathing hard. I again heard the bullet pass within a few feet of me.

"The firing stopped.

"Konrad slapped me on the back. 'You move faster than me, I think!' he said and then he laughed.

"I nodded and took a deep breath. I had not thought about what I was doing until that moment. I simply acted. It was like a reflex. I saw an enemy, and I killed him. I had also dodged two bullets.

"We continued walking behind the mountain-soldiers with metal detectors. The one who was shot earlier had been replaced.

"We followed the trail of the British army through the low-density minefield for most of the day. In the late afternoon, the trail ran through a small village. We did not see any civilians here, either. There were no mines inside the village.

"We marched through the village and found no more mines on the road afterward. We saw several signs, indicating that this was the road to the City of Retimo.

"When it began to get dark, we stopped and made our usual camp by digging foxholes. Ellis showed Konrad and I that the bullet had made a hole in his spade, as well as his helmet. Our equipment was most definitely not bulletproof.

"In an attempt to protect myself from the bitter cold, I experimented by piling soil on top of my legs. This actually worked quite well, and both Konrad and Ellis followed my example. Soon the three of us had a light coating of dirt all the way from our boots to our chests. It worked well as a blanket, but I found himself wondering if any insects or worms were crawling on me. Despite this, I slept much better that night than any of the previous nights on Crete.

"The night was unusually quiet. Gone were the sounds of artillery and machine-gun fire. The British must have been in full retreat to the other side of the island.

"The next morning we were served a hot breakfast and given our rations. We learned that the British forces had quietly evacuated the island during the night. This was radioed to us from the remainder of the 5th division, which was near Retimo.

"Apparently four companies of paratroopers had been picked up at Canae, flown to Heraklion, and parachuted onto the airfield there. They found evidence that the entire British force had evacuated the island during the night.

"After this our forces pushed across the entire island in a two-day advance.

"By June 1st, Germany controlled the entire island. The battle for Crete was over.

"Of the 8100 Fallshirmjager who either parachuted or glided onto the island, over one thousand were killed. More than sixteen hundred were wounded, and one thousand seven hundred and fifty nine of them were never seen or heard from again.

"The losses of the paratroopers were so great that they were never deployed in massive airdrops again. After Crete, we were nothing more than elite ground troops. Many of the replacements for those who died were never even jump qualified.

"It took almost a week for what was left of our division to be returned to our base in Berlin.

"Once we arrived, I was hopeful that I would be allowed to visit my home. I quickly learned, to my extreme disappointment, that this was not possible. The entire German army was being massed along the border of the Soviet Union and divided into three gigantic army groups. The blisters that I had acquired on the Island of Crete on my hands and feet had not yet healed, and here I was going to war again.

"I did, however, have a letter from Ingred waiting for me. I went to a Private place in the barracks and opened it.

"The letter smelled of her perfume. I smelled it with a long inhalation, and tears filled my eyes. I missed her and little Kurt so much. Kurt would be four years old in a few months, and I had hardly seen him since his birth. The thought of it made me furious.

"She wrote, 'Dearest Georg, I have heard about the invasion of Crete, and that your division was involved. The three of us have been praying for your safe return each night. I know that you will return to us.

When will this war be over? You have helped the Wehrmacht conquer all of Europe! I hope this nightmare comes to an end soon.

Business has not gone well at the bakery. The wheat and sugar we need for pastries have been rationed, and we were forced to raise our prices. Your mother and I have each been ordered to work at a local factory. We work different shifts so we can take turns watching Kurt and the bakery.

The factory makes airplane parts. There are many women who work there, since most of the men have gone off to war.

We have been making so many planes! The numbers they want keep going up! There must be something very big about to happen, Georg. I know that you will be careful, and keep yourself safe.

Sometimes an air raid Siren is sounded, and everyone must go to an underground shelter! It is a horrible experience. If the bombing becomes bad enough we might flee the city, and go to Uncle Fredrick's farmhouse. If we are ever missing, look for us there.'

"She signed it, 'Come home soon, Georg, Love, Ingred.'

"I immediately wrote back to her. I was unable to tell her any details about military operations, and I was very hesitant to tell her what had occurred on Crete. I did not want her to think of me as a killer.

"I wrote, 'I was in the invasion of Crete. I am unwounded, and quite well. I will come home as soon as I am allowed to, but I have no idea when that will be. I love and miss you all. Give Kurt a kiss for me and tell him that I love him very much. Keep saving my wages for after the war.'

I signed it, 'Love forever, Georg'

"The Fallschirmjager division received fresh new recruits to replace those who were killed or too horribly wounded to continue to be soldiers. Many of these young men were eager for battle after the recent whirlwind victories of the Wehrmacht. The invasions of Eben-Emael and Crete were legendary to them, and they regarded the emblems on my field jacket with awe. I had one each for the Polish campaign, for Belgium, Eben-Emael, and Crete. Each campaign was represented by a small gold rimmed patch, which was sewn onto my shoulder.

"I was also informed that my rank had been increased to Sergeant. My friend Ellis was moved up to staff Sergeant. Konrad was promoted to Corporal. We were among an elite group of paratroopers who had survived all three campaigns. Several others had also fought in Greece before the invasion of Crete.

"The division was transformed into an elite infantry division, with heavier weapons. These included larger artillery and anti-tank guns. Our special lightweight mines were upgraded to standard anti-infantry and anti-tank mines.

"Trucks, half tracks, and armored cars were our new modes of transportation. Gone were the days of parachuting out of planes or soaring silently in our gliders.

"I traveled with my newly upgraded division into Poland. We reached the outer edge of Warsaw on June 19th, 1941. We quickly dug our usual foxholes and awaited further orders.

"Ellis and I were each put in charge of an eight-man squad of snipers. Konrad was in my squad and served as my personal spotter. Konrad liked the idea of being a spotter because it kept him at least a few hundred meters back from most of the heavy fighting.

"We were informed that we were part of Operation Barbarossa, which was the codename for the invasion of the Soviet Union.

"This made Ellis and I furious.

"'This is insane,' said Ellis quietly. 'Let me show you something, Georg.'

"He unrolled a small map, which he kept in his pocket. It was a map of the world. He pointed to Germany. It was a rather large patch of land on the map.

"'This is the Fatherland' he said as he made a circle around the entire European continent. 'These are all the lands we've conquered.'

"Then his finger moved to the Soviet Union. I moved my eyes across it. It was many times the size of Germany. Even with all of the lands we had conquered included, it dwarfed them. How could we possibly attack such an enormous country? I imagined fighting for every square kilometer of the gigantic nation. The horrible thought of it was overwhelming.

"'And here we have the Soviet Union,' said Ellis in an ominous tone.

"'Do you think we will meet the same fate as Napoleon's army?' I asked. The story of the French army and their disastrous campaign into Russia was well known.

"'I don't know,' answered Ellis. 'Fate will decide. We have a lot of equipment that the French didn't have. Our motorized vehicles and tanks will give us an advantage, but the Soviets also have tanks.'

"'We must win to survive,' I said.

Ellis nodded. 'You are probably correct. We must win.'

"I made sure that I wore two pairs of socks. I stuffed a pair of gloves and a hat into my musette bag. It smashed my bread a bit, but I did not care. I also wore two undershirts. I did not want to sleep in the freezing cold without such protection again.

"I advised my friends and all of my men to do the same. Most of them did, including Ellis and Konrad. They also managed to stow several field blankets in their truck.

"We managed to keep our cache of over five hundred cartridges, which we acquired on the Island of Crete. These were also stored in the truck.

"Many of the Germans rode on horses, rather than motor vehicles. There was an enormous corral near the camp which contained thousands of the animals. Konrad and I walked over to the corral and fed the animals clumps of grass while we petted them. It relaxed us and made us forget about the upcoming invasion.

"I took a few minutes to look at the pictures of my wife and son in my locket. I closed my eyes and pretended I was with them. Then I pretended I smelled my son's hair as I inhaled deeply through my nostrils. This gave me a feeling of peace and drove away the fear which had been swelling in my heart. It also made me want to go home all the more.

Ingred could see how sad remembering was making Georg. She went and sat on his lap in the recliner. George grinned at them.

"I think that's enough," she said as she kissed him.

"Yeah, that *is* enough!" George said, getting up and heading for the cookie jar in the kitchen. "*Eew! Mushy!*" he mumbled as he left the living room.

CHAPTER 8

▼

OPERATION BARBAROSSA

George thought they would never finish with supper. He wanted to hear what else Grandpa had to say. As soon as the last bite of blueberry pie was gone, he jumped up to help Grandma clear the dishes from the table.

"Let's go!" he said excitedly, pulling on Grandpa's hand to help him up. As soon as they were all settled in their regular spots in the living room, Grandpa began.

"On the morning of June 22, 1941, I was once again riding in the back of a canvas-covered truck. Ellis, Konrad, and fifteen other snipers were riding with me. We all knew where we were headed. We were going to invade the Soviet Union—the largest country on the face of the Earth. Because the Soviets had taken over half of Poland, we would have to fight our way through that section of Poland before we even reached the Soviet Union. I felt sick to my stomach from the anticipation of combat, but I did not vomit as many of the other soldiers did. I simply looked out the back of the truck, and watched the countryside as we passed by it. Everybody was very quiet. The sound of the engine was very loud, like most engines which almost constantly roared around us. A great column of trucks, cars, and armored cars carried the division of Fallschirmjager.

"We were part of Army Group Central, which consisted of over one million German soldiers, one thousand tanks, two thousand artillery guns, two hundred thousand motor vehicles, two hundred thousand horses, and nine hundred aircraft.

"Attacking at the same time were two other army groups, including Army Group North, and Army Group South. Each was of similar size to Army Group Central.

"The Blitzkrieg was well underway by now. The Soviets had already been bombed and the army was now crossing their border in several places, like a great spear with many heads being thrust into their nation.

"Our officers assured us that we would not face the same fate as Napoleon's Grand Armee. The Fuhrer had it all planned to the letter, they said. Napoleon had no Panzer corps to spearhead his attack.

"The Panzer corps, in fact, were huge tank armies, consisting of hundreds of tanks, as well as supporting infantry, artillery, and air defenses.

"The 4th Parachute Division rolled behind one of the Panzer corps as it rolled into the Soviet Union. This Panzer corps consisted of three tank divisions, followed by forty infantry divisions—including mine—an armored car division, and an artillery division.

"The entire column halted at the Bug river, which divided the German and Soviet sections of occupied Poland.

"We spent several hours setting up a massive defensive formation. Infantry dug foxholes all along the western side of the Bug River. Tanks, anti-tank guns, mortars, heavy machine-guns, and other defenses were dug-in with the infantry, in case the Soviets counterattacked us while they were being shelled.

"Before we were even finished setting up these defenses, the hundreds of artillery pieces which the army had brought along began to fire. We could hear the shells landing only a few kilometers on the other side of the river.

"For about four hours, nothing happened. The guns continued to fire. I knew they must have been hitting something because they would never waste that much ammunition.

"After about four hours, a few artillery shells began to land on the German fortifications. They were probably coming from whatever forces were being shelled by the Germans. These were so few that they had little effect on such am enormous army.

"We all hid in our foxholes during all of this activity. We had been issued several periscopes, and we were watching the eastern side of the river during the shelling.

"Ellis, Konrad and I played cards while we waited. The other men, who were new recruits except for two who had taken part in the invasion of France, appeared very nervous. Ellis commanded that at least two of them keep watch through their periscopes at all times during the shelling.

"One of the new recruits announced that he needed to urinate.

"'Go in your helmet if you want to be safe from snipers,' suggested Ellis. The Private looked at Ellis for a moment, then got out of the foxhole and urinated on a nearby patch of weeds. He jumped back into the foxhole, saying 'I can't live in these conditions.'

"Ellis laughed. 'These conditions? This is nothing, boy! We've only been here a few hours! We haven't even seen the enemy yet, other than a few planes and artillery shells.'

"Within an hour, the artillery fire from the Russian side of the river had completely stopped.

"While the shelling was going on, we witnessed another battle that was being waged in the air. German and Soviet fighters were dog-fighting high in the sky. It was difficult to see very much detail of this, but the German planes seemed to be more than a match for the slower Soviet planes.

"German dive-bombers were dropping bombs about two kilometers east of the Bug River. This gave me a horrible flashback of the bombing incident in the mountains of Crete. I hoped that nothing like that would ever happen to me again.

"We heard an officer on a loudspeaker giving the order to prepare to move out.

"Within fifteen minutes, tanks began to roll across a bridge. They took up both lanes of the road and continued into the Russian-occupied half of Poland.

"While the tanks were crossing, the infantry began preparing to march across the bridge. I knew this meant that the enemy was probably close, because we had not been ordered into our vehicles. The infantrymen took all of their equipment and prepared to march.

"Two pontoon bridges were set up alongside the concrete bridge and eight hundred thousand men began walking across them, including some forty divisions.

"It was nearly dark by the time our division got across the river. We continued to march for about an hour, until we reached an area where the army was digging in again.

"The thunder of bombs had continued during this entire time. I had no idea what all of these shells and bombs were hitting, but it must have been either a fortress or a massive army. They reminded me of the fireworks show I used to love to watch in Hamburg each summer.

"The explosions continued throughout the night. Some of the men took turns watching through the periscope and listening for an attack. The rest of us attempted to sleep.

"Just before dawn, we were ordered to get ready for action. The normal breakfast and ration-giving routine did not take place.

"We were soon marching on foot behind the Panzer corps toward the east. The rising sun was blazing in front of us. We were surrounded by Polish farmland, which seemed to have been evacuated by all civilians.

"The tanks moved at a relatively slow speed to allow the infantry to follow behind them. We traveled in this manner for perhaps five kilometers. Then we saw an enormous Soviet army, which was dug-into a large area of farmland. We watched as several bombs were dropped on the Soviet troops.

"We continued marching toward the Russians, following the tanks. When we were about one kilometer away, all sorts of weapons began firing from both sides.

"The tracer bullets of hundreds of machine-guns fired at us. Several anti-tank guns and mortars were fired in our direction as well.

"Several German tanks blew up almost immediately when they were hit. Several German soldiers took hits from machine-gun and small arms fire, and fell.

"Those of us who were snipers began to crawl, using a ditch for cover. We heard the sounds of battle all around us.

"We reached a dirt farm road, which we used as cover while we studied the enemy army. They were about eight hundred meters away.

"We began to dig foxholes in the side of the farm road. We kept our heads down to avoid being shot. Some artillery shells landed on the advancing Germans, but most of the Soviet artillery guns were destroyed by the shelling and bombing which had taken place earlier.

"Several heavy weapons crews began digging into the side of the road as well, including MG34's, and 81mm mortars.

"Konrad and one other sniper spotted with binoculars, and the other snipers began shooting.

"'Remember to prioritize your targets,' reminded Ellis.

"I watched through my scope. I saw some brave Russian crews firing heavy machine-guns, but the vast majority of them were armed with rifles. They looked like they were less than one hundred and fifty meters away in my scope.

"I spotted a Russian officer. He was aiming at a group of snipers, and firing at them. He had no scope, but his rifle seemed to be semi-automatic. The muzzle-flashes were too fast for it to be a bolt-action weapon.

"I shot him in the chest, and he fell. I said to Ellis, 'They can see us, you know.'

"'I know, but we don't have time to set up anything more elaborate than this. Just keep shooting.'

"I continued firing. I hit a heavy machine-gunner in the forehead. I normally aimed for the chest, because it was a larger target, but the machine-gunner was concealed behind the gun and only his head was visible.

"I kept my crosshairs on the machine-gun. I knew that most of the Russians were armed with rifles and would probably go for the gun.

"Two seconds later a head popped up. "Bang!" the head disappeared.

"During the next five minutes I shot twenty-two men who attempted to work their machine-guns. After the third man, they had to move bodies to get into position. I could not believe their bravery and determination—or their stupidity.

"I saw an officer threatening a soldier by putting his pistol up to his head. He was ordering him to man the machine-gun.

"For a moment, I wanted to shoot this officer. The man was keeping his head down, but was still visible. I realized that he was actually helping me get targets. I allowed him to work.

"The frightened soldier dragged away one of the bodies behind the machine-gun, then grabbed the two wooden handles. A bullet hole appeared in his head.

"This scene was repeated five more times. Then no more soldiers attempted to man the machine-gun. It just sat there with a pile of bodies behind it.

"When the game ended, I moved the crosshairs to the officer, who was looking through his iron sights on his rifle. I shot him in the forehead as well.

"German mortar and artillery fire was landing all over the Russian positions. The planes were no longer visible. They must have had higher priority targets elsewhere.

"This slaughter continued for three hours. We had exhausted almost our entire cache of extra cartridges.

"One of the German machine-gunners who had been in a foxhole near the snipers was shot in the head during the engagement. I saw the soldier who was the loader of the two-man crew pack up the machine-gun and march along with the rest of the division.

"The Russians had been surrounded and cut off, and finally they surrendered. Their dug-in positions had been encircled by German troops.

"We advanced over the Russian positions. Dead Russians, with grotesque wounds on their bodies, were everywhere. Some of them were still alive, but I guessed they would not be for long. I had orders to kill any of the wounded I found, but I pretended not to see them.

"I had a chance to examine their weapons. Most of the infantrymen were armed with bolt-action rifles with an internal five round magazine, very similar to the Kar 98K. I later learned that these rifles were called Nagants.

"The officer's weapon was much more interesting. I had seen him firing shot after shot with it, without working a bolt. It had a ten-round removable magazine and fired 7.62mm ammunition.

"I took this rifle, along with the officer's belt which had six extra magazines on it. I tried not to look at the massive hole in the man's head. This gun fired the same ammunition as the other Soviet rifles, so ammunition was plentiful. I later learned that this weapon was called a Tokarev.

"Once I realized this, I began filling up the bag, which held the extra cartridges from Crete. I did this for several minutes, until the order to move out was given. I had gathered about three hundred rounds. The other snipers would not be able to use this ammunition, but I had a long-lasting supply.

"The other snipers had also been looting the Russians, but none of them found a Tokarev. They did take a few egg-grenades, knives, and two semi-automatic pistols.

"As we marched farther to the east, I showed my new weapon to Ellis.

"'You'll break your back carrying all that junk,' Ellis joked.

"The weight of two rifles, my other equipment, and the extra ammunition was taking its toll on my body. I asked Konrad to carry the bag of cartridges, which he did.

"We were allowed back into our trucks and rode for several more hours, until we reached the edge of the city of Bialstok. The Panzer corps and the special infantry squads, which were trained to protect them, had moved on farther to the southeast.

"Several infantry divisions, including ours, were ordered to enter Bialstok and destroy the defenders.

"We got out of our trucks three kilometers outside of the city. We marched up to within one kilometer and dug-in. Our artillery began bombarding the city.

"The sounds of shelling could be heard not only in Bialstok, but also to the north, south, and east. Several battles were going on at once.

"The defending Soviet troops, which were hidden inside the nearby city, began shooting artillery shells back at the Germans.

"All of us snipers were digging as fast as we could. Shells were already landing on our positions.

"One of the Soviet shells hit a nearby squad of infantry. Several of them had their arms and legs blown off. One man's body was cut in half. This sight inspired the men to dig much more vigorously.

"Within a few minutes, we had a shallow foxhole. We immediately got into it and continued to widen and deepen the hole with our spades.

"A shell hit within ten meters of our hole. One of our snipers was standing up too high, and a piece of shrapnel bounced off of his helmet. He fell down, screaming.

"We removed his helmet and examined the wound. It only cut his scalp. We put a bandage on it from a first-aid kit and told him he was fine.

"We began looking for targets within the city. After a few seconds, we spotted several Soviet soldiers. They were using houses and trees for cover. I realized that very few of them had spades, which meant they would not be able to dig foxholes.

"We snipers were concealed, not only by our foxholes, but also by tall grass which was all around us. We took clumps of grass and placed it in the webbing that covered our helmets. This hid the round shape of our helmets and made them much more difficult to see from a distance.

"When we were ready, Ellis gave the order to open fire. Several other infantry squads had already started shooting. Rifle and machine-gun fire was flying in both directions as the two armies attempted to inflict damage upon one another.

"German mortar crews also rained down 81mm mortar shells on the Soviets. These little shells were absolutely devastating, because the Soviets were not dug-in.

"We snipers began shooting enemy snipers, machine-gunners, and officers. I shot five heavy machine-gunner operators and two snipers. After this I was unable to find a target.

"The remaining Soviets on the edge of the city began retreating farther into the city.

"Within a few minutes, several German infantry battalions began cautiously advancing into the city. Our snipers covered them by watching the many houses for snipers and other enemy troops.

"After several thousand Germans had entered the city, we got out of our foxhole and began advancing into the city.

"The Soviet troops had already been looted by the time we reached them. Most of the useful weapons were already gone. I managed to grab a few replacement cartridges from two soldiers who had been shot and bayoneted to death. The bayonet wounds were distinctive bloody slits in the men's chests. I had seen them before in Poland.

"Many of the German infantrymen were now armed with MP-40's and other submachine-guns. This made their house-to house fighting abilities far superior to that of the Soviets, who were armed with bolt-action rifles. The sounds of hundreds of these machine-guns being fired could be heard a few hundred meters away. The Russians were resisting the Germans' attempt to enter the city.

"We snipers split up into two groups of nine: one headed by Ellis, the other by me. Our objective was to support the close-fighting Germans as they took the city by force.

"By now the shelling had stopped for the most part, since both armies were so close to one another. We could hear several shells landing on the north end of town, where the Russian artillery probably was. Their artillery was returning fire, landing shells a few kilometers to the South. I guessed that they had a poor idea of where our artillery was.

"I led my squad into a three-story tall warehouse. We cautiously entered the building, checking for any Russians who might be hiding in there. We found none.

"The warehouse was used for storage, and was filled with crates. We ignored these and continued on to the top floor. The stairs going up were made of wood, as was most of the structure. The outer wall was made of red bricks.

"The roof of the building had a large shell hole inside of it, and there were seven dead Russian soldiers near this hole. Their weapons and ammunition had already been taken.

"All of the windows had been blown out and much of the roof was damaged. The walls had a few holes in them, but were otherwise sturdy.

"I examined the thickness of the brick wall. It was about eight inches thick, which might offer some protection from bullets, but not much.

"We could see the fighting going on a few blocks away. Russian soldiers were attempting to make a stand, but were being overwhelmed by a superior number of Germans. Both sides were taking losses, but the Russians were getting the worst end of it.

"Our sniper team quickly began picking off Russian soldiers. Not that many targets were available, so we just shot any of them within sight.

"Konrad spotted for us. I stood by the stairwell and allowed my novice snipers to get some practice against these poorly trained Russian troops. I was tired of killing people.

"We took several shots apiece. Within about twenty minutes the line of Russians had been pushed back two blocks, and we could no longer see them.

"We decided to move to a new location. When we exited the building, Ellis and his men joined us. Several squads of German infantrymen ran by us toward the north end of town. This is where the remaining Russian soldiers were.

"A German Captain walked up to Ellis. 'What are you men doing here?'

"'We're snipers, Sir. We were using the warehouse and a few other buildings for firing positions. The Russians have been pushed too far north for us to see them, so we're moving to a new location.'

"The Captain saw the many campaign badges on Ellis' sleeve. The old Sergeant had not only his recent badges, but many from the Great War as well. 'Carry on, Sergeant. I'm sure you know what you're doing.'

"'Yes, Sir. Thank you Sir,' replied Ellis with a salute.

"The Captain and about fifteen squads of infantry marched past our snipers. Ellis motioned for the group to follow us.

"The infantry moved into a residential neighborhood, where every house had Russian soldiers inside it. They were firing their rifles out of windows.

"The Russians must not have realized how little protection they would get from the plaster and brick walls. German machine-gun fire turned the houses into deathtraps.

"Our snipers assisted the infantry-company. We shot several of the Russians as they attempted to shoot in their direction.

"The Russian soldiers began abandoning the houses before the Wehrmacht overran them. They pulled back into the center of the city, where there were many larger brick buildings.

"At this point, our infantry surrounded the southern half of the downtown area by taking over all of the houses. Ellis spoke with the Captain he had spoken with earlier.

"'Captain, we can keep this side of one of those buildings clear while your men attack. I would suggest burning them with flamethrowers.'

"The Captain seemed to like this idea. 'All right; let me know when you are ready.'

"Several of the infantrymen were already equipped with flamethrowers. These were easily visible because of the two fuel tanks on their backs.

"My snipers spread out until they all had some cover and a good line of sight.

"The Russians were firing from the buildings already, and as our snipers got ready one by one, they began shooting these defenders.

Ellis told the Captain that we were ready.

"The Russians on the south side of the closest building were soon either dead or too afraid to peek out of any of the windows. Two infantrymen with flamethrowers ran up and sprayed burning liquid into two of the windows. The building was quickly on fire, and the flames spread fast.

"Several Russians were shot as they attempted to flee out the north side of the building.

"Within a few minutes, flames were shooting out many of the windows on all sides. We then began shooting at the next large building's defenders. The whole process was repeated, and it worked very well.

There was little the Russians could do to defend against these tactics. Had they been equipped with heavier weapons, this might not have worked.

"Within a couple of hours, every Russian soldier within the city had either been killed or captured. The entire city was surrounded by German troops, so escape was almost impossible.

"It was getting late in the day. The division stopped for the night and a hot meal was served. The distant sounds of shelling and airplanes continued into the night. These were quite far off for the most part, so the troops in my division were not really concerned by them.

"The hot meal was a greasy stew, served with dumplings. I had once been a fussy eater; now anything hot tasted good.

"We were also given hot water to make coffee or tea with. We had coffee and tea among our cold rations, so all of us made one or the other. Some drank both. They did this by filling their field flasks with hot water, adding tea or coffee, and shaking it.

"I spat out coffee grinds. I liked coffee, but never quite got used to drinking it this way. Before becoming a soldier I never drank coffee without putting sugar in it. Now I drank it black, since no sugar was available.

"The snipers whom Ellis and I commanded were sitting in their foxhole, exchanging stories of the many Russians they had killed that day.

"Ellis, Konrad and I quietly played cards and cleaned our rifles.

"I decided to experiment with my new rifle. I removed my precious Zeiss scope from the Kar 98K and attached it to the Tokarev.

"'What are you doing, Georg?' asked Ellis. He sounded dumbfounded.

"'Just an experiment,' I said, 'to see how well it works at long range.'

"'It's got to be a piece of junk. I don't care if you don't have to work a bolt. You'll never hit anything.'

"The sounds of shelling continued all night. Ellis, Konrad and I slept quite well. The newer men were kept awake by the many discomforts of sleeping in a foxhole.

"In the morning, I had a chance to take a few practice shots. I set up a coffee can at six hundred paces, then I fired the Tokarev while looking through my scope.

"The recoil on the weapon was a bit heavier than the carbine I was used to. It had a flash suppressor on the barrel that concealed much of the muzzle-flash. I practiced snapping off several rounds in quick succession.

"This was difficult, because the recoil caused the sights to jump in between shots. I still was able to fire about once every second—this was three times faster than I could fire with the Kar 98K. I could also fire ten rounds per reload rather than six. Reloading was much simpler with my extra magazines. I simply ejected the old magazine, snapped in a new one, pulled back the slide bolt once, and all I had to do was pull the trigger ten times for ten consecutive shots. I practiced doing this, and soon could reload in less than five seconds. With my old rifle I had to push six individual cartridges into the top of the gun. This again was a vast improvement.

"I informed Ellis of the superior performance of this weapon. Ellis doubted its effectiveness at extreme range. I decided to hang on to my carbine anyway.

"I also still had my Walther PP, complete with silencer. All of the veterans of Eben-Emael still had them.

"Konrad had not only his pistol and carbine, but also an MP35. He was good with this weapon, and preferred it above all others for close combat.

"Our infantry division was soon preparing to move on. We were served a hot breakfast, given our rations, and prepared to move out.

"I gave my seven cartridges to Ellis, who was low on ammunition. I also gave him all of the extra 7.92mm cartridges, which were still in my ammunition bag. I still had sixty of them on my belt, and a full magazine inside of the carbine.

"Once again we were loaded into trucks and hauled toward the east.

"The Panzer corps had been waiting for us to catch up twenty kilometers down the road. Once we did, the army of tanks began rolling in front of us once again. The air was filled with gasoline fumes.

"The Panzer corps was commanded by the brilliant General Heinz Guderian. Guderian had led Panzer corps in Poland, Belgium, France, Yugoslavia, Greece, and now the Soviet Union. His presence made many of the soldiers confident of victory.

"After we had rolled a few miles down the road, we began to see several tanks heading in their direction from the east. The entire army slowed, then came to a halt.

"I looked through my scope at the oncoming tanks. They were definitely not German.

"'There's an army of Soviet tanks coming our way!' I told the others.

"Seconds later, officers began shouting. The infantry began exiting their trucks and moving up to the Panzer corps. We began digging in along the sides of the Panzers so they had room behind us to pull back if necessary.

"Our men dug as quickly as they possibly could. They took occasional glances in the direction of the Russian tanks and saw that their number was probably about equal to the three hundred tanks in the Panzer corps we were escorting.

"A division of some one hundred armored cars was also with the Germans. These included many "tankettes," which were like a cross between a car and a tank. They had armor, and a tank turret, but their weapons were light. They carried machine-guns, twenty-millimeter cannons, or other equipment. They had rubber tires, rather than steel tank treads. These vehicles were spread out behind the many foxholes, which were being quickly dug by the infantry.

"After digging a foxhole, we snipers began watching the Russian tank army as it advanced toward our position. The ground began to shake, and a great cloud of dust and smoke arose all around the Russians. The incredibly loud sounds of grinding metal filled the air like a chorus of demonic violins.

"'Oh, God! Oh, God! Oh, God!' shouted one of the snipers in the foxhole. "'We can't survive this!"

"'Calm down, soldier,' said Ellis in a calm but firm voice. 'We are Fallschirmjager. We fear neither the enemy nor death, remember?'

"The soldier was shaking with fear and breathing very fast. He ducked down in the foxhole and got into the defensive crouch which soldiers used to protect them from shelling.

"I could see many enemy infantrymen riding on the tanks. Each tank was being used as a personnel carrier. They were now about two kilometers away.

"'All right, boys, there are troops all over those tanks. We can start picking them off in just a moment.'

"Ellis pulled the frightened soldier up out of his crouch. 'We don't get paid to hide in foxholes. It's time for all of us to fight. Not just those who feel like it.'

"He nodded, and pointed his rifle at the enemy. His hands were shaking, and he began to weep.

"Ellis slapped the top of his helmet, 'Stop! This is not the time for that!'

"At that moment, a massive barrage of artillery fire began firing from the artillery behind us. Shells were raining down on the Russian tanks. Several of them were hit, and thousands of the troops with them were either killed or badly wounded. The tanks continued moving toward them.

"The two tank armies opened fire. Cannon and heavy machine-gun fire shot in both directions. Several German tanks exploded.

"We opened fire. I snapped off ten quick shots with the Tokarev. Each one hit an enemy soldier. By the time I put another magazine in the gun, most of them had jumped off their tanks and were scrambling for cover. A few of them had shovels and were digging. Others were just trying to hide.

"Seconds after that, the air was filled with so much smoke and dust we could no longer see the Soviets. Sounds of shells exploding and heavy machine-guns firing continued.

"I turned to Ellis. 'We might as well cover our heads. We can't hit anything now.'

"Ellis nodded. The eighteen men all got into a crouch. Sounds of explosions were all around. The sounds of the Soviet tanks got closer and closer. The shaking of the ground intensified, and I could see soil shaking off the sides of the foxhole. I clenched my teeth to keep them from chipping each other from the heavy vibrations.

"The only anti-tank weapons we possessed were four Panzerwurfmines. These were anti-tank grenades. I had witnessed one being used in Poland, and had received training in their use.

"These grenades consisted of a shaped charge on a stick with four canvas fins for stabilization. It could be thrown up to thirty meters, but it had to be a direct hit.

"Konrad took one of these anti-tank grenades from the soldier who was crying. He held it ready in his left hand. He held his MP35 in his right hand.

"The sounds of dive-bombers could be heard a few minutes later. Their engines whined as they dove down. I imagined them dropping a bomb right into the center of the foxhole. It would have killed all of us so fast we would never have known what hit us.

"There were several massive bomb blasts in the direction of the Soviet army. A gust of wind blew away some of the smoke and dust, but none of us dared to peek out of the foxhole.

"This intense battle lasted for half an hour. When the sounds of shelling finally ended, much of the smoke and dust was blown away by the wind. An officer ordered the infantry to move up and kill or capture any enemies still alive.

"My men and I stood up and began cautiously walking toward the burnt out Russian tanks. There were hundreds of them.

"About two thirds of these tanks were light tanks. They had been blasted apart in several places, and the armor was only one or two centimeters thick. They had 45mm cannons on turrets and one heavy machine-gun built into the body.

"The other one third of the Soviet tanks were medium tanks, with larger cannons which looked about seven or eight centimeters wide. Their armor was between two and six centimeters thick, and many of them had marks which indicated that cannon fire had simply bounced off of them. These marks were deep gouges in the steel, which did not penetrate. Some of them had damaged cannon barrels. My snipers examined them as they walked through the maze of burning tanks.

"One of the tanks blew up near us. *Some of the ammunition must have exploded*, I thought. The body of a Russian soldier was on top of the tank. The soldier's hair and uniform was burned completely off, and his skin was burned black.

"The bodies of other Russians were everywhere. Many of them were either burning, or black from having been burned. The smell of burnt flesh filled the air, and it was a horrible stench. In many places near the bodies I saw the dark colored mud—a mixture of blood and dirt. I had seen it before, but this time it caused me to become sick. I vomited.

"Following their orders, the infantrymen moved forward. They eventually found a few Soviets who were still alive, and captured them. Any who were mortally wounded were simply left to die. Their weapons and ammunition were confiscated.

"Ellis managed to find another Tokarev rifle and six extra magazines. He had seen me use the weapon successfully, and he wanted one for himself. Like me, he collected a lot of extra ammunition for it, and still kept his Kar 98K. He ordered two of his snipers to each hang on to one of the bolt-action Nagant rifles, which were carried by most of the Soviet troops. These were quite similar to the Kar 98K, but they could use the captured Soviet ammunition.

"Army Group Central spent the remainder of the day regrouping. They also attempted to repair many of their tanks, which had been damaged in the fierce tank battle.

"I was not surprised when I heard that many of the Russian tanks were superior in both firepower and armor to even the best German tanks. We had previously been led to believe that the Russians were technologically inferior. I wondered if this assessment of our enemy had been correct. What would the outcome of this war be if the Russians were, in fact, technologically superior to us? I hoped this was not the case.

"We then returned to the foxhole in which we had waited out the battle, and we prepared to spend the night. The distant sounds of bombs and artillery shells could be heard throughout the night, but otherwise it was quiet.

"The next morning, several divisions were diverted to the south to assist another army group near the City of Brest.

"My division was loaded into our trucks and other vehicles and followed the Panzer corps to the east, toward the City of Volkovysk.

"The Russian roads were made of dirt. There were many bumps and holes in these roads, and the many hundreds of tanks of the Panzer corps had made deep tank-tread tracks in them. The truck I was in bumped quite a lot for the many hours it took us to approach the city.

"To the north of the road was a forest. I watched it go by, from the rear of the truck. I expected enemy snipers or other troops to begin firing from the woods at any second. After a couple of hours, this fear passed and I began to wonder if we had advanced with such speed that the entire Russian army was behind us.

"Just before noon, my fears were confirmed. Enemy anti-tank guns had been concealed in the woods near Volkovysk, and we began firing at the many tanks of the Panzer corps as they rolled along on the dirt road.

"At the same time, enemy artillery shells began raining down on the Panzer corps. I could see that the road in front of the tanks had been blocked. This had been done with many fallen trees, and ditches. There were hundreds of foxholes behind these obstacles which were filled with enemy infantry.

"Within minutes a full-scale battle had erupted. The many tanks of the Panzer corps were firing both cannon and machine-gun fire at both the infantry and the anti-tank divisions which were attacking them. I watched as several German tanks were destroyed.

"The German infantry divisions behind the Panzer corps were instantly deployed. Thousands of them were ordered to advance into the forest and destroy the anti-tank guns. Others were sent to deal with the dug-in Russian infantrymen who were blocking the road.

"For several minutes there was utter chaos within the German ranks. Tanks and trucks attempted to manuver as some tanks tried to retreat from the vicious enemy fire. Trucks filled with troops were destroyed by artillery fire.

"A Captain ordered Ellis to bring his men along with his company into the woods. The sniper team was soon following the large group of soldiers into the tree line. The colossal sounds of many explosions filled the air this entire time.

"Within a few minutes I could hear the many companies in the front of the German infantry division fighting with Russian infantry. They had been hiding in the woods, waiting for them. The sounds of heavy machine-guns, rifles, grenades and mortars could be heard up ahead.

"We snipers spread out into two lines, and advanced toward the sounds of fighting. Trees and underbrush hid the battle from their view. After advancing about two hundred meters, we saw several mortar crews firing mortars at the Russians. We continued past these men, using trees for cover from shells and bullets.

"We heard bullets flying through the leaves above us almost constantly. The leaves which were hit by the bullets made a slight noise. It gave our soldiers a warning that enemy soldiers were firing in their direction quite heavily.

"Sensing the danger, all of our snipers switched to crawling very close to the ground. We came upon an area where several trees had been cut down by gunfire and explosions, and there were several dead and dying German soldiers.

"Ellis ordered the snipers to gather ammunition. We spread out to obey this order. I came across a soldier who had both legs blown off, and his intestines were outside of his body on the ground. He was still conscious and screaming. I knew there was no saving this unfortunate soldier, but I could not bring myself to take his ammunition. I moved past him and gathered several belts of cartridges from other dead German soldiers.

"Other German soldiers were continuing to pass through this area in the direction of the fighting. I saw many of them looking at the horrible scene of carnage all around them. Their faces were worried and sympathetic, and they were dirty from the last three days of fighting.

"After gathering ammunition, the snipers crawled to the top of a small hill and looked over the top of it. We were careful not to expose themselves too much to any enemy fire.

"On the other side of the hill there was another horrible scene of carnage, but this time it was one of many dead and dying Russian soldiers. Many of the Russians were crying out in agony for help, but none came.

"We ignored this scene for the most part, and looked beyond this area to another hilltop several hundred meters away. This was a large hill, covered with Russian heavy weapons crews. They were firing heavy machine-guns and mortars in the direction of the German forces, and were under heavy fire themselves. The Russians sat inside foxholes, which had sandbags and logs piled around them for extra protection.

"Ellis ordered all of us snipers to put weeds in our helmet netting. We quickly did as we were told. He then ordered us to spread out, hide ourselves, and begin picking off enemy snipers and heavy weapons crews.

"Konrad and I found a spot in some tall weeds on the side of the hill. We could see quite a few Russians from this position.

"We quickly began firing at the Russians. I used the Tokarev and had a much higher rate of fire than Konrad, who was using a Kar 98K.

"I moved the crosshairs across the Russian positions as I looked at them through my scope. I saw a heavy machine-gun firing one-second bursts, and I put a bullet through the head of the gunner. The loader instantly flattened and was hidden from view. I kept the crosshairs on the machine-gun for a few seconds, waiting for another soldier to attempt to fire it, but none did. I moved on to another crew. This time I shot the loader first. The gunner continued firing and one-second later I shot him as well.

"With the entire eighteen-man sniper crew shooting at them from only a few hundred meters away, the Russian heavy weapons crews were quickly decimated. The many German infantrymen whom the Russians had been pinning down were no longer pinned, and quickly advanced into their positions. I could see them throwing grenades into the Russian foxholes and trenches before jumping into them. Several of them were hitting fallen Russian soldiers with their rifle butts.

"As the enemy position was taken over, we shot a few Russians who attempted to fight back. Within five minutes, the entire hill was in the hands of the Wehrmacht. At that point, my squad advanced behind the many thousands of German infantrymen who were marching up the recently taken hill.

"By the time we reached the top of the hill, several heavy weapons crews had set up MG-34's, flamethrowers, and mortars on the top of the hill. When we looked beyond the top of the hill, we saw several Russian anti-tank guns. These were the same guns that were firing upon the Panzer corps on the nearby road. Their crews were now turning them to fire at the oncoming hordes of infantrymen. The Russian infantrymen who had just been wiped out had been guarding the southern flank of the anti-tank guns. With this barrier removed, the anti-tank guns were not very well protected from attack. Their crews were attempting to defend themselves, but were quickly overwhelmed by thousands of Germans. The snipers quickly got into prone firing positions near the heavy weapons crews, and began looking for targets.

"The closer enemy gun crews were overwhelmed so quickly that we concentrated our fire on other gun crews, which were several hundred meters away. Despite the great number of trees in the area, many of them were still visible at this range, due to the many clear spots in the forest.

"My first target was a Soviet officer who was waiving a pistol in the air in an attempt to get some of the gun crews to prepare for the oncoming infantry assault. My bullet hit him in the heart, and he instantly fell down. After this, I began shooting anti-tank gun crewmembers. After shooting a dozen of them, I spotted a large pile of anti-tank gun shells. These were two or three feet long and about two inches wide. I remembered the tremendous ammunition explosion that occurred on the Island of Crete when the enemies' artillery ammunition was hit.

"Hoping to create the same effect, I moved the crosshairs to the large pile of shells. I fired, but nothing happened. I fired again, and the whole thing went off like an enormous bomb. This was such a massive explosion that it dwarfed all the other sounds of the battle and drew the attention of all participants.

"I heard men cheering all around me, although I knew they had no idea what had caused the explosion. The woods were filled with gun smoke, and it saturated the air with its smell.

"The Soviet troops' morale was very adversely affected by the enormous blast. Several of them simply abandoned their anti-tank guns and ran. I watched as another pistol-waving officer attempted to order them to stop, only to be shot and killed by one of his own men.

"Several brave crews continued to fire at the Germans, despite being abandoned by their more cowardly fellow soldiers. A shell exploded on the face of the hill in front of me. The loud sound and dirt particles reminded me that I was not in a foxhole. I found the crew that had fired upon me, and I could see the head of a gunner peeking over the shield, which was mounted on top of the gun. He wore a green hat with a red star in the center of his forehead. I moved the crosshairs until they rested in the center of the star, then fired once. I watched as the bullet made a round hole in the center of the enemy soldier's hat. Unlike the better-equipped Germans, most of the Soviets were equipped with hats, rather than helmets. I did not envy them in this, or any other aspect. I thought the star made a good target, though.

"Another head peeked over the top of the shield, and I again put a bullet through the star in the center of his hat. After that, the gun was silent.

"During the next thirty minutes, almost every man in the entire Russian anti-tank division was killed, captured, or routed from the area. Many of them were killed while attempting to pull their heavy 45mm guns behind them. Several hundred men managed to flee to the northeast, with thousands of German soldiers right behind them. The Russian anti-tank guns, those that were still functioning, were taken by our countrymen.

"The Wehrmacht pursued the remnants of the anti-tank gun division for two hours. During this entire time, artillery landed close to them, but there were few actual hits. None of the German soldiers knew if the shells had been fired by the enemy, or friendly forces. The few Russian soldiers who managed to evade them ran into a nearby city.

"Our sniper team took a break from marching, and Ellis looked at his map. He informed them that the city was called Volkovysk. It was one of the major objectives of Operation Barbarossa and would most likely be well defended. German dive-bombers were already pounding the city with their extremely loud, high explosive bombs.

"An out-of-breath Captain informed us that the entire division had orders to dig in on the southwest side of the city and wait out the night. He also warned us that the artillery fire was coming from a Russian artillery battery, which was on the northeastern side of the city. This battery had been the target of the many bombs, which had been dropped that day. We chose a spot on a tree-covered hill that overlooked the city. Once again we dug foxholes to wait and sleep in.

"Ever-inventive, I decided to create a *deluxe* foxhole by digging a deep hole near the wall, which could be used as a toilet. Several of the men were soon trying it out, and they very much preferred this to using their helmets. Even Ellis was impressed.

"We wasted no time. The minute we had completed two medium-sized foxholes, we began eating our cold rations. Several of my fellow soldiers smoked cigars.

"There were far fewer stories of shooting enemy soldiers this day. The men had been in several battles by now, and it was more of a routine.

"I told the others of how I shot at the enemy pile of cannon shells, causing them to explode. They were very impressed, and had all noticed the blast when it occurred.

"The sniper team began scanning the outer edges of the city for targets. We had dug our foxholes in such a way that the tall weeds around us hid us from view. There was enough room on the front edge of the two foxholes that eight snipers could shoot at once. Ellis, Konrad and I used periscopes to spot for the newer snipers, while hiding behind the edge of the foxhole. The other snipers either rested or waited for a target. None of them allowed their heads to be exposed to enemy fire.

"Ellis spotted a pair of Russian soldiers looking out the upper floor window of a house. He ordered two of the other snipers to aim at the soldiers at once. When they were ready, he ordered them to fire. Both of the enemy soldiers were hit at once. The two snipers returned to the safety of the foxhole.

"Enemy artillery continued to rain down on our position. We watched as a Wehrmacht infantry division moved past our position to the north. They were moving around the city to flank the enemy artillery.

"After we had been dug-in for about two hours, we heard dozens of artillery guns firing from the southeast, and their many shells seemed to be landing on the far side of the city. This is where we presumed the enemy artillery was located, so the guns to the southeast must have been friendly. We were glad to finally have some artillery support.

"The Russian artillery began to fire back at the German artillery guns. The two of them fired deadly shells at one another all through the night. White explosion flashes lit the sky, and sent the sounds of massive shockwaves rolling through the Russian countryside.

"Shortly after midnight it started to rain. This made all of us very uncomfortable. We had nowhere to hide from the downpour. The dirt walls and floor of the foxhole quickly turned into mud. It was cold, wet, and we were very miserable. We attempted to shield our bodies and our precious rifles from the rain with our field jackets. Our jackets quickly became soaked and soiled with mud.

"Konrad spoke to me during the rainstorm. 'I wonder how long this will last!'

"'Not long, I hope,' I answered. Both of us had rainwater dripping off the edges of our helmets.

"'At least we'll get a shower!' laughed Konrad. I laughed with him. We had not bathed or showered for five days. Our hair was greasy, and the black soot of battle covered our faces. I attempted to wipe some of the soot off my face. I had no idea how much came off, for there were no reflective surfaces to see my reflection in. I imagined that I must look as filthy as all the other soldiers did.

"Konrad then got a bit more serious. 'Tell me something, Georg.'

"'What?'

"'Do you like to kill?'

"I could not believe he had asked such a question. 'Of course I don't! I'd much rather be home in bed right now!'

"'That's what I thought. I just wondered, since you seemed so accustomed to it.'

"This thought had never occurred to me. Had I become thataccustomed to it? The logic I had been using to justify killing enemy soldiers was merely that of survival. Kill or be killed. 'I'll never become accustomed to it. I just aim, and shoot. Kill or be killed. I kill only to survive. It's not something I like to do!'

"Konrad nodded. 'Understood. That is the same way I feel about it. It is much better to kill than be killed.' He paused a moment, 'So how many men have you killed, Georg?'

"I considered this a few seconds. How many had I killed? 'I'm not sure, perhaps a thousand or so.'

"Konrad's eyes widened. 'You can't be serious!'

"I shrugged.

"'You are serious! That's incredible!'

"'It's nothing to be proud of, Konrad.'

"'I know, but you must admit that is exceptional. Do you know how long you have to walk down the street before you pass a thousand people?'

"'I'd rather talk of something else,' I said quietly. 'I have enough nightmares as it is.'

"Konrad nodded. 'Whatever you say, Georg.'

"We spoke a few times about school. Konrad told me about his girl-friends, and I spoke of how fond I had always been of mathematics. Konrad found this fascination rather bizarre.

"After two hours of pouring rain, it finally died down to a light-drizzle. All of us were thankful that the downpour had passed.

"The shelling continued throughout the night, despite the rain. Rather than falling on my division, it was exchanged between the two armies' artillery batteries. They were obviously attempting to destroy one another.

"When the morning came, the air was damp and cool. The sky was filled with a blanket of low gray clouds, which probably meant no air-craft would be flying that day. We could still hear the two armies shelling one another.

"Ellis, Konrad and I began spotting again. Ellis spotted someone in the same house where we had shot the two soldiers the day before.I looked, and I saw just the top of a soldier's head peeking over the edge of one of the windows. The red star was clearly visible on the green hat, but no more of the face could be seen.

"The soldier who had been too frightened to fight during the tank battle two days before pointed his rifle and took careful aim. He fired once, but missed. The Russian soldier did not move at all. The young sniper spoke while looking through his scope. 'I missed him, but he didn't flinch,.'

"'Get down!' shouted Ellis. At the same instant, there was a metal-lic sound like a tin can being hit by a rock. The young sniper collapsed, and a second later they heard the crack of a distant rifle.

"I looked at the young sniper. His helmet had fallen off, and a bul-let hole was clearly visible in the top of his head. It entered through his left forehead, and exited out the back of his head. He convulsed, and his mouth opened and closed, as if he was trying to speak.

"'Damn it!' cursed Ellis. 'You take your shot and then you get your damn head out of the line of fire!' He spoke Konrad and I. 'Did either of you see where that came from?' We hadn't.

"Ellis put his helmet on the head of his spade and strapped it on. 'Watch for a muzzle flash.' He held it up above the line of weeds, care-ful to keep his hands inside the foxhole.

"Nothing happened. Ellis moved the helmet as if it was the head of a German soldier looking back and forth very slowly. *It looked very realistic*, I thought. No more shots were fired.

"'They've got a real shooter down there boys! He's a smart one!' Ellis scanned with the periscope while holding up the helmet. 'He's not going for a second shot!'

"For the first time since I had met Ellis, I could see fear in his eyes. 'This spot is no good,' said Ellis. 'We must find another.' He took half of the young snipers' identification disc. 'Someone get his ammunition.'

"Two of the other young snipers collected the dead soldier's ammunition. 'Get his scope, too. We don't want to leave it for the damn Russians.' They collected his 5x power scope.

"After hastily burying the dead sniper and placing his rifle in the ground, butt up with his helmet on top of it, we crawled out of the hole. We carefully stayed low so the weeds would conceal us as we crawled down the back of the hill. We expected the enemy sniper to shoot us at any second, but no shots came.

"We crawled to an area where there were several other foxholes, filled withour fellow airborne troops. Their holes too had turned to mud from the heavy rain.

"Ellis met with our Captain. 'We had to move. One of my men was killed by an enemy sniper.'

"'We're getting ready to move out soon, anyway. We have orders to take the city as quickly as possible." He added, 'I'm sorry about your man.'

"'We can support your advance into the city,' offered Ellis.

"'You can do more than that. You can advance right in there with us.'

"'We are more effective at long range.'

"'The enemy is hiding inside the city. There's nothing to shoot from out here.'

"'Yes, Sir,' Ellis relented. He returned to where we were standing. 'We've been ordered to accompany them into Volkovysk.'

"We looked at one another.

"During the next hour, the sounds of Russian artillery guns firing became less frequent by the minute. Finally, they stopped altogether. Our artillery began hammering the city.

"The Captain addressed our company all at once. There were about two hundred men, plus the two squads of snipers. 'Remember, advance slowly, check every house for enemy troops, let the artillery destroy enemy strong points.'

"We spent the following hour eating a hot meal and receiving our rations. The portions of breakfast were doubled, since no hot meal was served during the previous evening.

"After breakfast, we waited another two hours for artillery shells to soften up the defenses inside the city. We began advancing in several groups toward the city. It began to rain again.

"When we were within six hundred meters of the outer edges of the city, we began advancing in a much more cautions manner. We used every hill, tree, and clump of foliage for cover. All was quiet, except for the sound of artillery shells exploding deep inside of the city.

"As I climbed up a slippery grass covered hill, I heard hundreds of rifles and several heavy machine-guns firing from inside the city. I dove for cover, and could hear bullets passing through the air above my head.

"Our squad of snipers crawled up the hill until we could see several houses. Muzzle flashes were easily visible in virtually every window. We immediately began firing at them.

"I put ten rounds into ten muzzle flashes. I could clearly see the Russians' faces through my scope at this close range. A Russian heavy machine-gun raked the ground in front of me. I opened my left eye and saw the muzzle flash. I moved the crosshairs over and put a bullet through the gunner's face. I quickly shot the loader before he could take any action.

"German mortar crews began shelling the line of houses filled with Russian soldiers. Other Germans with rifles and heavy machine-guns filled the walls with bullet holes.

"I saw a Captain signaling a squad not to advance. A radio operator was nearby, calling in an artillery strike.

"One shell landed closer to the our forces than the Russians. The radio operator called in a correction, and another shell landed right in the center of a house. He then gave them a confirmation, and several shells began falling on the nearby houses. The sound was deafening.

"For several minutes, we hid while the shells continued to fall. Most of the nearby houses were flattened. Their windows, walls, and roofs burst from the many detonations all around and inside of them.

"Finally the artillery stopped and our company quickly got up and advanced before the Russians could recover. Several of them were already surrendering, holding up their hands with frightened looks on their faces.

"Our infantry division quickly advanced into the city through the gap in the Russian defenses. Our team of snipers followed the main body of men as we fought our way from house to house. We walked over the bodies of dead Russian soldiers.

"Two other infantry divisions were entering the city in the same manner. One came from the southeast, the other from the northeast. The latter was the division which had silenced the Russian artillery.

"All of our snipers and two other infantry squads were ordered to check two blocks of houses for enemy troops. We all knew this was hazardous duty.

"My squad checked out the third house. We scanned the windows for any signs of enemy troops, and saw none. We quickly walked up to the front door and kicked it in. A woman inside screamed.

"Inside the house we found an old woman sitting on the floor under a table. She was crying, and looked quite terrified. It was not unusual to find a civilian in a besieged city. Those who were able to do so usually left before the invaders arrived, but there were always people who did not.

"Lance Corporal Frantzen, one of the newly recruited snipers, began speaking to her in Russian. The woman shook her head. He spoke to me. 'She says there are no soldiers in here, Sergeant.'

"'Search the house anyway,' I ordered. The snipers cautiously searched the entire house.

"I realized that I had avoided speaking to most of the newly recruited snipers. I wasn't sure how long they would live, and I didn't want to feel bad if they should get killed. I spoke to Frantzen. 'I didn't know you spoke Russian, Frantzen.'

"'I think that's why I was conscripted, Sir. They pulled me out of college a few months ago. I was in my second year of Russian.'

I spoke to the others. 'Do any of you have any other special skills I should know about?'

"Private Hughes raised his hand. 'I am a master carpenter, and also fairly good at navigation." he was older than the other men, and spoke as if he was quite intelligent.

"The others shook their heads. They included Davey, who was a small dark haired man, and Harm, who was of medium build, with bright blue eyes. He was very quiet.

"Phillips was the only blond in the group. He found something to laugh about every few minutes.

"Remshart was the only man in the squad with a mustache.

"Achil was an ugly man with crooked teeth. He constantly spoke about drinking alcohol.

"As we left the house, I handed the old woman the box of candy which I had been rationed that morning, and told Frantzen to tell her not to be afraid.

"When we emerged from the house, fighting erupted a few houses down the street. Several Russian soldiers had been hiding inside two houses and were firing at several Germans who had the house surrounded. The house was hit with hundreds of bullets from all directions. A few seconds later, a flamethrower ignited the thatch roof.

"I ordered my men to take cover and shoot any Russians they saw. I put my own crosshairs on the house and shot a Russian rifleman in the head.

"Our sniper team quickly cleared the side of the house which was facing us. Another infantryman took this opportunity to run up and throw a grenade inside one of the windows. It exploded, causing the Russian troops to come out of the house with their hands up.

"We checked several more houses without incident. Most of these were abandoned shacks with few places to hide within.

"Other companies did not have such a quiet day. We could hear heavy fighting going on all over the city. Like in other cities which had infantrymen defending them, the downtown area had been the most heavily fortified. While my men and I checked houses all day, thousands of Russian soldiers defended the city center from attacks by the Wehrmacht. Artillery shells pounded downtown for the entire day.

"By nightfall, nearly every house in the city had been searched. Our snipers were re-deployed near the downtown area. Several buildings were still being fought over. We were ordered to watch for enemy snipers attempting to shoot from the upper floors of the many buildings still held by the Russians.

"Ellis and I took our squads into a large building. We began searching for Russian snipers. It did not take long to find them. There were hundreds of Russian soldiers firing from the upper floors of various buildings. We singled out enemy snipers first by looking for their scopes. We killed about a dozen snipers before firing at riflemen.

"It took the Wehrmacht and Fallschirmjager troops five days to take the many large buildings of the downtown area from the Russian soldiers defending them.

"For most of the buildings, we fought through them floor by floor. Two of the largest buildings contained hundreds of Russians, and they were simply burned down.

"Some desperate Russian soldiers even hid in and fought out of the city sewers. After making a few successful surprise attacks on German soldiers, they were considered to be a threat by the General commanding our forces. He ordered men to cover every manhole and storm sewer entrance with a mound of dirt. Several barrels of gasoline were poured into the sewer, and the fuel was ignited. The entire sewer system was filled with smoke, and the soldiers inside were presumed to be dead.

"Our snipers were able to sleep in a large house during the nights of this five-day period. We were also able to bathe and wash our clothes, which helped greatly to improve our morale.

"On July 1st the city was considered to be safely in our hands. There was no rest period for us. We were immediately ordered into our trucks, half-tracks, cars, or onto the backs of our horses. We again rode to the east.

"By now the Blitzkrieg had pushed beyond Volkovysk. The Panzer corps had pushed on to the City of Minsk and had met with fierce resistance. The three divisions of infantry which had been fighting for Volkovysk were sent to support the Panzer corps.

"On the way to Minsk, we passed the large City of Baranovichi. Heavy fighting was going on inside the city, and dive-bombers could be seen bombing the downtown area.

"The Panzer corps had been stopped in its tracks on the outskirts of Minsk. The city was defended by not only heavy tanks, but also several infantry divisions, artillery, air defenses, and fighter planes. The air defenses were keeping the German air force from bombing the defenders into submission.

"It took our snipers' division two days to reach Minsk. As we got close to the city, we could hear the sounds of shelling from several kilometers away. This sound instantly caused a feeling of foreboding among my snipers, as we each imagined what horrors awaited us within the besieged city.

"We stopped about one kilometer behind where the Panzer corps had been dug-into the farmland to the west of Minsk. The minute the trucks stopped all of the infantrymen who had been riding in them got out and began digging foxholes. We could see a division of Russian heavy tanks dug-in about one kilometer to the east of the Panzer corps. The two tank armies were firing their cannons at one another. To the north of our position, we could see hundreds of German artillery guns as they fired shells toward the east.

"Each infantry division had its own artillery. The many artillery guns of the three infantry divisions from Volkovysk quickly began adding their firepower to the siege.

"My snipers and I watched as a German Panzer general spoke with the general who led our division. We could not hear what was said between them, but they were pointing toward the enemy tanks quite a bit.

"Much to our surprise, we were pointed out to this Panzer general, and he approached us. This was indeed a rare event. I had never spoken with a general before. He addressed us after we saluted. 'I understand that you men are skilled and experienced snipers. I am in need of your help.' He pointed to the southeast. 'Do you see those batteries of enemy anti-tank guns there?'

"We had not noticed this before, but there was a long tree line in that direction, and there were several guns along this line. They were firing hundreds of shells toward the German tank divisions.

"'I need you to hit as many of those crews as you can. Kill them all, if possible!'

"Ellis spoke up. 'Yes, Sir! We would be happy to do this for you! I must ask you—can we deploy our men as we see fit?'

"'Certainly! Put them anywhere you want. Just don't get too far away. We've had a lot of partisan activity in all sectors. Watch your backs at all times for armed civilians. The Russians are also very bold at night, and have been caught sneaking up right beneath the muzzles of some of the tanks.'

"'Very well, Sir! We'll get right on it!'

"'Very well. Thank you, Sergeant." he saluted us, and left.

"Ellis began giving orders. 'All right, you heard the general. Frick, you take your men to the south and divide them up into two-man teams. We'll do the same from here.'

"'Yes, Sir!' I saluted my friend. I motioned my men to follow him. 'Move as I do if you don't want to get shot,' I told them. I then began crawling on the western side of the road, which we had just traveled on in our truck. I stayed low enough that I would not be visible from the east.

"We crawled in this manner for several hundred meters. I then ordered Davey to cross the road first. We all quickly crawled over the road one at a time. I went last.

"After safely reaching the other side, we divided up into four teams of two men each, plus one extra man in one of the teams. I chose Konrad as my partner, as usual. I told them all to spread out about twenty meters apart and dig a well-concealed foxhole before beginning to shoot. We began to crawl into the tall grass in the ditch between the road and a nearby farm.

"Konrad and I got our stomachs, hands, and feet wet as we crawled through this ditch. This was a mere inconvenience, and next to nothing compared to the hardships to which we were accustomed. We put fresh grass in our helmet nets before starting to dig a foxhole.

"I could hear some of the other snipers begin to fire before Konrad and I completed our foxhole. Within a few minutes we were ready to start shooting as well.

"Konrad and I looked through our scopes at the same time. I saw several Russian anti-tank gun crews. I scanned their positions for the many infantrymen who would surely be deployed around them for defense. I saw several foxholes which contained Russian infantry.

"'The Russians must have purchased some shovels,' I joked to Konrad. Many of the Russians we had previously encountered were very poorly equipped. They seldom had such basic equipment as spades, helmets, or grenades. Konrad laughed. 'Yes, I see that. I'll check around for enemy snipers.'

"The next few minutes were a bit frustrating. I looked at perhaps a hundred enemy soldiers, but I saw no snipers. Could they be that well hidden? Then I spotted one. The man was looking through a small black scope, affixed on top of his rifle. I fired, and watched as the bullet hit the enemy sniper in the side of the helmet.

"'You found one?' asked Konrad. He didn't look up from his scope.

"'Yes,' I said. 'There are not too many of them.'

"'Not that we can see, anyway,' said Konrad.

"'Let's just start on the gun crews,' I said. I moved my sights to the many anti-tank gun crews. They were continuing to fire at the Panzers.

"For a few seconds I looked for a shot at another pile of large shells. I saw none. They must have been storing them close to the ground to prevent them from being hit. I did see a few large piles of empty shell casings next to several of the anti-tank gun batteries.

"I moved the crosshairs to one of the loaders. The man was quickly loading shells one after another, as fast as the gun could fire them. I squeezed the trigger while holding the crosshairs on the man's back. The bullet took a couple of seconds to reach him, and then he dropped.

"The second crewmember had been pulling a chain to fire the cannon. He looked in my direction, using the gun for cover. I fired again. I watched as the bullet hit the Russian soldier in his forehead. The man disappeared from view as he fell behind the gun.

"Unlike our anti-tank guns, the Russian guns had no protective shields. This made shooting the operating crews quite easy for us. We began to methodically pick them off one after another.

"After shooting two magazines of cartridges and killing nineteen Russian anti-tank gun operators. I ordered Konrad to switch to scanning for enemy snipers with his binoculars. I knew that our skilled shots would quickly draw attention from the Russians. The other six snipers in my squad continued to fire, and I was sure that Ellis and his seven men were shooting as well. The sniper who had been killed earlier had not been replaced. As I looked down the line of anti-tank guns, there were not very many of them still being fired. The few crews still alive were either attempting to move their guns or running for cover, for the most part. A few of them continued to fire, and were quickly shot.

"In less than two minutes, the entire one hundred or so anti-tank guns had stopped shooting.

"I immediately ordered my men to stop firing. 'This position is no good now. We need to move!' We moved about one hundred meters to the south, where we were still concealed by the same high grass. I had my men dig in all over again. They did not complain. They knew I was an expert, and I would keep them alive.

"The Russians who were dug-in around the anti-tank guns were almost directly to the east. I ordered my men to help me scan their positions in an attempt to locate enemy snipers. We did this for several hours, and finally located about twenty of them. We took turns running back and forth to one another's foxholes and reporting the positions of the enemy snipers. Once we were confident that we knew where all of them where, we made a plan to kill them all. The anti-tank guns remained silent.

"We waited until the sun had almost set, causing sunlight to shine right into their enemies' eyes and making even our muzzle flashes impossible to see.

"Then we opened fire. We methodically shot all twenty of the enemy snipers in their known positions. We had about thirty minutes left until sunset. We used this time to shoot scores of heavy weapons crews manning machine-guns and mortars.

"Many of the Russians attempted to fire back at us. Rifle, machine-gun, and mortar fire was shot blindly in our direction with no effect. They apparently had no idea where we were.

"Once again, I felt a bit sorry for our enemies. I had put them at a great disadvantage, and they really had no chance to fight back. I knew this was necessary for our survival. I could not afford to give the enemy mercy. I had to be absolutely ruthless. I pulled the trigger again.

"As I looked through the scope, I saw the Russians close up. Many of them looked like Germans. Some of them looked Asian. They all looked terrified. I realized that for most of them this was probably the first time they had ever seen combat. For many it was also the last.

"I shot them one after another. I sometimes put one bullet through three of them if they were standing in a straight line. I shot a mortar spotter. A machine-gun crew. A frightened young officer. A rifleman, who was attempting to stay low as he urinated outside of his foxhole.

"It was like a shooting gallery. We killed hundreds of them. Finally the sun went down and we crawled back toward the main army group of Germans. Several of my men complained that they were almost out of bullets. I still had over one hundred rounds of captured ammunition, but my men could not use it in their rifles. I gave them some of my cartridges which had been rationed to me in the past week, but I knew it was not enough. 'I'll get you some more ammunition as soon as I can,' I promised them.

"We rejoined Ellis' squad and reported what we had done. Ellis and his men had the same success when the sun was setting. We saw that we had not only taken out the anti-tank gunners as ordered, but also inflicted a serious blow upon the defending infantry.

"We reported this to our commanding officer. He commended us for doing such an excellent job. He also ordered us to dig-in and get supper before getting some sleep. We knew there would be little or no sleep that night. The sound of heavy artillery shells exploding all over both armies filled the air almost constantly.

"We dug two foxholes in the area where the rest of the Fallshirmjager division was dug-in. This was north of the Panzer corps, and west of Minsk. We chose a spot on the outer edges of the division where we hoped few artillery shells would land.

"The shelling continued all through the night, as we had expected. We got some fitful sleep. Most of us just lay in the foxhole, listening to the sounds of shelling. The sounds of enemy shells falling tapered off shortly after dawn. The German artillery continued to fire, as did both tank armies.

"In the morning we were informed that our division would be attacking the city itself sometime that day. Two other infantry divisions had marched around Minsk to the north and flanked the enemy artillery. With their defensive artillery gone, they would be much easier to overwhelm.

"A few-hours later, German planes were flying over the city. Russian fighters raced to intercept them, and they engaged in a massive dogfight.

German 88mm anti-aircraft cannons had been set up behind the Panzer corps, and they shot huge explosive shells at the enemy planes. I watched as several of them were hit by flak and fell into the city. The Russians had lost not only their defensive artillery, but their anti-aircraft guns as well.

"Within two hours, all of the Russian fighter planes were either shot down or driven from the skies above Minsk. The German fighters flew to the south. They were probably heading to the now captured airfield at Baranovichi. I was amazed at how fast an enemy airfield could be taken over and used against the enemy.

"There were about fifty heavy Russian tanks still dug-in near the southwest side of Minsk. They were still firing their cannons at hundreds of tanks in the German Panzer corps. Shortly after the cities' air defenses were gone, several German dive-bombers appeared in the sky from the southeast. They immediately started dropping bombs on the Russian tanks. The effect of this was devastating. Several of them were direct hits on tanks, and they exploded in instantaneous green fireballs. I felt the shock wave and heard the sound of these blasts as I sat in my foxhole.

"Once the planes had dropped their bombs, not many of the Russian tanks were still in working order. The many German tanks immediately advanced upon them, firing everything they had. The Soviet tanks were larger, with better cannons. They could not withstand such overwhelming numbers, however.

"It was shortly after this tank engagement that those of us in my division were ordered to prepare for battle. The German artillery, which had gone from attacking the enemy artillery to their tanks, had now switched to shelling the city itself. I watched as a house exploded.

"More dive-bombers came, and several bombs were dropped on the city.

"The city was pounded for several hours by friendly artillery and bombs. While this was going on, a Corporal approached our unit. He saluted and spoke to us. 'The general would like to thank you for a job well done on the enemy anti-tank batteries. He wishes to know if there is anything he can do for you.'

"Ellis and I looked at one another in surprise. Ellis spoke. 'We could use some ammunition, and seventeen camouflage nets.'

"The Corporal saluted once again, saying 'I am sure we can accommodate you. The general is very pleased with your excellent skill.' With that, he turned to leave. Then he turned back, saying "Oh, I almost forgot. He has ordered that you and your men stay here with the Panzer corps while the rest of the Fallshirmjager assault the city.'

"'Why is that?' asked Ellis.

"'I think it's to prevent any of you from being killed.'

"'One of my men was killed the other day. Any chance of getting a replacement?'

"'I'll see what I can do,' said the Corporal. He turned and left.

"Within an hour the rest of the 4th Parachute Division, along with three other infantry divisions, shot their way into the city. A determined Russian division was dug-in all over the city and was putting up quite a fight.

"The Corporal returned with a box of one thousand rifle cartridges, eighteen camouflage nets, and a large Lance Corporal with a scope on his rifle. The sniper had black soot all over his face, but I recognized him immediately. 'Misha!' I called out to the large sniper.

"Misha looked at me for a few seconds, and then smiled in recognition, "Georg! I never thought I'd see you again, my friend!" he gave me a bear-like hug with his huge arms.

"The Corporal grinned. 'I thought you might need one extra camouflage net for your new man.'

"'Thank you very much, and tell the general we thank him as well,' replied Ellis. He shook the Corporal's hand.

"I introduced Misha to the squad, 'This is Lance Corporal Misha Gauss. We've been through school, basic training, sniper school, and combat in Poland together.' Misha waved to the other snipers as he was introduced. The others welcomed him.

"I lowered my voice so the others would not hear everything I said. 'So what happened to you after the conquest of Poland?'

"Misha told his story of how he took part in the invasions of Belgium, France, Yugoslavia, Greece, and the Soviet Union. Like me, he had seen more than his share of battles.

"'How is Anton doing?' I was still grinning from the joy of finding a friend so far from home.

"Misha's face abruptly changed from smiling to frowning. 'He stepped on a landmine in France, and lost both of his legs. He didn't live long after that.'

"'That's terrible!' I said, half-whispering. 'Thank God you're all right, Misha!'

"I told Misha how I had joined the Fallschirmjager, and I described the assaults upon Eben-Emael and Crete.

"The snipers spent the remainder of the day listening to Ellis and I give lectures on the finer points of being a sniper. They were each given a camouflage net, and Ellis once again demonstrated its effectiviness.

"We also watched as the Russian infantry battalion, which had been defending the anti-tank guns the day before, was driven from its fox-holes by a massive artillery barrage. We waited until the Russians had been gone for about an hour, and then decided to search their foxholes for weapons.

"We informed the artillery commander that we would be doing this so we would not be mistaken for enemy soldiers and shelled. Then we began marching toward the many enemy foxholes.

"The foxholes were filled with bodies of Russian soldiers. Several of the foxholes had been turned into craters by artillery shells. We imme-diately began taking 7.62mm cartridges from the ammunition belts of dead Russian soldiers. Many of the Russians were out of bullets, and few of them had more than thirty rounds. It was obvious that they were not very well equipped.

"We went to the various locations where we had shot Russian snipers the previous day. Many of their rifles had already been taken. We guessed that other Russian soldiers had taken them. However, three of the dead snipers still clutched their precious Tokarev rifles in their hands. These were the primary objective of the search.

"After searching an hour, we found two more Tokarev. This gave the entire team of snipers a total of nine of the semi-automatic weapons. Ellis, Konrad, Misha, myself and five other snipers each carried one. We got rid of our German rifles, so we would not have to carry so much. The remaining seven snipers still carried their Kar 98K rifles. We also collected several Tokarev magazines, and over one thousand rounds of ammunition.

"We also became curious about what the Russians had for rations. Searching their ration packs revealed little more than raw vegetables, including turnips, potatoes, and carrots.

"As we were examining the rations, a wounded Russian soldier attempted to fire his rifle at us. Davey, who was a small, dark haired sniper, noticed the man moving before he could fire, and quickly shot him in the chest.

"After this incident, we decided to leave the area. There was no telling how many of the dead Russians were feigning death, or merely wounded. We carefully watched all of the Russians as we walked over them back toward the German Panzer corps.

"The Panzer divisions were busy repairing and refueling their tanks for the remainder of the day. We listened to the sounds of the battle going on within the City of Minsk until nightfall. We were served a hot meal of bratwurst and sauerkraut. Once we were finished, we got back into our foxholes for the night. The artillery guns came alive several times during the night, as artillery strikes were directed onto the enemy positions within Minsk. This made sleep next to impossible, but we attempted it anyway.

"In the morning we were given our rations, and we were notified that the city was for the most part in German hands. One division of Wehrmacht remained behind to wipe out the last pockets of resistance, while the other three-infantry divisions prepared to move out. This included our Fallschirmjager division. The Panzer corps once again led the way.

"All of us snipers got into our trucks and were quickly bouncing down the dirt road. We headed north for a few hours, then turned to the east. We saw thousands of Russian civilians along the side of the road— refugees, who must have been ordered off the road by the Panzer corps.

"I took a few minutes to look at my locket. I looked at the pictures of my wife and son and missed them very much. I was very homesick. I had not been home for many weeks. I wondered when I would be allowed to visit them again, or if I would even live to do so.

"Misha and I exchanged stories of our war experiences for several hours. Misha had been through as much fighting as I had, if not more. He had seen a lot of action in France.

"Ellis was busily painting the light brown wooden stock of his Tokarev rifle black with shoe polish. When he had finished, he held it up proudly. He passed the shoe polish to Konrad, who began painting his rifle. As the truck traveled hundreds of kilometers, the entire team of snipers did the same.

"Another huge section of Army Group Central was following the 4th Parachute Division. This group had fought its way across the Nieman River near Grodno, which was northeast of Bialstok. When our division passed the northbound highway, which led to the City of Pastavy, this entire army group turned to the north. I was certain they meant to take the city from the Russian army.

"The truck rolled across a bridge which crossed the Dvina River. We rode down the bumpy dirt road for several more hours, and finally stopped for the night. The Panzer corps and three other infantry divisions had also stopped in the same spot. Thousands of Russian civilians resumed traveling down the road once the German armies were off of it. They moved to the east, in a futile attempt to outrun the Blitzkrieg.

"Our squad quickly dug a pair of foxholes and attempted to get comfortable. Several of our men had new Tokarev rifles, and had not yet sighted in their scopes. They set up a target shooting range and took several practice shots at candy boxes. Once they were certain that their scope settings were good, they returned to the foxhole.

"Ellis showed us a map of the Soviet Union. He showed us where Minsk was. We were well inside the border. The final objectives of Operation Barbarossa were the cities of Vitebsk, Mogilev, and Smolensk. We were within a one-day drive of Vitebsk, and the other two cities were not far behind. Another large city, called Nevel was on the way. We wondered if we would have to fight the Russians for it.

"The night passed without incident. We were all tired, and for the first time since entering the country we did not hear the sounds of shelling. After a hot meal, we all fell into a very deep sleep.

"Early the next morning, we were given our morning hot meal, rations, and ammunition. We were told to quickly board our truck. The army was moving out.

"We rode to the east for the entire day. To pass the time, we played several card games in the back of the truck on the wooden floor.

"I realized that each passing mile took me that much farther from home. I wished we were going in the opposite direction.

"We passed the road to Nevel, which meant that the fight for that city would go to other divisions. We continued driving to the east, and stopped about twenty miles west of Vitebsk. The city was across the Dvina River. We crossed this river the previous day, but it wound far to the south, and then to the north.

"Like the previous evening, this one was uneventful. We heard the distant sound of explosions to the east. We surmised that this was the sound of dive-bombers, since there were no German troops to the east of us that we knew of.

"We did not sleep quite as well that night. Wed all knew that we were almost certainly going to be in combat the following day. The outcome of the upcoming battle could be a quick and unexpected death for any of us. It could just as easily have been a horrible injury, such as a lost limb, blindness, or deafness.

"When we awoke in the morning, we smelled smoke. The air was filled with it. It was being blown across the Dvina River from the east. We were given a hot breakfast as we watched the mysterious clouds of smoke.

"After we had all eaten, we all followed the three tank and one armored car divisions on foot toward the east. We then marched for about five hours, until the river was within sight. We were then ordered to hold our position, and dig in.

"The bridge which had led to Vitebsk was visible. It had been destroyed, and was broken into huge sections of concrete. Several of these sections were partially underwater.

"We also could see the source of the massive clouds of smoke. The Russians had started an enormous grass fire on the other side of the river. This seemed like a very strange tactic. They were clearly getting desperate. I would later learn that this was the beginning of the Soviet "scorched earth" policy. The grass, brush, and trees were burned to deprive us of fuel for fires during the coming winter.

"Our squad split up into four groups and dug small, well-concealed foxholes. We selected a tree-covered hill with thick bushes all over it. We were about one kilometer from the river.

"I helped Konrad, Frantzen, and Hughes dig a foxhole. Before we had dug a foot down, the Russians began firing artillery shells at the Panzer corps. The Russians had seen them. The four of us quickened our pace. If a shell landed near us while we were out in the open, it would be disastrous.

"Within a few minutes we were inside the foxhole and throwing more dirt out to deepen it. After about ten more minutes and we had dug to a comfortable depth, and then covered the foxhole with camouflage nets. It would be invisible at even a few meters. We were ready to shoot. All four of us had Tokarev rifles. The other half of my squad was in another foxhole about fifty feet away. There were five men in that group, and only Davey had a Tokarev in that group. The other snipers all had Kar 98K rifles. The other captured Tokarevs were in the hands of Ellis, Misha, and two of the other snipers in Ellis' squad. They were on another section of the same hill.

"The other men of the 4th Parachute Division were digging in closer to the river. They were simultaneously digging over two thousand foxholes, each containing up to ten men. Three other infantry divisions were digging similar *foxhole cities* to the north of them. They were all evidently attempting to hurry. Enemy troops were already firing at them from across the river with mortars, heavy machine-guns, and rifles.

"The three Panzer and one armored car division were digging in south of the infantry. Across the river from them was a division of Russian heavy tanks, which were already firing their cannons at the tanks.

"The tanks were dug-in by piling sandbags in front of and on top of them. This made them much more resistant to enemy anti-tank weapons, which were absorbed by the sandbags. Their own cannons protruded from the sandbags and were still able to fire. They had their own special infantry squads, which were specially trained to protect them. These soldiers dug foxholes near the tanks so they could have some protection while building up the sandbag fortifications.

"We surveyed the scene for a few minutes. We watched the other soldiers and tanks of the German army dig in. We looked at the one hundred or so Russian heavy tanks across the river. These were larger than even the largest German tanks. The Russians undeniably had superior tank technology.

"I gave the order to begin shooting enemy machine-gun crews. Their muzzle flashes were clearly visible through the somewhat smoky air. All of the vegetation on the opposite side of the river had been burned black, so the enemy soldiers had no brush to hide behind. They had a foxhole city similar to that of the Germans. There appeared to be two Russian infantry divisions, which would have been some forty thousand men.

"The enemy soldiers were over twelve hundred meters away, but I had made longer shots than that before. I adjusted my vertical knob on my Ziess scope and began firing at muzzle flashes. I heard the empty shell casings landing all around me in the foxhole.

"Within five minutes we had fired hundreds of rounds. The Russians were definitely feeling the effects of the many well-placed shots on their heavy weapons. Only a few heavy machine-guns now fired from the Russian positions, and these were most likely replacement crews.

"The four German infantry divisions were now firing their own heavy weapons and rifles across the river. Mortar shells were exploding all over the Russian foxholes.

"Hundreds of German artillery guns began firing at the Russians. They were firing at the infantry, and their massive shells were wreaking havoc among them. Enemy artillery shells continued to hit tanks in the Panzer corps. It was obvious that something needed to be done about their artillery.

"This scene continued for four hours. The two armies inflicted massive damage upon one-another. We snipers shot hundreds of Russian soldiers as they attempted to fight.

"At about four o'clock, nearly one hundred German dive-bombers appeared in the sky from the west. They began dropping bombs somewhere behind the enemy infantry divisions. I supposed that this was where their artillery was located.

"Our artillery changed their direction of fire. Instead of pounding the enemy infantry, they began shelling their artillery, which was farther to the east. I was amazed that artillery could fire that far. The shells must have been landing more than six kilometers away.

"The fighting continued all through the night. We snipers took turns resting and sniping during the night. Those who were resting could not sleep, due to the sounds of battle. Those who sniped only fired a few shots at those on the other side of the river foolish enough to fire long machine-gun bursts. A few German flares were also fired above the Russians during the night. These were fired from special flare pistols, and fell suspended from tiny parachutes as they burned a bright white light into the dark sky. The Russian positions were illuminated, but few of them were foolish enough to stick their heads out while so revealed.

"The next day the assault on the enemy artillery guns continued. Bombs and artillery shells hit them all day, until barely any artillery was fired from the eastern side of the river. By late in the afternoon the our artillery changed its direction of fire again and shells began raining down on the many Russian tanks across the river. Another group of dive-bombers appeared and began dropping bombs upon them.

"The unfortunate Russians must have had very strict orders not to retreat from this spot. They held their ground and took a very bad beating for their stubbornness. For the us, it was like a crash course in extreme range sniping. We all became quite skilled at it. After realizing that this engagement could last some time, we slowed down our rate of fire to two shots per hour per sniper during daylight hours. We had several thousand rounds of captured ammunition, but used up one third of this in the first two days. The vast majority of our shots resulted in kills. We only fired at targets which were clearly visible and not moving. We only shot enemy machine-gun crews, mortar crews, snipers, and officers. We left the enemy riflemen for the artillery to finish off.

"The Russians were joined by reinforcements on the second day as well. Two more infantry divisions crawled into the many foxholes filled with dead Russian soldiers. Many of the dead soldiers were piled onto the sides of foxholes and used like sandbags.

"The battle for Vitebsk continued for twenty days. Our forces killed thousands of Russians each day, then they would be reinforced the following morning. Some of the foxholes were so filled with dead enemy soldiers that there was no room for a living soldier to get into the hole. The entire area smelled horrible. Rotting corpses and human waste filled the air with a horrible smell, which made me and the other snipers feel as if we were about to vomit. It was almost unbearable. We were sure that it must have been much worse closer to the river, as it worsened considerably when the wind blew from that direction.

"The Russian tanks were all destroyed within the first week. They never retreated from their position, and were constantly pounded by artillery and bombs. So thick was their armor that only direct and very close hits could destroy them. When they were destroyed, internal ammunition explosions shot green and white flashes out of every hole in them, and often blew the turrets right off the top of the tanks.

"On the eighteenth day of the siege, the entire Panzer corps mobilized and headed back to the west. Two divisions of infantry were left in their dug-in positions. The other two infantry divisions, including the paratroopers, were ordered to move out. Our snipers quickly moved from our foxholes on the hill and marched to our truck, which was waiting for us a safe distance to the west with a large number of other trucks, armored personnel vehicles, cars, and horses.

"All of us smelled terrible from spending eighteen days in a foxhole. We were all very happy not to have been killed or wounded in the many days of fighting. The Russian soldiers never even fired at us. We had fired at long range from their safely concealed position the entire time.

"The tanks of the Panzer corps turned off of the dirt highway and rolled over Russian farm roads. We headed east for a while, then to the south. Shortly after noon, we reached a spot in the Dvina River where several pontoon bridges had been constructed. Our Fallshirmjager division was sent across first, to make sure the other side of the river was safe. Our truck was at the very front of the column. We had moved out of our foxhole much faster than most of the other infantrymen, and got to our truck much sooner. We were a bit apprehensive about crossing the river first, but it was uneventful.

"After crossing the pontoon bridge, our army rolled to the east toward Smolensk. We traveled for several hours—until nightfall. At that time, we finally came to a halt, and dug our usual foxholes in yet another huge army encampment filled with thousands of foxholes.

"We snipers had used up most of our precious ammunition. Running out of cartridges was the thing we feared most. We decided to attempt to acquire ammunition for at least the German rifles.

"Each man contributed one of their cigars from our morning rations. Konrad and I did not smoke, and we had saved up several cigars. We each contributed a handful.

"Davey was chosen to attempt to trade the cigars for ammunition. He was the smooth talker of the group. He walked around the camp until he found a machine-gun crew. The first crew refused to trade, so he found another. They were willing to trade. He gave them forty cigars for one box of five hundred rounds. If questioned, they could easily say that they had used it up the previous day.

"As it got darker, we ate our usual hot evening meal. We could hear the sounds of distant explosions to the north, east, and south. It was obvious that the other factions of Army Group Central had made progress while they had been tied down at Vitebsk.

"In the morning, the army was split into two groups. Two tank and one infantry division headed to the east, toward Smolensk. One light tank, one armored car, and the paratroopers' infantry divisions were sent to the north. Their mission was to cut off the supply route and stop any reinforcements headed for Vitebsk. In effect, they would strangle the determined Russian army that had been stubbornly defending the city.

"As our squad rode in our truck to the north, all was quiet for most of the day. We ate our cold food rations as we bounced along in the truck, playing our usual card games.

"Then, at about three o'clock, we heard the tank division in front of us open fire with machine-gun and cannon fire. A whistle sounded somewhere and we all began leaping out of the truck, which had suddenly come to a halt.

"We had encountered a Soviet supply caravan. It consisted of about fifty trucks, four tanks, and about one hundred infantrymen. This force was absolutely tiny, compared to our force, which contained one hundred light tanks, one hundred armored cars, and twenty thousand paratroopers.

"By the time we started looking through our scopes for targets, almost all of the Russian infantrymen had been killed already. The four Russian tanks were still in action, but were being hit by cannon fire from all directions. Their own massive cannons were blasting as quickly as they could at our tanks, and the tanks were backing up, heading away from us at what was most likely their maximum reverse speed.

"We infantrymen were ordered to attack the tanks with any means possible and destroy them. Our eighteen-man sniper squad was soon running after thousands of other infantry, with our four anti-tank grenades in hand. We could no longer see the enemy tanks because of all the German tanks, armored cars, and soldiers in front of us. The air also was quite smoky already.

"We could hear heavy machine-guns firing ahead of us, and we were unsure whether bullets were heading in our direction or not. After we ran several hundred meters, we passed the burnt out remains of three light German tanks. They each had a single hole in the front of them from the large cannon of one of the enemy tanks. We could hear the pop of machine-gun rounds as they went off inside the burning tanks.

"After that, we encountered a burnt out Russian tank. Both of its treads were broken, and it had dents from small caliber cannon hits all over it. The barrel on its main gun was bent from a direct hit on its side. There was a black hole in the side, which was most likely caused by a German anti-tank grenade.

"Soon afterwards we found several more German tanks, and finally the three Russian tanks. All were destroyed in a similar fashion. It was obvious that the light German tanks were no match for these behemoths by themselves, but as a group they stood a good chance. It was also apparent that our anti-tank grenades inflicted more damage on the Russian tanks than one of our tank's cannons could.

"After this relatively small battle we continued to the north inside our truck. Within an hour we reached the Dvina River east of Vitebsk and effectively cut off the Russian troops inside the city.

"Instead of digging a large round camp, we formed a massive line of foxholes. This went from north to south for several miles. The foxholes were spaced fifteen meters apart and had one tank and one armored car in between them. This made a massive line of foxholes thirty kilometers long.

"We snipers did our best to conceal our foxhole. We took turns watching for any signs of danger. The remainder of that day was uneventful.

"We listened to the massive shower of shells which hit in and around Smolensk, a large city to the southeast. We could also hear the Russians in Vitebsk being shelled. The distant shelling sounded like thunder or fireworks. When it became dark enough, they actually lit up the sky like lightning.

"Several large anti-tank mines were concealed beneath the dirt of the road on which the supply caravan had been destroyed. These were cunningly concealed out of view of the foxholes, so any Russian tanks would hit them before they were aware there was any danger present.

"We looted the Russian supply trucks which had been attempting to reach Vitebsk. We found boxes of ammunition. Other German soldiers were not interested in this treasure since our rifles could not use the smaller caliber bullets. We took as much as we could carry, which added up to about seven thousand rounds.

"There were also boxes of hand grenades, food, barrels of water, and other supplies. Some of my snipers took some of the Russian grenades, which were similar to German egg grenades. The food was mostly raw vegetables and stale bread. We also took a few carrots and some potatoes. The latter were baked in a campfire next to our foxhole. It was nice to have some extra food. We walked back to our foxhole, which was two miles to the south of the road on which we had ambushed the supply caravan.

"We paratroopers spent the next two months in our foxholes. The 4th Parachute Division destroyed three more supply caravans meant for Vitebsk. All of my men had become very good friends as we played cards and talked in our foxholes. I realized that my own survival depended upon their skills as well as my own. Realizing this, I decided to train them the best I could. I taught them every sniper trick I could possibly think of, which took many days.

"August 5th, 1941 was the 46th day of Operation Barbarossa. It was on this day that the Soviet armies in the cities of Vitebsk and Smolensk surrenderd. They added up to over 100,000 soldiers. On the same day, Army Group South trapped some sixteen to twenty divisions, and captured over one hundred and fifty thousand men.

"On August 8th, Army Group Central captured another 38,000 prisoners in the forest near Smolensk. This entire force, along with the rest of the defenders of Smolensk, had been cut off from their supplies and emerged from the woods out of ammunition and starving. On the same day, all of Army Group Central's tanks, of which there still remained some one thousand, were sent back to Germany for refitting. The Blitzkrieg was halted. They had traveled some three hundred and fifty miles inside of the Soviet Union.

Grandpa suddenly stopped, with no warning, pushed his recliner into the upward position and asked, "Ingred, have you got any of that fruit soup left?"

George chuckled. His father had often told him about "Grandma's fruit soup," but he had never tasted it. Looked like tonight was his lucky night.

CHAPTER 9

▼

OPERATION TYPHOON, THE PUSH FOR MOSCOW

"As each day passed in the foxhole, my snipers sensed that the Russians were preparing for them. We all knew that the next three hundred and fifty miles would probably not be taken as easily as the last.

"I and the other snipers were already tired of constantly being out in the open. We had to deal with insects, heat, constant sun, and occasional rain. The night brought anxiety. We had no way of knowing if each little sound we heard was a wild hare, or an enemy soldier sneaking up on our position. We were all under a lot of stress from being constantly on alert.

"I received two letters from Ingred. She wrote that she missed me dearly and prayed for my safe return. She also mentioned that there had been several air raid scares, and described how the people of Hamburg panicked when they heard the sirens. There were several underground shelters, but they simply hid in the cellar under the bakery. After reading this, it was my turn to worry. I pictured my wife, child, and mother sitting in the cellar, listening to the sirens. I was hopeful that I would be allowed to return home on September 1st. This was the date on which my four year conscription ended.

"On September 1st I received a letter from Berlin. It was a notification that my conscription had been extended an additional four years. 'Damn it!' I screamed.

"'What is it, Georg?' asked Konrad. All of the men were watching me.

"'My four years are up, and guess what? I get to fight for another four damn years!' I opened my locket and looked at the pictures of my wife and son. 'I might as well memorize them, it's all I'll ever get to see of them!'

"'Calm yourself, Georg!' ordered Ellis.

"I began to rationalize my situation. 'I'm going to kill every damn Russian I see. I'll slaughter them all, and then I'll get to go home!' I did not speak for the rest of the afternoon.

"On October 1st, 1941, Army Group Central's tank divisions returned. They had been refitted with new parts, including additional armor and larger caliber cannons for many. They still lacked the heavy armor and firepower of the Soviet tanks.

"There were many brand new tanks which took the place of those that had been destroyed in previous fighting. We were also given four new divisions of tanks which had previously belonged to Army Group North.

"The infantry and artillery divisions were also reinforced. Many thousands of soldiers had been killed or wounded and were replaced by fresh recruits. There were several new divisions of recruits as well. Heavy weapons were issued in much greater numbers. Each sniper was given a Panzerwurfmine (anti-tank grenade), if he did not already have one.

"It was quite obvious from the rapid pace in which new recruits were marched to their new units that something very big was going to happen very soon. My fellow snipers and I were certain that our days of sitting and waiting in the foxhole were soon coming to an end. Compared to combat, we considered enduring the elements to be a mere inconvenience. We would much rather stay where we were and guard the front line.

"That evening it was confirmed that we would be attacking the Soviet front line in the morning. We all found it almost impossible to sleep that night. This new offensive was called Operation Typhoon. The objective was Moscow, the capital of the Soviet Union.

"In the early hours of the next morning we were told to quickly gather our gear and be prepared to march. We were soon marching to the southeast.

"After marching several kilometers, it was about eight in the morning. We had marched into a large forest which surrounded Smolensk. We stopped after marching up beside a division of heavy German Panzers. We were told to dig in, which we promptly did.

"As usual, we dug two large foxholes and divided into two groups of nine men. The ground was uneven, so there were foxholes all over hills and lower areas for several thousand square meters of forest. We chose a large hill toward the rear of the division. As snipers, we were given much more freedom to choose our position than regular infantrymen.

"Soon after finishing our foxhole, the sound of shelling began. Thousands of artillery shells were fired from somewhere to the west. The shells landed somewhere to the east. We soon heard Russian artillery very close to wherever the German shells were landing answer with their own deadly rain of shells.

"This barrage of shells continued for the entire day. We also heard the sound of German dive-bombers dropping their incredibly loud bombs. These were very distinctively louder than artillery shells or other such explosions because of the sheer size of the bombs. Even the largest artillery shells weighed only about one hundred pounds. A bomb dropped from a dive-bomber could weigh around five hundred pounds. This sound caused Ellis and I to remember the time the German Air Force had mistaken us for enemy troops and bombed our position in the mountains of Crete.

"A few hours after noon, we still had not actually seen any enemy troops. The sounds of explosions still filled the air of the forest. Several of us ate our cold food rations as we listened to the sound of shelling.

"Suddenly the sound of our infantry division's artillery guns erupted into the already loud afternoon. We could hear shouts of excitement all around us. Something was coming.

"Fifteen minutes after hearing the sound of our own artillery firing, we heard the distinctive sound of heavy enemy tanks. Their steel wheels and tracks made a horrific sound. The ground shook from their massive fifty-ton weight as they rolled into the forest. They were headed right for us.

"The sounds of fighting began. We could hear the cannons firing. The Panzer division, which had been sitting to the southeast of our position, came to life and began moving to meet the Russian tanks. A Fallschirmjager officer shouted at all the soldiers within hearing. We were to move alongside the Panzers and attack the Russian tanks!

"We could not believe what we were hearing. Attack tanks with infantry? This sounded suicidal. We had no choice in the matter, though. Together we stood and followed our fellow paratroopers toward the sound of fighting.

"We could hear the sound of machine-gun bullets passing through the foliage above our heads as we approached the enemy tanks. It was quite clear that heavy fighting was taking place just a few hundred feet away.

"As we walked over the next hill, one of the massive Soviet tanks headed right at us over the top. We were shocked by this sight, as we had expected to encounter the enemy much farther away. We scrambled for whatever cover we could, as the tank opened fire with three heavy machine-guns.

"I ran to the side and dove behind a small lump of earth on the side of the hill. I heard bullets cutting through trees all around me as I did so. I knew that someone was shooting at me. There was little I could do but wait in this somewhat safe position as the tank continued to roll toward me and my men. Konrad then joined me in this spot.

"The tank boldly rolled down the trail which we had been walking up. Its turret turned in the opposite direction from me as it attempted to fire at the snipers who had rin to the other side of the trail.

"Seeing an opportunity, Konrad readied his anti-tank grenade and took a few steps toward the tank. It was twenty feet away from him when he hurled it. The tank's machine-guns could not fire at him, as they were mounted on the front of the tank as well as the front of the turret. The main gun was turned away from him. He was in the tank's blind spot.

"The anti-tank grenade hit the rear of the tank, and exploded. I thought it would be impossible for such a crude weapon to damage such a large tank. I remembered the tank in Poland which had been blown apart by the same type of grenade. The Polish tanks, however, where many times lighter and smaller than this behemoth before me.

"To the surprise of all of us, the Russian tank began to explode from the inside. Multiple explosions echoed and flashes of light shot out of the many peek holes on the tank. After about six of these, there was a huge single blast and the turret was blown off of the tank. We scrambled to get as far away from it as we could as this was happening.

"It was at this point that I saw Phillips. He was in a prone position on the ground near the tank and had been shot by several machine-gun bullets. He was moving, but I could see that there would be no saving him. I could not get near him because of the exploding tank. All I could do was watch him die.

"There was no time for ceremony. After the tank finally stopped exploding, Ellis ordered that all of Phillips' ammunition be taken, and gathered his identification disc. By then my unfortunate comrade was already dead. We continued marching up the hill.

"As we reached the top of the hill, we crawled on our hands and knees. We could not believe the scene which was before us. German soldiers were everywhere. All were fighting. Only a few meters away from these soldiers were three Russian tanks and their protective infantry squads.

"I took a few seconds to take in what was going on. I saw three German infantrymen cut down by the heavy machine-gun fire from one of the Russian tanks. A German anti-tank gun crew fired a 50mm cannon at one of the tanks. It bounced off the thick armor. A mortar shell landed behind one of the tanks and exploded. Six Russian infantrymen actually flew up in the air from the blast. One of them was decapitated. A German anti-tank grenade hit one of the Russian tanks at the wrong angle and did not explode. Heavy machine-gun fire raked the Russian tanks, killing several of their protective infantrymen. The German anti-tank gun fired again, and this time found its mark. One of the Russian tanks exploded. The massive explosion instantly killed two of the Russian infantrymen who had been crouching behind the tank for cover. This occurred when the ammunition inside went off in one huge blast.

"One of the other tank crews responded to the explosion by turning the turret on the top of their tank. They aimed it at the anti-tank gun crew which was in a foxhole with their 50mm cannon. The heavy 7.62mm machine-gun, which was built into the Russian tank's turret, opened fire on the crew.

"It was at this moment that I saw an opportunity. 'Cover me!' I shouted to my men. They were already firing at the Russian infantrymen with their sniper rifles, and the effect of this fire was murderous. Most of the snipers were armed with Tokarev semi-automatic rifles, and soon almost all of the Russian infantrymen were dead or seriously wounded.

"I pulled my anti-tank grenade from my belt and stood up. I took a few steps down the hill. There were only two tanks now, and the Russian infantrymen were too busy dodging bullets to fire at me. One tank was firing at the 50mm gun. The other was firing in the opposite direction at a squad of Germans who were hiding behind large trees. This tank's main gun fired and one of the one-foot thick trees exploded, killing several Germans. The 50mm gun crew had stopped firing, as they were dodging bullets. I threw the grenade at the turret of the tank firing at the gun crew. I hurled it underhand, as I had been trained to do in basic training. The second or two it was in the air seemed like it was in slow motion. I watched the finned tail of the dart-like grenade open to stabilize its flight. I turned and ran back toward the top of the hill. I knew the grenade was going to hit. It was flying straight at the tank when I last looked at it. I dove for the ground.

"I heard the grenade explode behind me. It was about three times louder than an S-24 grenade, as it was considerably larger. I knew the shaped charge on the tip of the grenade would cause the blast to go inside the tank rather than toward me. I crawled up the hill as fast as I could. I heard the blast as the shaped charge blasted through the tank's steel armor. When I reached the top, I joined the other snipers and turned to see what effect my grenade had upon the monstrous tank.

"This time the ammunition inside the tank did not explode. The tank simply sat there with its loud diesel engine idling. The crew must have been either dead or seriously stunned. The other snipers cheered.

"The last tank was now alone. The German infantrymen surrounded it, as all of its protective infantrymen had been killed. It began backing up the hill behind it, in an attempt to retreat.

"Another German soldier appeared beside it with yet another anti-tank grenade. He hurled it, and his grenade too hit the side of this tank. It exploded on the side of the turret, blasting right through the armor. Once again, the ammunition inside of this tank did not explode. The tank continued to back up for a few meters and then turned into a group of large trees, as if unguided. The trees snapped off as the fifty-ton tank slammed into them, then the tank began rolling down into a rather steep drop between two hills. It finally dropped out of sight.

"We all got up and ran forward. We fired several rounds into the bodies of the dying Russian soldiers and into the view slits of the two tanks. This was rather dangerous, considering the amount of ammunition inside of them. We climbed on top of the tanks and attempted to open them, but their hatches were locked from the inside.

"We checked on the 50mm gun crew and found that one of the three soldiers had been hit in the head, and was dead. The other two were frightened, but otherwise all right. They thanked us profusely for our help. The sounds of fighting continued all around us.

"'We need to put this gun to good use,' said Ellis. We helped the anti-tank gunners pull the weapon out of the hole. We also helped them carry several wooden crates of ammunition, Each one holding four rounds for the weapon.

"One of the anti-tank gunners told us, 'This fifty millimeter is one of the only guns we have which can penetrate the thick armor of these Soviet tanks. It fires a special armor-piercing round with a tungsten core.'

"We moved to where we heard a nasty fight going on nearby. It was over yet another hill. Beyond this was another panorama of brutal fighting. Two Russian tanks and about fifty Russian infantrymen were fighting about two hundred paratroopers, who were still in their fox-holes. We watched as one of the tanks fired its 76mm cannon right into one of the foxholes, killing the five soldiers inside.

"8cm mortar shells rained down onto the Russians from some-where. These killed about half of the infantrymen who were with them. We immediately began firing at them. I shot five of them within a few seconds. After this there were no more of them standing any-where that I could see them. Ellis' men and I had shot the rest.

"With the protective infantry gone, the tide of the fight instantly changed to our favor. Several anti-tank grenades were hurled at the tanks. One of the behemoths was hit and exploded.

"The two 50mm gun crewmen aimed their weapon at the remain-ing tank and loaded a shell into the breech of the weapon. They fired once and watched as the shell went into the side of the tank. It hesi-tated for a moment, then began turning its turret toward them. They quickly reloaded and fired again. Again it penetrated the armor. This time the tank exploded. The turret was blown off.

"At that moment, my men and I came under fire from several more Russian infantrymen. Frantzen, the soldier who could speak Russian, was hit in the left thigh. He screamed in shock and pain.

"These enemy soldiers were firing from a hilltop one hundred feet away. They were to the south of where the enemy tanks had been. We all scrambled for cover from this new threat.

"After getting behind a large tree, I began firing back at them. I shot three of them as they were firing their bolt-action Nagant rifles at me and my men. I shot each of them through the red star on their Russian soldier's hat.

"The fire from the other snipers was just as deadly. Within seconds, the twenty or so Russian infantrymen were all dead. Ellis and I ran to assist Frantzen as he fell, writhing in pain. We put a tourniquet on him using his own ammunition belt and a spade. We also applied pressure to the wound and bandaged it.

"Ellis ordered two of his men to help Frantzen get to a medic. They quickly carried him away. All around us were dead and dying soldiers, both German and Russian. We spread out and shot the wounded Russians. Once this task was completed, we began helping the many wounded German soldiers.

"They had all sorts of injuries. Some had bullet wounds to their limbs, or heads, or torsos. Several had shrapnel wounds from grenades and tank cannon fire. Others had been wounded when the 8cm mortar shells had hit. They informed us that their officers had been killed. Ellis ordered them to carry the wounded to safety, and told the others to stay with him.

"The sounds of fighting were now somewhat quieter. The battle was coming to an end. We later learned that fifty percent of our division was either killed or wounded. The German tank division, which had also been fighting the Russian tank division, had lost thirty percent of its tanks. The Russian tank division had been annihilated. We learned that the Russian tanks were known as KV-1 heavy tanks, and were even more powerful than the heavily armed and armored T-34's which we had encountered at the beginning of the invasion of Russia.

"Our division was told to hold its position and dig in. We once again dug foxholes and ate our cold food rations.

"My men were all very stressed from the deadly battle in which they had just participated. They all considered themselves lucky to be alive. I felt guilty about Phillips. I wondered if I had done something wrong. Perhaps if I had ordered the men to walk off of the trail, he would still all be alive. This thought made me sick. I was a good sniper, but I still was new at commanding other men. I hoped that Frantzen would be all right. We had managed to stop his bleeding. I hoped the poor man would not get a lethal infection. I also realized, to my horror, that I was getting accustomed to this. That thought was almost as terrifying to me as death itself. The killing and danger hardly bothered or surprised me any more. It had become routine. How many men had I killed? How many had I watched die? I had no idea. I did not know when it would end. It was as if I had been sent to hell, and sentenced to spend eternity fighting a never-ending war.

"The 4th Parachute Division had once again made a good account of itself in battle. Had we not been an entire division of veteran soldiers, we might have been overrun.

"The following morning the 4th Parachute Division was reinforced with new recruits. Some of them were veteran soldiers who had been injured in previous battles. Most, however, were fresh out of basic training.

"Two new snipers were assigned to me. They told me their names, which were Lederer and Williams. I ordered Remshart and Achil to teach them both how to be good snipers. I also gave Frantzen's Tokarev to Private Harm.

"The sounds of artillery shells continued throughout our entire stay in our new camp. The war had unquestionably not stopped without us, but we were not attacked. We were told by a runner that the entire division would be moving out that night. We were going to attempt to flank the enemies' artillery batteries to the east. There were two large groups of artillery guns behind four dug-in Russian infantry divisions. They had been firing at our artillery positions during the entire battle. German artillery shells and bombs had failed to knock all of them out, and it was impossible to attack the infantry divisions in front of us without getting shelled mercilessly.

"Just after dark, the entire division of paratroopers began to march in an enormous column. As they did so, it began to rain very heavily. The rain did very little to lift our spirits. It was not long before all of us were entirely soaked from head to toe. We heard the booms of artillery over the sound of millions of raindrops falling everywhere.

"The division marched in the dark to the northeast. There were not supposed to be any enemy troops in this area, but anything was possible.

"After marching for several hours, we turned and began to march to the southeast. We were carefully marching around a division of Russian infantry, which was supposed to keep us away from the massive 15cm Russian artillery guns behind it. We all hoped that the combination of darkness and rain would hide our passage. We could only see a few feet in the darkness, so the chances of moving the twenty thousand men of the division without the Russians noticing must have been quite good.

"After marching to the southeast for several more hours in the pouring rain, we again changed direction. This time we were marching to the southwest. The paratroopers were well-trained soldiers, and they marched at a rapid pace, despite being weighed down with heavy weapons.

"My men and I were about fifty meters behind the front of the column. The column was twenty soldiers wide and one thousand soldiers long. Also in this column were several artillery guns, which were part of our division, and our division's company of medics. We could hear the Russian guns firing into the sky in front of them, only now the shells were heading away from us, toward our artillery. We also heard massive explosions as German artillery shells hit the Russian positions. This did not look like a good place to be out in the open.

"Massive muzzle flashes from the 15cm Russian artillery guns began to be visible. We were getting very close. The division was ordered to spread out, and attack the enemy at will. We must have been within two hundred feet of them.

"We snipers knew that the weather would make long range shots next to impossible. We would have to get in close, alongside the other infantrymen. We readied our weapons and leaned down as far as we could as we ran. We were travelling across Russian farmland, and the soil had all turned to thick mud.

"Heavy machine-gun fire then opened up in front of us. We all dove down into the mud and began crawling forward, while staying as low as possible. We heard weapons being fired in both directions. A grenade went off about fifty feet in front of us.

"I saw a muzzle flash from a heavy machine-gun. It was firing in my direction. I aimed at it and fired three quick shots with the Tokarev. The machine-gun stopped firing. I waited. The flashes started again, and I fired once more. I saw several rifles being fired near the heavy machine-gun. I was at first not sure if these were friendly or enemy troops, so I hesitated. When I heard a bullet zip past my head in the air, I decided to shoot. I methodically fired at each spot where I thought I saw a muzzle flash. Then I had to put in a fresh magazine of ten rounds.

"The other snipers were alongside me, doing much the same thing. We crawled forward, using what little cover there was from small patches of uneven ground and holes which had been made by friendly artillery.

"The thousands of paratroopers who were with us made quick work of the small infantry squads attempting to protect the artillery guns. They were hopelessly outnumbered, and we had better and heavier weapons. The artillery crews could not use their weapons effectively at this close range. Several of them simply ran, leaving their field pieces. Our comrades shot them as they attempted to flee.

"We fought our way into the large area of foxholes, where the artillery guns had been dug-in. As we advanced, the first light of dawn began to make the horizon glow. This made it much easier for long range shooting. We each shot dozens of Russian soldiers as they attempted to stand their ground against the Fallschirmjager.

"Within twenty minutes, the entire artillery division had been over-run. Our superiors radioed our success to command, and then watched as a second Russian artillery division, which was positioned about one mile to the south, began to get shelled by both of the friendly artillery divisions to the west.

"We then moved into a position where we could shoot at this second division. We made several long-range shots and hit dozens of artillery crewmen. Some of the crews turned their weapons to fire in our direction, although they could not see us. We all were covered with mud and lying prone. We could easily see the Russians through our scopes, which made them appear to be about three hundred feet away.

"There were four Russian infantry divisions and one heavy tank division in between the paratroopers and the rest of their main German army group. The paratroopers watched as the Russian tanks were attacked by two divisions of German heavy tanks. Artillery shells rained down upon the Russian heavy tanks as well. Three of the Russian infantry divisions were attacked by two divisions of Pioneers—highly trained German infantry with heavy weapons—and the division of heavy tanks, which had assisted the paratroopers earlier with the tanks in the forest.

"The enemy tanks were destroyed. The Russian infantry fought throughout the next day. They finally surrendered, after being cut off and surrounded. When an army was cut off, it was like being suffo-cated. They got no ammunition, food, or replacement soldiers. To lose your supply lines meant either surrender or death.

"After the last of the Russians moved out of their large area of fox-holes to surrender, our snipers went into this area to search for weapons. Many other paratroopers were doing the same thing. We found most of the ammunition boxes to be empty. The Russians had run out of bullets. We also found dozens of grenades, and two more Tokarev rifles. Ellis and I each kept one for their respective squads. I gave mine to Private Remshart. He was one of only four of my men who still carried a Kar 98K. With the acquisition of this new weapon, six of the nine men in the squad, including me, had a Tokarev.

"Destroying this first Russian army should have meant pushing the Blitzkrieg ever closer to Moscow, but the intense rains continued for days and slowed the advance to a crawl. It was almost impossible to drive tanks on the Russian roads, none of which were paved. If they had been, nothing would have stopped the advance into Moscow.

"The City of Safonova was only a few miles to the east. Our army dared not venture out without its armor and artillery. They tried having men pushing and pulling trucks and tanks, but it was hopeless. It was also difficult to dig in. The foxholes continually filled with water, and all of the soil in which they were dug turned to mud.

"The next month was very quiet. The rains continued. Our army moved only one or two miles per day. The Russians kept their distance. We all were miserable. We were constantly wet and covered with mud. The nights were extremely uncomfortable, even for us, and we were accustomed to hardship.

"The sounds of distant battles could be heard to the north and south, but only occasionally. We frequently witnessed aerial dogfights between fighter squadrons, and we heard both dive and strategic bombers strike Safonova, and the surrounding area. We were sure that an enemy army awaited us there.

"Finally, on November 3rd, the rains stopped. The soil was still wet and muddy, but I was glad that I could at last dry off.

"The following morning the mud roads began to dry and the army surged forward toward Safonova.

"The city was a natural fortress, with the Dnieper River around its southern and eastern sides. The Russians had fortified it with anti-air-craft cannons, artillery, several divisions of infantry, and two divisions of tanks. Even as we approached, the German bombers were pounding the city. The sound of bombs rumbled through the air every few minutes.

"The 4th Parachute Division was assigned to defend a bridge over the Dnieper River, which was to the southwest of Safonova. It was vital that the bridge be kept in the hands of the German Army, and not the Soviets. If the Russians took it, they would be able to cut off the main army group as it attempted to destroy the army defending Safonova.

"The division moved to the other side of the bridge. We had been told that there were no enemy units in the immediate area, but we were still on alert. Every bush, house, and tree looked suspicious.

"Upon reaching the other side, we once again began digging hundreds of foxholes. We made four, rather than the usual two foxholes. We were again near the rear of the division, where the artillery was located.

"After we had eaten a meal and talked a while, a runner jumped into the foxhole where Konrad, Hughes, Davey and I were. He was out of breath and saluted me saying, 'Excuse me, Sir. We need your help. There's at least one Russian sniper shooting at us from long range, Sir. He already hit five of our guys, and we can't even see where the bastard is. Someone told me that you guys are good at killing enemy snipers.'

"'All right Private. Lead the way.' I did not want to lose any of my men, so I motioned Konrad to follow me, then I picked up my rifle and one of the periscopes. The Private crouched down low, as did Konrad and I as we ran behind him. It took us several minutes to reach the front of the division, and I expected to be shot at any second. We jumped into another foxhole near the front.

"The sounds of battle were already intensifying to the northeast. The main army group must have reached the outer defenses of Safonova. I was glad I wasn't in that battle.

"'What now, Sergeant?' asked the runner. There were several other men in the foxhole, and they were all looking at the two of us snipers hopefully.

"'Now we try to find out where he is,' I replied as I peeked over the top of the foxhole with the periscope. The terrain seemed endless before me. There were farmhouses, trees, bushes, wheat fields, barns, and many more good hiding spots. It was like looking for an ant in a yard that needed mowing.

"I spoke to Konrad. 'Put your helmet on your spade and tighten the strap very tight.'

"'All right,' replied Konrad. He did as he was ordered. He handed me the helmet on the spade.

"I held the helmet up in plain sight. I turned it back and forth, as if it was looking left and right. For almost a minute nothing happened.

I pictured myself looking at this area through my own scope at long range. I might or might not shoot at a helmet. If it as a heavy weapons user or a sniper I would not hesitate.

"'Give me your rifle,' I said to Konrad. I took it from Konrad's outstretched hand. I placed it in front of the helmet, keeping my hand as small a target as possible. I held the rifle upright, as if the pretend soldier in the helmet was aiming it around.

"'Ping!' a bullet went through the helmet. I let go of the rifle and looked up into the helmet. I could see one hole in the front, and another in the rear of it. A few seconds later I heard the crack of the sniper rifle, which had been fired at me. I estimated that the enemy sniper was about one kilometer away. I kept the helmet up, as if it had not been hit. I turned the periscope toward the direction of the sniper. I saw nothing at first, other than farmland and a few trees, then I saw a muzzle flash in the window of a farmhouse.

"'Ping!' the helmet was struck again. I dropped the helmet, as if it had been hit. Konrad recovered his helmet, which now had four round holes in it. 'This ought to keep the damn rain off!' he said, laughing.

"'Be glad your head wasn't in it," I joked. I continued watching the farmhouse with the periscope. 'Keep your heads down, boys. This sniper is good, and he has no idea we've spotted him.'

"I closed my eyes for a moment. I kissed my locket and said a silent prayer. I handed the periscope to Konrad and ordered him, 'Tell me if you see a muzzle flash, and do it quick!'

"'Yes, Sir!' replied Konrad.

I quickly took some mud and rubbed it all over my helmet. I also put it on my face. I hoped this would give me a few extra seconds. I then pictured where I had seen the house, and quickly popped my head up, aiming my rifle. I frantically moved the crosshairs around, searching for the house.

I saw it. I moved my crosshairs to the window, and fired. At the same instant, I saw a muzzle flash. I ducked. "Flash!" yelled Konrad excitedly. A second later, the sound of the bullet whizzing through the air above my head could be heard.

I then spoke to the runner. 'Private.'

"'Yes, Sir?'

"'Now put your helmet on your spade and do the same thing Konrad was doing.'

"'Yes, Sir!' He tightened the chinstrap with shaking hands and held up the helmet. Nothing happened.

I stuck my head up and aimed at the house again. I fired two more rounds into the window, and one into each window of the farmhouse.

"'Order a mortar crew to turn that house into a crater!' I told the runner.

"'Yes, Sir!' The runner ran off to follow his orders.

Konrad and I took turns watching the house, making sure nobody left it. The sniper could have gone out the back of the house, which was not visible to us, but I was pretty sure I had hit him. After a few minutes, mortars began landing near the house. Then three of them landed right on the roof, blowing most of the upper floors off. They continued to land on it, demolishing the entire structure. The runner returned.

"'Problem solved.' I tapped the runner on his helmet and waved goodbye. We headed back to our foxhole.

"The sounds of fighting continued through the night and into the next day. It sounded ferocious. Later in the day, a Panzer division of heavy tanks crossed the bridge and came to a halt alongside the 4th Parachute Division. The tank division was considerably smaller, since it contained one hundred tanks and about one thousand men. The 4th Parachute Division had over twenty thousand men and about five hundred motorized vehicles.

"We witnessed the commanding officers of our division and the Panzer division speaking to one another. After a brief meeting, the word spread throughout the division that at least one division of heavy Russian tanks was on its way to our position.

"There was a main road that went over the bridge and to the east. It eventually went to a large city called Vyazma. It was on this road that the Russian tanks were travelling. The engineers of the 4th Parachute Division quickly began lying anti-tank mines along the road and alongside it. We also positioned all of our anti-tank guns in such a way that they could easily target anything coming up the road.

"Later in the day, an artillery division moved across the bridge and dug-in behind our division. The men of the Panzer division began putting sandbags around the Panzers to increase their armor protection from the heavy Russian tank cannons.

"About six o'clock that night we could see about one hundred dive-bombers dropping bombs on something moving in our direction from the east. We were all quite certain that it was the enemy tank division.

"My snipers and I began looking through our scopes and binoculars. It was not long before we could see the many KV-1 and T-34 tanks heading in our direction. There were more than one hundred of them, and each one of them had about ten soldiers riding on top of it. The Russians used their tanks like transport trucks.

"Our artillery guns began firing at the tanks. We snipers started taking extreme range shots at the infantrymen riding on the tanks. All of the snipers in our foxhole scored several hits as the tanks approached.

"When the enemy tanks were perhaps one thousand meters away, all sorts of weapons began firing at them. The infantry riding on them jumped off and began running behind them and using them for cover. Machine-guns, mortars, rifles, and artillery shells hit the Russians from several angles as they rolled forward. I was amazed that any of them were still alive.

"We heard the high pitched screech of the tanks' steel wheels on their treads as they got closer and closer to us. The Russian tanks began firing heavy machine-guns and cannons at the Germans, who killed several of the paratroopers as they fired their weapons.

"When the tanks were about one hundred meters away, they began hitting anti-tank mines. These blew the tracks off the steel giants, immobilizing them. The cannons of the German tanks and anti-tank guns were pounding them all badly now, as there were only perhaps seventy Russian tanks left. There was no sign of any protective infantry. A dive-bomber dropped a five hundred-pound bomb on a squad of three Russian tanks right in front of me. They all were destroyed by the massive blast.

"Some of the Russian tanks reached the first foxholes of the 4th Parachute Division. They had been dug extremely deep so the Russian tanks would not be able to cross them. Several of them plunged into these deep holes, which were half filled with water, as the ground was still very wet. Other tanks stopped, as if their crews realized that this was an impassable barrier. The tanks in the deep muddy water experienced engine failure as their engines sucked in water. German infantrymen sealed their doom by throwing anti-tank grenades onto their roofs as they sat helpless in the deep water.

"At this point, there were about forty Russian tanks remaining. Over one hundred tank cannons, artillery shells, and scores of anti-tank guns pounded them mercilessly. They were exploding left and right. Several crews attempted to back up and leave the area. This only divided their forces, as some crews stayed to fight.

"Ten minutes later, every Russian tank had been destroyed. The entire division had been wiped out.

"I did not know if the Russians believed their extremely good tanks to be invincible, or if they were so desperate that they would sacrifice an entire division of them for little or no reason. Whatever the case, I was glad to have faced them in this situation rather than if they had been dug-in waiting for me.

"The German Panzer commander ordered his mechanics to salvage any of the Russian tanks they could. They were extremely well-built machines. Their armor and weapons were superior to the best German tanks, and several had already joined the ranks of the Panzers from previous battles.

"They got right to work, hauling tanks out of the muddy water. We snipers simply sat in our foxholes and waited. The defenders of Dnieper surrendered that night. The following morning was November 6th. Our army was soon in trucks and on the move.

"The City of Vyazma was defended by an enormous Russian army. Rather than attack this huge force head on, The Germen army spread out and dug-in to the west of the city. Two other armies moved around the city to the north and south, until it was completely surrounded. Another city, called Bryansk, was to the east of Vyazma. It, too, had a huge Russian army dug-in and prepared to defend it. We Germans simply surrounded these huge armies, and on November 11th they surrendered. Army Group Central captured 663,000 prisoners that day. It seemed that victory was not far off. The rains continued off and on the entire time and the ground was still quite muddy.

"The next day the army would have headed for Moscow, which was only about two hundred miles away. Instead, a cold front moved in and the temperature dropped well below freezing. Our tanks, which were sitting in about one-foot-thick mud, were frozen in their tracks. We could not move an inch. Hundreds of infantrymen were put to work in an attempt to free them, but it was not possible. They even tried surrounding them with burning logs to thaw out the mud. They did manage to free a few tanks, but nowhere near all of them. It was obvious that Army Group Central was here to stay.

We did not have any winter clothing. We had no hats, gloves, or heavy coats. We all sat in groups around campfires shivering. My friends and I had brought gloves and extra clothes, so we did not suffer quite as badly as the other men, but we were still extremely cold. I wrote a letter home and told Ingred and my mother how miserable I was. There was little else to do.

"On November 15th, 1941, the weather improved. The ground thawed somewhat, and the army surged forward in an attempt to attack Moscow before even colder weather set in. The Soviets could only muster a few divisions of poorly trained and equipped conscripts to oppose us. Most of these unfortunate units were pounded by dive-bombers before they finally surrendered.

"On November 27th the Panzer corps had divided into two huge Panzer groups which were attempting to encircle Moscow and cut it off. The northern group was within twenty one miles of the city. The southern group was about forty miles south of Moscow. We stopped for the night. My snipers and I were part of the southern group.

"That night another extremely cold front moved in. This time it was so cold that the very oil inside of our tanks froze. They were once again frozen in rock hard mud, which was about a foot deep. Several men died that night from exposure. I could not stand the cold. There was no escaping it. Everything in our world was cold. The ground. The air. Every piece of equipment became a piece of freezing metal which could tear a man's flesh from his bones by instantly freezing it. My lungs filled with freezing air each time I inhaled. I put my mouth inside my shirt and breathed in and out of it to conserve body warmth. I soon had ice on my mustache, beard—I had not shaved in weeks, and eyelashes. My hands and feet were almost constantly numb from the cold. We rarely had fuel for fires, but burned whatever we could. Liquid water was a rarity. We usually sucked on ice or snow to quench our constant thirst. The bitter cold wind howled constantly, biting at us through every opening or thin spot in our inadequate clothing.

"Many of the Russians who were captured had heavy winter coats, gloves, hats, and boots. All of these articles were quickly taken by the Germans. There were still far too few of them to equip all of us from the bitter cold. Several prisoners died of exposure only minutes after being stripped of their winter clothing.

"I heard a rumor that this was the coldest Russian winter in over fifty years! I believed it. I was always cold. It seemed there was no escape from it. I was thankful that the cold nights on the Island of Crete had convinced me to bring at least some protection from the cold. We all huddled together in our foxhole we had dug the night before. It was a good thing that we had dug it then, because the ground was so frozen that digging became nearly impossible. Pick axes and saws had to be used for digging, rather than spades. It was more like concrete than soil.

"The army stayed in this position for several days. It snowed every day, and it was piling up. In most places, it was a foot deep. The wind blew hard, and the snow drifted everywhere. In some places the snow was three feet deep or more. My squad secretly went into the truck that normally carried us and took the long boards that made the benches in the back. These we placed on top of our two foxholes, then we covered them with snow. We left peek holes, which we could fire out of, on all sides. After being snowed on a few times, the foxholes looked like two large piles of snow.

"Before the sun rose on December 6th, the Russians began a massive counteroffensive from their positions around Moscow. Artillery shells began to rain down upon our position as we attempted to keep from freezing to death in our foxholes. The frozen tanks were silent.

"I could tell by the sound of them that these were 15cm shells. They made a deafening shock wave when they hit. I could hear my fellow soldiers screaming for it to stop all around me. They all just wanted to go home. The cold froze not only their bodies, but their spirits as well.

"It was actually somewhat good that the ground was frozen. It prevented the shells from breaking up the ground as they hit. It was about as strong as concrete, so only a direct hit could be effective. There was little we snipers could do other than try to keep warm and keep our heads down. We were on the outer edge of the division, on the west side. This put us much farther away from the Russians than most of the paratroopers.

"I hoped that the Russians did not have any tanks in this area. I could not imagine how we would be able to stop them. Our tanks were useless for the moment, and it would be impossible to dig a hole to place an anti-tank mine in.

"As the shelling continued, it began to snow quite heavily. A freezing wind accompanied the snow out of the north. It felt as if the arctic had been moved from the North Pole to this God-forsaken place.I wished that I could be anywhere other than where I was.

"The shelling continued for several hours. Again and again the air was filled with the sounds of explosions. It reminded me again of the time Ellis, Konrad and I were bombed in the mountains of Crete by our own army. The 100-pound 15cm shells were much smaller than the massive bombs which weighed almost 250kg (about 500 pounds). We had been through worse. We huddled together in the cold, dark foxhole, and held our helmets tightly over our heads as our positions were shelled.

"We Germans were not completely defenseless. Our own artillery answered back with its own barrage of 15, 12, and 10cm guns. Planes fought for air-superiority in the clouds above the army. It seemed that the German airforce was once again defeating the Russians in the sky. This is probably what saved us more than anything else. We could hear bombs being dropped on the enemy artillery positions. This lessened their rate of fire, but the shells continued to fall.

"Whew!" Grandpa said. "I'm tired. Anybody else?"

Grandma looked at George. He was curled up on the end of the sofa, nearly asleep. She took an afghan and tucked him in, turned off the light and joined Granpda on his way up the stairs.

"Maybe it's too much for him," she suggested.

"We'll see," Granpda said. "We'll see tomorrow night."

CHAPTER 10

▼

A LONG COLD WINTER

As the trio finished supper, Grandpa asked George, "Am I boring you with my stories? Do you want to forget hearing more?"

"Oh, no, Grandpa!" George insisted, remembering his father's admonition to remember everything Grandpa told him if he talked about the war. "I want to hear all of it."

Grandpa began where he'd left off the night before.

"Late that afternoon, as we snipers hid in our foxhole to keep away from the shelling, we could hear machine-guns begin to fire. We could tell that they were close, so they must have been friendly. We also noticed that the shelling began to subside. That probably meant that the enemy infantry was getting close.

"I looked out and saw what looked like thousands of Soviet troops advancing toward our dug-in army. For a moment I thought, *How can we possibly shoot all of them?* Then my men and I began shooting at them.

"The Russians were advancing quickly, using whatever they could for cover. They hid behind any sort of hill, tree, rock, or other thing which would protect them from the thousands of bullets being fired at them. Many of us were already firing back. It was difficult for snipers to target men who were running, so we concentrated on those who had stopped to shoot.

"I shot several riflemen, an officer, and a machine-gun crew within the first few minutes. I watched as German mortar shells landed near several advancing groups of Soviets. I then saw a few of the outer foxholes get overrun. I put my crosshairs on a Russian soldier as he raised his rifle, as if he was about to bash in the skull of a German soldier. I fired. The bullet passed through his head, which was covered with a warm-looking fur-covered hat.

"This assault continued for hours. Russian squads would reach the edges of the 4th Parachute Division, only to be slaughtered. Their bodies piled up like cordwood.

"Late in the afternoon we snipers noticed several Russian snipers taking long- range shots from a wooded area about one kilometer away. Ellis and I ordered our men to concentrate their attacks on the snipers and keep a sharp eye out for them. We shot over thirty snipers before nightfall.

"The attacks only intensified after dark. Our squad could do little but listen to the sounds of fighting. A thick fog rolled in and visibility was reduced to a few feet.

"We found an extra German helmet. This item was used as the toilet. We took turns dumping it behind the foxhole. A patch of filth and yellow ice developed back there. We dared not venture far from the foxhole. For ration and mealtime we took turns going out to get food and ammunition. We ran from foxhole to foxhole as we went, and several Russian soldiers in the surrounding hills took shots at us.

"On December 8th we were informed that Hitler himself had ordered the army to stand its ground. There would be no retreat. We were to defend this miserable piece of land to the last bullet and the last man. This did little to boost anyone's morale. Most of the men still did not have proper winter gear. Every morning, I heard of two or three more who had frozen to death the night before. Several of them had pneumonia. Frozen German corpses were everywhere. They had been placed outside of foxholes, where they were covered by blowing snow.

"We were also told that The United States was now at war with Germany. This seemed like very bad news, but any problems the US might cause were a long ways off. All of the men were well aware that this was the nation chiefly responsible for Germany's defeat in the First World War.

"The Russians continued to lay siege to our positions for weeks. Every day we would be shelled, shot at, and charged. We paratroopers were fearsome fighters and stood our ground, day after day.

"On December 19th General Brauchitch, who commanded the entire German army and air forces, resigned in protest. It was rumored that he wished to pull the army back, while Hitler had ordered it to stand its ground.

"On December 31st, the three generals who led Army Groups North, Central, and South all resigned in protest. Still we were ordered to stand our ground. Replacement troops arrived every week to replace those who had been killed or died. These were fresh conscripts who had just gotten out of basic training. They did not have proper winter clothing, either. Several of them were sick when they arrived, and died shortly after reaching the front.

"On January 10th there was a general state of alarm. Officers announced that an enormous Soviet army, which included infantry, tanks, artillery, and air-defense cannons, was headed our way. We still were unable to withdraw. We would stand our ground, or die trying.

"The many tank crews frantically lit fires under their tanks in an attempt to start them up. The oil in their engines had frozen solid. The enemy was about three hours off, and I wondered if this would be enough time to thaw the frozen tanks.

"After about two and a-half hours, our defensive artillery began to fire. We were certain that the enemy must be very close.

"Shortly after this, the sound of enemy tanks could be heard echoing throughout the countryside. They were getting nearer. The enemy tanks were soon rolling over the horizon to the east. This included a large area of Russian farmland, which was now covered with snow.

"Riding on top of the tanks were thousands of infantrymen. We looked at them with our scopes. They were all dressed in fur-lined coats and hats.

"'Fire!' I ordered. The snipers in my squad began to fire well-placed shots at the Russian infantrymen riding on top of the tanks. I fired as well. I hit several of them. Some of my bullets went through three or four men. This murderous fire prompted many of the infantrymen to jump off the tanks and run behind them. Several of the tanks stopped to fire their cannons and machine-guns. They bounced so much that it was almost impossible for them to aim without doing so. Their fire still had no effect upon us Germans, as we were all dug-in with rock hard frozen ground surrounding us.

"Several of our tanks were now operational, but most of them still had not started. They were also dug-in, with sandbags piled all over the vulnerable spots. It would be difficult for the Soviet tanks to damage them.

"Our artillery and mortar shells rained down upon the tank army as it surged forward in the snow. This had more of an effect upon the infantrymen than the tanks, although several tanks were destroyed by direct or very close hits.

"As the tanks approached, several anti-tank guns began firing from the paratrooper positions. A battery of 88mm anti-aircraft cannons was also firing at them. The effect of these guns was devastating. They knocked out dozens of the massive T-34 tanks with single hits at long range. They made excellent anti-tank guns, as well as anti-aircraft cannons.

"When they reached the foxholes, several of the Russian tanks began firing their weapons at the many holes all around them. German anti-tank grenades flew at them from all over, and even more tanks were destroyed. We snipers continued to shoot Russian infantrymen as they attempted to catch up with the tanks. Several machine-gun crews were also firing at these men, with devastating effects.

"Behind the tank division, what looked like two divisions of infantry were heading toward our army group. Several of our paratroopers began firing at these men as they ran in groups of thousands. Bodies of dead Russian soldiers and burnt out tanks covered the landscape.

"For two hours, the attack continued. The Russian tanks were all destroyed within the first half-hour. Several artillery shells then began to land on our positions. The Russians must have finally gotten their artillery into position. The Russians' infantry units retreated, and allowed the artillery to do its damage.

"The air forces did battle in the sky as the land forces were attempting to destroy one another as well. We paratroopers did not pay much attention to this, as they were too busy keeping our heads down.

"The intense sound of the shelling penetrated the thick roof of the foxhole, and once again shook my entire body. I hated being shelled more than almost anything. It was extremely uncomfortable, and the stress of wondering which shell was going to land right on top of me was unbearable. All my fellow snipers and I could do was duck down and pray that we would be spared.

"After about an hour, the shelling stopped. We could hear the guns of the German artillery battery firing nonstop. This must have been how the Russian guns had been silenced.

"The Russians did not attack with such force for the next few days. On January 15th, winter clothing began to arrive at last. Much of it was civilian, and must have been donated to the army by patriotic German citizens. All of us snipers were given heavy coats, gloves, hats, boots, wool socks, and long underwear. We all stripped down and put these items on immediately. We were so happy to finally have winter clothing that many of us wept.

"On that same day, we were ordered to withdraw from our position. We snipers assisted thousands of other soldiers in digging trucks and tanks out of the icy ground. It was exhaustive work, but it had to be done for our survival. We had to stop several times to fight off Russian snipers who mercilessly shot at us as we attempted to retreat.

"At last our army was ready to move. We removed the boards from our foxholes and placed them back in the truck. We were soon rolling along over the snow-covered road.

"We did not travel far. About forty miles down the road, we stopped. We had been ordered to pull back eighty-five miles from Moscow. We were ordered to dig in and around the City of Obninsk. There were several positions inside and around the city where the Soviets had dug foxholes and other fortifications in an attempt to defend the city from the German Blitzkrieg.

"We snipers were ordered into a large concrete building, along with about one hundred other infantrymen. This is where we would all make our stand.

"The building was located on the northeast side of the downtown area. Having taken part in the sieges of several cities,I knew that it would certainly be one of the first downtown buildings to be attacked. The building was made of concrete and cinderblocks, and the upper floors had already been damaged by our conquest of the city several weeks earlier. We had to clear out the remains of several frozen corpses.

"The many windows on the building, which was once a factory, were broken. Bullet holes were everywhere, indicating that this had been a location in which heavy fighting had once occurred. We paratroopers prepared our defenses as best we could. Heavy machine-guns, a few anti-tank guns, and riflemen were strategically positioned on the upper floors. Two squads with submachine-guns guarded the lower floors. Our snipers divided up into groups of three and spread out to various upper floors. There was no need to blacken our faces, as we were already black from filth. None of us had seen a bathtub, or even a shaving mirror, for weeks. All of us were unclean, and we smelled terrible. There was no escaping the soot and grime.

"Also positioned within the city were thousands of additional troops, several tank squads, artillery pieces, and flak cannons. An artillery division was dug-in to the west of the city, as were several anti-aircraft cannons. Infantry and tank divisions formed a great line to the north and south of the city, which stretched for hundreds of miles.

"We were ordered to secure our positions inside of our building and then to assist in fortifying the city. We helped lay mines, which included both anti-tank and anti-personnel. We all also helped dig several ditches and foxholes. We had to dig with pick axes and saws, as the ground was too frozen to dig with spades. We covered the mines with loose soil, gravel, and snow.

"The anti-personnel mines included mines made of metal, glass, wood, and cardboard. All but the metal mines were undetectable by metal detectors and had to be found with probes. Most of the mines were designed to blow a man's foot off. There was also an extremely deadly mine called a *shoe mine*, which shot up into the air after being triggered, and fired 360 projectiles in all directions. These were much like bullets and could kill people hundreds of feet away. Paratroopers placed most of the shoe mines on the far side of town, where the Germans would not be subjected to their horrible effects. Some were set to go off when triggered by remote control, which consisted of wires buried just under the ground leading from the mine to an electric controller.

"Anti-tank mines disabled enemy tanks by blowing their treads. The enemy tanks would serve as huge roadblocks once they could not move. Squads of German soldiers waited in position to shoot anyone attempting to fix the tread. They would also have their anti-tank grenades handy, to destroy the immobile tanks.

"The Russians did not give us long to prepare our defenses. On the third morning after our arrival, which was January 18th, 1942, we could hear word of an enemy army approaching. Less than an hour later, our artillery division to the west of the city began firing its guns. An hour after that, enemy artillery began to fire back. We also heard many of the mines on the far side of town going off. The 4th Parachute Division's 8cm mortars and many artillery guns began firing at the enemy troops, who were setting them off. We were already inside of our assigned building and were preparing to defend it.

"For two hours the enemy troops got closer by the minute. 'I see them!' shouted Konrad as he looked through the periscope. 'They're probing for mines!'

"I motioned for Remshart to have a look. At the same time, I leveled my own Tokarev rifle on the windowsill. I looked through the scope, while attempting to look in the same direction which the periscope was pointed. I quickly saw them: three Russian infantrymen, using the cleaning rods from their rifles to probe for mines. Without speaking, I quickly snapped off three shots, hitting all three of these soldiers in rapid succession.

"Remshart gasped in surprise. 'How the hell can you aim that thing so fast? Doesn't the recoil throw you off?' He spoke as he ducked back behind the safety of the wall.

"I did the same while Konrad answered for me. 'He's had lots of practice.'

"'They're sending men out to take their places!' said Konrad. I looked once again and saw three more men crawling over the still quivering bodies of their comrades. They all looked terrified. I shot them as well. 'Bam! Bam! Bam!' The empty cartridges clattered onto the concrete floor. I camly ducked down once again.

"'This group is running!' said Konrad excitedly. We heard an explosion, followed by several more gunshots. Other German soldiers must have heard the sounds of my shooting and were shooting at them. 'One of them hit a mine,' Konrad reported. 'He's not dead. Foot's blown off.'

"'Never mind him, just watch for more!' I said.

"For several minutes, no more Soviet troops attempted to come down the street. Then we could hear the sounds of tanks coming. Their wheels made the usual high-pitched sound as they approached. 'Tanks!' shouted Konrad. Then we heard a loud explosion. 'One of them hit an anti-tank mine! He's blocking the street!' There were several gunshots. 'Protective infantry attempted to move up and got hit hard by someone downstairs.'

"'Did any of them get through?' I asked calmly.

"'No. All are down. The tank is trying to back out with one tread, and it's turning into the building.' There was another explosion. 'Infantryman got him with an anti-tank grenade. He's hit bad.' We could hear the after-explosions as the tank's ammunition went off.

"We could hear similar fights going on all around us. Every street leading to the downtown area from the east had become a small battleground. Russian tanks fired at the large buildings with cannons and heavy machine-guns. They were hit in return by anti-tank guns, mortars, grenades, and hundreds of rifles. All of the streets were mined heavily with anti-tank mines. With their infantry unable to find the mines without being shot, the tanks were unable to move forward safely. Their commanding officers must have been ordering them to attack despite the danger. It was almost suicide.

"Then several mortars hit the area in between the Soviets and the many large downtown buildings. 'They're trying to blow up the mines,' I suggested.

"'Yeah, and they're throwing smoke grenades too!' shouted Konrad. Seconds later the sound of dozens of MG34's firing began all at once. The rifle fire intensified considerably. 'They're rushing!'"

"'Everybody shoot!' I ordered. Remshart and I started firing down into the thick smoke below. We could no longer see what we were shooting at. Konrad hurled an egg grenade which he had previously taken from dead Russian soldiers. It fell to the ground some sixty feet down and exploded. He then fired both his Tokarev, and his MP35 at the same time. He held one weapon in each hand.

"The smoke began to clear as a breeze blew through the area, and we could see hundreds of Russian infantrymen attempting to rush forward. There were piles of dead Russian soldiers everywhere in the street below. Scores of them were cut down at the same time by machine-gun bullets, but they continued to run forward. It was obvious that at least some of them were reaching the lower floors of the building, which our snipers were shooting from. We were able to aim, rather than fire blindly now. We each shot several Russians as they attempted to scramble for cover. I fired one bullet through a soldier's throat, and I watched in stunned horror for a moment as he fell screaming in pain. I was not used to shooting men this close. I could see every detail of agony upon their faces as the bullets tore through them.

"A few seconds later we heard the sounds of fighting in the lower levels of the building. Several riflemen ran downstairs to help the SMG squads defend the lower floors.

"I thought for a moment. There was so much smoke outside that we could not see anything. Sniping would be impossible, at least for the next few minutes. I knew that critical battles were taking place at that moment downstairs. I also knew that their outcomes could easily be changed. I ordered Remshart to remain in his position and continue to snipe. I ordered Konrad to come with me to the lower levels. Konrad gave me an intense look, then nodded in agreement. We were both experienced at this sort of indoor fighting and could be of great assistance to our comrades downstairs. Both of us knew that it was extremely dangerous.

"We soon reached the stairs and began to descend. Even though we were quite sure that the Soviets had not reached the upper floors of the building, we were extremely cautious. We walked in silence on the concrete floor, listening to the sound of fighting downstairs, and a few more riflemen descending the stairs above us.

"When we reached the second floor we met up with several of the riflemen who had gone down before us. They, too, were proceeding cautiously, unsure what to expect. We walked down together and quickly entered the first floor, which was a maze of offices.

"It did not take us long to reach an area which was being fought over. We saw the backs of several more riflemen who were shooting down a hallway. A grenade exploded near them, and several of them were injured. I heard the clicking of boots running down the hall. The Soviets were advancing on the stunned riflemen! Konrad and I ran forward and saw about ten enemy soldiers running down the hallway. The two of us began firing at them with our Tokarev rifles. The bullets tore through several of them before stopping, and all ten of them fell after being hit! The German riflemen stood up to finish them off with their slower firing bolt-action rifles.

"There was a German Lieutenant commanding the riflemen. He signaled them to advance down the hallway. I watched them as they cautiously advanced. A grenade was hurled around the corner at them. They ran for their lives back in the direction they had come from. The grenade exploded harmlessly. A Soviet soldier's head appeared around the corner as he attempted to shoot at the retreating men. I shot him in the forehead. I had been waiting with my crosshairs on that very spot. One of the riflemen threw an S24 grenade down the hall, and it exploded loudly.

"After the grenade went off, a squad of riflemen advanced down the hall once again. I heard them firing and Konrad and I followed them. We soon saw what they had been firing at. Two Soviet soldiers had been wounded by the grenade, then were finished off by the riflemen.

"There were no more Russians inside the building. The riflemen secured the lower level and found several of our fellow soldiers who had been guarding the first floor. Most of them were dead, but we did find a few who were wounded, and three who had been hiding in an office. The Lieutenant thanked us for our help and told us to get back upstairs. We ran up to join Remshart once again.

"Remshart was firing his rifle when we reached him. He waved at us and pointed frantically. We ran up to look. Down on the street below, there was a huge pile of Soviet bodies. Some were moving, but most were obviously dead. Other Soviet soldiers were attempting to advance toward the building, and Remshart was shooting at them. We could still hear several heavy machine-guns firing from other floors.

"The Soviets stopped attacking for several hours. There were sounds of fighting in isolated places, but no more large attacks took place until dark. We dreaded fighting the Soviets in the dark. It would be much more difficult to hold them off.

"An hour after sundown it became very dark and very cold. My men and I were shivering, despite our heavy winter clothing. We were thankful to be indoors, out of the wind. As we sat on the floor shivering, we heard the sounds of hundreds of weapons of all types start to fire in the streets below. We all stood and looked down. We could see Russian soldiers running down the street. All three of us began firing at them, as did several machine-gun crews. Tracer bullets were everywhere, shooting like tiny orange darts in the night.

"A German flamethrower sprayed burning fuel onto the enormous pile of dead Russians, and it began to burn. This lit up the entire area and made shooting much easier. It also created a horrible smell as their flesh burned.

"What followed looked like a scene from hell. Hundreds of Russian soldiers attempted to rush toward the building in a wicked hail of bullets and mortars. They ran in large waves, and they died in large waves. None of them reached the building. Several bullets hit in and around the window, which we were firing from. Luckily none of us were hit. We attributed this more to luck than to our blackened faces.

"This continued for many days. Almost every day the Russians would hurl infantrymen and tanks at us, and we would repel them over and over. I could not believe how the Russians could throw away so many lives, and yet gain next to nothing.

"On the third week we were shooting at enemy troops in the street, as we had many times before. Suddenly, Remshart was hit in the forehead by a bullet, and he fell dead. Konrad and I ducked down and began scanning with the periscope. We had a rough idea where the shot came from, because of the way Remshart had been standing and the two holes in his helmet.

"I spotted a church steeple. 'He must be in there!' I shouted. Konrad looked at it as well. The church was about five hundred meters away. A bullet would reach that distance in less than a second. There would be no time to duck. 'We have to tell the other snipers about him quickly!' We both moved out of the room carefully, while staying out of the snipers' line of sight. We told the other groups of snipers about him, and Ellis promptly shot him. We gave Remshart's Tokarev to Achil.

"The Soviet counteroffensive finally ended on February 15th, 1942. We had held our ground.

"This was followed by a break in the fighting. Both armies needed time to lick their wounds. Remshart was replaced by Frantzen, the Corporal who had been shot in the thigh months earlier. He did not look at all pleased to be back. 'I thought I would be going home. They told me that as long as I can still walk and see, they'll keep sending me back!'

"This statement gave all of the men a feeling of dread. There was no escape from this madness, except by death, capture, or horrible disfigurement. The war could also end, but there was no chance of that happening in the near future. The Russians were certainly not going to surrender.

"I was repeatedly denied the chance to travel back to my home for a leave. I was told that the Soviets could attack at any moment, and that it was very dangerous to travel behind the lines. Partisan activity was extremely heavy behind the lines. Supply caravans were repeatedly attacked.

"I did send and receive several letters to and from home. I stopped discussing the war, even when asked. I did not want my family to picture me in this nightmarish scene. I instead wrote of the future, and what we would do when I returned home.

CHAPTER 11

▼

THE SUMMER OFFENSIVE, MAY 1942

"On May 8, 1942, the German army was once again on the offensive in Russia. We paratroopers were again with Army Group Central, attacking the Crimean region of the Soviet Union.

"The Russians attempted to halt the unstoppable army, but were again unsuccessful. By June 4th Army Group Central had fought its way to the Soviet City of Svastapol. This enormous city had been turned into a super-fortress by the Soviets. There were dozens of divisions within these fortifications, which included infantry, T-34 tanks, 15cm artillery guns, 7.6cm flak air-defense cannons, and anti-tank guns. This force was so massive that it dwarfed anything our war-weary army had faced so far in the Soviet Union. It had already been under siege by Army Group South for eight months. It was hoped that Army Group Central could break the stalemate.

"We snipers spread out in small groups and made cleverly hidden foxholes from which to shoot. Over the next month we killed hundreds of Russian soldiers as they attempted to defend the city. Enemy snipers, heavy weapons operators, observers, officers, riflemen, and other types of soldiers fell victim to our long-range attacks.

"I had become accustomed to killing. It was nothing unusual for me to kill a dozen men or more during each day. I wanted the war to end. If I had to kill every Russian soldier in the entire Soviet army to end it, fine. Whatever was necessary to go home, I was willing to do.

"On the second week after our arrival at Svastapol, Ellis and I were told that a cunning enemy sniper was killing several soldiers each day near the City of Mekenziery. This was a city just to the north of Svastapol. We were ordered to take our men to this location, find the enemy sniper, and eliminate him.

"We attempted to locate the sniper by pinpointing his victims. We were dismayed to learn that his suspected kills were spread out all over a three kilometer span on the front line. The German infantrymen were afraid to stick their heads up out of their foxholes.

"The sniper was very good. He fired once, then moved to a new location. This is how our snipers were trained to operate, too, but many of them often ignored their training and fired several shots from the same position. At extreme range, when there were a lot of noises from a battle, this was not a very risky thing to do. When it was quiet, firing and moving would keep a man alive for a much longer period of time.

"All of us snipers split up into nine groups of two men. I again went with Konrad, who was by now my best friend. One of us never went anywhere without the other. We had both saved each other's lives many times, and each considered going solo quite unhealthy.

"The first day we saw no sign of the sniper. Five German soldiers were killed by the enemy sniper that day. We saw several opportunities to fire at enemy soldiers, but did not. We instead waited for a sign of our prey. We held up our helmets on spades several times, but none were shot at.

"On the second day one of Ellis' men was shot while running from one foxhole to another. We were almost positive that he had been killed by the enemy sniper. The man's partner dove into another fox-hole and waited until dark to move.

"The third day we decided to try a new tactic. Half of our men set up well-concealed foxholes about one kilometer behind our lines. It would be almost impossible for the enemy sniper to see even our muzzle flashes at this range. The other nine snipers moved up closer and set up several helmets on spades. In front of some of these they propped up their rifles with sticks. The scopes were clearly visible, and they made convincing snipers.

"When all was ready, the long-range snipers, including me and my men, began firing at every Russian soldier we could see. We shot dozens of them. We kept this up for about three hours.

"Finally someone took the bait. One of the helmets behind a sniper rifle was shot through the center. One of Ellis' men looked through the two holes in the helmet and saw the enemy snipers' general position. After looking through a periscope, he saw him. This time the enemy sniper was not moving around. He must have seen the five German helmets and sniper rifles and thought he had an entire squad of snipers in his sights. Before he could fire a third shot, Ellis shot him in the head.

"The enemy air defenses were so good that our air force was afraid to fly over them. This is what was causing the stalemate. Without bombing, it was difficult to destroy the enemy artillery. As long as they had artillery, it was impossible to defeat them on the ground.

"On July 1, 1942, this stalemate came to an end. My snipers and I were firing at targets of opportunity, as usual. Then, without warning, there was an incredible sound behind us, as if a thousand artillery guns had fired at the exact same time. Seconds later, there was a titanic explosion within the area of one of the many Russian artillery batteries. We looked at this area through our scopes and saw that the entire area was covered by a huge cloud of black smoke which was rising quickly into the sky. An immense artillery gun had been driven to the area on rails. This gun, which was nicknamed "Dora" by the troops, fired shells which were 60cm across and weighed seven tons. It was the largest artillery gun ever used in warfare. After firing fifty of the enormous shells, the enemy air-defense and artillery batteries were in ruins and the airforce was able to begin bombing them. Two days later the defenders of Svastapol surrendered. On July 5th, all resistance within the Crimea came to an end.

"We also learned that our Allies, the Japanese, had suffered a major defeat at the Battle of Midway Island. This was a naval battle which took place in the Pacific Ocean. The Americans were finally on the move.

"On July 9th the combined forces of Army Group South and Central began the drive toward Stalingrad. Yet another mighty Russian army stood in our path.

"As the two huge armies approached one another, a massive air battle took place in the skies above. Thousands of planes were dog-fighting and attempting to attack one another's ground forces at the same time. The Russian planes were inferior, but their numbers were greater than their German counterparts. Several bombs were dropped on our artillery divisions as they attempted to drive forward. Many of our artillery guns were on armored vehicles, which resembled tanks. This gave them good protection from bombs, but like tanks, they were vulnerable to close hits. Bombs were, after all, much more powerful than any tank cannons or artillery guns, with the exception of Dora.

"German 88mm air defense flak cannons were pulled behind trucks and rolled along with the army. When the air battle began, they were deployed around our artillery guns. They shot down great numbers of Russian planes and were a formidable defense against them. Many of the artillery batteries which received the worst of the bombing were too far from the 88mm guns to be defended by them.

"The size of the field of battle was enormous. The front was hundreds of miles long from north to south. As usual, infantry and tank divisions were in front, with artillery and air defense units behind them. I could not believe the number of enemy troops, tanks, and planes, which were sent against us. We had destroyed so many armies and captured so many prisoners…How many Russians were left? There seemed to be no end to them.

"For two and a half months, my men and I fought every day. We killed thousands of Russian soldiers of all sorts. We used our most cunning tactics, for the Russian snipers were plentiful—and deadly. Another one of Ellis' men was shot in the head by one of them during the second week of the battle.

"Ellis received a replacement sniper, a sixteen-year-old boy named Rolfe. All of my snipers were very interested in this boy. We had heard rumors of young boys being conscripted, but had not seen any up close. We listened as Ellis questioned him after his arrival.

"'Have you ever been in combat before?'

"'No, Sir!' the young man looked straight ahead as Ellis sat next to him, asking questions. They were both sitting in a large foxhole with the rest of us snipers. It was evening and we had all been shooting the entire day, except for Rolfe.

"'Are you a good shot, Rolfe?'

"'Best in my squad at basic, Sir!'

"'Excellent. I like to work with green snipers. They don't have any bad habits which I have to break. Do what I tell you, Private, and you'll stay alive much longer than if you do not. Understood?'

"'Yes, Sir!' I thought Rolfe looked as if he were about to cry. I felt very sorry for the boy. He should have been in school that day, not here on a battlefield. Sounds of explosions echoed through the air as this conversation went on in the foxhole.

"Ellis must have felt sorry for Rolfe as well. He took him with him every time he went out to shoot. He took Rolfe under his wing and personally trained him, just as he had done for me. I wondered how many killers the old sniper had trained. Ellis had personally killed thousands of men, and his trained assassins had killed thousands more. That's essentially what we were. We murdered men as they attempted to fight, or have a cigarette, or relieve themselves. We fired their bullets through their heads, or hearts. Both were equally deadly. The metal-jacketed bullet would hit several seconds before the sound of the rifle could be heard.

"The Russians made several great lines with their armies. The first stretched from the forest near a city called Stary Oskol to the south to a port city called Rostov. They were just north of the Sea of Azov, which was a northern extension of the Black Sea.

"The Russians used natural barriers such as rivers and forests to great effect. After our army smashed through their first line of soldiers, they formed a huge army behind the Don River near Voronezh. This was a very formidable obstacle. Hundreds of Russian tanks were just on the other side of the river, with artillery and air defense cannons behind them. It took weeks for bombs and artillery to soften them up enough to enable troops to cross the river.

"I saw thousands of dead and dying soldiers during the ten weeks of battle. Many of them were German, but the vast majority of them were Russians. We marched past hundreds of dead Russian soldiers as we moved ever closer to Stalingrad.

"By late August, German bombers were beginning to bomb Stalingrad heavily. An enormous army was in and around the city, protected by natural barriers. The Don River was to the west and the great Volga River was to the east. Hundreds of heavy tanks were waiting for us just on the other side of the river. Enemy artillery shells rained down upon our infantry and tank divisions, which dug-in on the western side of the Don River.

"It was about this time that the first German Tiger tanks began to appear on the battlefield. These were enormous tanks, which weighed more than twice as much as previous German heavy tanks. They were more than a match for even the heaviest Russian tanks, such as the T-34. Armed with the powerful 88mm cannon, they could easily blast through Russian armor.

"On September 23rd the Battle of Stalingrad began. We paratroopers were informed that we would not be taking part in the battle. We were sent back to Germany, along with several other divisions. The Fatherland needed to be protected from possible invasion from the west. The Americans and the British were massing troops in England. The armies of occupation which guarded the Atlantic Coast from invasion were no match for them without the help of some veteran divisions of tanks and infantry. It was for this reason that we were sent back home.

"My men and I, along with all of the other soldiers who were going back, were extremely happy to be going back. We were even more excited when we were told that we would be given a one-week leave to visit our homes. We would have thrown a party if we had not been so exhausted from weeks of fighting.

"By now all eighteen of us snipers were armed with Tokarev rifles. We had also accumulated several thousand rounds of ammunition. We put this cache of weapons on the truck, along with the rest of our equipment. Soon afterward, we began the long ride back to Germany.

"It was like a dream come true for me. I had begun to think that I would never again see my home or my family. Even one week with them was precious to me. I could not wait to see them. Young Kurt was five years old already! I had missed so many years of his childhood.

"It took us three weeks to reach Berlin. We bounced along on the dirt roads of Russia, Ukraine, Poland, and finally reached the paved roads of Germany. We all spoke of the many things we would do once we reached the city. Most of the men just wanted to go home and get drunk. Ellis wanted to visit his family. He seldom spoke of them, but I knew he had two teenage boys. Ellis was very concerned that if the war dragged on they might be conscripted. Misha was not married, but wanted very much to see his mother. Konrad had a girlfriend he very much wanted to visit. Every man had someone he had wanted very badly to see.

"Stalingrad had turned into a hellish battleground. The Russians sent reinforcements over the Volga River each night. Tens of thousands of soldiers had perished on both sides. It had become an enormous battle of attrition between infantry platoons and snipers. We paratroopers were kept informed by rumors of unknown origin, but which seemed to be true. Most of the news we heard came in such a manner, and it was more often true than not. By the time the battle for Stalingrad would end, more than one million soldiers would die.

"I finally reached home on November 1st, 1942. I had not expected to see so much of Hamburg in ruins. It had been bombed heavily. Several blocks of the downtown area were nothing but rubble. The street where the bakery was located was still intact, and I was thankful for that. It horrified me that the war had reached so close to my own home. I was completely unprepared for this.

"When I entered the bakery, the familiar smell of baked goods filled the air. I saw my mother and Ingred behind the counter. *They both look a little older*, I thought. They looked at me as if I was a stranger. I must have been unrecognizable with my face and uniform covered with the filth of battle. I wearily walked into the bakery and attempted a smile.

"A small boy stood by the counter looking up at me. "Kurt!" I shouted jubilantly. I opened my arms. My son ran to Ingred and hugged his mother.

"'Is it you, Georg?' asked Ingred. She approached me with open arms. I hugged her with an iron grip. Years of digging and marching had made my muscles as strong as ropes. I realized that I must smell and look awful. 'I'm sorry,' I said. 'I need to bathe.'

'It's all right, son!' my mother sobbed as she rushed forth to embrace me. 'We were so worried about you!' she put her arms around me and sobbed. She could no longer speak.

"'I'm all right!' I said, trying to assure her. Kurt just looked at me, without recognition.

"'It's your father, Kurt,' urged Ingred. 'Give him a hug.'

"'Papa!' Kurt blurted as he ran forward with his arms open wide. He too began to cry. The four of us hugged each other for several minutes, weeping.

"Finally my mother spoke. 'What happened to you during the winter, Georg? We heard how it was so cold that men were freezing. The army asked us to send coats and boots. They said that you had no winter clothing. Was it true?' Tears ran down her cheeks as she asked me this.

"'It doesn't matter. I'm here and I have all of my fingers and toes,' I said softly.

"'Is it over? Is the war over?' asked Ingred.

"I shook my head. I closed my eyes in anger as I spoke. 'I have one week.'

"'Damn them!' my mother shouted. 'Will this ever end?'

"'Calm yourself, mother! I am to be guarding the Fatherland from attack. I am not going back to Russia.'

'Thank God for that!' said my mother. 'Guarding us from what, Georg? The Russians?'

"'No. Guarding you from the British and the Americans. They have a large army gathering in Britain.'

"'They bombed us, Daddy,' came Kurt's little voice matter-of-factly. 'Boom! We hid in the cellar.'

"This made me furious. War was for soldiers, not for women and children.

"I finally had a chance to bathe and wash my uniform. It had many holes in it from the many years of wear and tear. My mother patched it for me.

"On the third day of my visit, the inquisitive young Kurt came me and asked, 'Daddy, did you kill anybody?'

"I was taken by surprise by such a question from my young son. I did not want to lie to him, nor did I want his son to think that I was a mass-murderer. I was silent for several seconds. 'I shot my gun at some people. I might have hit some of them.'

Kurt gave me a hug and said, 'I hope nobody kills you, Daddy.' He began to cry.

"It was then that Mother explained that two of my uncles and a cousin had been killed in action. Two of my other cousins were missing in action. She asked me if I had any idea what happened to men who were missing in action.

"I just shrugged. I actually did have a fairly good idea what that could mean, though. They could have been blown to bits by an artillery or mortar shell. They could have been captured. They could have been killed while their unit was withdrawing, leaving their bodies to the enemy. Their commanding officers may have simply been too busy fighting to pick up their identification discs, or they could be dead. In any case, they would most likely never be seen or heard from again. This made me very sad, as I knew all of these men. I had grown up with my cousins, playing with them on family visits. I had wrestled with them. Played hide-and-seek with them. I had slept in their houses. Now they were forever gone.

"She named off several more relatives who were on active duty. All of the fit adult males between the ages of sixteen and sixty were either on active duty, missing, or dead.

"'We have to get out of this country,' was all I could say. "'Before it destroys us.'

"Ingred had saved all of my wages, plus much of the money she had made while working at the bakery and the factory. She and my mother both worked a shift there five days a week. I asked them if they could quit, and they said they could not. 'You know an airplane factory is a prime target for bombing, don't you?' I asked. They did.

"'We have an air-raid shelter at the factory. We have to get into it about once every three weeks,' Ingred replied.

"At the end of the week, they again told me to be careful. I assured them that I was extremely cautious. "I'm a survivor," I told them. This answer only hinted at the many horrors I had seen.

"My mother presented me with yet another gift: a set of two books; one was an English-German dictionary. The other was a

Russian-German dictionary. 'I hope that these will help you,' she said. I had a feeling that they might.

"The same day I returned to the base in Berlin, I was informed that the Americans had invaded German-occupied North Africa.

"Three days later our army invaded the southern half of France. This region had previously been left under French rule, even though the Germans controlled the northern part of the country. I knew that they were turning Europe into a fortress, the likes of which the world had never seen. They were met with little resistance. The French had no real army left.

"Christmas of that year was as joyless as the previous five had been. I was still a conscript in the German army, with no end to my tour of duty in sight. I was away from my family, waiting on an army base in northern France. We snipers were extremely thankful that we were no longer on the eastern front, but knew that it was only a matter of time before we were once again called into action.

"I learned that on January 10th the Soviets counterattacked German forces near Stalingrad. It was a massive offensive and was sure to overwhelm Army Group South. Within three weeks the Germans were surrounded and forced to surrender. This was the beginning of a long series of defeats for the Germans on the eastern front. The Russians were taking back their land, kilometer by kilometer. I could only imagine the horrors my comrades on the eastern front faced during this second Soviet winter.

"Things were quiet for the entire winter for us. We were quite thankful for that. We spent many days talking about our lives and how we would change when the war was over. That was all we could speak of—what we would do when the war was over. The truth was that we did not know what the world would be like when the war was over. We were fairly certain that Germany would emerge victorious, but with war nothing is ever a certainty.

"In May of 1943 we heard more ominous news. The Africa Corps surrendered in North Africa. They had been defeated by American and British troops. *Where would they strike next*, we wondered.

"I think they would strike in their stomachs," George said, causing Grandpa to laugh.

"Why do you say that?" Grandpa asked.

"Because your stories make me hungry." With that he wandered into the kitchen. Georg and Ingred smiled at each other as they heard the refrigerator door open.

CHAPTER 12

▼

THE INVASION OF ITALY

"On July 9,[th] 1942, it was announced that the combined armies of the United Kingdom and The United States had landed on the Island of Sicily. German defenders were being overwhelmed with incredible fire-power from enemy battleships and bombs.

"My division, along with several other infantry and tank divisions, were mobilized to stop the Allied offensive. I was once again going to war. I was not at all thrilled about it. I was, in fact, extremely upset. I kept this to myself, as usual. For a few minutes I seriously considered jumping out of the back of the truck and walking home. I knew I would be shot for doing such a stupid thing, so I eventually decided that it was better to just go along with the others.

"During the past few months, the armaments of the 4th Paratrooper Division had been upgraded significantly. Our divisional anti-tank guns were increased from 37mm to 75mm. These larger guns could knock out all Allied tanks, we were told. Other new anti-tank infantry weapons also appeared, including the RP 43, which was a rocket-launching tube which could be fired from the shoulder. It fired an 88mm shaped charge, which also could supposedly knock out all Allied tanks (this weapon is often referred to as the 'Panzerschreck'). Our anti-tank grenades were replaced with a new weapon called the Panzerfaust, or 'tank fist.' These were similar to our old Panzerwurfmines, except that they had a rocket propulsion system in the handle. They could be fired about thirty meters and had a shaped charge 100mm in diameter. We were assured that these weapons could also knock out any Allied tank.

"A new rifle was distributed to some of the paratroopers, called the FG 42. It was similar to the Tokarev in that it had a ten round magazine, but it fired in fully automatic mode only. Most of the men in the 4th Parachute Division still fought with either Kar 98K rifles or MP35's. Other weapons, such as the MG 42, MG 34, and 8cm mortar, were still standard and very deadly and effective equipment.

"All of us snipers had expected to be put into combat almost within the hour of our arrival in southern Italy. Instead, we were put to work. Our forces were preparing the entire region for invasion. High command had begun a 'scorched earth' policy to slow down the invasion. For the next two months, we cut down and removed phone lines, burned motels and apartments to the ground, placed mines in and around large buildings and houses, destroyed bridges, tore out large sections of rails, and destroyed all types of automobiles and other vehicles. We also destroyed water towers, slaughtered cattle and other animals that could be used for food and pumped every liter of petrol from the fuel stations and vehicles.

"We were also put to work building a hastily constructed line of defense about twenty five miles north of the City of Naples. This was known as the 'Barbera Line,' and would be our first line of defense, if we should have to fall back. We dug several kilometers of trenches, laid thousands of all types of mines, and placed many obstacles for tanks. These included anti-tank mines, 'dragon teeth,' which were small pyramids made of concrete, and sections of rail stuck into the earth in a way that would cause them to damage a tank's treads should it drive over them.

"The paratroopers joked that they had gone from being skydivers to infantrymen to engineers. This was not normally the type of work which paratroopers would do, but the situation was desperate. The Allies were surely planning something. It had taken the Allies thirty-eight days to conquer Sicily. It was reported that they had a fleet of over three thousand ships, including six battleships, two aircraft carriers, eighteen cruisers, and more than one hundred destroyers.

"Every day air battles raged in the skies above as we worked. The Allied airforce was attempting to destroy our airforce. They fought over Italian soil, and our pilots were assisted by anti-aircraft fire from batteries of 88mm cannons on the ground below.

"Over one hundred thousand German and Italian troops had managed to escape from Sicily before the Allies overran their positions. This was accomplished at night, using hundreds of commandeered civilian boats.

"I studied my English-German dictionary at every opportunity. There was not a lot of idle time, so I had to read during meal times. I said several English words aloud, and the other snipers laughed at me. The language sounded bizarre to me. It was similar to German, and yet very different. One of the phrases I secretly memorized was 'Don't shoot! I surrender!' I seriously doubted that I would ever have to surrender, but it was certainly possible. It was a very unpalatable thought, but preferable, I hoped, to death. I wondered what had happened to the millions of Russian soldiers our army had captured. I also wondered about the hundreds of thousands of soldiers from Poland, France, Belgium, Yugoslavia, Greece, and other nations. Hitler surely would not waste millions of kilograms of food on them all. I wondered what the Americans would do to me if they captured me. Would they execute me? Torture me? Anything was possible. I had heard of some men who were captured by them in the Great War who did return home. Perhaps they were merciful.

"Working on defenses and destroying things became routine for those two months. It became our life. It was much like any other routine, but we got to do something different every day. I found some of the tasks, such as burning down hotels, to be somewhat entertaining. The placement of mines was also exciting. I would picture an Allied soldier moving about and try to guess where he would step. I had seen many mines used to great effect in Russia, and I knew a great deal about where to put them. Mines placed just around the corners of buildings were particularly effective, so I placed many of them in that manner. I also placed them on footpaths. About half of the mines were made of wood, and therefore undetectable by metal detectors. The only way to find them was by using a probe. In some areas we would also bury things such as stones or boards, so that anyone using a rifle cleaning rod or similar item to probe for mines would become frustrated by finding several harmless things just under the surface of the ground. This might cause them to become careless, or foolhardy. We had learned these tricks from the Russians, who were quite good at them. The Russians had also employed a 'scorched earth' policy, which included destroying communications, bridges, water sources, fuel, food, and anything else of value to an army. The unfortunate civilians who remained in such areas would be begging the Americans and the British for food and other necessities. The civillians probably also stepped on more than a few landmines.

"On September 8th, 1943, the routine ended. It was announced that Mussolini had been arrested more than two weeks earlier and Italy had surrendered to the Allies. My division was immediately dispatched to disarm the Italian Army. Within minutes we were in our various trucks, cars, and other vehicles, and were speeding toward a nearby Italian army base.

"My men and I watched as a German officer walked up to the front gates, and demanded that the guard open it immediately. The guard seemed unsure what to do for a moment and the officer shot him in the head with his pistol. A second Italian guard quickly opened the gate.

"Before the garrison could react, paratroopers were everywhere. They had their weapons drawn and ordered the Italians to surrender their weapons. Most were not armed, as their weapons and ammunition were in storage. This was standard for a military base. The soldiers were issued weapons only when either training or going into combat. They held their hands up and gave us a fearful look as they were disarmed. I could not believe that we would turn so fiercely upon our former ally. On the other hand, the Italians had betrayed us to the Allies. They were traitors, and deserved to be treated as such.

"We loaded several tons of weapons and ammunition into our vehicles, and ordered the Italian soldiers out of the base. They were loaded onto trucks and transported to Germany, where they would be put into labor camps. We spent the remainder of the day taking an inventory of what we had taken, and driving it back to our base near Salerno.

"In the late hours of the night we were awakened by the sounds of thunder. Blast after blast was echoing throughout the countryside. I knew it was not thunder, but artillery. 'Wake up, boys!' I shouted at my fellow snipers. Something was happening. The City of Salerno was being shelled. The shells made an enormous sound. I thought they sounded almost as loud as a one thousand-kilogram bomb. I had heard many of these when they were frequently dropped from German dive-bombers.

"The bombardment continued for hours. We soon realized that what we were hearing was a barrage of enormous shells which must have been fired from Allied naval guns. We were ordered to move into the hills surrounding the city and dig in. The force of the blasts could be felt in the air as we walked in the darkness and dug our foxholes. We were not with our entire division, but we were a mixture of several battalions from several different divisions. Many of these troops had never seen combat, and several of these men were panicking in the anticipation of combat. I witnessed several of them vomiting and praying. I then said a quick prayer myself before choosing a good spot to dig in with my men.

"Our two squads of snipers, including Ellis, Misha, Konrad, and I, had managed to stay together. We had all participated in the destruction of Italian buildings, vehicles, and bridges together. Now we would once again face danger together. Each of us knew what to do. We had now been in so many battles that we had become accustomed to it.

"Rolfe, the young teenage sniper, was extremely frightened. He had seen some combat, but would probably never get used to it. *He should be sleeping in his bed, waiting to go to school in the morning*, I thought.

"All of us snipers were soon digging. We tried to ignore the massive artillery barrage which was causing colossal sounds not more than one kilometer away.

"Three Panzer divisions were not very far away. These included the 3rd and 15th Panzer divisoins to the west of Naples and the 16th Panzer division to the southeast of Salerno. In total, they had over three hundred tanks, including several of the new Tiger and Panther D tanks.

These were heavy battle tanks, capable of holding their own even against the heaviest Soviet tanks.

"As we snipers were digging our foxhole, I noticed that the shells were systematically destroying huge areas of land. The explosions were getting closer to our position. I pointed and tapped Ellis on the helmet. Ellis nodded in recognition. 'We have to get out of here!' he shouted. Our snipers moved to other holes and told several other squads that they needed to move as well. Within seconds we were running for our lives, as the sound of explosions became deafening. The night sky and landscape were lit up, as if lightning bolts were flashing right behind us. We could hear the sound of sand, dirt, small rocks and other debris landing all around us as things erupted into the air in huge dust clouds.

"I held onto my two rifles and ran hard. My fellow soldiers and I ran for several hundred meters, before topping a large hill. It was not until then that we decided to stop and rest. The explosions did not seem to be coming this far inland.

"The naval guns continued to fire for twenty minutes, then they finally reduced the number of shells they were firing. A few could be heard exploding in the hills far to the north. Perhaps they were attempting to destroy some of our artillery or air defenses. We snipers crawled up the nearby hill and looked at the beach to the southwest of the City of Salerno. We could see hundreds of landing craft and thousands of enemy soldiers landing on the beaches. We knew immediately that this was a large invasion force which probably included more than one division. Several other friendly units were already firing at them with heavy machine-guns, mortars, and rifles. The Allied troops were returning fire with similar weaponry.

"'We'll hit a few of them, then fall back!' shouted Ellis. 'Everyone fire one magazine, then we'll go!'

"We could see the dark shapes of enemy soldiers with the white tips of waves behind them. I unscrewed the dust covers on my Zeiss scope and looked at them through it. I could see the familiar muzzle-flashes of enemy machine-guns. One by one I moved the crosshairs around, firing rounds right into them. I could hear the other snipers firing at the same time.

"Within seconds we could hear enemy bullets flying over our heads. I felt the wind of one as it passed next to my ear. The enemy had definitely seen our muzzle-flashes as well. My men and I then backed down our side of the hill and we hid ourselves from the enemies' line of sight. Several other German soldiers were firing from the hill as well, and they stayed to fight.

"A Lieutenant stopped us and said 'Where do you men think you're going?'

"Ellis saluted him and said, 'We're snipers, Sir. We're going to move back to a better position for long range shooting.'

"I could tell that the officer was unaccustomed to combat. He seemed unsure of what to do or what to say to Ellis. It was obvious that he was waiting for the old Sergeant to give him some advice.

"Ellis must have picked up on this, too, as he said 'We should all move back Sir. We are badly outnumbered. We need to let artillery and tanks hit them hard before we dare to take on a force that large. We need reinforcements as well. Our only chance is to keep them from breaking out of this position.'

"The officer nodded. 'You men move back. We'll follow.'

"As we moved back about five hundred meters, several hundred men followed us, along with the Lieutenant and several other young officers. Allied mortar fire hit a few places near the group of men, but none of them were hit.

"As we dug-into another hill, the sky began to glow with the approaching dawn. This gave us a better view of the enemy positions. We could see tens of thousands of enemy troops on the beaches and the surrounding area. My snipers frantically dug several good foxholes and covered them with leafy branches. We divided up into nine groups of two men, as we had done many times before. I was once again paired with my favorite spotter and friend, Konrad.

"I noticed that several German mortar crews had dug-in behind another nearby hill. They were out of the direct line of sight of the Allied troops and had a spotter up at the top of the hill. He was holding a periscope, and directing the fire of the crews.

"Konrad and I watched intently through binoculars as several mortar rounds fell short of the nearest Allied foxholes. The spotter made a hand gesture, holding up three fingers, and pointed toward the enemy troops. One mortar round struck the center of one foxhole, and the spotter gave a thumbs-up signal. The mortar crews began saturating this entire area with mortar after mortar. They adjusted their fire slightly after each shot so they would not waste ammunition on the same location. The effect of this was devastating to the front line Allied troops. They were struck again and again by mortar shells. Several of the Allied mortar crews attempted to strike back, but it was obvious that they had no idea where the battery of German mortars was located.

"Knowing that our fellow snipers were probably shooting at enemy snipers and heavy weapons operators, Konrad and I decided to target the enemy mortar crews and spotters. Konrad spotted and I shot them, one after another. Looking through the scope, I had a smaller field of vision, so Konrad had to say things like, 'To the left of that large piece of driftwood' or 'Fifty meters to the left of the man you just shot' to help me find the target. As soon as I saw the target, I would say 'Got him!' before I fired a shot. I very seldom missed, and usually did so only when the target suddenly moved in the one or two seconds it took for the bullet to reach him.

"Other German infantry units were dug-in closer to the Allied troops, and were coming under heavy fire. Konrad and I witnessed several of their foxholes taking direct hits from mortars and artillery shells. When this happened, the hole simply exploded. Dirt, sand, dust, bodies, body parts, and equipment were thrown high up into the air. The shallow foxholes were replaced with a smoking crater much wider and deeper than the foxhole had been.

"For four days we snipers fired into the ranks of the Allied army. The American, British, and Canadian forces attempted to break out of their position, but their four divisions of infantry were surrounded by three Panzer divisions and two German infantry divisions. Our own 4th Parachute Division was quite fearsome, with many veteran soldiers in its ranks. Several of them, like me, had participated in several of the campaigns of the war, including Russia and others. Despite our fierce defense tactics, the Allies managed to capture Salerno and the land to the north of the city.

"On September 13th, the fifth day of fighting, some of my snipers had run dangerously low on ammunition. Several of them had switched from using their captured Tokarev rifles to standard Kar 98K rifles. We were still only issued seven cartridges per day, but they were definitely not going to get any more Soviet cartridges any time soon. Many of us, including me, had been hoarding our rationed cartridges for several months. We had hundreds of them. Two of the Tokarev rifles had damaged internal parts and were being used for spare parts for the other guns.

"On this same day, the Allied troops' position was becoming precarious. Our artillery shells were landing all over the beach, and it was quite obvious that their infantry had an extremely difficult time dealing with the Tiger and Panzer tanks. Their bazookas and other anti-tank weapons simply bounced off the thick steel armor of these fifty ton-plus vehicles. Our forces were gaining ground each day, and the Allies' small pocket was becoming smaller.

"The following morning, we were given an order for an all-out attack. We were ordered to push the Americans back into the sea. This attack began with a massive artillery barrage, which destroyed much of the Allied artillery and most of their air defense units.

"Suddenly, in the middle of this attack, scores of Allied heavy bombers flew high overhead and the world seemed to turn upside-down. Five hundred pound bombs were raining down all over our positions. The other snipers and I watched in horror as blast after blast hit right in the center of one of the Panzer divisions. The enormous shockwaves were visible in the smoke, and they overlapped one another again and again. I wondered if anyone at all could possibly survive such punishment, even inside a heavy tank.

"This utterly halted the German offensive. The tide of battle turned in favor of the Allies, and they began gradually expanding their area of captured land around Naples. Tens of thousands of land mines had been planted around the Allied troops to slow their advance, and our forces began a series of tactical withdrawals.

"For the next week, we snipers would take a few choice shots and then move back to another position. The Allied force was growing as more and more men were brought to shore. They had over ten divisions now and were pushing our badly outnumbered forces back every day.

"A few miles to the north was a hastily constructed defensive line called the Volturo Line. We all had had implicit instructions that the Allies were not to be allowed to cross this barrier before October 15th. They were to pay the price for each meter of ground which they gained in blood. We continued our scorched earth policy, which included burning hotels, destroying vehicles, and other acts of subterfuge in any area about to be taken by the Allies. This included the populous City of Naples, which was a few miles to the west of the Allied lines around Salerno.

"Placing mines was often dangerous, and many of our troops were poorly trained new recruits. I heard of more than a few who were killed or maimed while placing mines. Others simply got careless and walked on one of the mines which was intended for our enemies.

"We snipers were involved in a particularly fierce battle on September 23rd, while helping a battalion of paratroopers defend Sorrento Hill, not far from the City of Naples.

"Hours after withdrawing from another position and preparing new camouflaged foxholes, we could see an enormous enemy force advancing toward the hill. There were thousands of enemy soldiers.

"My heart began to pump hard. We were dug-in, and it was the early part of the day. We could not withdraw without orders, and getting out of our foxhole in the middle of a battle could be disastrous. 'Get ready, Konrad. I think the devil is coming for us today,' I said with a shaky voice as I looked through my scope at the advancing army. I could see that the troops were British.

"Konrad gasped as he looked through his own scope. 'Look at them! We've got to get out of here!'

"'We can't!' I snapped. 'We have orders to hold this position at all costs.'

"The enemy was just over one kilometer away when all hell broke loose. All manner of weapons were fired at the British, including small arms, machine-guns, mortars, anti-tank and artillery shells. I watched as a shell exploded right in the center of a group of British soldiers as they attempted to advance behind some trees. Bodies and body parts flew into the air. I could hear the explosion, but although the men looked like they were close in my scope, I could not hear their screams. I could see their mouths opening wide, and I knew that those who still lived were screaming in pain.

"Several groups of British soldiers began returning fire. Without even thinking about it, I noticed an enemy sniper and put my crosshairs on him. I squeezed the trigger and felt the familiar kick in the shoulder from my Kar 98K. I watched for a second or two as the bullet flew through the air and saw the perfectly round black hole appear in the man's helmet. His head snapped back, and his eyes opened wide. His body then began convulsing. I ignored the pandemonium around him and watched this one man for several seconds in grim fascination. How many times had I done this? How many lives had I destroyed? It was not just the man I was destroying, but all who knew him. He might have a wife and children. He must have family of some sort.

"At that second, an artillery shell exploded on the hill about fifty meters to the south of Konrad's and my foxhole. At first we ignored it. Then we heard shouting and screaming. I looked and saw that a foxhole had been directly hit.

"'That's Ellis' foxhole!' screamed Konrad.

"'No!' I screamed. I dropped my rifle and picked up the binoculars. I looked. I frantically moved the binocculars around until I could see the hole. I saw grey smoke floating out of the hole, then I saw a severed arm on the grass a few meters from the hole. I knew it was Ellis'. 'Damn you!' I dropped the binoculars and picked up the rifle once again. I pointed it toward the enemy troops and quickly targeted and killed five enemy soldiers. I used no methods of prioritization. I just found a man, shot him, and searched for another. I quickly reloaded my rifle and repeated this spree.

"'Georg, what are you doing?' asked Konrad. 'You can't kill them all.'

"I hesitated. Konrad was right. 'Find me a target then. Artillery spotter.'

"'All right, Georg.' Konrad looked around with the binoculars. 'Damn it, why did it have to be Ellis? That shell could have landed anywhere!'

"'He forgot rule number one.'

"'What?'

"'That's what Ellis used to say. Rule number one: don't get killed.'

"'What was rule number two?'

"'Refer to rule number one.' I sat down and continued. 'Ellis has been in enough battles. His time just came, that's all. We'll all get our chance, I'm sure. This damn war isn't going to be over any time soon.'

"'I hope you're wrong about that.' Konrad interrupted himself. 'I think I see one!" He pointed.

"I opened both eyes. I moved the crosshairs to a hilltop. I saw a British soldier looking through binoculars. He did not have a weapon pointed in our direction. He definitely fit the description of an artillery spotter. I put the crosshairs on the man's face and fired. In the seconds while the bullet traveled through the air, I saw the man speak into a radio handset. He was a spotter. Probably the very one who had called down the shell on Ellis' hole. I watched with grim enjoyment as the brass-jacketed bullet passed through the man's head.

"The battle raged on for hours. The British shelled our hill, and they were shelled in return. They attempted to storm the hill with several large waves of soldiers, only to be repelled by withering fire from hidden machine-gun and mortar nests. The 4th Paratrooper Division, another infantry division, and several Tiger tanks were all firing at them. These tanks proved to be an insurmountable obstacle to the Allied soldiers. Their rocket-propelled anti-tank weapons bounced off of them, while the Tigers returned fire with 88-mm cannons and 8mm machine-guns. Later in the day one of the Tiger tanks was hit by a bomb that was dropped by a dive-bomber, which was in turn was shot down by a hidden 88mm flak cannon.

"By nightfall, countless soldiers on both sides were dead or wounded. We had held the hill. When it was dark enough, Konrad and I crawled over to Ellis' foxhole. We found some remains, but there was not much left of Ellis or his spotter. We could not find their identification discs.

"We laid mines all over the hill throughout the night. Just before dawn, they withdrew. Konrad and I buried what remains we could find of our friend Ellis. We placed his rifle on the grave, barrel down, with his paratrooper helmet on top of the butt. 'Goodbye Ellis,' I said to my friend's grave. 'I've got to get going now. Maybe I'll come back some day and visit you here.' I wept, and attempted to console myself, knowing that my friend had died instantly. He had lived the life of a soldier, and died the death of a soldier.

"I learned that Konig, one of Ellis' men, had been with him in the foxhole. We also learned that the Italian dictator Mussolini had been rescued by German paratroopers, and had retaken control of the Italian government. Perhaps Hitler had turned things around for us! It was impossible to be encouraged by this news after the death of Ellis.

"I was given command of the sniper squad. I accepted this duty from my commanding officer with a nod. I told the CO how Ellis and I had been together since the invasion of Poland, and the officer seemed to be impressed by that. 'You're a survivor, Georg. I need men like you. Don't fail me.'

"'Surviving is what we do in the infantry, Sir! It's all we can do.' I saluted. The officer returned the salute, and dismissed me.

"The fighting continued for weeks, then months. Our forces were pushed back again and again. Our primary mission was to delay the Allied advance, and delay it we did. On most days my men and I would set up ambushes. We would team up with other specialists, including engineers, heavy weapons crews, and riflemen. They learned that I had acquired a great deal of knowledge in my years as a sniper. Officers listened to me. I would have them set up several mines, including many types. My favorite was the 'shoe mine.' These jumped up a few feet into the air and sprayed bullet-like projectiles in every direction.

"We would find a good ambush sight with natural terrain. We would mine all the approaches, with one clearly visible approach only lightly mined with shoe mines. These were attached to detonator cords. The co-ordinates of the ambush area were pre-targeted by mortar crews. All they had to do was drop shells into the mortar tubes when the signal was given.

"An enemy force would move into the target area and the shoe mines would be activated. They would jump up, spray their deadly ball bearings all over, and cut several men down. Then the mortars would begin to land and the MG-42 crews would begin spraying the entire area with bullets. If any enemy soldiers were foolish enough to charge us, they ran into more mines. These were the small wooden ones that were designed to blow a man's foot off.

"On a good day we would ambush and kill fifty men. On one day we ambushed an entire company. We killed over one hundred of them before the stubborn British soldiers finally decided to retreat. Our platoon would move on before artillery or bombs could be dropped on our position. We dug some of the mines up and took them along. Others we left as gifts for the invaders.

"My character had changed. I was no longer just a tired soldier who killed for survival. Now it was personal. They had killed one of my best friends. A man with whom I had hoped to have a lifetime of friendship. Now only a few pieces of that man were in a shallow grave marked by a sniper rifle and a helmet.

"Ellis was not the only reason for my rage. I had heard reports that the Allies were bombing Hamburg. I worried every day about the safety of my family. I was not even sure if they were alive.

"I had been part of an invading army for so long that I knew just what they would try to do when they came into my traps. I designed each ambush better than the one the day before. I watched with grim fascination and satisfaction when the traps worked. It was like hunting an extremely dangerous animal. You just had to stay one step ahead of it.

"We also looted the enemy troops. The Americans were our targets of choice for looting. They were armed with M1 rifles, which were far superior to our Kar 98K rifles. These weapons were semi-automatic with an eight round detachable magazine. Each soldier carried fifteen such magazines, giving each of them one hundred and twenty rounds. This was unheard of to we Germans who, even when fully equipped, were sent into battle with only sixty rounds and a bolt-action rifle with a five round internal magazine. It was like finding treasure. The Americans were the most well supplied troops we had yet encountered.

"Most of the other American weapons were very similar to their German counterparts. Their anti-tank weapons were inferior, however. Their 'bazookas' only had a caliber of 60mm, compared to the German RPzB 54, which was like a bazooka, but had an 88mm shaped charge. The German Panzerfaust, or 'tank fist' weapons had a shorter range, with even larger 100mm shaped charges.

"There was one other American weapon, which we Germans liked to capture very much. This was the Browning .50 caliber heavy machine-gun. This gun fired bullets half an inch wide the way the MG-42 fired bullets which were roughly two-thirds their size. It was incredibly powerful, and could be used effectively against personel and even armored vehicles. My platoon captured two of these weapons and several hundred rounds of ammunition.

"We continued to ambush and harass the invading Allied army for weeks. Every day we would either wait in ambush, lay mines, or guard an important bridge. We continually improved our tactics. After ambushing and destroying a company of British tanks and infantry, we placed over a ton of enemy ordinance into a crater in the road. We then put an anti-tank mine on top of it and concealed everything under a large pile of dirt.

"On November 20th it began to snow. We were enthusiastic about this, because we had learned the hard way in Russia that winter weather greatly improved defense. It was on that very day that my platoon and I were in charge of guarding a bridge over the Volturo River at the same time it was attacked by a substantial Allied force. We were not guarding it alone. In addition to my platoon there were two companies of Panzer grenadiers, armed with the heaviest anti-tank weaponry.

"I was giving myself a badly needed shave. I was looking into a small mirror which someone had probably stolen out of one of the many apartment buildings we had burned down as part of Hitler's "scorched earth" policy. It had a brass frame, which was held up by a brass figurine of a naked woman. I had not shaved in many days, and my whiskers stung as I shaved them off with a straight razor that I had found. It sounded like sandpaper scraping over leather.

"It was at that moment that one of the scouts who had been hiding on the hill above came running down into the area of the bridge, and began yelling, 'Get ready! They're coming!'

"'Who?' someone yelled, and all the men began urgently rushing to their assigned positions.

"'The British! And they have tanks!'

"A few seconds later I heard the tanks. The distinctive sound of their squeaky wheels and their loud engines always let it be known that they were on their way. I had heard that sound many times before. I was sitting in a covered foxhole, about two hundred meters away from the bridge. Konrad and Misha were with me, but Misha quickly excused himself and rushed to his assigned foxhole. My snipers had dug their usual eight foxholes with two men in each one.

"We were confident that the Allied soldiers would not bomb or shell this position. The bridge was too valuable to their invasion. We also knew that the Allies would have to confine themselves to the road leading to the bridge. The tanks could not climb the steep hills nearby, and they were heavily mined with anti-personnel mines.

"Our men, however, enjoyed many well-chosen dug-in positions. There were heavy weapons crews with machine-guns, mortars, and anti-tank guns. There were also many Panzer grenadier squads with heavy anti-tank weapons. All of these men were in foxholes which were surrounded by sandbags, and were well concealed with nets and other camouflage.

"When the tank column came around the corner, I was watching them through my scope. I could see several infantrymen running behind the second tank. A vanguard tank was out in front, with no infantry protecting it. I watched them advance, listening to the terrible sound of the tank wheels as they screeched forward. I, like the other German soldiers, knew that we were not supposed to fire until the enemy reached a certain point. This was a fallen log which acted as a roadblock to automobiles. I knew that the thirty or forty-ton British tank would smash it into splinters. I watched the log intently as the vanguard tank got closer to it. Finally, the treads began to crawl over the log and crush two one-foot wide track marks into it.

"At that moment, four well-concealed S34 shoe mines shot up into the air. These were between thirty and fifty feet behind the log, right in the center of the protective infantry squads behind the second, third, and fourth British tanks. The mines shot about four feet into the air, and exploded. I saw the white flash of the explosions a second before I heard the bang. I then heard many of the British soldiers begin to scream in agony. Deadly bullet-like shrapnel had been fired in every direction by the mines.

"The vanguard tank began to back up. The crew must have thought this would be better than pushing forward into the ambush. They were firing both their cannon and their machine-gun as they did so, but doing so blindly. The shells hit the side of the hill far below my position.

"Mortar shells began raining down on the tank column. The shots were perfect, as they had been pre-sighted weeks before.

"Panzer grenadier crews hidden on the hill above the British force fired their anti-tank weapons down onto the tops of the tanks in the front of the column. All of the five tanks that were visible to me were blown up one by one. It was a massacre. Tanks in the rear of the column were destroyed first, creating a roadblock.

"The shelling continued for several minutes. A half-hour later, a runner climbed up the steep hill and crawled into my foxhole. He told us that British engineers were attempting to move up the far side of the hills on the opposite side of the river. The colonel in charge of defending the bridge had ordered me and my men to move to the opposite side of the river so we could harass the engineers as they attempted to probe for mines. With a loud whistle, I signaled my men to move out, and we quickly ran across the bridge and split up into two eight-man groups. One was headed by Misha, another by me. We were down to sixteen men, as Ellis and Konig had not yet been replaced.

"There was a hill on each side of the road which approached the bridge. I took my group up the east hill while Misha's group began climbing the west hill. We moved as quickly as we could, knowing that each minute we wasted would only give the British more time to locate mines.

"We snipers looked like piles of green rags as we climbed up. We each had a camouflage net with leaves and twigs stuck into us, covering our upper body. This made it almost impossible to see when we were not moving and hiding in natural terrain. Ellis was dead, but his tricks lived on.

"The hills were covered with snow, which revealed every place that each man took a step. We were marching on virgin snow, which had been free of footprints. It crunched beneath our booted feet as we quickly marched along. I could see my breath, but I did not feel cold. The air actually felt warm in comparison to the harsh Soviet winter I had endured.

"I and my men finally reached the top of the large hill and cautiously peeked over the top. We used a large group of trees for concealment from the eyes of the enemy. There were a few Panzer grenadiers up there, and they pointed down the southern side of the hill, making a sign to be quiet. I followed their direction and looked with my scope. I could see several British soldiers probing for mines with metal probes. They were poking them into the ground, and marking the mines with flags.

"I motioned for my men to spread out. They all knew just what I meant. I put my crosshairs on the closest British soldier's head and waited for my men to get into position. I was only about two hundred feet from my target. This range was extremely close for me; I was used to long range shots.

"I heard a few grunts and quiet whistles from my men, indicating that they were ready. With a mild sigh, I squeezed the trigger. The soldier in my crosshairs was hit in between the eyes. At the same instant the other snipers began firing beside me. I knew that they were hitting targets as well. They could not miss a still target at this range. I worked the bolt action with amazing speed and precision, and chambered another round. I then targeted another British soldier. This man was getting his own rifle up to fire back when my bullet hit him just below the chin.

"At that moment a bullet struck me. I suddenly felt my hand and rifle jump. I fell backward and saw that two of my fingers had been shot off in the middle. I looked at the rest of myself and saw that there was no more damage. The bullet had passed through my pinky and ring finger on my left hand. It also damaged the wood on my rifle just under the barrel. 'I'm hit,' I said rather loudly. I was attempting to bandage myself when Lance Corporal Frantzen came to my aid. 'Don't worry, Sergeant. We can take good care of you.' He bandaged the wound and applied pressure to it. The other snipers continued to fire as he was doing this. After being bandaged, I considered going back down the hill. I was in intense pain. I could feel what was left of my fingers throbbing with each beat of my heart. I was thankful that my wedding ring was still intact. For a moment I felt light-headed, as if I was about to pass out. I managed to prevent myself from doing so.

"Mortars began raining down upon the British soldiers who were climbing the south side of the hill. Large artillery shells also exploded on the column below. There was a battery of 105mm artillery guns concealed on a nearby mountain. They too had the road leading to the bridge already sighted in their guns, and only had to load and fire their

weapons. The British column was a sitting target. The valley below
became filled with the sounds of explosions and screams. Gray smoke
covered the area like a dense fog.

"I managed to join my men once again, despite the pain from my
severed fingers. I shot three more of the engineers before I could no
longer see any of them. It appeared that all of the engineers had either
been killed, had fled, or were hiding.

"After a few minutes, two squads of riflemen joined us on the hilltop. The artillery and mortar shells continued to rain down. I thought
I should check on Misha and the other men who had climbed the hill
to the west. I looked with binoculars and saw them involved in a similar shootout with British engineers. I alerted the other snipers, and
they began helping them with long range fire.

"I targeted one of the engineers with my scope. I put my crosshairs
on the soldier's back. They shook a bit. The pain from my hand was
getting worse. The shock was wearing off, and just an intense ache set
in. Then I realized that I would never have those two fingers again.
The thought made me sick to my stomach. What would Ingred say? I
then saw the engineer aim his rifle up the hill. This awoke me from my
thoughts, and I fired my rifle. The bullet struck an inch lower than
where I had aimed, but it was still an unquestionably fatal wound. The
British soldier jumped and rolled down the steep hill. I heard the other
snipers firing around me, and I knew that any engineers who were visible had probably just been killed.

"What was left of the British forces retreated from the area. We
observed them with binoculars as they dragged hundreds of wounded
men out of the cloud of smoke. Several tanks and light vehicles were
still functional, although most of them had black powder marks all
over them. I watched them through my scope. I saw an older British
soldier giving orders. He had to be an officer. I squeezed the trigger
and sent a long range shot right through the officer's heart. Several of
the British soldiers nearby scrambled for cover. A few looked in my
direction with their rifles in their hands, looking for me. One of them
was looking through a scope. I shot him as well. After this, the other
men nearby got out of sight. One of them stepped onto a mine, which
blew him into the air. He landed with one of his legs blown off just
below the knee. Another British soldier ran to his aid as he unbuckled

his belt. I shot him in the chest before he could reach the wounded man. None of the other soldiers would go near the one I was using as bait, and he slowly bled to death. My men and I kept the men pinned down until nightfall. I was certain that several of their wounded soldiers had died because of a lack of medical attention. I knew this was extremely cruel, but this is the sort of thing snipers did: they killed people.

"After nightfall, we finally climbed down the hill. We walked into the area around the bridge, and I finally was given medical attention for my fingers. The colonel commended us for keeping the enemy off the hilltops. Misha and the other snipers joined us. They were very surprised that I had been shot. They knew that I was an extremely cautious soldier.

"Two days later the British returned with an enormous force. We saw them coming and decided to blow the bridge and pull back rather than fight. When the British reached the river, we snipers harassed them with long range fire for several hours. German mortar and artillery shells also landed on their position, until the British moved their own artillery into position and began to fire back.

"Every day we lost ground to the Allied army. Our army had three defensive lines, which had been prepared to slow the advance of the Allies. The Barbera Line, which was the first of these lines of fortifications, had already been overtaken. The Reinhard Line, which was the second line of defense, was under attack in several locations. The southern half of it had already been overtaken.

"I heard that many of my fellow paratroopers had been taken prisoner near Cassino. My men and I had by now unofficially become a part of the 14th Panzer Grenadier Division. Much of this division was made up of what remained of several divisions which had been partially destroyed or scattered.

"I also heard that Hamburg had been nearly leveled by some of the most intense strategic bombing of the entire war. Thousands of tons of bombs had been dropped onto the city, and I had no idea if my loved ones were alive or dead. I was furious when I was told that this had happened in late July.

"We were also informed that Italy, our former ally, had declared war upon us. Any Italian soldiers encountered were to be treated as enemy soldiers, which meant kill them on sight.

"On January 14th, exhausted, we accompanied the rest of the Panzer Grenadier Division to the Gustav Line, which was the final and by far the most heavily fortified line of defense in Italy. It had concrete bunkers, with built-in artillery guns, air defenses, anti-tank guns, and heavy machine-guns. I was amazed when I saw that old tank turrets had been built onto the wall in such a way that their cannons could still be fired, and the turret protected the gun crew from enemy fire. I had never seen such a thing.

"The Gustav Line also used natural defenses and had been built next to rivers and dangerous cliffs. It was truly a formidable obstacle which the Allies would not easily cross. It was here that the 14th Panzer grenadiers would make our stand against the Allied invasion. We were ordered to assist the garrison at the Garigliano-Liri-Rapido River area, which was part of the Gustav Line. When we arrived it was January 16th and the garrison had just opened the floodgates on the dam. They were in the process of turning the farmland on the opposite side of the river into an immense barrier of mud, which would bog down Allied tanks and trucks. I laughed when I saw this. I remembered the days of living in the mud in Russia, and trying to push trucks and tanks in it. It was almost impossible.

"We snipers were assigned to guard a section of the wall, which had several concrete bunkers. Some of the other paratroops set up some MG42's and 8cm mortar nests on the wall. We were well protected by eighteen inches of concrete, which was sharply angled to deflect projectiles. We also had concrete over our heads within the bunkers, which would give us good protection from artillery, bombs, and mortars. The ground in front of the wall had been cleared of trees, brush, or any other sort of cover. It had also been heavily mined. We were only a few hundred feet from the river, and we spent the remainder of the day cleaning our weapons and studying the terrain, which was visible from our position on the wall. The other snipers and I hoped that our duty would be boring and uneventful. We all felt we had already had enough excitement for one lifetime.

"As we attempted to sleep on the hard floor of the bunker that night, we once again listened to every sound. The bunker and the close proximity of the minefield gave us some measure of safety from attack, but we were still cautious. We all knew that only a fool let his guard down when in a war zone. One second of complacency could mean instant death.

"The thump of distant artillery guns awakened us. The sound came from the south, which meant it most likely was unfriendly. We soon heard the whistle of incoming artillery shells, which exploded nearby. We each moved our backs against the concrete wall of the bunker, held our helmets over our heads, and covered our ears. It was all we could do. The shells continued to rain down for several minutes. Even as the shells continued to fall, I managed to get up and look out the murder hole, which was a small firing hole on the side of the bunker, that over-looked the river. I looked through my binoculars, hoping that no shells would land close enough to spray shrapnel into the hole. I jumped once, as a shell exploded some one hundred feet away. It lit up the horizon with a flash, followed by a tremendous thunderclap-like explosion. As I jumped, I realized that during the bright flash I had seen something. I looked again with the binoculars, and clearly saw men on the other side of the river. They looked as if they were attempt-ing to construct a pontoon bridge.

"'Look alive boys!' I shouted. 'We've got company!' I gave Konrad the binoculars, and grabbed my rifle.

"Konrad looked out another murder hole. 'Bridge engineers!'

"We had been given a radio to report any sign of the enemy. I told Konrad to get on it, which he quickly did. 'This is sector two-one-one-seven, over.'

"A moment later came a reply. 'This is Tiger den. Report two-one-one-seven, over.'

"We are under bombardment. Enemy bridge engineers attempting to construct pontoon bridge directly across from our position, over.'

"'Acknowldedged two-one-one-seven, one moment please.' There was silence for about a minute, then the voice continued. 'Observe enemy engineers for artillery placement, over.'

"'Acknowledged, over!' Konrad looked at me. 'Georg, watch for a shell near them!'

"I watched, and I saw a shell explode about fifty meters to the east of the enemy engineers. They all dove for cover. 'Correction, fifty meters to the west,' I said.

"Konrad relayed this information into the handset. A few seconds later another shell landed, this time about ten meters to the west of the engineers.

"'Another correction, ten meters east,' I said, as I watched through my scope.

"Then a shell landed right in the center of them. 'Direct hit!' I said. Konrad repeated this into the handset. Then shells began raining all over the engineers' position. The shells made large holes in the mud and I could see bodies and severed limbs being thrown into the air. I knew that none of them could survive that. 'Tell them to save their ammunition. Nothing left but pieces out there,' I said unsympathetically.

"Several heavy machine-guns opened fire from far across the river. Tracer bullets lit up the air as they sped toward us in our bunker. It looked like a show of fireworks. The bullets arced through the air, as if they were shooting water with sparks in it rather than bullets. The sound of bullets striking concrete could soon be heard as hundreds of rounds hit all around the bunker. All of us moved away from our murder holes to avoid being hit by any well-placed shots. It was not long after we moved when one round flew into the room. We could hear it bouncing off the walls. It also bounced off Lederer's helmet with a metal-sounding clang. 'Shit!' he exclaimed with surprise. 'That one was a little too close!'

"'Let's move into the corridor!' I shouted. There was a corridor leading to another bunker, which was now empty. We all quickly moved into it and attempted to make ourselves small targets by sitting in a crouch with our faces covered. 'We'll stay here for a few minutes. They can't keep up that much firepower for long!'

"Lederer had been with me since the invasion of the Soviet Union. He was normally a man of few words, but at that moment he looked at me with a very sincere face and said 'Thank you for being cautious with us, Sergeant Frick. You know how to keep us alive.' The other men quickly agreed with him, and they all thanked me. Konrad and Misha nodded in agreement.

"'You don't have to thank me, men. Without you, I too would have died long ago. We keep each other alive.'

"At that moment we heard a knock on the steel door at the rear of the bunker. All of the men looked at me as I crept over to stand beside the door. 'Who goes there?'

"'We've come to reinforce you! Let us in, for God's sake!' Sounds of explosions and the thick steel door muffled the reply, but it was clearly German. I opened the peek hole slit and looked out. I then opened the door and let them in.

"Twenty Panzer grenadiers entered the room. They had two MG 42 crews of two men each, and sixteen riflemen. One of them was a master Sergeant, who outranked me. 'Why are you men hiding in the corridor?' he barked. 'I thought you Fallschirmjager were supposed to be tough!'

"'They were raking us with heavy machine-guns so heavily that rounds were entering through the murder holes,' I answered.

"'Well, too bad! It's time to bring the fight to the enemy!'

"I had no choice but to obey the order. I looked at my men and said'"Everyone move to a hole and start shooting those machine-gun muzzle flashes as fast as you possibly can. Understood?' They all nodded, and gave the other sergeant a dirty look. As we spoke, the Panzer grenadiers set up their two heavy machine-guns, and some of the riflemen began looking out through murder holes. Heavy enemy fire could still be heard all around the bunker.

"Doing as they were ordered, my snipers moved into position. Each of them moved to a murder hole, which was a small hole in the wall through which they could shoot. Seconds after looking out, they began shooting back at the enemy machine-gun flashes. I did the same, and within seconds I had fired into the center of three muzzle flashes. The machine-gun fire hitting the bunker began to falter.

"The Panzer grenadiers also began firing. The tracer bullets from their MG 42 could clearly be seen arcing back at the enemy, and sixteen of those armed with rifles fired what were probably wildly inaccurate shots in the direction of the enemy force. The sound of these machine-guns was extremely loud inside the concrete bunker, bouncing off of the walls, floor, and ceiling. It sounded like a cross between a sewing machine and a string of firecrackers. The sound of brass bullet casings hitting the floor could also be heard as they fired dozens of rounds from each machine-gun.

"Minutes later we could see hundreds of enemy soldiers running while carrying large objects. As they got closer, we could see that these objects were small boats. The boat carrying soldiers came under fire from the heavy machine-guns within the bunker, as well as several others from other adjacent bunkers which also must have contained Panzer grenadiers. Many of the teams of enemy soldiers carrying boats had some of their men fall down, but they ran on. The mud slowed their advance, and I knew they probably were thinking that they were running into hell. Mortars were landing all around them, and blowing some of the men into the air. These explosions created brilliant flashes which lit up the entire area.

"Then a flare was fired high into the air, revealing every detail of the battlefield. Some of the enemy soldiers reached the river and quickly got into their boats in a desperate attempt to cross the river. Mortars continued to hit all around them, even in the water. Bullets could be seen splashing in the water all over their position. I watched as one boat exploded, after being hit by a mortar. I knew that whatever the fools were attempting to do, it would end in dismal failure.

"After about ten minutes of taking intense fire while crossing the river, only about one hundred of the enemy soldiers managed to get across. This was perhaps one tenth of the men who had started out carrying boats. Some of these men came too far inland and stepped on landmines. Their screams were heard by all of us in the bunker. The other enemy soldiers began digging foxholes in the mud as fast as they possibly could. We paratroopers and Panzer grenadiers did not give them respite, despite their hopeless position. We shot about half of them as they dug their holes.

"'I wonder if they know they're digging their own graves,' I said softly. I watched as mortars began pounding the area where the enemy soldiers had just dug-in. They left huge craters in the mud. I felt a bit sorry for them as I heard their screams, but I realized that they would have done the exact same thing to me and my men if the situation were reversed.

"This fighting continued through the night. The entire enemy force which had made it across the river was destroyed. Artillery fire was exchanged until the following morning between the German guns, which were far behind the Gustav Line, and the Allied guns, which must have been dug-in to the south somewhere.

"In the morning things quieted down. The enemy force on the riverbank could not be looted or examined because they were completely surrounded by mines. It was so utterly quiet, however, that it was presumed that all of them had been killed.

"The next day I got a letter from Ingred. 'Dear Georg, I don't know any other way to tell you this, but your mother has been killed. I am terribly sorry. She was working at the factory when it was bombed.

There is more bad news. The bakery was destroyed as well. I managed to save some of our things, and we are now living with Uncle Fredrick at his farm. I have been helping with chores on the farm, although there are not so many now that it is winter.

I hope that you are still alive, Georg. I know that you are a survivor. Be careful, and please come home to us soon. All my love, Ingred.' I could see that the letter had been dated several months earlier, which meant that her funeral was long since over.

"If I was younger, I probably would have broken down and wept over the death of my mother. Now that I had seen four years of brutality and warfare, not much phased me. I showed no sign of emotion.

"As I attempted to sleep that night, however, thoughts of my mother filled my head. I remembered how she taught me things, and played with me when I was a boy. I also remembered how concerned she was that I would be killed in the war. I thought it was ironic that she was killed by an enemy attack, after I had escaped so many. Then the tears did flow. I finally realized that she was gone forever. She could never be replaced. All that was left of her was that which I could remember. I strained to remember everything—every moment I'd spent with her, every line of her face, and every word of wisdom which she had bestowed upon me.

"After an hour of weeping silently among the sleeping soldiers, a rage came over me. It was unlike anything I had ever experienced. I wanted to destroy something. The rage swelled within my bowels, and I clenched my teeth as tightly as I possibly could. I wondered exactly who was at fault in this matter. Should I be angry with the Allies, or with Hitler?

"We got a four-day break from the fighting while waiting for an attack. On January 21st that attack came. It began in the pre-dawn hours of the morning as Allied artillery shells began to whistle down from the sky before they exploded with thunderous booms. An entire division of American infantrymen attempted to cross the river in the same spot where the previous attackers had tried to cross. This was not a good thing for the Allied soldiers, because there were four times as many artillery, mortar, machine-guns, and other heavy weapons trained on that area as there had been four nights before. We assisted with long range fire, and each of us hit several targets. A few of the Allied soldiers did cross the river, only to find the decaying bodies of their comrades who had crossed four days earlier. The entire division was either killed or captured before noon.

"The next day, January 22nd, 1944, the Allies landed an army behind the formidable Gustav Line on Anzio Beach. This was done with the same massive fleet of ships that had shelled me and my fellow snipers a few months earlier.

Grandpa's eyes were moist from the memories of his mother. Grandma looked very sad. George wondered if he should let him stop telling his story, but he again thought of his father telling him to find out as much as he could of Grandfather's tales. Yes, tomorrow night they would go back to the war.

CHAPTER 13

▼

ANZIO

"My men and I were awakened early on January 22nd. We were informed that a massive Allied invasion force had landed on the beaches at Anzio, which was about fifty miles to the west of our current position.

"We expected that we would be put into action immediately, as things were quiet on the Gustav Line. Instead, we were put on high alert. We also heard a rumor that the Soviets had pushed all the way into Poland. This did nothing to raise our spirits. It seemed that we were caught between two angry giants.

"Later in the afternoon we paratroopers were informed that we were to rejoin the 4th Parachute Division. It had been reorganized and reinforced with fresh troops. We gathered our gear and got into the back of a truck, which carried us to the City of Cassino. This is where the 4th Parachute Division was stationed.

"The city was under siege at the time of our arrival. We could hear artillery shells exploding all around us. We watched a shell blow the top of a church into thousands of pieces. Dust, bricks, and small particles were hurled everywhere around the structure.

"On the north side of the city were hundreds of large foxholes. It was here that the 4th Parachute Division was riding out the attack. We all got out of the truck and quickly found a command bunker. I entered it while my men waited outside in a foxhole.

"Inside the bunker stood a colonel and several lower ranking officers. They seemed to be talking about something other than the war, and several of them were laughing. I snapped to attention and saluted. 'Sergeant Frick reporting as ordered, Sir!'

"'At ease, Sergeant,' began the colonel. 'Are you the snipers from the Gustav Line?'

"'Yes, Sir!'

"'Very good. We will be moving out in a few days. Welcome back to the Fallschirmjager. We have had to collect several of our men from other divisions. They were scattered all over Italy.' He then pointed to a Lieutenant, saying 'Lieutenant Werlin, will you see to it that these men are divided up among the new recruits?'

"This alarmed me. I did not want to be seperated from my men. 'Excuse me Sir, but my men and I have been together for years. Some of them have been with me since the invasion of France. Please do not split us up.'

"The colonel seemed to be irritated, but spoke politely. 'I am sorry, Sergeant, but there are so many new recruits among our ranks that I feel it is necessary to put at least one veteran soldier in each squad.'

"I saw hope dwindling for staying with my men. 'We work best as a team of snipers. We can hit targets at extreme range. Every man in my squad has killed hundreds of enemy soldiers. If you put them into regular infantry squads, they won't be very effective.'

"I could tell the colonel had already become tired of this line of conversation. He spoke with a measure of finality. 'Your men will be divided up. You may choose three of them to work with you on your long range shooting. Dismissed.'

"Unable to speak further, I saluted, snapped my heels, and exited the bunker with the Lieutenant. I approached my men ahead of the Lieutenant so I could speak first. The snipers saw a distraught look upon my face, and each was eager to hear the news. I spoke to them, 'They're going to split us up.' The men all became vocal and were palpably angered by this news. 'I can only choose three of you to remain with me. The others are going with the regular infantry.' As I said this, I realized that I would be choosing more than snipers. I probably would be choosing survivors. Regular infantrymen were killed all the time. They died by the dozen. I had come to know all of these men, and I hated to assign any of them to such a fate. I looked them over and could see that they too realized this.

"'Konrad, you have been with me since Eben Emael. I can't let you go.' Konrad nodded. 'Thank you, Sir!'

"'Misha, you were with me in basic training. You has as much experience as I do.' Misha shook his head, saying, 'I'll be all right. Choose someone else.'

"'No. I want you to stay with me.' Misha relented and walked over beside me. Then I looked the others over. How could I choose just one more of them? They were all good snipers. Any one of them was worth his weight in gold, as far as I was concerned. *Which one?* I thought to myself.

"My eyes fell upon Rolfe. He still looked like a schoolboy. He was kicking dirt clods, as if he knew that he did not have a chance of staying with me. He had accepted his fate. 'And Rolfe,' I heard myself saying. I could see a look of shock on everyone present. Even Rolfe could not believe it. None of the men questioned my decision. 'I wish I could keep all of you, but I can't. I'm sorry.'

"The Lieutenant showed the other three snipers and I where we should go. The rest of my men went to their new units.

"'Why did you choose me?' asked Rolfe. I did not answer, so he asked again. 'Why'd you pick me, damn it? Those other men all have a lot more experience than I do.'

"'Because you look like my son,' I said quietly, 'and you're a hell of a good spotter.'

"We moved to our patch of ground, and dug our usual foxhole. The sounds of shelling could be heard all the while. It was coming from the south. The Allies now had two armies on the continent—one was to the south, attacking the Gustav Line, and moving northward, and the other was on the beach of Anzio, and would surely attempt to attack the Gustav Line from the north. We were caught in between two pincers.

"We remained in this area for three days. After that we were moved to an area near the town of Campoleone, where an army was massing in preparation for a counterattack upon the Anzio beachhead. We were not going anytime soon, however. We were told to dig in and wait. We remained in our foxhole for over a week. During that time, we were joined by the 715th Motorized Infantry Division, the Hermann Goering Division, and about half of the 3rd Panzer Grenadier Division. The other half of this division had been delayed by Allied air strikes, which had destroyed several bridges.

"In the middle of the night of January 31/February 1 we heard the sounds of fighting breaking out very close to us. Small arms, mortars, machine-guns, and cannons could be heard. The sound was to the south, which was in the direction of Anzio.

"After about half an hour of tense waiting and listening, a runner found us and told us to sit tight until further orders. When we asked what was going on, he said that one or two Allied divisions had attacked us. We were waiting for artillery to soften them, and for the light of dawn.

"Instead of just waiting, the snipers crawled several hundred meters to the south until we could see several muzzle flashes. We were still several hundred meters away from the enemy, but they were within sight. It was here that we quickly dug-in under the cover of darkness. We concealed our two holes with nets with grass and twigs woven into them. We did not sleep much that night.

"The fighting continued until dawn. When the first light of dawn came, the sounds of battle intensified all along the western front. It was extremely loud to the southwest, where the 715th Motorized Infantry had been dug-in. We later learned that the 715th had ambushed a battalion of US Rangers, and almost completely annihilated them.

"'All right men, let's show our new comander what we can do.'

"My men and I had managed to hang on to about five hundred rounds of extra ammunition. I felt a bit bad about letting the others go with the standard sixty rounds, but I knew that almost every bullet we fired as snipers resulted in an enemy casualty. Ammunition was spent on the front line often just to let the enemy know that you had not run out of bullets.

"Konrad and I were in one of the holes together. We both looked through our scopes, scanning the enemy line. The terrain was flat, which was perfect for us. Rain began to fall as we looked for our first targets. The water was cold. It was the middle of the Italian winter. It was cold, but not cold enough to snow. I had to wipe off my scope several times. I was soon very wet, and I tried hard not to shiver.

"As I was thinking of several other places I would rather be at that moment, I spotted an enemy sharpshooter. The soldier had a small scope fixed on the top of his Springfield rifle, and was looking through it intently. He had leaves all over his helmet, and was lying flat to avoid detection. I almost missed seeing him. I put the crosshairs on the green helmet and squeezed the trigger slowly. The gun fired, and I scrambled to put the crosshairs back on him after they had leaped with the recoil. I managed to find the enemy sniper again at the same instant the bullet hit. I could see the man's head snap, and then sag to the ground. The Springfield fell to the wet ground and was still.

"I imagined crosshairs on my own head. The combination of my own paranoia and the intense cold made me shiver.

"We continued to find and hit targets throughout the day. We witnessed several bloody fights, which we could do little about. I watched as an American soldier charged a German machine-gun nest. The gunner was changing barrels and the American leaped into the hole, skewering him with his bayonet. The loader reached for his rifle. The American's bayonet was stuck in the gunner's chest, so he detached it and quickly fired a bullet through the loader's chest. Then the American attempted to turn the MG 42 in our direction. He fired a few rounds before my bullet went through his forehead.

"This fighting went on for days. The Allies pushed us back every day. The 4th Parachute Division was hit every day by hundreds of enemy artillery shells. Some of these were enormous shells which must have been fired from enemy battleships in the Mediterranean. Our artillery shells were far fewer in number and smaller in caliber.

"Each day we would fire about fifteen shots each. We were rationed the usual seven bullets per day. A runner would bring us our rations each night. It consisted of bread, potatoes, onions, beef jerky, water, two cigars, and seven cartridges. Gone were the spices, tea bags, and hot food. It was obvious that our supplies were being cut, either because of Allied bombing, or some other reason.

"On February 3rd the Allies reached the City of Campoleone. Rather than allowing them to take the city, the 4th Parachute Division fortified the city. Every house and building became a strongpoint, either for infantrymen or heavy weapons crews. The naval guns seemed to be out of range, for their powerful 1000 pound shells did not fall upon the city. Smaller shells did fall in great numbers, and several houses were hit.

"My men and I moved into a battered apartment building. All was quiet. The civilians had fled from the battle. The stairs were covered with broken glass, as every window in the building had been shattered. I guessed that this had been caused by shock waves from artillery shells. Our booted feet crunched on the glass as we ascended to the upper floors.

"We finally reached the sixth floor and moved to a room which overlooked the farmland to the south of the city. We had an extremely good view of the battlefield.

"The room had already been damaged, as if looters or perhaps rampaging soldiers had already been there. There were large sections of wallpaper torn off the wall, and some of the plaster had been knocked off in the bare spots, revealing small horizontal boards. The ceiling had a few bullet holes in it. The bullets had probably come in through the window. A container of uncooked noodles had been shattered on the kitchen floor, and there were pieces of broken glass, as well as noodles, everywhere. In the center of the room was a bed, with one corner of the sheet and blanket opened up as if someone had just awakened and left.

"According to the scorched earth policy, we should have burned this building down. However, it made a very good snipers' nest. We decided to stay here a while and see what targets we could find. We hung a camouflage net over the window, so we would be difficult to see from the outside. We could see through the many holes in it quite well. We began looking with binoculars and our naked eyes.

"We could see many craters, and witnessed many artillery shells hitting the ground to the south of the city. We could also see groups of Allied soldiers advancing from crater to crater. They were getting ever closer to the edge of the city. Mortar, artillery, small arms, and machine-gun fire harassed us, but it seemed that all of the German soldiers had retreated into the buildings of Campoleone.

"We heard an explosion and looked in time to see an Allied soldier in mid-air. He must have stepped on a mine. He landed, screaming, his leg blown off. Others moved to help him. I saw an opportunity.

"'Bait them!' I said and pointed. The other snipers and I grabbed our rifles and began aiming at the company of US Army Rangers. 'Remember to line up your targets if you can. Ready?' I asked. They all nodded and whispered that they were. 'Fire!'

"It took the bullets a couple of seconds to travel the one-kilometer to the enemy soldiers. I watched as nine enemy soldiers were hit by the four bullets. One of them was the medic, who had been attempting to assist the soldier who had stepped on the land mine. The other soldiers were confused. They had not yet heard any shots. My men and I continued to fire at them. Some were hit in the leg and screamed for their comrades to help them. Others scrambled for cover. A mortar crew must have picked up on what was happening, because an 80mm mortar landed only a few meters away.

"The Rangers were pinned in three artillery craters. They dared only to glance for a moment to see where the enemy fire was coming from. Another mortar hit even closer to one of the craters. The mortar crew was adjusting their fire. The Rangers must have known what was going to happen next, for they all scrambled out of the three holes and retreated as quickly as they could. A third mortar hit directly inside one of the abandoned craters.

"We snipers took a couple of shots at the Rangers as they fled. As usual, the bullets went through several of them. One Ranger attempted to help a wounded comrade run and was subsequently hit through the pelvis. He screamed in agony. Three more Rangers turned to help those two, and they were all shot seconds after turning around. I spotted an officer or Sergeant yelling for the others not to turn back. He himself was holding still. He fired at the man, but he turned to run a second later, and escaped harm.

"My men quickly reloaded their Kar 98K rifles. By the time they reloaded, all of the unwounded Rangers were out of sight behind a hill. The wounded were attempting to crawl toward it. We simply watched them. All the while, artillery and mortars continued to fall all over the landscape. We also watched the top of the hill, waiting for the other Rangers to check on the progress of their friends. Finally, a face appeared. It was well over a kilometer away.

"'Don't shoot!' I ordered. 'Let them think they're out of range!'

"The wounded soldier who had been shot through the pelvis had stopped crawling. He had probably lost too much blood. One of the Rangers who had been shot in the back of his right leg was still crawling at what seemed to be a fairly good speed. Finally, one of the other Rangers ran out from behind the hill and ran to help him. I waited until he reached the wounded man and hoisted him onto his shoulder. Then I fired once and watched as the bullet struck the rescuer's leg. Both men fell and began to crawl.

"For several tense minutes the Rangers behind the hill only dared to peek at the two wounded men as they crawled on their bellies. When they were about fifty feet from the hilltop, I ordered the others to aim carefully at one of the peeking faces and squeeze off a shot. 'On my mark, three, two, one!' We all four fired at once. Three of the faces were hit. A dust cloud was kicked up right in front of a fourth. All of the Rangers behind the hilltop hid completely from view.

"Two more bullets ended the lives of the two crawling Rangers. 'Good work,' I said. 'That will make them afraid. They won't come again before dark, I'll bet.'

"As the hours of the day passed, more and more Allied troops arrived and dug-in. They stayed behind the hill where the others had hidden, but their numbers could be estimated, as hundreds of them began digging in just out of sight on the top of the hill. Then both armies were pounded by artillery. We heard two shells hit the upper floors of the apartment building. It caused the entire building to shake and we were frightened for a moment, but the building held. We also noticed several extremely powerful shells landing among the enemy positions. We later learned that a 280mm (about 11 inch) artillery gun mounted on railroad tracks (like a miniature Dora) had been deployed in the Alban Hills to the northwest. This monster boosted our morale a bit each time one of its massive shells landed. Even this huge gun was dwarfed by some of the US naval cannons, which could be as large as 18 inches across, and fired 1000 pound shells.

"During the night the Allied soldiers attempted to rush into the city under the cover of darkness. They hit several mines and alerted the Germans to their attack. Our troops quickly fired some flares into the air and began hitting the Allied soldiers with heavy fire of all types. The attack penetrated a few blocks into the city before dawn. More and more friendly reinforcements were arriving each day, and the we held a numerical advantage over the Allied troops. We could hear fierce house-to-house fighting going on in the many houses below. We were concerned that some of the Allied soldiers might enter the building we were firing from. Just as we were contemplating this, about fifty German paratroopers entered the building and set up defensive positions all over it.

"Fifteen minutes after these troops arrived, the building was attacked from below. The sounds of fierce fighting could be heard in the lower levels. We heard the sounds of grenades, rifles, machineguns, and screams. At the same time, I noticed a column of Allied tanks moving up the road toward the city. I had no time to worry about them. 'We've got to help our comrades downstairs!' They all nodded in agreement and began to move out of the room.

"We descended the same set of stairs which they had come up with caution and stealth. I shouldered my rifle in favor of my silenced Walther PP pistol, which I had carried ever since it was issued to me before the assault upon the Fortress Eben-Emael. I chambered a bullet by pulling back on the action. Konrad readied his MP35. Misha and Rolfe did not have any close-range weapons other than bayonets, so they held their rifles ready. They had grenades, also.

"We quickly reached the first floor and heard fighting just down the hallway. We heard the sound of an M1 rifle firing one shot after another. It was an eight shot, semi-automatic weapon. When the last shot was fired, we heard a distinctive 'ping' sound, followed by the sound of the magazine bouncing on the tile floor. Konrad looked around the corner and fired twice with his MP35. He then motioned for the others to follow. We saw that he had hit an American soldier twice in the back. Misha picked up the M1 rifle and took the chest belts, which were filled with magazines, off the dying soldier's chest. He had eight extra magazines left, which amounted to sixty-four shots. Misha slapped one into the weapon and pulled back the action.

"I knew that the soldier must have been firing at someone. 'Don't shoot!' I whispered in German before looking around the corner. At first I saw nothing, but then two frightened paratroopers came into view. They had been hiding around the corner down the hall. They motioned for us to join them and pointed down the hall to the left, signaling danger. I nodded and peeked down the left hall. All was quiet. The hallway was long, lined with many apartment doors. All of these had been kicked open, so it was impossible to tell where the enemy was hiding.

"Then a hand appeared and hurled a grenade in my direction. Remembering Konrad's actions in Eben-Emael, I smacked the grenade in midair with my bare hand. It flew back in the direction of the thrower. I then ducked around the corner as the grenade exploded.

"The grenade had been thrown from the apartment to our right. Only a plaster wall stood between us and the enemy soldier. I pointed at it, and we all fired several rounds through the wall. Konrad ran up to the doorway and tossed an S24 grenade inside. We heard a scream just as the grenade exploded.

"We could hear more enemy soldiers approaching down the hall. I motioned for Konrad to duck into the room which he had just thrown the grenade into and switched his pistol for his rifle. He saw an enemy run around the corner and fired a bullet through the man's chest. The soldier's eyes widened in shock and he fell. I quickly worked the bolt on my weapon as another enemy soldier attempted to fire a Browning automatic rifle at me. The Browning, also known as the BAR, was a machine-gun that looked like a large rifle. It could cut a man in half in less than a second. Before the ranger could even fire his weapon, I fired a bullet into his chest. I was using the mechanical sights below my scope, and did not want to take any fancy head shots. I quickly worked the bolt again. Misha stood at my side, ready with the M1.

"We stood there for several minutes, waiting to see if any enemies would appear. We were unsure if we had killed all of the Rangers, or if more were silently waiting for us to let down our guard. Konrad finally chanced a quick retreat from the shattered room which he had grenaded. He had also obtained an M1 rifle and several magazines. He handed these to Rolfe.

"I noticed a door with a sign on it. It was written in Italian, so I had no idea what it said. I pointed to it, and the others shrugged. Rolfe tested the doorknob and found it locked. Misha kicked it solidly, and it burst open with a loud crash. Stairs going down into a dark basement were revealed.

"'If we have to retreat, we can go down there,' I whispered. The others nodded in acknowledgement.

"We watched the hallway for about half an hour. We finally decided to move up and see what was there. The six of us moved as silently as we could, and snapped around every corner, looking into all of the appartments on either side of the hall. Each appeared empty, but we did not search them. We continued down to where the two enemy soldiers lay. We took their guns, ammunition, grenades, and even their food. I had developed a taste for the American rations. They were much better than the new mainstay of the German's rations, which were potatoes and onions.

"As we were taking these items, a grenade was hurled through a window near our previous position down the hallway. It exploded loudly. We all pointed our weapons in that direction and listened to the sounds of someone climbing into the window. We all moved quietly down, as the window was not in our direct line of sight. When we were close to it, I moved quickly around the corner and saw the enemy soldier climbing in. I shot him through the chest with one of the M1 rifles. The man screamed, and attempted to shoot me before he died. I put another round through the soldier's forehead.

"Konrad hurled an American grenade out the window. It exploded loudly on the ground below, and we heard screams. Then we heard more men moving into the hallway in which we had just fought the three other soldiers. I signalled the others to follow, and we all moved down the stairs into the dark basement.

"The basement was pitch dark, and the floor was made of dirt. It smelled of mildew, and we ran into a network of spider webs that spanned from the floor to the ceiling. The only light we could see by was coming in from the open door above. I lit my field lighter, which lit up a large area. We could see that the basement was a huge labarinth of tunnels; each led to a storeroom of some sort. We all found positions which allowed us to see the stairway, but gave us some cover from the many brick walls. The stairs went down in the opposite direction, so we would have a view from behind anyone who came down as they descended the wooden stairs. There were spaces in between the stairs, which we could see through.

"After a long while, an American 'egg grenade' (which is what the Germans called them, although the Americans called them pineapple grenades, or M1 grenades) was hurled down the stairs. My snipers and I all simply ducked behind brick walls, and held our ears. The grenade exploded, and two more grenades were hurled back away from the stairs. This was in the direction which we were hiding. Once again we ducked for cover. The explosions were much louder because of their proximity. My ears rang painfully. I quickly recovered and pointed my weapon at the stairs. Two American soldiers attempted to run down the stairs, to reach the cover of darkness. All six of us opened fire, and the Americans were hit several times before even reaching the dirt floor.

"Then one of the Americans upstairs shouted something, probably an obscenity. A second later, bullets were fired through the floor down into the basement. My snipers responded by firing their captured American rifles up through the floor. Misha fired a whole magazine out of the BAR, creating several holes in the floor. Light danced down to the dust filled basement through these holes. It was still very dark, however.

"We also began to move away from the stairs to avoid being hit by the wild gunfire through the floor. One of the two paratroopers whom we had found earlier had been wounded by one of these stray bullets, and we had to bandage him in the dark. Misha and Konrad watched the stairs as the others either bandaged him or held a lighter to provied some light on the process.

"The Americans did not attempt to enter the basement again. After about ten minutes we heard the sounds of fierce fighting above, and the Americans were driven from the building. We then emerged cautiously from the basement and sent the wounded paratrooper to the medical platoon. It was in a building on the other side of town. His companion went with him. As we were seeing them off, we could hear the sounds of intense combat about one block to the south. There was a loud explosion and the distinctive sounds of tanks rolling on their steel treads.

"There were hundreds of paratroopers all around, watching the enemy tank column as it was repeatedly pounded with anti-tank weapons from the many buildings above. Rocket-propelled grenades were hitting the tanks, and they were trapped in between burnt out tanks both in front and behind them. Some of the tanks attempted to fight back, while other crews opened their hatches and tried to surrender. Within a few minutes, all of the tanks in the column had either been destroyed or captured.

"Throughout the night the Allied soldiers were pushed out of the city. This began when several heavy Panzer tanks, backed up by a division of Panzer grenadiers, took the land to the south of the city. This effectively cut off the Allied soldiers who had taken buildings inside the city, and denied them supplies and reinforcements. Several of them surrendered soon afterward. Others were stubborn, and the Germans had to destroy the buildings with tank or mortar fire. By dawn the city had been completely retaken, and the Allied army was withdrawing to the south.

"That date was February 4th. Our forces launched a new offensive. I remembered it well. German and Allied aircraft battled in the skies above and repeatedly harassed one another's ground forces with machine-guns and bombs. The Allied soldiers repeatedly attempted to dig in and stand their ground, only to be pushed back by hordes of our troops.

"This advance was costly, however. Several of our tanks were hit dive-bombers, and were destroyed in a fiery blast. Many of our infantrymen were also killed either by bombs, artillery shells, or enemy gunfire.

"We drove back the Allied forces for two days until finally reaching the Town of Aprilia, where the Allied soldiers attempted to hold their ground in an Italian factory. This consisted of three large brick buildings. Our artillery shelled the buildings repeatedly, and hundreds of troops finally took them by storming them. We paused for the night, and occupied the factory.

"The next day two Allied infantry divisions counterattacked the factory. Our forces were dug-in both inside and all around the factory.

We were well prepared. The ferocity of the attack took us off guard, however. We were bombed by dive-bombers. We were also shelled quite heavily. It seemed that twenty Allied artillery shells landed for every one German shell. I could not believe how heavily we were being shelled. I had never seen anything like this in all my years of fighting. There were more craters than foxholes, and many foxholes took direct hits.

"My men and I were dug-in about half a kilometer behind the factory, and decided to move late in the afternoon when the shelling got very close. We did this by crawling for two hundred meters to the north and quickly digging another foxhole.

"Minutes after we dug a new one and covered it with nets, the shells and bombs subsided, and we could see thousands of enemy soldiers advancing upon the factory. They were crawling, or running in a crouched position from cover to cover. German machine-gun and mortar fire hit several groups of men as they tried to advance.

"We began looking for priority enemy targets. We shot and killed several snipers and heavy weapons crews before nightfall.

"The fighting continued well into the night, until the attack was finally broken off.

"During the next few days, the two mighty armies dug-in. The foxholes on both sides of the line could be seen as far as the eye could see to the west (toward the coast) and to the southeast. We snipers found this type of fighting much more to our liking than the fight in the apartment building a few days ago.

"As each day passed, more bodies were carried out of the many German foxholes. This was primarily done at night to avoid attracting the attention of enemy snipers. Fresh troops were also arriving. They were paratroopers, but they were fresh out of basic training. None of them were jump-qualified. This meant that none of them had ever parachuted! I wondered how they could be considered to be paratroopers at all.

"There were many young faces among these new recruits. Some of them were as young as fourteen years old. There were also men who were older than fifty-five. It was obvious that our army was becoming desperate for troops.

"Things were relatively quiet for several days. The armies fought one another, but it was more a battle of snipers and mortar attacks than attempts to gain ground. My men and I shot scores of snipers during this period.

"The number of troops on both sides grew every day as each army poured in fresh troops. Finally, on February 16th, we launched yet another offensive. My men and I helped where we could, but we were astonished at the ferocity of the attacks of our fellow soldiers. Enemy foxholes took direct hits from mortars, and were quickly overrun. Each hour we gained ground.

"Late in the evening, a large hole had been torn in the enemy lines to the south. One division of German infantry and sixty tanks poured through the gap and began turning upon the flanks of the nearby dug-in enemy troops. My snipers and I could see everything through our binoculars. It was apparent that the situation was becoming desperate for the enemy. They were outnumbered, and their line had been broken.

"The Allied forces made another line of foxholes behind this one, creating a second line. They also pounded us with thousands of artillery shells, bombs, and naval cannon shells. This caused our offensive to grind to a halt.

"We kept the enemy inside a pocket, which was about ten to fifteen miles away from Anzio. This situation continued for two weeks. The two dug-in armies took shots at one another, but little else changed.

"Finally, on March 4th, we began what was to become our last offensive at Anzio. We attempted to push forward as we had two weeks before, only to be met by withering fire by a well-prepared and dug-in enemy. Thousands of our infantrymen were killed. The offensive lasted a bloody six days, and was finally cancelled on March 9th.

"At that point, a lull in the fighting began. We were told to fight defensively. We were to give as little ground to the enemy as possible, and make every meter extremely costly. My snipers and I continued to kill enemy snipers and heavy weapons operators every day.

"On May 12th, we were told that the Gustav Line had been attacked by an Allied spring offensive. One week later, the Allies captured the City of Cassino. This created a breach in the mighty Gustav Line.

"At that point, the Allied VI Corps, which had been contained around Anzio, renewed their offensive. Our 10th Army, which included the 4th Parachute, and several other divisions, began a tactical retreat to the north.

"On May 25th the Allied II and VI Corps met up, creating one enormous army. This united their army, which had been trapped near Anzio, and the army, which had been attacking the Gustav Line. All we could do was retreat and continue the scorched earth policy. We got very little sleep. We moved by cover of night and slept in foxholes during the day. We finally retreated all the way to the north of Rome.

"On June 4th 1944 Rome was liberated by Allied forces. High Command had decided not to attempt to fight for the city. This surprised me. With so many buildings and places to hide, we might have held up the Allies for months. It could have even turned the tide of the war, like Stalingrad had for the Russians.

"Two days later, the Allies opened a second front in France. They attacked the Beaches of Normandy with massive sea, air, and ground forces. I remained in Italy for another six months, until my men and I were ordered to travel to Germany. We were to be part of a major counteroffensive in the Ardennes, which was code named 'Wacht Am Rhein' (which means 'Guard on the Rhine), or as the Americans would call it, "The Battle of the Bulge."

"Are you tired, Grandpa?" George asked when Grandpa paused for a few minutes.

"Yes, son, I'm tired. I'm tired of remembering, just like I was tired of the war."

"You can stop if you want to," George said.

"Yes, I think I will stop for tonight."

"No, Grandpa. I mean you can stop—altogether, if you want to."

"Soon I will stop." He smiled a bit as he gazed at Ingred. "The war is almost over."

CHAPTER 14

▼

WACHT AM RHEIN

"In November, the lines in Italy were holding. Both the our army and the Allies removed divisions from Italy to participate in operations in Western Europe. The 4th Parachute Division was one of the divisions sent to fight the battle.

"The 4th Parachute Division also received soldiers to replace the thousands who had been killed or captured. Many of these new recruits were, in my opinion, unfit for duty. Some were as young as twelve years old, some as old as seventy-five. Others were veteran soldiers who had been hospitalized for serious injuries which had now healed. Many were poorly equipped. Some were sent to fight, armed only with Panzerfaust anti-tank weapons.

"I had not been allowed to return to my home since before the invasion of Italy. I did not learn of my mother's death until months after the fact. This made me furious, as I was now about to begin my eighth year of service.

"By now, my superiors had come to greatly respect my abilities as a sniper. My three men and I were allowed to operate in whatever manner we saw fit for the most part. We were also now secretly given more ammunition per day than normal infantrymen. The vast majority of the shots we fired resulted in enemy casualties, so the ammunition was not wasted.

"We were amassing an enormous army, which included 600,000 men in 6 corps. These were divided up into 31 divisions, with about 20,000 men in each. We also had at least eight armored divisions, with over one hundred tanks each. Many of these were the extremely armed and armored Tiger and king Tiger tanks. The Allies had nothing like them. They could only counter these juggernauts with air power, and the sky was thick with a dense winter fog.

"The other paratroopers and I had been put into the 6th Panzer Army. We were stationed near a city called Prum, just a few miles to the east of St. Vith.

"The invasion began in the early morning hours of December 16th, 1944. It was still dark, and things were quiet. The ground and the trees were covered with snow, and things looked quite peaceful as we snipers marched behind a column of armored vehicles. We marched in this manner for about two hours; I guessed we must have traveled about twelve kilometers. At that point we could hear the sounds of shelling ahead, and were ordered to move up with caution. The enemy was close.

"The army had moved into the front lines, where the Americans had their infantry divisions spread along a very long front. As my men and I cautiously moved forward in the trees, we could see many of our fellow soldiers digging in. We were waiting for the enemy to be softened up by artillery shells. The sounds of shells exploding could be heard in an area about one kilometer to the west.

"The snipers and I moved northward until we found an unoccupied spot which had a good view of enemy lines. We found some bushes which we could hide underneath, and cunningly dug-in just under the western edge of them. This gave us concealment from the enemy, as well as a good view.

"We all began scanning westward with binoculars. It took a while to see anything. Finally, we saw several enemy bunkers made of logs. They had walls as well as roofs. They looked much more comfortable and protective than foxholes. Artillery shells then began landing near several of these log bunkers.

"I spotted an enemy soldier. He was firing a large machine-gun from one of the bunkers. 'Konrad,' I said, 'enemy machine-gun operator near that small hill.' I pointed.

"Konrad looked through his scope on his Kar 98K for a few seconeds before answering, 'Ya, I see him!' He then aimed carefully before taking one shot. I watched as the gunner was hit in the head. The gun abruptly ceased firing.

"We watched the enemy positions for about half an hour, and hit five more enemy soldiers. At that point we heard the sound of 88mm anti-aircraft guns firing. Normal artillery guns fired their shells high into the air, causing them to fall like bombs. Flak cannons fired their shells in straight lines, much like an enormous rifle. They were aimed directly at their targets. The 88mm flak cannons were primarily used for protection from enemy aircraft, but they were equally deadly to ground targets. The shells were hitting a line of trees, which was closer than the bunkers. I saw that several trenches and foxholes were in that area. I had failed to notice them before. The flak shells were hitting the trees and exploding. These were called 'tree bursts.' They caused wood to fly like shrapnel. A piece of wood could go through a man's arm or leg after being hit by a shell. I watched in morbid fascination as the thick tree trunks of the many fir trees exploded one by one.

"The Americans were almost completely defenseless, as they had no artillery of their own. Most of them just got low to make as small a target as they possibly could. A few attempted to fight back, but they were at extreme range, and our infantrymen were doing a good job of hiding from view.

"I witnessed one Wehrmacht sniper crawling very close to the Americans. I hid behind a large tree and then began shooting at the few Americans who were attempting to fight back. The sniper hit several of the Americans before he was then spotted by them. They then began to shoot at him, and he was pinned behind the tree.

"Several American mortars soon landed all around him, and he was blown to pieces.

"'Did you see that?' I asked the others. They nodded. 'That's why we don't want to get that close.'

"'No shit!' said Rolfe. 'Don't they train those Wehrmacht snipers?'

"'I was in the Wehrmacht. They mostly just taught me how to shoot. Ellis taught me everything else. He has kept me alive all these years.'

"'His tricks didn't keep him alive,' continued Rolfe.

"I shrugged. 'Sometimes no trick can save you. An enemy sniper or spotter sees you, and boom, you're dead!'

"After another hour or so, the Americans in the trenches had had enough. They surrendered. I watched several of them hitting their weapons on trees to break them. The order was then given to move forward and sieze the enemies' weapons. The snipers and I waited a few minutes, until the bulk of the division had moved into the Americans' position. Then we left our hiding place and followed.

"Although many of the enemies' weapons had been damaged, many had not. Several of our lightly armed soldiers armed themselves with M1 rifles, M1 carbines, BAR's, Thompson SMG's, bazookas, and 81mm mortars.

"Behind the hills which the American soldiers had fortified, we found several buildings and bunkers. There were more Americans here, however they were not willing to surrender. Our soldiers were already fighting with them. As we cautiously moved over a hilltop, we could hear gunfire and the sounds of grenades going off. We saw a squad of paratroopers throwing grenades into an American bunker. Suddenly one of them was hit by gunfire from another bunker, and a grenade exploded in the middle of their squad. I looked through my scope and saw an American sniper firing out of a window of one of the buildings. I fired once and watched the sniper fall out of the broken window through the glass. He hung half in and half out of the building. I spotted two infantrymen just standing straight up and firing their M1 rifles. They were lined up, so I fired a bullet through both of their chests.

"Some of the Americans must have located me, because we soon heard the sound of bullets flying through the leaves of trees all around us. My men and I quickly got behind a clump of trees. Several more of our comrades ran by us in the direction of the buildings. We heard more intense gunfire, and finally decided to move up to help.

"My heart pumped hard as I quickly ran up to the nearest bunker. I knew that I could be in an enemy's crosshairs at any moment. As I neared the bunker, an enemy soldier ran around the back corner of it. We saw one another at the same moment. I aimed my gun without hesitation, and fired a bullet through the soldier's head. I then motioned for my men to follow, and advanced up to where the soldier had fallen. There was a growing pool of dark red blood getting larger by the second all around the soldier's head. His body flinched and jumped, but I realized it was only the man's reflexes.

"An entire company of paratroopers moved into the area, and the sounds of fighting quickly died down. We paratroopers took the fallen soldier's ammunition magazines, which fit the M1 rifles the three of them carried as backup weapons. These same cartridges also fit Misha's BAR.

"Our soldiers proceeded to loot the many buildings of the American base. The area had been a German strongpoint before the Americans reclaimed it a few months ago.

"The 4th Parachute Division stayed in the area for the night as it regrouped, rested, and took charge of several thousand prisoners.

"Over the next eleven days, our enormous army moved to the west. American infantry and tanks in small groups attempted to slow our advance, but the we crushed them. We saw several aerial dogfights, as American and German fighters chased each other through the foggy sky. I wondered if this operation would be going so well if the weather had cleared. I guessed that it would not. The Americans had a fearsome air force. The British air force attacked our forces by night. The American air force attacked by day. Our unit was strafed a few times, but it was mostly ineffective, thanks to the fog. The 88mm guns shot two of the American fighters down while my man and I watched.

"On December 19th we reached St. Vith. The US 7th Armored Division had dug-in both in and around the city. They were ready for a fight. They had already ambushed several of the small advance units, which scouted in front of and around the main corps.

"The 4th Parachute had been harassed by air attacks on the way to St. Vith, and thus was broken into several smaller groups. My men and I did not arrive in the city until December 19th. Other battalions of the 4th Parachute Division had already arrived, and there had been fierce fighting. There were burnt out tanks (both German and

American) just to the east of the town. There were also several dead bodies lying in the snow.

"I saw dozens of American foxholes to the east of the town. They had been deployed on either side of the road. Two destroyed German tanks sat in between these two rows of foxholes. The snow in this area had been blackened by gunpowder from explosions. I saw several machine-gun and bazooka crews in the foxholes, as well as riflemen. I watched them through my scope from a safe distance, some eight hundred meters down the road.

"The Blitzkrieg had not halted because of the stubborn defenders of St. Vith. They had simply gone around it for the most part. Columns of tanks, trucks, and troops moved around the city to the north and south. The Americans had caused a costly delay, however. The three roads, which crisscrossed through the center of the town, were needed to move the armies with greater speed, so the order had been given to take the city by force.

"We snipers knew that our fellow soldiers were not yet ready to assault the town. The preparations would take a few more hours. Instead of sitting and waiting, we began taking shots at the heavy weapons crews in the not-so-distant foxholes.

"I waited carefully as three US soldiers in a foxhole smoked and talked with one another. They seemed to be unafraid, and I saw them laugh several times. I was certain that they had no idea what they were up against. They probably thought that a relatively small German force was attacking them, when in fact it was an enormous army of hundreds of thousands of men. The Americans had less than a division around the entire town, and were unknowingly being encircled by two divisions. The 4th Parachute was to the east, while the 18th Volks Grenadier was moving around to the north.

"After several minutes, one of them leaned over to allow another soldier to light his cigarette. I instantly fired. I watched as the bullet traveled toward the enemy in less than a second and went through two of their helmeted heads. I quickly worked the bolt on my rifle in preparation for another shot.

"The third soldier in the foxhole dropped the cigarette out of his mouth as he jumped in surprise. He then set his rifle on the edge of the foxhole, and looked to see where the shot had come from. A second bullet then hit him in the forehead.

"I expected the other Americans to put their heads down. Instead, the other dozen or so crews with heavy machine-guns began firing blindly in my direction. I ordered my men to shoot them all. Soon all four of us snipers were firing with deadly accuracy. Within one minute, at least one man in each of the enemy foxholes had been hit. Then they did put their heads down in fear.

"My snipers kept the enemy crews pinned down for half an hour. During this time, some of the other paratroopers advanced upon them and began throwing grenades into some of the closer holes. As the Americans popped their heads up to fight back, we shot them down.

"This fighting continued until it was dark. Shortly after dark, a column of American Sherman tanks rolled out of St. Vith in an attempt to push the attackers back. They got about two hundred yards out of the town when two bright red fireballs streaked in their direction. I watched as the two lead tanks exploded. They had been hit by German RPzB54's, which were a German 88mm version of the American bazooka. The other Sherman tanks quickly went into reverse, and rolled back into the town.

"This initiated a wave of intense fighting, both to the east and the north of the town. Our comrades fired flares above the American positions, and shelled them mercilessly. Using the light from flares, we continued to take long and deadly shots at our enemies. The fighting continued all night, and the town was not taken until morning.

"As the 4th Parachute was moving out of the town the following morning (Dec 21st), the sky began to clear and the temperature plummeted. It had been cold before this, but I imagined that it was now well below freezing. I noticed that many of the dead American soldiers and POW's I saw had newspapers stuffed under their uniforms for protection from the cold.

"With the sky clear, the Allied air attacks increased in frequency and intensity. Every time we heard an incoming aircraft, we ran from the road in a scramble for cover. Several men did not make it in time, and were raked with .50 cal bullets. Many of the trucks and horses were hit as well, creating costly delays in the advance.

"My men and I also got our first up-close look at an artillery weapon called the 'nebelwerfer.' It was an armored vehicle which fired large rockets. As the rockets sped to their target, they made a terrifying screaming sound.

"Over the next week it became clear that the attack on the Americans would fail. Our army was harassed by constant air attacks, and our enemies fought us bitterly at every opportunity. As in the Soviet Union, several men died simply from exposure.

"On January 8th our army was forced to retreat. Many of our tanks had either been destroyed by aircraft, or simply run out of fuel and had to be abandoned. Two days later we were ordered to stand our ground. Hitler commanded us not to give an inch.

'Well, doesn't that sound familiar?' I mused. We had been given the exact same order during their first winter in Russia. It had been horrible, but our lines had held. The same order had been given in Italy to give engineers time to prepare defenses. It seemed to be Hitler's favorite tactic.

"Then came an entire month of sheer horror. We had to fight in bitter cold and snow. The two armies dug foxholes and fought as if they were replaying World War I. The snipers and I killed every day, and watched our fellow soldiers die.

"The nights were terrifying. Every strange sound could be an enemy. Every tree seemed to move in the darkness.

"We fought on the western front for almost four more months.

"At last, in the third week of April of 1945, we were ordered to ride all night in a truck to Berlin. The Soviets were about to make an assault upon the city, and Hitler had called for any soldiers who could be spared to take part in the defense of the capital.

Grandpa yawned and stretched. "Tomorrow night my tale will end," he said and got up and walked upstairs.

CHAPTER 15

▼

BERLIN, THE FINAL STAND

George was anxious to hear the end of the story, which Grandpa had promised would be tonight. Once again, as he listened, he could see it being played out, like he was watching Grandpa perform in a play. It began, as usual, slow and steady, with more of the general information that Grandpa loved to tell so well.

"The 4th Parachute Division was hard pressed by the American forces. It was for this reason that they could allow only one regiment (about 6000 soldiers) to travel to Berlin. We set out for Berlin on the evening of April 17th. We did not have a very long way to go, as the western lines were also dangerously close to Berlin. After driving about thirty miles, we reached a bridge which had been destroyed. It was only going over a shallow river, so we were ordered to walk the rest of the way.

"We walked all night and into the next day. We came upon a small city, and saw that thousands of civilians were clogging the road from Berlin, abandoning the city. Several of them gave us cold looks, and were visibly furious with us. I realized that we were being blamed for all the terrible things which had befallen the nation. The war was all but lost, and the army was being blamed. *If only they could know what we have been through*, I thought.

"We reached the outskirts of Berlin on the evening of April 17th, after a forced eighty-mile march. We were absolutely exhausted. Our equipment and weapons felt as if they were made of lead, rather than steel. I was accustomed to marching, but this march made even my rock-hard feet hurt. My boots were so worn from the many years of marching and fighting in them that they each had a small hole developing in the sole. This was most unusual, as boots of this kind normally lasted for years. I had lived in those boots since they were issued to me in 1940. I could have taken new boots from the many dead German soldiers on numerous occasions, but had never thought to do such a thing.

"My old Kar 98K was showing its age, as well. I cleaned it carefully every day, but the wooden parts were covered with nicks and gouges from the many rocks, trees, holes, destroyed buildings, tanks, and other things I'd had to hide behind at various times. My field flask was covered with dents, and my clothes were worn with age. They smelled terrible. There was no time or place on the battlefield for a bath. The other paratroopers were equally filthy.

"As we entered the city, I could see many destroyed buildings. They were formerly houses or businesses, but were now only blackened skeletons of steel and brick. There were civilians here and there. Some were preparing to leave, while others just went about their daily tasks. I saw a mailman, and my mind flashed back to the one who had given me my draft notice. For a moment I let my mind play with the idea of shooting the poor fellow. I wondered if I suddenly shot him if they would imprison me. That would be one sure way to avoid the upcoming battle. Then I came to my senses, and I scolded myself for thinking such a cold thought. What had I become? A mass murderer, or an excellent soldier? What was the difference? A murderer killed for amusement and a soldier killed to survive, I supposed. I was feeling a little unbalanced at the moment. I walked into Berlin, a place I feared and hated. I was going there to defend it from the Soviets. I hated the Soviets, and had hoped that I would never again in my lifetime see another Soviet soldier. Now I was sure I was going to see more of them than I ever wanted to see. The Red Army was coming—like an impending storm.

"We marched until we reached a checkpoint, which consisted of a barbed wire fence with a gate across the road. A dozen soldiers guarded the fence and asked the new arrivals what they were doing. Our commanding officer, a colonel, spoke to them. I could not hear what was being said. At last we were ordered to move to the city center and await orders. The colonel went to find the high command bunker, and was gone for hours.

"We were ordered to sleep in an apartment building. It was abandoned, as the civilians had been ordered to leave. It had several floors. Despite being large, it was not large enough to house so many men. We were sleeping in every room on the floors and even in the hallways. The other snipers and I slept in the living room of one of the apartments. We considered this to be quite comfortable, compared to sleeping in a hole, which is where we usually slept. Holes were nice and soft, but I constantly imagined worms touching me during the night. I hated them.

"The following morning, we paratroopers were informed that our unit had been renamed the "9th Parachute Division," even though we were far short of division strength. Divisions generally had twenty thousand men. The Colonel had briefed his subordinate officers, who then informed the various Sergeants of the situation.

"We also were told that thousands of other troops were preparing to help in the defense of Berlin. These included the Mucheberg Panzer, the 20th Panzer Grenadier, the 18th Panzer Grenadier, the 11th SS Panzer Grenadier, the 1st Flak, 3rd Kriegs Marine (war marines), 4th SS Police Grenadier, SS Frundsberg, SS Bodyguard, Friedwick Ludwig Jahn, Hitler Jugend (Hitler Youth), and various Volkssturm and Gestapo units. All of these units were called "divisions," although they all fell far short of division strength. In total, we had about 60,000 men. This was equal to about three peacetime divisions. During the war, they were seldom ideal size, due to various factors. The Mucheberg Panzer Division was named after the city where it had been formed a few days earlier, and consisted of several types of soldiers from different divisions.

"The Mucheberg Panzer division included sixty tanks. This was not even one full division of tanks. There were normally one hundred tanks in a division, and I knew that the Soviets would bring lots of tanks. Their tanks were also much heavier and more powerful than the ones which the Americans and British put into the field. I had a flashback of watching them take hits from various anti-tank weapons, only to have them bounce off. The thought gave me a feeling of dread. I had heard that the Soviets had developed tanks even larger than the ones I had seen on the eastern front.

"The city had air defenses, which included about 100-88mm guns of the 1st Flak Division, and six special air defense towers around the city center. These towers were bomb-proof and held enormous 12.8cm flak cannons.

"Various artillery and mortar batteries were concealed throughout the city, and the entire city had artillery support.

"The city was divided into nine sectors, which were called sectors 'A' though 'H,', with the city center called 'sector Z.' This was where Hitler's bunker was located, along with the most heavily built buildings in the city. Sectors A-H were pie shaped, with the tips cut off for the city center.

"The pattern of city defenses was further divided into three rings of defense. The outermost ring was sixty miles in diameter, and consisted of hastily dug trenches and roadblocks. The second ring was twenty-five miles wide, and used the S-Bahn railway, as well as many solidly-built houses as a defensive wall. This section of town had many wide streets, which would be used as deadly kill zones to trap the invading Soviet soldiers. The third and final ring of defense was the city center, where Hitler's bunker and the various government buildings stood.

"Our 'division' was informed that we were needed to help build the outer ring of defenses. If the attack came unexpectedly, we were to attempt to hold this line, but fall back if necessary. We were to use the civilian telephone system to communicate with high command. We were all given a slip of paper, with the telephone number typed on it. 'You must check in at least once every day. If you can find the number of the telephone which you are near, you must report it,' we were ordered.

"We paratroopers spent the next two days working in the sun. We dug trenches, laid mines, and instructed policemen and Hitler Youth members on how to lay and detect mines. I showed them how to use a cleaning rod for a mine probe, at least a hundred times. I became sick of it. What made me even sicker was that most of my fellow defenders had never been in a real fight before! *This is hopeless,* I thought to myself.

"All the men knew it was hopeless. Our only chance of survival was to hold the Soviets off until the Americans and British could take part of the city. We would much rather surrender to them than to the unmerciful Soviets. I dreaded the thought of being taken prisoner by the Soviets. I had heard plenty of horror stories of them torturing and murdering my fellow soldiers.

"As we toiled, we could hear the sounds of battle growing closer by the hour. It was obvious that the Russians were not far off. On April 21st, we were told to move into the city and prepare a fallback point. The distance between the outermost ring of defenses and the second ring was about seventeen miles. I chose a solidly constructed bank. There were areas of unpaved land around the bank, in which small trees had been planted. We were able to get some S-mine-35's, which we buried near the trees. We were unable to bury the wires, because the areas of soil were surrounded by pavement. Instead, we laid boards over them. The wires led to a field detonater, with a crank for generating power. We had to return to the outer ring quickly, so we had time to do little else.

"Once again we snipers were allowed to operate independently. I was told that I might later have to take charge of stragglers who had lost their units. It was an unwritten rule that if a soldier got separated from his unit, another one would take him in as one of their own; it was safer than looking all over for your unit during a battle.

"As we were marching back to the outer ring, the sounds of fighting had already begun. We doubled our pace to get back in time. We could hear artillery shells, and all sorts of other weapons. The Russians had arrived. I felt the fear swell in my breast, as if this was my first time entering combat. I was afraid it might be my last. I had not felt such anxiety in years. Konrad gave me a few worried looks as we ran, and I finally said 'Men, I want you to know, if I don't make it, you were all...' They interrupted me all at once, saying 'We know, Frick, we feel the same...' and other similar things. We all shook hands. I finally managed to swallow the lump in my throat and tell them, 'If I don't make it, please tell my wife that I did everything that I could to survive.' I looked at the ground as I said this, and the three other men all said they would relay the message if they needed to. They also expressed their wishes for words to be passed on. Misha and Rolfe had only their parents. Konrad had a girlfriend, as well as his mother. His father had been conscripted a few months previously, and Konrad had no idea where his father was.

"When we arrived, we could see that the Russians had not even bothered to soften our section with an artillery barrage. They had chosen instead to attack with large numbers of men. German machine-gun crews were mowing them down in large numbers. Some of the Russians had hit the outer edge of the minefield, and were being blown into the air. I watched as an S-mine 35 shot into the air and sprayed deadly pellets in every direction. The Russian soldiers were screaming in agony as they were cut down.

"Mortar fire began to rain down on the Russians outside the minefield. The mortar crews had been told not to fire into the field, to avoid destroying precious mines. Several squads of Russians were blown to bits as they surveyed the situation.

"Several of the Russian soldiers were obviously very experienced. Many squads of them dug foxholes and simply ignored the danger. They knew it was their only hope. Others fought back, firing rifles and heavy machine-guns in the direction of the German defenders.

"We snipers had earlier prepared a concealed foxhole to shoot from. We crawled into it and began scanning the Russian units for targets. I was amazed at how many of them there were. I saw thousands of them getting out of trucks and off of tanks. The numbers made my stomach tighten up. There were probably as many Russians attacking this one section of the line as there were German defenders in the entire city. 'My God!' I whispered.

"'What is it?' asked Konrad, as he looked through his own scope. 'Mary, mother of God! There are thousands of them!'

"At that moment, we snipers were certain that we had no chance for victory. Our only hope was to delay the Russians as long as possible, and to make their victory as costly as we could. I fired a bullet through a Russian officer's head, hitting two more soldiers behind him. I worked the bolt and moved the crosshairs horizontally until I saw a machine-gun crew. I waited a few seconds, until another soldier crouched behind the gunner, then I fired. The bullet passed through the gunner's head, and through the thigh of the infantryman behind him. I could hear the other snipers firing as well, and knew that they were also hitting targets.

"Moments later, a massive artillery barrage began raining down upon the Russian soldiers. Trucks, tanks, and large groups of soldiers were hit. Bodies and pieces of bodies flew through the air. The shells were very accurate. The entire area had been pre-sighted by our artillery and mortar crews.

"Three large Russian tanks boldly attempted to cross the minefield. One of them was hit by an RPzB54 shell—an 88mm bazooka, which fired a rocket propelled shaped charge capable of piercing the heaviest armor—and began exploding from the inside. A second tank hit a Tellermine-29 anti-tank mine, which blew the right tread off. It ground to a halt, but continued to fire its two machine-guns and cannon. Seconds later, it was hit and destroyed by another RPzB54 shell. The last tank got about ten feet closer, and also hit an anti-tank mine. Several 88mm shells hit it, and it exploded as well.

"Rather than simply attacking another section of the defensive ring, or retreating—as I believed any sane commander would do—the Russians continued to send countless troops to attack this one section of the line. They fired mortars into our ranks, killing several paratroopers. German machine-gun crews were desperately screaming for ammunition as they continued mowing down groups of Russian infantrymen. They fired their MG42's in one-second bursts, as they had been trained, but this was not enough to conserve their ammunition. The Russians were very numerous.

"The mines continued to take a horrible toll on the attacking Russians. I watched many of them advancing with looks of horror on their faces, as if they knew they were about to step on a mine. The air around the entire area was full of smoke, and it was difficult to see. We continued to hear the sounds of explosions and machine-gun fire.

"The battle continued like this for about half an hour. After this, the Russian infantrymen were able to use the cover of smoke to move some of their infantry up to the nearest foxholes of the paratroopers. The well-armed paratroopers promptly shot them, but it was obvious that there were at least a few safe paths through the minefield. Any experienced soldier knows that all you have to do is follow the tracks of another through the minefield, and you'll make it fine.

"An enormous Russian tank rolled through the concealing smoke and dust and moved within spitting distance of the outermost German foxholes. Its two machine-guns and its cannon began blasting away, and one foxhole took a direct hit. Three paratroopers' bodies were blown into the air by the 90mm shell. A Panzerfaust rocket propelled anti-tank grenade slammed into the side of the tank, and it exploded. The sound of more tanks moving up behind it could be heard, and several officers shouted that it was time to pull back.

"The Russians had breached the outermost line in less than an hour. This was not a good sign at all. We were so badly outnumbered that there would be no chance to counterattack. Any ground the Russians took was theirs.

"We did not run all the way back to the bank. Instead, I kicked the front door of a large house in and we quickly ran upstairs. The family that lived there had fled the area and the house was ominously quiet, despite what was going on outside. It was surrounded by thousands of other houses, but the we had a good view of the lines from the upstairs. We saw paratroopers retreating and Russian soldiers and tanks moving over the area of foxholes. Other foxholes still had Germans in them, as the ring spread out to the north and south. We paratroopers had been placed in B sector, as we were some of the most heavily armed and well-trained of the city's defenders. As the Russians moved across the outer ring of defenses, they were surrounded by a half-circle of defenders. This included those who were falling back from the front line, and foxholes still filled with soldiers to the north and south. The Russians were taking concentrated fire from all directions.

"We then heard the sounds of another Russian attack striking the north section of the outer defensive ring. I knew there must be yet another enormous force of Russians there. The area to the north was far too distant for us to see, so it was not possible to help them, not even with extreme range shots.

"For the next several hours we snipers shot several Russian soldiers each hour. We attempted to assist our fellow paratroopers as they retreated. It was difficult to see the entire battlefield because of the houses all around. We had been ordered not to engage large numbers of Russians in this mainly residential area. The houses were packed too closely together, and it would have been suicide.

"We heard the sounds of aircraft flying overhead. Several bombs were dropped upon the city, and several planes were shot down. 88mm flak shells were exploding all around the Russian planes as they dropped their bombs. I witnessed a plane as it crashed into a group of houses. The houses caught on fire, and flames were soon shooting high into the air.

"I picked up a telephone in the kitchen and called headquarters. I reported that the enemy had breached the eastern outer defensive ring and that the defenders were falling back while fighting. The voice on the other end was that of an officer, and he did not sound very encouraged by the news. He did thank me for reporting in, however.

"As the outer ring defensive line collapsed we defenders spent the next ten days fighting in retreat. We destroyed hundreds of Russian tanks and other vehicles, as well as killing tens of thousands of Russian soldiers. Losses among the defenders were in the low thousands. We had given the Russians a bloody nose, but the juggernaut refused to slow its advance upon the capital city.

"The nights were very dark, and extremely terrifying. I and my men would sleep in a house with other soldiers, and we heard fighting all night. An enemy probably could have stood on the front porch and not been heard because of all the background noise. We posted sentries to watch the outside of the house, but that did little to ease our paranoia. Sentries could be killed quite easily in the darkness, especially with the constant roar of battle masking all but the loudest of sounds.

"The wounded defenders were carried past us constantly, either on stretchers or a fellow soldier's shoulder. We saw men with horrible wounds on all parts of their bodies. Some would obviously not make it, but they were being taken anyway. There was a medical company in one of the downtown hospitals. A few brave civilian doctors and nurses stayed in the city to help as well—probably under orders from Hitler.

"Supplies were brought by the boys of the Hitler Youth. They all were rightfully terrified to be in this situation, but managed to perform their duties well. They brought precious ammunition to us each day.

"Three rivers inside the city made the advance very costly for the Russians as well. The Spree River ran through the heart of the city, running from the northwest to the southeast. It made a "V" shape with the Landwhehr River around the downtown area. The Teltow River ran along the south side of the city and the Russians were unable to move across it during the initial invasion. The bridges had been destroyed, and a combination of snipers and heavy weapons crews made bridging it impossible.

"Despite the proximity of the enemy, we snipers had still not yet been in any close-in fighting. We kept our distance and made remarkable shots over and over. We managed to acquire extra ammunition from fallen comrades, as well as a few dead Russians. We were not conservative with our ammunition. When we saw a target, we fired. The American rifles we had captured months earlier were still in our possession, but we were saving that ammunition for an emergency. The Americans and the Russians both used .30 cal ammunition, but the shells were of a slightly different length. We were afraid to experiment with one type of ammunition in the wrong gun, fearing an explosion.

"May 1st was the tenth day of the battle, and the defenders had been pushed almost completely out of the outer defensive ring on both the east and north sides of the city. This included the 9th Paratroopers' sector, and we were falling back into the larger buildings of the inner city.

"While we snipers were falling back, we came upon a Hitler Youth who was carrying supplies. While running by us, he was hit by a sniper's bullet. The boy screamed and fell to the ground. I shouted at him, "Don't move! He might think you're dead!" We did not venture out to where the boy was. He looked like he was about thirteen years old, and he began to cry.

"'It hurts! Please help me!' he pleaded. He was only a few meters away from me.

We agonized over how we could help him. Konrad took the periscope and began looking for the sniper. Rolfe was anxious and said 'Can we please help him, Sir?'

"'The sniper is waiting for someone to do exactly that!' I told him. I knew. I had used wounded men for bait many times.

"'I see him!' shouted Konrad. 'He's on that high roof. I'll shoot the bastard!' He prepared to fire his rifle, removing the dust covers from his scope.

"'Can you see his entire body?' I asked Rolf.
"'Yes."

"'How far away is he?'

"'About one hundred meters.'

"'Wait a moment, Konrad!' I shouted. I strapped my helmet onto my spade and moved it the sniper's line of sight slowly, as if it were a cautious head peeking.

"*Poink*! a bullet instantly cut through the steel helmet. 'There goes your head,' I said sadly.

"Konrad froze. I had just saved his life. 'That was damn fast!'

"'He was waiting for you.'

"The boy cried out again, 'Please help me! I don't want to die!'

"Misha suddenly moved out with surprising speed. I yelled for him to get back, and I attempted to grap the huge man's arm as he ran by. Upon seeng that this was hopeless, Konrad and I both swung our rifles around the corner and attempted to shoot the sniper before he shot us. I did not even know where he was, and my crosshairs raced around to every spot where he thought the sniper could be.

"We heard the sound of Konrad firing, and I finally saw the enemy sniper as he fell. I sighed in relief, and took my eye away from my scope. I saw Misha rolling back onto the ground, with a small red bullet hole in his chest. He gasped, and looked at me. His mouth moved, as if attempting to speak, and then his body relaxed in death.

"'Damn it!' I shouted. 'If I tell you to stay behind cover, you stay there, damn it!'

"We dragged Misha and the boy behind the brick house we had been hiding behind. The boy had been shot in his knee, and had lost a fair amount of blood. Misha was dead. We closed his eyes, then I took half of his identification disc and ordered Konrad and Rolfe to check his weapons and ammunition. I tended to the boy's leg by removing his belt and using it and the boy's sheathed bayonet as a tourniquet. 'You'll be all right,' I assured him. The boy looked very frightened. I thought to myself that the boy was lucky the sniper's bullet had not passed through his head before striking Misha.

"We needed a way to get this boy back to the hospital. We spotted another Hitler Youth soldier, and I ordered him to help the wounded boy get to the hospital.

"Misha had been carrying a Kar 98K, an American Browning automatic rifle (BAR), three stick grenades, and a lot of ammunition. I took the BAR. Rolfe was about to discard the Kar 98K when I told him to keep it, in case of an emergency.

"By this time I was carrying four rifles, including my Kar 98K, the BAR, a Tokarev, and a US M1 rifle. I also had my pistol with a silencer in a holster, three stick grenades, and a thirty-pound load of ammunition, which I kept in a large bag. I was overburdened, but I did not want to lose all of this equipment. I wanted to bury Misha. We could not risk digging anywhere outside the second defensive ring, so I decided we should move.

"We dragged Misha's body for about two kilometers, until we reached the S-Bahn railway. This was the outer perimeter of the second ring of defense. There were Panzer Grenadier soldiers guarding this barrier, using the tracks as cover. I knew that these troops badly needed me and my two remaining snipers to cover them from enemy snipers and heavy weapons crews. We would have to work fast.

"We moved to the bank, which was about two blocks from the S-Bahn. We were all almost at the point of exhaustion. The constant fighting, sleepless nights, poor nutrition, and heavy equipment load were taking their toll upon even their well-conditioned bodies. We took Misha into the bank and kicked open the door that led to the basement. Behind it were some wooden stairs which led down to a dirt-floored basement. Miraculously, the electric power was still on, and we were able to negotiate the dark basement under some yellow light bulbs on the ceiling.

"We hastily dug a shallow grave and buried Misha. We placed his bayonette on top as a marker—it looked somewhat like a cross, as it had a small crosspiece—and placed his helmet on top of that. I supposed that when the fighting was all over, someone would eventually find him, and he would be properly buried.

"We stashed our extra rifles in a storage closet, along with a few extra grenades and the bag of ammunition. Inside the storage closet were several cans of coffee, bags of sugar, and several boxes of crackers. We all looked at one another and smiled. We had not had much to eat in the past few days. Within minutes, we were pouring water into the coffeepot upstairs and eating crackers. We still had a half dozen wooden mines, which were designed to blow the foot off of an infantryman. We buried each of these near the windows, which were in the basement. The windows had already been burglar-proofed, with steel bars on the outside. These were probably installed to keep out bank robbers. The windows were below ground level, with a window well around the outside of them. One of them was in a room filled with coal for the boiler, so we planted a mine outside the door.

"Konrad lamented about Misha, 'Poor old bastard just couldn't live with himself if he would have let that kid die.'

"'Misha was a big man with a big heart,' I said. 'I went to school with him.'

"Rolfe began to cry. I had to remind myself that Rolfe was little more than a boy himself.

"'We're all going to die, aren't we?' he managed, in between sobs.

"'Not if I can help it!' I said with determination. I went over and spoke to Rolfe rather sternly. 'You must not let this happen to yourself, Rolfe!' I grabbed Rolfe's shoulders firmly. 'Emotion is good, but don't let it be fear. Let it be hatred for those who would take your life! We must fight—or die!'

"Rolfe's eyes narrowed. 'You're right.' He wiped the tears from his eyes. 'I'll take a hundred of those communist bastards with me!'

"Konrad interrupted us. 'You know, there might be a third choice.'

"Rolfe and I looked at him, listening.

"Konrad continued. 'I have thought of one way in which we could escape from this situation.'

"'What is it? We're surrounded by the Red Army,' I observed skeptically.

"'If we could get into one of the rivers at night, I think we could just swim down river.'

"I thought for a moment. What Konrad was suggesting was punishable by death—fleeing a battle as a cowardly deserter. However, who would be left to kill us? Was it desertion if the entire German Army was killed or captured, and the entire country taken over? I found this idea to be very promising. I knew we would not be able to tell anyone what we had done.

"'What would we tell people if they asked us how we escaped?' I asked.

"'Tell them it was too horrible to speak of. That's what my father used to say,' answered Konrad.

"Rolfe and I liked the idea. However, we would have to wait until we were certain that the Russians would be victorious. We were almost certain now, but what if the Russians lost their resolve to take the city? How many casualties was it worth to them to take the capital of an all-but-defeated Germany?

"We were not aware of it at the time, but Hitler was already dead. He had committed suicide in his bunker, called the *Fuhrer Bunker*, the day before. Had we known this fact, we might well have fled sooner.

"Minutes after we finished this conversation, we heard the sounds of battle get closer. We rushed to the windows on the eastern side of the bank and saw that the S-Bahn was being attacked. Russian infantry squads were hurling grenades over the barricade, while others shot at the defenders. We watched as several defenders who had been positioned on the S-Bahn were shot by enemy sniper fire. The others put their heads down, which allowed the Russians to begin crawling over the railroad tracks.

"The bank windows had been shattered long ago. We began shooting at the Russian infantrymen on the S-Bahn. We could see that a lot of other defenders were shooting at them from nearby buildings. Machine-gun fire was raking up and down, killing scores of them.

"At that point, a large group of men, women, and children entered the bank through the main doors. I cursed myself for not having asked Konrad to watch the door. It could have been the enemy coming in. I told Konrad and Rolfe to keep shooting, and I moved down to inspect the group.

"The group of people, 32 in all, stood in the large entryway of the bank and looked around cautiously. I hailed them with a wave as I quickly walked down the stairs toward them. 'The enemy is coming here. I don't think you civilians want to be here.' I then saw that they were not all civilians. Six of them were Hitler Youth soldiers, and three were Berlin policemen. All were armed with various weapons, ranging from rifles to sub-machine-guns. They all looked terrified. One of the policemen stepped forward to speak 'There are over a million civilians trapped inside the city. The other buildings are filled up. Isn't there anywhere we can hide them?"

"I did not need these distractions at a moment like this. 'Are you people insane? Why didn't you get the hell out of the city?'

"'There was no time!' said a very overweight civilian. I could see how he had escaped being conscripted. Most of the other men were too old. There were four old men, three old women, four young women, and eleven children who all looked younger than twelve years old. One was an infant.

"'Very well. The women, children, and old men can hide in one of the second floor offices. You,' I pointed at the large man, 'you're going to help us fight.' The man's eyes opened wide and he held up his hands in protest, 'But I'm not even trained!'

"'We'll teach you all you need to know.'

"One of the other policemen looked doubtful, saying 'Can you do that, Soldier?'

I noticed that Konrad was standing behind me, and that made me feel a bit braver, 'During a time like this, I can do just about anything I want to. We have been ordered to hold this building for at least a few hours.'

"The plan to defend this part of the city was a desperate one. The large buildings each had men in them for defense, and the streets would be turned into deathtraps. The success of the defense depended upon the soldiers in each large building holding off the enemy for as long as possible and assisting the defenders in other buildings. The Russians were advancing about three kilometers per day, and I knew we could only hold out for a few hours at best. It would be dark in about three hours, and we could attempt to escape then. Hopefully we would not be mistaken for Russians by other German defenders as we escaped.

"Rolfe and Konrad continued to shoot enemy soldiers on the S-Bahn for the next half-hour. I positioned the ten other men at various defensive points around the building. I questioned them about their abilities and placed them accordingly. Two Hitler Youth, armed with Panzerfaust anti-tank grenades, watched the streets from the fourth floor of the bank. It was their job to destroy any Soviet tank attempting to pass by the building. I placed them on the far side of the building, which I hoped would keep them safe from enemy snipers. I positioned a policeman with them, so at least one adult would be up there. I still considered the Hitler Youth to be little more than children, which is what they were.

"I positioned two Hitler Youth and one policeman armed with rifles on the third floor and ordered them to shoot at any enemy infantry they saw in the streets. I told them to especially watch the entrances of the other buildings, to assist the defenders inside.

"Aside from a fire escape on the back of the building, there was only one way into the bank. It was the main entrance, which was ideal for defense. It was easy to defend, because it led to a large open room, and could be clearly seen from the second floor balcony. It was also visible from the bank teller booths, which stood about forty feet away. I placed two Hitler Youth and the civilian man up on the second floor balcony, overlooking the main entrance. The first floor of the bank had no windows, so we did not have to worry about the Russians entering there.

"The third policeman and I waited in the teller booths across from the main entrance. I told Rolfe and Konrad to help the second floor guards if a fight broke out in the building. Their sniping window was only about fifty feet away from the balcony overlooking the main entrance.

"The next several minutes were very tense. The sounds of fighting could be heard as if it was just outside the building. Then I distinctly heard one of the riflemen upstairs fire two shots. I considered running up to see what was going on, but decided not to. I watched the main entrance and listened to my pulse as my heart pounded with fear. I felt like an animal cornered by hunters. I wondered how long we would have to sit there and wait for someone to come through that door.

"Then three men appeared in the doorway. 'Don't shoot!' one of them shouted in German. Two of them were carrying a third. They entered the building, and I could see that they were some of Hitler's SS bodyguard division. The wounded one had been hit in the abdomen, and the front of his uniform was dark and wet with the stain of blood. The two unwounded men were carrying MP43 assault rifles on their shoulders. The wounded man was unarmed.

"I stepped out of my booth to tell them to go to the hospital. Before I could speak, one of the SS soldiers pointed outside saying, 'They're right behind us!'

"At that precise moment, a Russian soldier appeared in the doorway and aimed a sub-machine-gun at me. Two bullets instantly hit the Russian soldier in the chest as he attempted to fire. He fell down screaming in the doorway. The three SS soldiers moved behind some desks near the teller booths and I ran back to the teller booth where I had been earlier. I heard more shots and saw another Russian fall in the doorway as I went into the booth. I readied my American M1 rifle, and pointed it at the door.

"A few tense minutes went by as we all watched the doorway. One of the SS soldiers told the wounded man that he would be all right, while the other kicked a large desk over and aimed his MP43 at the door. It was a newer type of weapon which had been introduced in 1944. It had a 30-round magazine and fired a shorter 7.92mm cartridge than other German rifles did.

"Konrad and Rolfe spoke as loudly as they dared, letting me know that they too were watching the doorway. Seconds later, a Russian egg grenade was hurled into the main entrance and sat there on the floor for about two seconds before it exploded. I hid until the grenade went off, and then reached for the crank of the detonator for the mines outside. I had already attached one of the mine's wires to it, and when I turned the crank, it set off one of the mines. I heard the explosion, as well as many projectiles bounce off the outer stone walls of the bank. Some of them flew into the main entrance, bouncing off the marble interior like bullets. I heard the screams of several men outside, whom I presumed were the Russian soldiers who had hurled the grenade.

"'What the hell was that?' asked one of the SS soldiers in a frightened and anguished voice.

"'S-mine thirty five,' I said calmly. I could tell that the man had no idea what the hell that was, but he nodded anyway.

"The sounds of shooting and explosions could then be heard out-side. I guessed that the defenders of the building across the street were shooting at Russian infantrymen in the street. We could hear the sound of a huge tank rolling near the eastern side of the building, and I shouted for the three men with anti-tank weapons to get ready. Konrad said he would go up and help them, and I acknowledged by shouting, 'All right! Move *now*!'

"As the tank pulled around the corner of the building, we could hear both the squeaky sound of the steel wheels and treads and the sound of the massive diesel engine which powered the monster. Then we heard the sound of a Panzerfaust hitting it. The sounds of after-explosions filled the air.

"The SS soldier who was helping his wounded comrade announced that the wounded man was dead. I ordered one of the SS men to take a position in one of the teller booths to help watch the main entrance. I then ordered the other SS soldier to watch the entrance to the base-ment and to listen for mines going off down there. 'If you hear a mine, let us know. I'll send someone down to help you keep them off this floor.'

"The SS soldier who was to watch the door nodded in acknowl-edgement. He took several ammunition magazines off the body of the dead SS soldier. I told them to keep the floor secure, and I ran upstairs.

"When I reached the second floor, I saw Rolfe, the two Hitler Youth soldiers, and the civilian—whom I had ordered to help fight—holding their weapons on the doorway, hiding themselves behind the stone railing; only their heads and rifles were visible from the main entrance. The civilian man was visibly shaking. He was visibly terri-fied.

"Rolfe smiled and pointed at the civilian. 'He shot one of them, Frick.' Rolfe smiled as if he thought it was funny. The civilian man attempted a smile, but he was still palpably terrified.

"'I'm going upstairs. Don't let any of them get in here,' I ordered. Rolfe nodded.

"As I climbed up to the fourth and highest floor of the bank, I heard gunfire downstairs. I knew that more Russians must have been trying to get in. I almost went back down, but knew that a greater threat needed to be dealt with. I walked to the room where I had stationed the policeman and two Hitler Youth soldiers. It was one of the many offices of the bank which had a desk, file cabinet, two chairs for customers, and a large fan. Papers were all over the floor and the window was shattered. They were not in the room. I remembered that the Russian tank had been hit on the south side of the building. I began shouting for the men, trying to find them. They shouted an answer from one of the other offices, and one of the two teenage soldiers peeked out into the hallway.

"I hurried over to the office to which they had moved, and saw that it was almost identical to the other office, with the exception that the wallpaper was covered with faded flowers. Konrad was there with the other three soldiers, and they nodded to me in recognition, then they excitedly pointed downward to the tank, which they had just destroyed. Black smoke poured from it, and we could still hear thirty caliber machine-gun bullets popping off inside the metal monstrosity.

"'Excellent work,' I said in my usual calm voice. 'We have to make sure that none of them attempt to destroy the building.'

"Not only had they destroyed the tank, they had also created a fifty ton roadblock. There was enough space in the street for one tank to move by it, but it would make destroying it all the easier. They had started with three crates of Panzerfausts, with six to a box. The boxes were filled with a new type of Panzerfaust, which had a one hundred and fifty-meter range.

"I told Konrad to watch for enemy anti-tank guns, tanks, or anything else that might be put in a position to destroy the walls of the building.

"'You can count on me, Georg,' answered Konrad. His expression was serious.

I patted him on the shoulder and added "Stay alive, soldier,"

"Yes, Sir!"

"'I'm going back down to watch that damn front door!" I turned to leave, but as I did I noticed a telephone directory collection on a bookshelf. I saw a 1941 directory for Hamburg, and my heart sank. I picked it up with trembling hands and began paging through it.

"'What is it, Georg?' asked Konrad. I did not answer. I was too emotional.

"'The phones work. Do you think I could call Hamburg?'

"'I don't know...I suppose you could.' Konrad snapped his fingers. 'We forgot to check in today!'

"'That can wait a minute!'

"'Of course.'

"I found my Uncle Fredrick's telephone number and quickly dialed it. My fingers shook. I heard a busy signal, and my heart sank. I wondered if it was busy, or if the Russians had cut the phone lines going out of town.

"Konrad must have seen my sad expression. 'I'll check in, Georg. You can try again later.'

"I looked into my friend's eyes. 'We're going tonight.'

"Konrad nodded in recognition. His lips curled upward in a tiny smile. 'All right!' he said softly. The other men clearly wondered what we were talking about, but asked nothing.

"Then I heard ferocious gunfire downstairs. 'Stay here!' I commanded and left the room.

George awoke with a start. He wasn't sure how long he had been sleeping, but he was sure that even his subconscious had heard Grandpa's story. It was a fascinating story, but he was ready for it to end. He knew it had a happy ending; Grandma and Grandpa were here—in America. They were free.

He shifted his position and settled in to listen to what he hoped was "the rest of the story."

Grandpa continued, not even aware that George had dozed off. It felt good to get this all off his chest. Yes, the time was right. He sighed and rolled along.

"As I got to the second floor, I could see a large pile of bodies downstairs in the main entryway. They were all Russian soldiers. Several of them were still moving, and the white marble floor was covered with a growing pool of dark red blood. Rolfe, the two Hitler Youth soldiers, and the overweight civilian were watching the door, as if it was a Tiger about to pounce upon them. The Russians had attempted to rush an entire squad into the room.

"With the stealth of a cat, I slowly walked down the stairs. I kept my M1 rifle pointed at the doorway with rock-solid steadiness. I moved around the pile of dead and dying Soviet soldiers and pulled a stick grenade from my belt. I unscrewed the bottom, pulled the detonator cord, counted two seconds off, and threw it outside. I quickly ran toward the teller booth were I had hidden previously and scrambled over the counter as I heard the grenade go off outside. I heard the screams of several Russian soldiers.

"A few tense minutes went by and I untied the wire of the spent S-mine-35 from the small generator. I tied one of the other two wires onto it, then I watched the door again.

"For about two minutes, nothing occurred. Then, without warning, a hand appeared and tossed an egg grenade into the main entrance. It landed right on top of the dead and dying Russian soldiers who lay there and exploded a second later. I turned the crank on the generator as hard as I could. It would not go off. I panicked. What could have happened? Did the wire get cut? Did the Russians find the mine, or was it a dud? I had no idea.

"As I scrambled to place the third mine's wire on the detonator, I heard more shooting. I looked up and saw that several Soviets were attempting to quickly climb over the four-foot pile of bodies in the doorway as dozens of bullets were fired into their midst. I watched as a bullet passed through three men lined up in the doorway. They fell into the room, writhing. One of the SS guards shot them point blank with his MP43 set on semi-automatic. He snapped off ten shots in a few seconds from his thirty round magazine.

"'Don't waste ammunition on dead men, soldier!' I said. The SS guard nodded and kept watching the door intently.

"As more enemy soldiers attempted to squeeze through the doorway, I wrapped the third wire around the generator. I ignored the loud sounds of shooting around me and turned the crank handle once again. This time I heard a mine detonate outside, then I heard the screams of at least a dozen men.

"The doorway was a very quiet place for the next half-hour. The Russians must have figured out that this was a strongpoint which could not be taken by throwing large numbers of troops at it. I knew it would not be long before they found another way in.

"'Is anyone low on ammo?' I asked as loudly as I dared. The two Hitler Youths and the civilian—who had been given an extra Kar 98K—said that they were. I cautiously approached the pile of bodies. I held my captured BAR in one hand as I grabbed weapons and ammunition from the dead Russians. I looked for signs of life among them. All of them had either been shot, or shot and blasted with the grenade. They seemed to all be dead and were piled six feet high in the doorway. The Soviets had either been armed with Nagants, which were rifles very similar to Kar 98K's, only with a slightly smaller caliber bullet, or with PPSh-41 sub-machine-guns. These weapons had a drum-shaped magazine which held 71 rounds of 7.62mm cartridges and were quite powerful.

We utilized their thirty-minute respite as well as we could. I gave each man a PPSh-41 and two extra drums of ammunition. I also made sure each of them had at least three egg-grenades. They were small and easy to carry.

"All three of us were overloaded. We knew that we only needed a few weapons to get through the night, so we got rid of a lot of our weapons and ammunition. We each kept our Kar 98K with scope, a PPSh-41, two stick grenades, three egg grenades, one Panzerfaust, and we also each kept a third weapon. I kept my silenced Walther PP, Konrad his MP35, and Rolfe found a PO-8, commonly called a "Luger" pistol, on one of the dead Russians. It was a German pistol, which the Russian soldier must have captured.

"I really hated to get rid of my BAR and Tokarev. I was tired of carrying them, however. I had always wanted to shoot one of the legendary PPSh-41 sub-machine-guns. The Russians had entire divisions equipped entirely with these weapons and hand grenades and used them as shock troops. This was very unusual, as infantry divisions were normally made up of riflemen supported by heavy weapons crews. They were very effective units for urban warfare, but they lacked the long-range firepower to be very effective outside of the cities.

"We told the other defenders and the civilians to be ready to move out after dark came. We did not want to be trapped in this bank when the lines moved beyond it. The sounds of fighting could be heard in the buildings to the east, north, and south. The Russians had not yet begun assaulting the large buildings to the west, but it was only a matter of time. We kept a close eye on the door and the surrounding streets as we changed weapons, and we were all trembling with stress and fear.

"When a half-hour of relative quiet ended, we heard the sound of a dive-bomber diving down from the sky, followed by a massive explosion inside one of the buildings to the east. Along with the sound came a strong shock wave, which hammered through the bank. I ran upstairs to see what was going on, and saw that the building had collapsed. I then heard the buzz of the plane's propellers as it pulled out of its dive overhead. I saw a cloud of dust and smoke as it engulfed the streets below. I decided this was a good time to get out of the building. The smoke cloud would be perfect cover for all of us, even better than darkness.

"Just as I was about to announce my decision, I heard another smaller explosion, which I knew was a cannon of some sort hitting the bank's eastern side. I looked out the window, and through the dust I could make out a gun crew two blocks away. There was a small opening between the other buildings through which they could fire shells at the bank. Without hesitating, I aimed and fired at them. I shot the gunner, two loaders, and then fired the last three rounds in my magazine at the nearby crate of ammunition for the cannon. It did not explode, so I ran up to the forth floor, where the Panzerfausts were. I aimed one of them at the box of ammunition and fired it. The weapon's back blast filled the room with heat and smoke as the rocket shot at the box like a bullet. When it hit, the ammunition exploded and several nearby Soviet soldiers were either killed or severely injured.

"I yelled 'Let's get the hell out of here now!' and began moving downstairs, along with the policeman and the two Hitler Youth members who had been on the fourth floor. They carried the precious Panzerfausts with them.

"As the rather large group began preparing to exit the bank, Russian infantrymen hurled grenades into a large hole which the anti-tank gun had blasted in the wall on the first floor. The SS soldiers hurled S-24 stick grenades out through the hole and hid behind cover to avoid being harmed by enemy grenades. I told the three policemen to watch the main entrance while three Hitler Youth members pulled enemy bodies out of the doorway to make some room. I fired a few bursts from my PPSh-41 through the large hole in the back wall. This was answered by hundreds of bullets from small arms fire.

"After we pulled perhaps ten bodies off the ghoulish pile in the doorway, I heard the sound of a heavy machine-gun. I knew immediately it was a Soviet DSHK 12.7mm—.50 cal—machine-gun, and watched in horror as the armor piercing bullets began flying through the first floor.

"One of the SS guards was hit. A 12.7mm bullet went through his head, and it exploded. The women and children were screaming in terror as the soldiers began running out of the bank's main entrance.

"'Run if you want to live!' I shouted. Konrad and I sprayed bullets while the remaining SS soldier threw one grenade after another out of the hole. The women, children, and other people in the room ran out as quickly as they could into the smoke-filled street and headed toward the large buildings to the west, which were still held by German soldiers.

"Once they were all gone, my men and I ran out as more 12.7mm bullets shot through the building. The only surviving SS soldier was following close behind.

"We could hear bullets shooting past us in the smoke, but we did not turn to fight. Instead, we ran. We ran as fast as possible, and did not look back. The cover of smoke and dust became thinner with each meter we traveled. The civilians, policemen, Hitler Youth soldiers, and the SS soldier ran into the very first building they came upon. The three of us kept going, and ran for several blocks.

"When we finally stopped, we knew we were safe, at least for the moment. We laughed off the fear that had been in our hearts.

"'That was a close one!' I said. I was out of breath from the long sprint. My body was a bit out of shape from all the time we'd spent in foxholes.

"'Too close!' answered Rolfe. He too was winded.

"'Look at this,' Konrad said curiously. The rest of us looked, as he pointed at his shoulder. It was covered with blood that was dripping down his side. 'I must have been hit!'

"'Lay down!' I shouted. Konrad did. He looked worried, as Rolfe and I looked at the wound. They removed Konrad's ammo belt and used it along with the cleaning rod for his Kar 98K to make a tourniquet.

"'We'll get you to the hospital,' I said.

"'What about the river?' asked Konrad. His voice was filled with a dread, which I had never heard before. He was terrified of the prospect of being left to the Russians.

"Rolfe and I looked at each other. We would either have to wait a few days or leave our friend in the hospital.

"We could wait for you," I suggested. There was silence for a moment.

"Konrad spoke. 'No, you two would probably never find me again. Besides, you would probably get killed fighting those damn communists for two or three more days. You should just go.'

"'Don't be ridiculous,' argued Rolfe. 'we're a team. We can't just leave you here,'

"'Just go,' Konrad spat. 'I can swim by myself. Think of your families. If you don't go tonight, you might not have another chance.'

"'All right. We'll go,' I finally said. 'I'm sorry, Konrad.'

"'It's not your fault. I'll be all right.'

"I know I must have looked solemn. I put out my hand for a handshake and said 'Konrad, it's been a pleasure.'

"Konrad shook hands with me with his good arm and responded, "It has for me also, Georg. We've been through so much together. I won't feel the same without you watching my back. I hope we can find one another again one day."

"'Look me up. If I'm not in Hamburg, talk to my uncle, Fredrick Frick, if you can't find me. He'll know where I am. I'll feel strange without you watching my back as well.'

"I patted Konrad on the back and looked away to avoid my friend seeing a tear fall from my eye. "You stay alive, Konrad.'

"'You too, Georg." he then looked at Rolfe, who without a doubt felt out of place 'You stay in one piece also, Rolfe!'

"'You don't have to worry about me. I'll be fine.'

"We walked Konrad to the hospital, which was already full of thousands of wounded and dying German soldiers. Bodies were stacked like a giant pile of firewood outside. I was not shocked to see this, and had in fact expected such a sight. Rolfe, however, was visibly affected. His eyes widened in terror. He looked at me and said, "I'm glad he insisted that we get the hell out of here, because I would have gone anyway.'

"An officer approached us and asked, 'What the hell are you two doing, just standing around?'

"Rolfe and I snapped to attention and saluted. "We just brought our comrade to the hospital, Sir!" I replied.

"'Well, you've taken him. Now get back out to the front line!'

"We saluted once again and turned to run. We ran east for one block, and then turned to go south. I saw the officer start to run after us. My adrenaline began to flow, and to my surprise, I wanted to kill the man.

"'In here,' I told Rolfe. We attempted to avoid the officer, and stepped into the entryway of a large hotel. I opened the door and we hurried inside.

"Inside the building was an abandoned lobby. It was very quiet. I wondered if the defenders of this building were on the upper floors.

"The officer was visible through the hotel windows, and we watched as he saw the empty street before him. He noticed the door of the hotel closing, and he stepped inside.

"The officer had a furious look on his face as he entered the dark lobby and saw the two of us snipers just standing there. He reached for his pistol, which was in a shiny holster on his belt.

"I had expected that move. I had my Walther PP already in my right hand, and had been holding it behind my back. I pointed it at the officer's forehead and fired a bullet through it before the man could even draw his gun. The gun made a coughing noise, which did not sound at all like a pistol shot. The glass behind him shattered as the round passed through, and was freckled with blood. The officer fell down like he was a bookshelf being knocked over. He hit the ground with a loud slapping noise.

"Rolfe jumped in panic. 'Christ, Georg! What the hell do you think you're doing?'

"'I did exactly what he was about to do to us," I answered as I calmly took the officer's pistol from its holster and put it into the dead man's hand. I then laid his hand on the floor to make it 'obvious' that the man had killed himself.

"'Let's get the hell out of here,' I said. Rolfe nodded, and we exited the building through the door we had come in.

"We still had about two hours before it would be dark. We moved to the south side of the German controlled part of the city, avoiding large groups of German troops. We did not want to be ordered into some strongpoint, where we could not easily run.

"It took us three hours to reach the southernmost edge of the German controlled territory. By then it was quite dark. We entered a large house, which had not a single unbroken window in it.

"'What is it?' asked Rolfe.

"'We need to blacken our faces.'

"'With what?'

"'I'll tell you as soon as I see something.' I searched the house as I answered Rolfe's questions. Then I found something: a wood-burning stove in the kitchen. I opened the cast iron doors on the front and reached inside.

"'What are you getting in there?'

"I ran my fingers along the top of the stove, then pulled them out. They were as black as coal. I told Rolfe to do the same.

"We went into the bathroom of the home and looked in the mirror. Only a small amount of light shone in the window, so there was not much light to see by. We smeared the soot all over our faces, ears, and necks. We were almost black already from the filth and smoke of battle, but we needed a little touch up.

George was startled. This was the first time, as he recalled how odd they looked, that Grandpa had laughed during his whole long tale.

"While the eastern and northern areas were under heavy siege, the southern area was relatively quiet. The river created a natural barrier, which was nearly impossible to cross under heavy fire. I knew it would not be easy to even get into the river, let alone float down it without being seen by either army.

"We walked into the master bedroom of the huge house and began searching for clothes. We quickly found the owner's clothes hanging in a closet.

"'You know, Rolfe, you can still turn back. We'll have to pretend that we're civilians. If we're found out to be soldiers by either army we'll be shot as either deserters or spies.

"'I don't care. I just want to get out of this damn city, and this is the only way we're going to get out as free men. The other options are prisoners of war, or corpses.'

"'Very well, then." With that being said, we took off our uniforms. It felt strange doing this, as I had worn it like a second skin for eight years. The trousers and shirt I put on were of a dark color, and felt too soft. I was used to a Spartan life. My calloused fingers fumbled with the buttons one by one. We also found two heavy work jackets with large pockets. The pockets had zippers on them and were ideal for carrying equipment. We found some men's leather shoes, which we put on in place of our jack boots. The shoes were slightly too small for me, and too large for Rolfe, but we put them on anyway.

"'What about our dirty faces?' asked Rolfe. 'How do we explain that?'

"'We got caught in a house fire. They're all over the city.'

"'That sounds believable, until you consider that these clothes are too clean.'

"'You're right. We'll have to remedy that, won't we?" We went back to the wood burning stove, and rubbed soot all over the clean clothes.

"'We also don't have any papers.'

"'They burned!'

"We went into the house's garage and searched for anything that might float. We found some old tires and spent the next half-hour removing the inner tubes from two of them. We also found some rope and tied a twenty-foot piece around each tire as a tether. We decided that it was still too early to attempt to sneak down to the river, and decided to wait a while.

"While we waited, I explained the dangers we would face just getting to the water. 'We'll have to watch for both German soldiers and mines. Follow me, and try to look as much like a shadow as you can.'

"Rolfe looked a little scared, but nodded. 'I can do that, don't worry about me.'

"'I know. You've been through a lot. I just want you to be as ready as you can be. Hopefully this will be our last brush with death for the next decade or so.'

"'That sounds like a good thought!'

"We left all of our weapons behind, except for our pistols, two magazines of extra ammunition, two egg grenades, a bayonet, and our scopes. We hid the weapons and scopes in the pockets of our work jackets. We also each kept our field lighters. We each had a small portion of our rations left in our musette bags. We ate these quickly, but were still quite hungry. We went to the kitchen and found some bread, a pie, and some potatoes. Since it was getting dark, we smelled them to see if they were moldy. The pie and the bread definitely smelled of mildew. The potatoes were all right, so we each ate three of them, then we found a bottle of wine and we each drank some, but not enough to get drunk.

"At two in the morning we got all of our equipment and placed our camouflage nets over ourselves. When we exited the house, we crawled out. The night was very dark, and we could only see a few feet in front of us. We carried our PPSh-41's with us, but we planned get rid of them as soon as we reached the water. I felt strange without my rifle. It was like a part of me. I felt almost naked without it.

"We were only a hundred meters from the water, and we carefully moved forward about fifty meters. We spotted two German foxholes, about thirty meters apart. Each had only one helmeted head keeping watch. The other soldiers must have been sleeping. We didn't have to worry about being heard, as the constant sound of explosions made a perfect background noise.

"We crawled very slowly in the thirty-meter gap between foxholes. I kept imagining I heard the soldier on watch alerting the others. This surely would have meant our deaths. Even though we were dressed as civilians, any soldier spotting us sneaking near his hole at this hour would have shot us on sight. I wondered if we should have left so many of our weapons behind.

"I felt the ground in front of me before I crawled onto it. I knew that sod was safe. The defenders' mines had not been there long enough to have grass growing over them. When I was about five meters from the water, the sod ended and I felt bare moist soil. Rolfe was right behind me and had been as quiet as a mouse.

"I had brought my rifle-cleaning rod along to use as a mine probe. I pushed it gently but firmly down through the soil, feeling for a mine. It had taken us almost an hour to crawl this far, so I had plenty of time. I would space my probe spots out a few inches, making sure I kept them closer together than the width of a mine. They only went off if they were pressed upon with more than twenty or so pounds. I would stop the instant I hit anything.

"Five feet onto the bare earth area, I hit something solid with my probe. I was extremely careful not to push too hard on the object, which was probably a mine. Rather than disarming it and removing it, I simply took another path, moving around it. It took another ten minutes to go the next two meters. Sweat was dripping down my face into my eyes, so I kept wiping my face. I had tapped Rolfe's head and then pointed to the place where I thought the mine was. Rolfe nodded in recognition. It was strange not wearing a helmet, and Rolfe looked awkward without one. I laughed at the thought. I looked ahead and saw that we had only about two meters to go. I began probing once again, and became very nervous. I hoped that the Russians on the other side of the river would not suddenly fire a mortar or a flare, which might light up the area.

"I felt another mine four feet from the water. Once again, I notified Rolfe. Instead of going around this one, I crawled over it and slid silently into the cold water. Rolfe did the same. We released our PPSh-41 sub-machine-guns into the river and took our inner tubes off our backs. Soon we were floating down the river, kicking to get as close to the center of the river as we could. We floated to the north, toward Hamburg. I was at last on my way home!

"We kept our heads close to the water, in the centers of the inner tubes. If someone saw us floating down the river, they might just think it was garbage. Or they might just shoot at us. It was impossible to know, but we both thought it would be better than just swimming.

"I listened to the many sounds of fighting as we floated silently. I imagined the thousands of men who were dying by the hour, and wondered if I had been wrong to abandon them. I felt especially terrible for deserting my fellow paratroopers.

"Several times throughout our trek down the river, we distinctly heard Russian soldiers speaking in the darkness. We knew that we had moved into enemy territory. I fully expected to catch a bullet in my head at any moment. Several times I put my entire head underwater and held my breath for a few seconds. I felt the inner tube, waiting for it to suddenly pop from being shot. The shot never came, and we floated through the entire night.

"When dawn came, we swam to shore. We had no idea how far down the river we had gone. Hamburg was about three hundred miles away from Berlin. Somewhere in between were the 5th, 6th, and 7th German armies, as well as several Allied armies. Running into any of these groups could well mean our deaths.

"The water was quite cold, and we were both shivering when we got out. We found a secluded spot in the woods where we made a small campfire. We hung our jackets and pants up to dry. I estimated from the fading sounds of battle that we had floated about twenty miles down the river. This put us only a few miles outside of the city. The Russians were too busy fighting for the city center to worry about us.

"We slept for most of the day. We were both extremely tired. We awoke in the afternoon, and after cleaning the water from my pistol I shot a rabbit for our evening meal. I cleaned the rabbit with my bayonet and drove my rifle-cleaning rod through it to hold it over the fire. I balanced the rod on two large rocks, which I had placed on either side of the fire. The rabbit tasted excellent. Much better than any of the rations we had eaten for the past year or so.

"When the sun went down we put our dry clothes back on, and once again draped our camouflage nets over ourselves. We began walking in the darkness to the northwest. We left our inner tubes and were glad to be out of the water.

"The date was May 2nd. It was much later that I learned that that was the day all the German forces in Italy surrendered.

"We had only to walk for about six hours before we reached the front lines. We could not believe how close the two fronts were to one another. Almost the entire country had been taken over by foreign armies. I thought this was just as well. We now wanted the Allies to win, so the German army could not shoot us for desertion. I planned to get out of the country as quickly as possible. I was not sure how I was going to do this, however.

"The front lines were easy to find, with the sounds of artillery shells and bombs going off here and there. We also saw a few burnt out German vehicles, including several trucks and a Tiger tank. All had been attacked from the air.

"As dawn approached we found another wooded area with lots of underbrush. In this area, we used our bayonettes and our hands to dig a foxhole. It took us more than an hour to cover it with branches. We hid in the hole and waited through the day. We became quite thirsty; I wished I had brought my field flask. I knew that I would not be able to conceal it or explain why I had it. We lay in the hole and thought of home.

"I knew that Rolfe was from Munich. It was probably behind enemy lines by now, and it was hundreds of miles to the south.

"'You should come to my home in Hamburg with me until this war is over. I don't think it'll be too long.'

"'I don't have anywhere else to go. Hamburg sounds as good as any-place to me!' Rolfe said sadly. 'I bet you can't wait to see your wife and your son.'

"I let out a loud sigh. 'You have no idea. I have been gone for so long. I hope they're all right.' I opened my locket, which still hung around my neck. I looked at the pictures of my wife and child. Kurt was a baby in the picture, but was now seven years old. I didn't even know what my son looked like! Tears rolled down my cheeks.

"'Don't worry, Georg. I'm sure they're fine.'

"'I heard that Hamburg had over three thousand tons of bombs dropped on it in less than a month. I *hope* they're fine.'

"Rolfe shook his head. 'How did it come to this?'

I laughed. "We took on the world and lost. What did you expect?"

"'Not this.'

"'It was the same in the Great War, but Germany surrendered before anything like this happened. The Allies never attacked our cities with such ferocity.'

"As we waited in the foxhole that day, we heard the sounds of vehi-cles moving from the front line toward the east. At first we had no idea what that meant, then I realized, "They're pulling back. The lines are moving!"

"We could do nothing but watch as German trucks, and a few battered tanks, rolled down a nearby road. There were many trees in the way, but we could still make them out.

"An hour after the last Germans had passed, the Americans followed. They drove new looking trucks, tanks, and armored vehicles in large columns. Thousands of American infantrymen also marched by. It was like watching a column of giant ants.

"After the Americans passed, things were very quiet. We could hear more shells and bombs explode to the west. We had passed right through the front line by not moving!

"Each day we would move at night, avoiding contact with people. We passed through a battlefield, filled with rotting bodies, broken weapons, and destroyed vehicles. Most were German, but there were some Americans as well. We could have picked up weapons, but we chose not to. We did find two field flasks filled with water, and each of us drank thirstily.

"Five days later, we finally reached Hamburg. We cleaned the black off our faces in the river, then we drank from it.

"We entered the city cautiously. There were American troops there, driving armored vehicles and tanks around. They were announcing on megaphones that all German forces had surrendered unconditionally, and that if any German soldiers were there, they needed to surrender immediately.

"The bombing raids had flattened Hamburg. I had a hard time even recognizing which part of town we were standing in. The devastation was unbelievable. It was as if much of the city had been part of a painting which had been painted over with ashes and fragments of buildings. Huge bomb craters were everywhere.

"At last we reached my uncle's farm. It was almost lunchtime. A young boy was playing with some toy soldiers and milk cartons on the front porch. When he saw Rolfe and I coming, he looked up and ran inside the house, yelling for help.

"Ingred came to the door and looked at me as if I was a stranger. I had not cut my hair or shaved for a month, so I had a beard and mustache.

"'What? You don't recognize your own husband?'

"Without speaking, she opened the screen door and ran to me. She opened her arms, and grabbed me with surprising strength in a loving hug. She began sobbing almost instantly, to the point where she could not speak. I hugged her, too, and stroked her hair.

"'It's all right. I know you've been through a lot. I'm so sorry.'

"'Are you home for good now?' she finally managed to ask.

"'I'll never leave home again!'

"'Kurt, come here and give your father a kiss!'

"'I want one from you first!' I said, and I held her close while we kissed for about a minute. I did not want to let her go. Not ever again.

"Kurt ran up to me and exclaimed, 'Daddy!' He hugged my waist with all his might. He squeezed so tightly it made my breathing difficult.

"'That's quite a grip you've got there, Kurt!'

"Kurt was weeping as well. 'I missed you so much, Daddy! We thought the Russians killed you!'

"'Where is Uncle Fredrick?'

"'They drafted him a few months ago. He was too old, but they took him anyway.'

CHAPTER 16

▼

INGRED'S GOLD

George stared in amazement. It had taken his entire vacation to hear his great grandfather's story. When he looked at his great grandfather, he no longer saw just an old man. He knew he was a very corageous man who had endured unbelievable hardship. He had survived, where millions of others had perished.

"That's the most incredible story I've ever heard!" George was amazed. His great-grandmother had wept through the entire story in silence, not wanting to interrupt. "What happened after the war was over?"

Still sitting in his recliner, Georg answered his great-grandson's question "For the next several weeks, both Rolfe and I had to lay low. The Allied soldiers were searching for German soldiers and imprisoning them. We simply stayed inside the farmhouse, and Ingred did not tell anyone that we were there. After a month, things began to return to normal."

"On June 5th, the Allies divided Germany into two sections. The Soviets controlled the eastern portion, while the western Allies controlled the rest. Berlin was divided in half, even though it was well inside Soviet territory. The German high command and provisional government was imprisoned, and charged with war crimes."

"The western Allies eventually let some of their prisoners-of-war go home. The vast majority, however were given to the Russians. This was a great betrayal. The main reason the Germans had fought so hard during the Battle of Berlin was because they did not want to be captured by the Russians. They killed over three hundred thousand Russians in the Battle of Berlin alone."

"I did not learn the fate of my fellow soldiers for years. The Russians were very cruel captors. They shot hundreds of thousands of German prisoners of war. Hundreds of thousands were either sent to Siberian labor camps, or used as slave labor on communal farms. The majority of these men were worked or starved to death. A few of them served about five years imprisonment and were then released to go home. In any event, this was cruel punishment. They were conscripted into service for the most part, and all they had done was follow orders. There had been units of SS soldiers who had committed atrocities, such as killing Jewish and other civilians, but even regular army troops were brutally punished."

"Uncle Fredrick, like millions of other German men, was never heard from again. Konrad was listed as a prisoner-of-war, and I later learned that he was one of the hundreds of thousands who had been executed. I guessed that it was because Konrad had been wounded and would not have been much use as a laborer."

"Ingred had taken my idea of leaving the country very seriously. She had saved all of my army wages, and on the advice of Mother she bought one-ounce gold ingots with it. She had also used all of the money from her factory work and bakery pay to buy gold. She had over one hundred ounces buried in a coffee can behind Uncle Fredrick's house. The German economy had been devastated by World War I. When the tide of World War II began to turn in their enemy's favor, they knew what was coming.

"Rolfe eventually rode home on a bus. I bought him a ticket and wished him farewell. We both wrote letters to one another for years.

"Three months after the war ended, I took my family and moved to America. We had enough money to buy a farm and start all over again. We've been here ever since, but have sold off most of our land."

George looked around the old farmhouse. It took on a whole new meaning to him. It was like looking back in time. Every piece of wood trim around every door and window reminded him of the past. Rather than being something obscure, historical things took on a whole new meaning for him.

George moved over beside his great-grandfather and gave him a big hug. "I love you, Grandpa. Thank you very much for sharing your story with me. It means a lot to me."

"You're welcome, George. Just promise me one thing"

"What?"

"You'll never forget. Don't forget about me after I'm gone."

"I promise I won't! I'll be telling that story to my great-grandchildren!"

"You have to remember the mistakes of the past before you can make a better future. Remember that hate is wrong, and war is wrong. Never forget that."

They heard a car pull into the driveway. Ingred rose and said, "Your father's here, George."

George told his family his great-grandfather's tale. One year later, Georg Frick passed away, but his tale lives on...

ABOUT THE AUTHOR

Tim Erenberger has extensively studied the history of various wars since childhood. *Grandfather's Tale* is his second book. He has also written *Fangs of the Serpent,* under the name Timothy Summers.

0-595-16462-5

Made in the USA
Lexington, KY
06 June 2010